A MONSTER'S COMING OF AGE STORY

THE OUROBOROS CYCLE, BOOK ONE

A MONSTER'S COMING OF AGE STORY

G. D. FALKSEN

WILDSIDE PRESS

For Evelyn

THE OUROBOROS CYCLE, BOOK ONE:
A MONSTER'S COMING OF AGE STORY

Published by Wildside Press LLC.
www.wildsidebooks.com

Ebooks available at
www.wildsidepress.com

FOREWORD

There is much that is uncertain, but this much is true: the beasts that from time to time plague our lands are not an isolated occurrence. In my travels I have seen shrines and icons and statues of these monsters, creatures not quite man nor wolf nor bear but an unholy mixture of the three. I have found sacrificial pits dedicated to them beneath the forgotten cities of Sumeria. I have seen statues and masks of these same creatures in the lands beyond Abyssinia. I have walked through temples dedicated to their likenesses lost in the forests far to the south of Kanem and Mali, in the mountains of Bactria, and in the great deserts of Tartary. In the lands of the Franks there are caves in sacred groves decorated with paintings of these beasts. In Greece, Palestine, and Egypt I have found no less than seven monasteries adorned with these icons, and many others that refused my entry to examine the rumors about them. And to my horror, I learned upon my journey that the worship of these creatures is not a practice that has been forgotten by time.

In the great cities of the world, in Constantinople, Jerusalem, Baghdad, and Rome, I have found cults that to this day give men, women, and children as offerings to their beast-gods. They congregate in the deep places beneath these cities where their foul acts go unnoticed, but they count among their number many of the great lords of the civilized world. There are stories of unnatural congress between the beasts and their followers, of men who are born in God's image but with age transform into the unholy. I have heard similar stories in other places: tales of the Norse berserkers who become as bears, and of the Turks who claim lineage from the wolf Asena. Let us remember that Rome was founded by Romulus and Remus who were nursed by a she-wolf, and that the Bible tells us of Benjamin, who is as a ravening wolf. Such tales would not haunt me so were it not for what I have seen.

In Paris, I met a cultist who I persuaded to tell me of his beliefs. Among other things I asked him how the cult of these creatures could exist in so many disparate places and among so many peoples. He called the creatures "Scions", though he pronounced it as if it were "Skion"; perhaps a derivation of an older word from another tongue. He used this analogy to illustrate the point thusly: A man walks through a forest and encounters a tree hidden behind a mass of bushes, each different from the next. Only the twigs of the tree's branches may be seen, but these all bear beautiful flowers that are clearly of a similar nature. The man does not understand how so many flowers can be so alike growing, he thinks, from different bushes. He does not see that they all spring from the same tree. These Scions, said the cultist, are all descended from the lineage of a great wolf-god older even than the God of Abraham. The truly faithful are blessed by allowing unnatural congress with these beasts, creating offspring that are born as men but in time become as wolves. This much I knew, or perhaps hoped, could not be true, but I dread to think how many of the world's great kings and nobles come from families that have sought to mix their blood with these creatures.

I slew the cultist of course, and his congregation. My conscience would not allow otherwise. I am left now to wonder how old and how widespread this cult can be, and just how much of its blasphemous doctrine may be true. What can these Children of the Wolf intend for mankind? Do they mean to one day feed us all to their ravenous gods?

—Konstantine Shashavani,
excerpt from *On The Nature of Beasts and Men*
(unfinished, c. 1300)

CHAPTER ONE

Spring, 1861
Normandy, France

It was a spring evening still touched by the chill of the season past. William Varanus smelled the familiar scent of winter as he walked down the spiral passage that descended into the depths of the unfathomable earth. Torches lined the walls of the tunnel, casting weird shadows that flittered about him as he passed. They almost seemed possessed of life, darting away the moment his eyes turned toward them.

How typically theatrical, he thought. *Like we are still in the depths of the Middle Ages.*

Or like they were still at Versailles.

His hosts had difficulty familiarizing themselves with the concept of the 19th Century. One would have thought that having escaped the horrors of the Revolution, they would have learned to adapt to the changing world. But no, they still wallowed in their pageantry and superstition.

Then again, they were French.

Finally the narrow confines of the tunnel ended in a black chamber lit only by the feeble glitter of a few lanterns. Of course, he had little difficulty seeing in the darkness, possessed as he was with the senses of his ancestors. But capacity did not justify excess. Just because his kind could manage in the darkness did not mean that they should flock to it so eagerly. Not yet, at any rate.

William stepped into the chamber and made for his appointed place at its center. It was an amphitheatre of tremendous proportions, carved from the rock seemingly by the hand of God. An historian might have assumed it to be the work of the Romans during their occupation of Gaul. Such a man would be wrong.

William did allow himself a hint of pride as he walked down into the central pit of the chamber. It had been carved from the stone by eager worshippers at the behest of his ancestors—or cousins to his ancestors, at any rate—in the time of the Celts.

He stopped before a raised dais hewn from the stone at one end of the pit. He saw the elders seated in their glory, hunched over like beasts with their features concealed behind hoods and cloaks. They had summoned him, but why?

"I am here!" William announced, his voice echoing off the rock and into the farthest depths of the cave. "As my elders have commanded!"

He paused, waiting as the reverberations of his announcement spread, faded, and finally vanished.

"What do you wish of me?" he asked, as silence finally returned.

That had gotten their attention. The elders' eyes glinted in the darkness as they studied him, and all around the multitude in attendance—businessmen, landowners, and soldiers in their finest attire—leaned forward in their seats around the amphitheatre and waited to hear what would be said next.

Pathetic, William thought. *Dogs fawning about the feet of their masters, hoping for a scrap of meat or word of approval.*

In England things were different. There men of the Blood had dignity, not this perverse hierarchy of submission and spite.

"William Varanus," rasped one of the elders, its voice so far gone as to be no longer recognizable as human, "you have been called before us to answer for a crime against your blood."

Crime?

Out of the corner of his eye, William saw gray-haired Louis des Louveteaux step out of the shadows at the edge of the pit. Louis was like all the rest of them: tall, broad, and powerful, with the same gray hair as William. Once they reached a certain age, certain qualities of appearance became almost universal. It was the way of the Blood.

"I have committed no crime!" William answered. "Who says otherwise?"

"I do," Louis said, crossing the pit to join William before the seat of the elders. "I do," he repeated, more softly, as he gave William a half snarl, half smile.

"William Varanus," the head elder said from on high, "you are accused of offending your blood...*our* blood...by failing to adhere to our most basic of laws."

"The sanctity of the Blood!" proclaimed a second elder.

The call was taken up by the assembly, which began chanting aloud: "*The Blood! The Blood!*"

William growled softly and felt his hair rising, but he kept himself calm. Losing his temper here and now would not only lose him face, it might lose him his life.

"What is my sin?" he asked.

Louis was the one who answered, smiling all the while:

"You have offended the Blood by taking a mortal woman to bear your offspring."

William scoffed.

"There is no crime in that," he said. "I know that here in France you seek to in-breed as much as possible—"

"Blood must be mated with Blood," someone said. Soon the entire assembly was chanting those words with ever-growing fervor.

"—but I took my son's mother in England," he continued, "where things are different."

"And see how you have been repaid," Louis said. "Your bitch is dead, your son is a pathetic wreck kept ignorant of his heritage for his own *sanity*, and his surviving offspring is a *runt!* You would seem to be the last Scion in your line."

William bared his teeth.

"So you say. What of it?"

"You have a granddaughter, William," Louis said. "What a shame it would be if she were to go to waste."

William felt the warmth of anger rising through his body.

"What do you propose?" he asked.

"Mate her to someone fit," Louis said. "Someone of the Blood. That way, if she does nothing else, at least your granddaughter can bear a new generation of our people. Your line is diluted. It must be reinvigorated."

"And who do you propose to father these 'reinvigorated' children?" William asked.

He already knew the answer. Indeed, he already *smelled* the answer as it waited dutifully in the shadows.

Louis smiled and motioned for someone to join them. A burly young man in a cuirassier's uniform approached from the darkness.

"My son Alfonse," Louis said. "Can you suggest a fitter man among our number?" He patted his son proudly on the shoulder. "Strong, brave, filled with vitality. A perfect specimen of the Scion race."

So that was the plan! William had wondered at it ever since receiving the elders' summons. Of course, he doubted the des Louveteaux cared a damn about young Babette. They were after the Varanus fortune, the company that William had spent decades building amid the smoke and fires of industry.

What typical Frenchmen.

"I thought," William said, "that good Alfonse was intended for his noble cousin, Mademoiselle de Mirabeau." Alfonse des Louveteaux and Claire de Mirabeau were first cousins. "And what a fine match they would make. Blood with Blood."

Louis's mouth twitched.

"I feel that our race shall be better served by Alfonse redeeming your bloodline," he said, all but snarling. "Alfonse and Claire are both ideal in their purity, but unless we act wisely, Babette's offspring may not be."

There were murmurings among the elders in their high seat. At length, the leader spoke:

"This proposal pleases us. There is great wisdom in it. William Varanus, you shall see to it that your granddaughter is wed to Alfonse des Louveteaux, to redeem her taint of humanity by bearing his offspring."

"My lords—" William began, seething with rage.

"So it has been decreed," the elder continued. "Let it be so."

"*My lords!*" William repeated, a roar hidden at the back of his throat. "This is folly. Shall I sow discord among my household by forcing my only grandchild to marry a man she does not love?"

"Love?" Louis scoffed. "Why should we care about a matter of love? The best families in Europe are filled with loveless marriages."

Your own in particular, Louis, William thought.

"We are in a new age, my brothers," he said, his voice resonating from the stonework. "We know that love has nothing to do with marriage—"

There were murmurs of agreement from the crowd.

"—and yet, more and more the idea of love, of a marriage based on love, has infected the youth of the civilized world. And even without love, there is still choice. A woman may be swayed by a father's directives, but it is she who must choose with whom to entwine herself. If we force Babette to marry good Alfonse here, she will be angry and resentful, and she will cause disruption between our families. Worse, because she has not been inducted into our mysteries—as our elders have ordained—"

"Because she is a runt," he heard Alfonse murmur.

"—then she will not know to measure her dissent. Her outcries against the arrangement may draw unwanted attention. And that is no good to anyone."

"What alternative do you propose?" the elder asked in his rasping voice.

"Give me one year's time to find Babette a suitable match. One of her own choosing." When Louis began to protest, William held out his hand to silence him. "It will likely be Alfonse. But give Babette a year to accept him, to choose him of her own accord. She is yet young. A year's delay will be of no great significance. And if—unlikely a chance as it is—she chooses another, then let us be content with that. I will ensure that any match is suitable. No matter who Babette's husband is, their children will be Scions in mind, even if not in body. At worst, *they* will provide acceptable breeding stock for a 'purer' family. What more can be asked?"

The elders whispered among themselves for a time. William waited in silence, returning Louis's furious glare with a cold expression. Like his brethren, Louis was an inbred dolt. The French Scions had once been among the greatest of their race. How far they had fallen over the centuries.

"We have decided," the head elder said, drawing itself up to its full height. Even in the darkness and shrouded by the cloak, the perverse structure of its massive body was clearly seen. "William Varanus shall be granted one year's time to find a suitable mate for Babette Varanus, one that the child will accept with accord. Should he fail in this task, Babette *will* be given to Alfonse."

"Thank you, my lords," William said.

He bowed deeply and turned his head sideways in a symbolic gesture that showed his throat. Louis and Alfonse did likewise, murmuring their gratitude through clenched teeth. There were some among the Scion order who would go so far as to lie upon the ground and show their bellies to the elders. William had far too much dignity for that.

"And now," the elder rasped, "let us sing a hymn to He from whom all goodness flows, He who holds all life in His jaws."

William smiled to himself. The politicking with the des Louveteaux was annoying, but he could manage it. Now, with that nonsense passed, the assembly would turn to something worthwhile. A few hymns to the ancestors, and then…

He smelled blood. Fresh blood. Young blood. And the delicious scent of meat.

The feasting would soon begin.

CHAPTER TWO

Babette Varanus sat by herself in a mountain of ruffles and lace, amid the gaiety and splendor of her grandfather's ball, wishing with all her might to be somewhere else. Dancers spun past, all smiling in delight. Babette could think of little to smile about.

Much better to be in Grandfather's library, she thought, dressed in less ostentatious clothes and surrounded by books of substance. Instead, she was dressed like a pastry and surrounded by a confederation of the most useless people in all of France. Never mind that they were among the wealthiest and most powerful—the aristocracy of the new empire. Babette doubted very much that they had a single thought between them that did not pertain to matters of politics, business, or clothes.

Or war. There were far too many men in uniform prancing about like dashing dragoons. And except for the odd hussar in braided dolman, Babette could picture none of them riding into the jaws of death with sabre brandished high....

Dashing indeed. Many of them were old and gouty. Even the young were overfull with their own pride. Hardly inspiring stuff. They had all gone for glory in the Crimea; but as Grandfather said, it was the English who had done all the real work there.

She shook her head and felt her auburn hair buffet the sides of her face. For a moment she felt like screaming. Her father had insisted upon ringlets for the ball. Even Babette's protestations to Grandfather had been for naught.

"And how does the evening find you, my dear?" asked a voice at her elbow.

Babette nearly jumped with fright. She turned in her seat, looked up, and saw her grandfather, William Varanus, standing above her in his finest evening dress. His was a kindly face, strong and masterful, with penetrating blue eyes and framed by elegantly graying hair. Babette's temper softened for a moment as Grandfather smiled down upon her dotingly as he had done since she was a child.

"Hello Grandfather," she said, folding her hands in her lap and forcing a smile. "It finds me...well."

"Have I not always taught you never to lie?" Grandfather asked, his smile never fading. "May I sit?"

"In your own house, Grandfather? Of course." Babette motioned toward the chair beside her.

Grandfather sat and gave Babette another smile, showing his teeth as he always did. He looked out across the ballroom, his smile fading into a dignified frown.

"Abysmal, is it not?" he asked.

By God, yes it was.

"What is?" Babette asked, feigning ignorance. It was only polite to do so.

"Look at them," Grandfather said, ignoring the question, as he was wont to do. "My friends and neighbors, business associates, well-wishers, and some of the most highly placed people in France.... And all here to celebrate the coming of the new season on my *shilling!*"

Grandfather was English, of course. Even in France he preferred English vocabulary. Indeed, if not for the ball, they would have been speaking in English, as they always did at home when not intruded upon by guests. Even the staff were required to understand the language, for which they were paid extra.

Grandfather turned back to Babette and smiled again as he regarded her. "And all for you, my darling: the daughter I never had."

Babette laughed lightly, as was proper, but sincerely.

"I thought that was Father," she said. She could only have spoken so to Grandfather.

Grandfather barked a laugh and slapped his knee, drawing shocked looks from a gaggle of women standing nearby.

"Ah, dear James," Grandfather said, studying the throng with his eyes. "Yes, where is my son? No doubt ensuring that everything is *parfait* for your *début* into society."

"My *début* is not until Paris," Babette reminded him.

"You *avant-début* then," Grandfather said, still searching the crowd, every once in a while sniffing as if he could smell is son.

Babette giggled slightly and hid her mirth behind her fan. Grandfather was such an eccentric at times.

"Your blasted mother may have had the good sense to die," Grandfather said gruffly, "but I daresay she has *possessed* your father. He was never so insufferable until after *her*." He paused and looked at Babette. "My apologies," he said. "I should not have spoken so of your late mother, God rest her soul."

Babette looked away, for the moment stricken not by the pain of loss but by the pain of lacking.

"No need, Grandfather," she said. "You remember, I never knew her. How can I mourn someone I never knew? Besides, I rather suspect that had she lived, she would have hated me."

"Nonsense," Grandfather said, momentarily placing a hand upon her arm. "No, your mother would have loved you. She would have treated you like a doll."

"A doll?" Babette asked.

"Oh yes. She would have dressed you up in more frills and bows and shackles of lace than exist on God's green earth." Grandfather shrugged. "At least, that was what she did to her poor dogs."

He spoke with such distain that Babette was silent for a moment. Presently, she asked:

"Like father has done to me?"

She motioned to her gown. Though it was impeccably tailored, her tiny waiflike body was all but overwhelmed by the mass of fabric.

"Now that you come to mention it…" Grandfather said.

"Yes, Father no doubt *is* possessed," Babette said. She sat in silence for a moment, gently fanning herself. Though the weather outside still held a twinge of winter's chill, the ballroom was ever so slightly warm. "Are you certain I cannot have a book, Grandfather?" she asked at length. "A small one. I could hide it behind my fan. No one would ever know."

"Are you dreadfully bored?" Grandfather asked.

Babette sighed and her shoulders slumped briefly.

"As you cannot imagine," she said. "There is nothing to do. No one speaks to me, you know."

"What of your dance card?" Grandfather asked.

Babette almost laughed.

"Empty, as it has been all night," she said.

Not that she minded. All of the possible claimants were unbearably *French*, a quality that Grandfather had raised her to distain. And all were unbearably boorish besides. She doubted any of them had half a sentence of intelligent conversation. The only thing wrong with her situation that evening was the lack of a book.

And the damned dress.

"It will be different in Paris," Grandfather said.

"Will it?" Babette asked, disappointed at the prospect.

If Grandfather recognized her tone, he ignored it.

"You are the heir to the Varanus fortune," he said. "In Paris they will all flutter about you like moths"

"Or flies around rotting meat?" Babette asked. "Truthfully, I would prefer otherwise, Grandfather." She looked up at him, her green eyes big and pleading. "Must I marry, Grandfather?"

From what she had heard about marriage and motherhood, it seemed like it would all be such a dreadful waste of her time.

Grandfather looked at her sternly, like he always did when she was being difficult. After a token staring match to defend her independence, Babette relented and lowered her eyes.

"Babette," Grandfather said, "do not ask foolish questions. You are sixteen. You are a woman now. And you are your father's only child. Of course you must marry. If you do not bear children, our line dies with you. And you would not bring that shame upon me, would you?"

Babette gritted her teeth. Damn Grandfather for asking such a question! He knew that he was her greatest weakness!

"No, Grandfather," she said softly. After a moment, she added, "But why cannot Father remarry? He could choose a young wife, and she could bear him *sons*. And I could happily become a spinster."

"You are far too young to speak of becoming a spinster," Grandfather said, chuckling. "Wait until you are twenty before harboring such thoughts."

"Perhaps," Babette said.

She fell silent as a gaggle of young, beautiful women walked past with their heads held high in distain. They were led by the insufferable Claire de Mirabeau, who paused and bowed her head to Grandfather in the most courteous manner possible. The others did likewise, but they walked on without so much as acknowledging Babette.

Babette bristled at the slight, more on principle than for the source of the insult. Claire and her little company had antagonized Babette for as long as she could remember. Father had tried to force friendship between them once. Thankfully that had finally ended at age ten, when Claire's torments had earned her two black eyes.

"Will she be in Paris?" Babette asked.

"Of course," Grandfather said. "Everyone will be in Paris."

The idea of Paris was becoming more and more displeasing by the minute.

"I spy Alfonse des Louveteaux," Grandfather murmured, directing her gaze midway across the room.

Babette looked where Grandfather indicated. True enough, there was Alfonse: tall, robust, brutal, and handsome, with thick black hair, a broad moustache, and heavy sideburns. He wore the uniform of a cuirassier, and Babette even admitted to herself that he cut quite the figure in it. If he were not such an insufferable bore, she might even have found him attractive; but Alfonse was not a man in whom a self-respecting woman could delight once she had passed words with him. Some things were simply impossible.

"Indeed," Babette said, looking away. "No doubt we shall have to see much of him in Paris as well."

"No doubt," Grandfather said. "His family wishes an alliance. And it may even come to pass."

"Oh?" Babette asked. "I'm to *marry him* then?" She scoffed softly at the notion. "Father's idea no doubt."

Grandfather was far too sensible to have suggested such a thing. Babette was certain of it.

"You dislike the notion?" Grandfather asked.

"It is not my place to say, is it?" Babette asked.

"Of course it is."

Babette considered and then answered, "Yes, I dislike the notion." She raised her chin firmly. "In fact, I consider Captain des Louveteaux to be most unsuitable. I believe that he and I should have nothing to say to one another across the dinner table."

Grandfather chuckled and said, "Yes, I suppose you are right. But you must marry, Babette. And you must marry soon." After a lengthy pause, he added, "But enough words with your old grandfather. I must see to my guests."

So saying, he rose, bowed to Babette, and rejoined the throng of guests.

Babette watched her grandfather leave without protest, though it was the last thing she wanted. Now she was left alone again, forced to pass the dreary evening in silence. Aside from Grandfather, there was no good conversation to be had.

She opened her fan and studied it intently, wishing that it were a book. Instead, she was rewarded with pictures of flowers. They were the last things she cared to see at such a time. She much preferred the idea of returning to Grandfather's library and perusing one of his books on zoology. Animals were vastly more interesting than plants in her estimation.

A shadow fell across her and she looked up. A man stood before her, and the sight of him made Babette's breath catch in her throat.

The man was tall and slender, clad in the uniform of a hussar. The uniform was a fiery red, with braid and trimmings of black. The man's hair was also colored black, like raven's wings. His poise was flawless, and he held his chin high with pride, dignity, and just a hint of arrogance. He was handsome, beautiful even, with a narrow jaw, high cheekbones, and a sharp nose. He could not be much older than twenty. Despite herself, Babette stared at him, for the first time in her life enjoying the experience of simply looking at another person.

Who was he? Certainly not a local. Babette had seen them all. Could he be a Frenchman from further south? English perhaps? Or a Russian? Her mind whirled at the possibilities.

"Good evening," the young hussar said. His accent was German and remarkably charming. "I wonder if I might have the honor of introducing myself to you."

Babette was silent, unsure of what to say. But, she reflected, conversation had suddenly become unnecessary, if only for the moment. At length she shook herself and said:

"Shouldn't someone else introduce us to one another?"

The hussar shrugged sadly and motioned around the room. "It seems there is no one on hand to manage the introduction. They are all far too busy."

"Well, then we must take it upon ourselves, mustn't we?" Babette asked, extending her hand delicately.

"My thoughts exactly," the hussar said, taking her hand gently in his and bowing over it. "I am Korbinian Alexander Albrecht Freiherr von Fuchsburg. And I am at your service."

Babette felt her heart pounding in her chest. It was all she could manage to keep breathing properly as Korbinian held her hand. The sudden excitement was intolerable, though far from unpleasant. But doubtless she looked a complete fool.

"I am called Babette," she said, keeping her chin up and her expression controlled.

"Surely you have a family name?" Korbinian asked.

He was joking, of course. How could he not know that she was the granddaughter of William Varanus? She was the shortest woman in the room. Everyone knew her by sight, and most of them avoided her for it.

Babette smiled pleasantly, prepared to play his game. "Babette shall suffice for now, sir. How can I give you my family's name? Surely that is the job of a third party, when we are finally introduced properly."

A slow smile crept across Korbinian's face as well, and he bowed his head.

"Of course you are right," he said. "Babette is more than sufficient for our purposes."

He spoke as if he assumed it was a pseudonym. Well, no matter.

"It is delightful to meet you, Baron von Fuchsburg," Babette said.

"For me also, it is delightful," Korbinian said.

"Fuchsburg?" Babette asked, trying to remember her German geography. "On the Rhine?"

Korbinian smiled and nodded.

"That is the one."

"What brings you to Normandy?"

"I am pursuing my baronial duties," Korbinian said, his pale gray eyes twinkling. "I am here to find a wife. Or so my family has instructed me."

"How unromantic," Babette said. "To find a lover would be understandable, but a wife? Surely you have wives aplenty east of the Rhine."

Korbinian grinned savagely and looked into Babette's eyes, making her feel warm and heady with the intensity of his gaze.

"The wise man does not seek a lover among the French nor a wife among the Russians. Austria suffices for both."

"Personal motto?" Babette asked.

"Family proverb," Korbinian said. "Though having seen the Austrians fight in Italy not long ago, I have been given cause to doubt it."

Babette regarded him dubiously and asked, "Does your family have many proverbs of a similar nature?"

It would explain a great deal.

"Many," Korbinian said. "And worse. You may have heard rumors about us."

He said this as if it were something to be proud of. Babette made a note of it.

"I am beginning to think I ought to have," she replied, disappointed that she had not. Clearly Father was keeping choice bits of international gossip from her. While she despised local gossip as boring and irrelevant, on the scale of nations, it made politics and diplomacy much more understandable.

"Tell me, Baron," she continued, placing her fan in her lap and sitting up as tall as she could. "Is your family very scandalous?"

"Very," Korbinian said.

"Well, if you are going to be scandalous, I hope you have the good sense to make it something interesting. Otherwise it would be a waste of everyone's very important time."

Korbinian tilted his head and made a great show of being deep in thought for a few moments.

At length he said, "We eat meat during Lent."

"Well that is of no great importance," Babette said. "So does my family, and so do many of our neighbors."

"We *are* Catholic," Korbinian said, no doubt referencing the holy fast.

Babette ignored his meaning.

"That is a fault easily forgiven," she said. "I am as well, as is my father. My grandfather is not, of course, but he is English and therefore above reproach. Most of the fine people assembled here tonight are

Catholic, at least in name, as is the Pope himself, who would never be foolish enough to follow a scandalous religion."

Babette snapped her fan open and began cooling herself in triumph. "So as you can see, Catholicism does not suffice as scandal. Please try again."

Korbinian drew himself up and took a deep breath, fighting to conceal a smile.

"We were very nearly excommunicated once," he said proudly.

Babette's ears perked up. That was interesting.

"On what grounds?"

"For opening our university to women," Korbinian said.

Now that was *very* interesting....

"Why would you do such a thing?" Babette asked.

Korbinian shrugged.

"It was during the Thirty Years' War," he said. "All the men were out fighting."

"That sounds most unseemly," Babette said. "Most unseemly indeed."

It also sounded rather promising.

"You needn't worry," Korbinian said. "There was nothing improprietous about it. The women were all relatives, and they all dressed as men while on the university grounds. The sanctity of knowledge was preserved, and the scandal was kept in the family."

"And do they dress as men still?" Babette asked.

"Often, yes. It's no longer required, but it's all in good fun isn't it?"

Babette countered with a repeat of the question: "Is it?" She continued, "Still, that seems hardly decent grounds for excommunication."

"It is slightly more complicated than that," Korbinian said. "An Italian cousin who attended the University of Fuchsburg to study divinity apparently went to Rome and passed herself off as a man for many years. She successfully became a cardinal and was very nearly elected Pope. She would have succeeded as well, had she not been found out."

"The Church took exception?" Babette was not surprised.

"The *Pope* took exception. She would have beaten him for possession of the Holy See."

Babette covered her mouth with the fan to conceal a titter of laughter.

"But surely that is a thing of the past," she said. "And a scandal of the past is something of little consequence. Your family may be eccentric, but quite acceptably so, I have no doubt."

She sighed in disappointment. It was exaggerated of course. This was the most fun she had enjoyed without the company of a book in some time.

Korbinian leaned down until he and Babette could look at one another eye to eye. Babette took a breath and smelled his scent. It was pleasing and exotic, not like the stench of perfume or the smell of wet horses that permeated the likes of Alfonse, Claire, and their ilk. Korbinian smelled of roses and jasmine, lemon and orange, rosemary and smoke....

Babette caught herself as she began to drift away on her thoughts.

"Would you believe," Korbinian said, "that my own mother is a great khan who rules over a kingdom in Asia?"

Babette looked at him very seriously and replied, "No, I would not." She paused. "Does she?"

"Upon the name of our Lord, she does," Korbinian said. "She sends chests of silk and opium home each year for my birthday."

"How thoughtful of her," Babette said.

Well, he certainly sounded sincere, she thought.

"Baron von Fuchsburg," she continued, "it seems to me that you are a peculiar character possessed of an eccentric and not altogether respectable lineage, and that you have a talent for implausible stories about your family. I rather suspect that I should not be speaking to you. I am certain that my father would not approve."

"I have been told that fathers seldom approve of me," Korbinian said.

"This comes as no surprise."

"I have also been told," Korbinian continued, "that this is one of my most desirable qualities."

"And are you possessed of many desirable qualities?" Babette asked.

"Enough that I am satisfied," Korbinian replied.

"It is rare that a man is satisfied with himself," Babette said. "It speaks well of you."

"I am glad that you approve," Korbinian said, "but I have a confession to make."

"Oh?" Babette asked, so intrigued by the curious statement that her lips formed a perfect little O as she spoke. She quickly hid her mouth behind her fan again. Had Korbinian noticed? How foolish had she looked?

If Korbinian had noticed anything odd, he gave no indication. His eyes were still fixed upon Babette's.

"I fear," he said, "that I have shown very poor manners tonight. Upon arrival I have sought out the most beautiful woman in the room, addressed her without introduction, spoken candidly to her without any respect for decorum or polite conversation, and all before I have even introduced myself to our host."

Babette nodded firmly and said, "Shameful, Baron von Fuchsburg. Your conduct has been nothing short of shameful."

"Have I terribly offended you?" Korbinian asked, grinning wickedly.

"No," Babette answered. "Not in the slightest."

"In that case," Korbinian said rising up to his full height and extending his hand, "perhaps you would be kind enough to join me for the next dance. I have no doubt that you have many suitors for the evening, but you see, the next dance a waltz, and you have not danced the waltz until you have danced it with a German."

Babette felt her breath catch again at the invitation. Her heart pounded almost painfully. She really shouldn't.... Not with a man to whom she had not actually been properly introduced. What would Father say?

All the more reason to do it.

She stood and snapped her fan shut, letting it dangle from her wrist. She placed her hand in Korbinian's and felt the energy in his long, elegant fingers.

"It would be my pleasure," she said, "for you to show me how a German dances."

CHAPTER THREE

Despite his better judgment, William loved his son. But James Varanus was of an especially nervous nature that often set William on edge. Put simply, James fussed. He fussed about everything. He fussed about the furnishings. He fussed about meals. He fussed about the servants and about what the neighbors would think—regarding what, he never said. Whenever there were visitors, he always fussed about whether the family was being sufficiently hospitable. And above all, he fussed about his daughter.

"Where has Babette gone?" James asked, craning his neck to look in every direction.

William sniffed the air and turned toward the dance floor.

"Dancing," he said.

He could not see her yet, but he knew she was there. After a few moments he finally spotted her amid the sea of dancers, held in the arms of a tall man dressed in red. William was immediately on edge. To see his granddaughter on the dance floor was curious enough, but who was the strange young man dancing with her?

William watched Babette and the stranger dance. In spite of the huge difference in height, they moved with remarkable grace. And the way that Babette smiled.... William had never seen her so happy in the company of others.

A thought began to form somewhere in the back of William's head.

"Oh my!" James exclaimed. "What is going on here?"

He was looking toward Babette and the stranger.

"It would appear that your daughter is dancing," William said. "And having a wonderful time while she is at it."

"But...but who is he?" James asked. "They haven't been introduced, have they?"

William sniffed the air again, testing for the young stranger's scent. It was difficult in the crowded room, with so many smells polluting the air. The room was thick with the strong musk of Louis des Louveteaux and the other old Scions and the weaker scent of the young ones, like Alfonse and his cousin Claire. They were all practically in heat. William scowled for a moment.

But though he could not find the stranger's scent clearly, he knew that the man was no Scion.

"I could not say," he told James. "I am certain I have not met him, but if he is here, he must have been invited."

The servants were always very careful with the guest list. William made certain of that.

"Shouldn't we stop them?" James asked, fidgeting.

"Why? You would rather she spend the night sitting alone? Or perhaps I should allow her to retire to the library. You know that she would much rather be there than here."

"Nonsense," James said, but his voice sounded uncertain. "Why isn't she dancing with someone respectable, like Captain des Louveteaux?"

Alfonse.... William's lips drew back in a snarl for a moment. James was foolishly impressed by Louis's damnable son. For that matter, where *was* Alfonse? Surely his father had instructed him to begin courting Babette.

William followed Alfonse's scent and spotted him to one side of the room. He was deep in conversation with Claire de Mirabeau. Alfonse was busy murmuring something of no importance, and Claire seemed to be enjoying every moment of it. William knew the look on their faces. If they tried to excuse themselves to some other part of the house, he would kill them.

Human youths were bad enough, but among the Blood the arrival of spring was like a curse from Nature.

"I believe young Alfonse is otherwise occupied," William said, smiling at James. "But no matter. Your daughter appears to be having a wonderful time entirely without him."

William looked back toward Alfonse and saw Louis berating him. It made William smile a little. His argument in the pit had been well founded. Louis was a fool if he thought he could attach Alfonse to anyone but his cousin, least of all William's granddaughter.

"But is he of a good family?" James asked.

"Of course not," William said, only half listening. "His lineage is rotten and inbred, like a bush in a swamp."

"But you said you didn't know him!" James exclaimed.

William looked back at him. "Oh, you mean the man who is dancing with Babette."

"Of course!" James said. "Father, please take this more seriously! We are speaking of our own flesh and blood!" He looked back toward Babette and the stranger. "Is he even French?"

William place a heavy hand on his son's shoulder.

"James, my boy," he said, "do not fret. It is one dance. What could happen?"

* * * *

Babette felt like she was flying as Korbinian held her in his arms and they twirled together across the dance floor. She had never danced before, not properly at any rate. There had been lessons, of course, and childish dancing with Grandfather. But she had never before danced with a young man who was not her tutor.

She could not describe the exhilaration, not even to herself. Her heart pounded against her ribs and her head swam. The other dancers flashed past in a blur. All she could see was Korbinian's face looking down upon her, the light of the lamps encircling his head like a gilded crown. Everything else melted away into a delicious haze until time itself drifted into the distance.

Babette was brought back to the world by the absence of music. She and Korbinian slowly spun to a stop. Babette blinked a few times to clear her head and saw that the dance had finished. She quickly pulled away from Korbinian. The others were looking at them. Babette suddenly felt very self-conscious. She was not used to caring about the opinions of others, which made the experience even worse.

"*Dankeschön, fräulein*," Korbinian said, bowing. "You are a spirited dancer. Most delightful."

"Thank you, Baron," Babette said, concealing her pleasure at his words. "You are quite agreeable yourself."

Korbinian chuckled and asked, "Are you already engaged for the next dance? Or might I impose upon you further?"

"It would be my—" Babette began. She was interrupted by her father's voice.

"Babette!"

She turned and saw him step out of the crowd, moving toward her with as much haste as he could manage without causing undue attention.

"Babette," Father said, taking her arm, "come with me. There is someone I wish you to meet." He gave Korbinian a quick look. "Good evening, young man."

Korbinian drew himself up proudly and bowed his head to Father.

"Good evening, sir," he said. "I am Korbinian Alexander Albrecht Freiherr von Fuchsburg."

"A pleasure," Father said, clearly lying. "I trust you are enjoying yourself at my family's ball. Good evening."

Babette shook her head. Even in anger, her father maintained perfect decorum.

She cast a last look over her shoulder at Korbinian as Father led her away. Korbinian stood on the dance floor watching her with a small smile. His eyes never wavered until the crowd finally swallowed them up, and they vanished from sight.

Babette followed Father out of the ballroom and into the hall.

"Father, what is all this?" she asked. "Why did you take me from the ball?"

"Why did you dance with that man?" Father asked.

Babette stared at him.

"Because he asked me to," she said. "That is the purpose of a ball, is it not?"

Father looked at her sternly.

"Now is not the time for wit, Babette. Do you even know who he is?"

"Of course," Babette said, drawing herself and setting her most stubborn face. "He is the Baron von Fuchsburg."

"Yes, but who introduced you?" Father demanded. "*I* did not, nor did your grandfather."

Babette held her breath for a few moments before exhaling. Why did Father have to arrive and pull her away after only one dance? For the first time she had been enjoying herself in the company of her peers.

"We introduced ourselves to one another," Babette said.

Father's face went pale.

"You did *what?*"

"It seemed more civilized that way," Babette said. "The Ancient Greeks—"

"Damn the Ancient Greeks!" Father cried. "Babette, you must not do such things! Least of all with your introduction to Society looming in the future! What will people say?"

"They will say that we danced wonderfully," Babette said.

Father ignored her and continued on:

"I knew I should not have asked you to attend! But your grandfather insisted. 'Tradition' he said. Why did I listen to him?"

That is quite enough, Babette thought.

"Father," she said, taking him by the hand, "I appreciate your concerns, but I assure you that nothing scandalous has happened nor will happen. I danced with a guest at Grandfather's ball. That is all. And he is a guest of *noble birth*, so I cannot see what you have to complain about. This is the year when I enter Society, is it not? Which means that I must make myself available to dance with young men." She fixed Father with a hard look. "It's my duty, isn't it?"

Father sighed, his mood suddenly altered from anger to regret.

"'Duty,' Babette? You make it sound so unromantic." Father placed his free hand atop hers. "Babette, you are on the threshold of marriage and motherhood, the greatest aspirations of any young woman. You need not be so callous about all of this. Rules of conduct are in place for your protection."

"My protection?" Babette asked skeptically. Rules always seemed to be in place for her inconvenience.

"To safeguard you," Father explained, "so that you can find true love with a respectable and upstanding man. Monsieur Bazaine, perhaps—"

Babette's eyes bulged in horror at the suggestion of the noted banker.

"He is nearly *fifty!*" she snapped.

Father smiled and spread his hands, offering a more pleasing suggestion. "Then perhaps young Alfonse des Louveteaux..."

Babette scowled and put her fists on her hips. They were difficult to find beneath the mass of frills that was her dress, but she managed without too comical an effect.

"Father, Alfonse des Louveteaux has yet to pass two words with me this evening. Yet you offer him up as a man I ought to regard in a favorable manner. Baron von Fuchsburg asked me to dance! Alfonse has *never* done that."

Father cleared his throat and said, "Then let us return to the ball. You may be surprised at what you find."

He looked so pleased and hopeful that Babette knew he was up to something.

He's meddling! she thought. *My God, if Alfonse asks me to dance now, I'll scream!*

But independent of her private thoughts, Babette smiled pleasantly and cocked her head to one side.

"I'm never surprised by anything, Father," she said, taking his hand and allowing him to lead her back to the ball.

After sixteen years as your daughter, how could I be?

When she returned to the ballroom, Babette looked about carefully but intently, searching for Korbinian. He was tall enough to stand out in the crowd, but he was nowhere to be seen. Babette frowned and made her way toward the stairs leading up to the second floor balcony. Small as she was, the throng of guests made her view difficult. Perhaps he was simply on the other side of the room, too far away for her to see from her angle.

Suddenly a queer sensation came over her. A familiar and displeasing scent assailed her nose, and she felt her hair stand on end. She spun about in time to see Alfonse loom over her as he reached out to grab her arm. Babette drew back and snapped her fan open, holding it out before her like a weapon.

"Captain des Louveteaux," she said, nodding politely. "What a pleasure to see you this evening. I trust you are well?"

Alfonse bowed his head and smiled at her hungrily.

"Very well, Mademoiselle Varanus," he said. "And you?"

"Well enough."

"Good," Alfonse said. "Give me your hand. We dance now."

He reached out again, and again Babette withdrew.

"We do, do we?" Babette asked, trying hard not to snarl for the sake of appearances. Dealing with Alfonse was always a trial. He little understood the concept of conversation. To him the word was synonymous with dictation.

"We do," Alfonse said, nodding. His expression was twisted with growing frustration at Babette's refusal to follow his command. "So give me your hand and accompany me to the dance floor."

"I am not so inclined," Babette replied, the hint of a scowl crossing her face.

Alfonse was a bully, and if he thought he could simply order her about—her, the granddaughter of William Varanus no less—he was in for a surprise.

"It is rude for a lady to refuse a man's request to dance," Alfonse said, growling.

"It is customary for him to *ask* her," Babette said.

She was not entirely certain how to describe the sound that Alfonse made, but it reminded her of one of her Grandfather's hounds being denied a piece of meat. The similarity did little to make Alfonse's behavior any more palatable to her.

"Mademoiselle Varanus," Alfonse said, his tone still that of a growl, "would you do me the great honor of accompanying me for a dance?"

Babette bared her teeth and forced a smile.

"Of course, Captain," she said. "It would be *my* honor. I will put you down for the next quadrille."

That at least would buy her some time. The quadrille was scheduled three dances away.

"I would prefer the next waltz," Alfonse said, speaking in such a way that it made Babette's hackles rise.

"That is most unfortunate," Babette said. "But I fear that the quadrille is the next dance for which I am available. Not sooner."

She had no intention of allowing Alfonse to hold her in any sort of close manner.

The two of them fixed eyes and stared at one another for a long while. Babette felt Alfonse's seething anger at her impudence, but she refused to back down. Finally, Alfonse forced a smile and said:

"Very well, the quadrille."

Satisfied, Babette bowed her head and smiled back.

"The quadrille," she said. "Now, if you will excuse me, Captain des Louveteaux, I must…see to something."

So saying, she snapped her fan shut and plunged into the crowd, eager to put as much distance as possible between herself and Alfonse.

Shaking with anger at Alfonse's presumptuous treatment, Babette stole away from the ball and took the servants' passage down into the kitchens. Father would be cross with her for leaving, but she could tolerate his anger. What she could not tolerate any longer was Alfonse. Five minutes with the man was worse than hours of her father's fussing.

Alfonse was simply so intolerably arrogant! And boorish as well. And to think that Father actually held the man in high regard! Like the rest of his family, Alfonse was an insult to Frenchmen everywhere, that much was clear.

Babette stole a bowl of strawberries when the kitchen staff was not looking and settled in by the outside door to enjoy the cool breeze blowing in from the grounds. The ballroom had been extremely stuffy.

As she savored the taste of the berries, thinking about the strange events of the past hour, Babette heard someone approach her from behind. She looked over her shoulder, expecting to see one of the servants. Instead, she saw Korbinian striding along the corridor with a devilish grin upon his lips. Babette felt her heart leap with excitement at the sight of him, and she quickly looked away to conceal her delight.

"Good evening, Baron," she said. "I am surprised to see you down here among the common people."

"Nonsense," Korbinian said. "Here are only you and I, and there is nothing common about either of us. Clearly this is where the ball ought to be, and the company upstairs is simply too parochial to realize it."

"How very astute of you," Babette said. "But tell me, what brings you here? This is quite a coincidence, surely."

Korbinian thought about her words for a moment, as if trying to discover some hidden meaning.

"Isn't it obvious?" he asked. "I wanted to see you again, and so I followed you. Why should I pretend otherwise?"

"Well, when you put it that way..." Babette said. "Would you care for a strawberry?"

"Yes, *dankeschön*," Korbinian said, plucking a berry from the bowl. "Mmm, most delicious."

Babette prepared to take another for herself, but Korbinian reached out to stop her.

"No, no," he said. "Allow me."

He selected another strawberry and gently fed it to her. Babette felt a shiver of excitement as his fingertips brushed her lips, and she swallowed the fruit eagerly.

Keeping her composure despite her impulse to the contrary, she said, "Baron, I feel that you should not have done that. It was most inappropriate, and I should not have allowed it."

"But you enjoyed it," Korbinian said, smirking.

"It is often the inappropriate things that we enjoy the most," Babette said. "Like reading. Or setting off firecrackers in the garden."

"The last I heard, Our Lord had not ordered an injunction against fruit."

"Oh, you think you're so clever," Babette said, not at all displeased.

Korbinian nodded.

"Yes," he said, "and I think *you* are clever too."

He took another strawberry and placed it against Babette's lips.

"So," he continued, "why don't you and I spend a little time being clever together?"

Twenty minutes later the bowl was empty, and Babette was in paradise. She could not remember a time when she had spoken so freely to another person. She and Korbinian talked of everything and nothing, delighting in conversation for its own sake, but even in their verbal meanderings they wandered close to matters of intellect and substance.

"And that," Babette said, looking into Korbinian's eyes, "brings us to the Ancient Greeks."

Korbinian laughed and replied, "I find the Persians to be of far greater interest."

Babette gave him a playful shove, which he did not seem to mind.

"How can you?" she demanded. "Persia? The great Asiatic horde seeking to invade Europe?"

"Nonsense!" Korbinian said, catching Babette's hand and holding it with gentle fingers. "The great *civilized* horde seeking to bring order to a fractured people."

"You are a terrible classicist," Babette said, looking at Korbinian with a firm expression.

"My tutor always said so," Korbinian agreed. "He said I was always too easily distracted by beauty…."

He raised Babette's hand to his lips and kissed it softly.

Babette swayed a little, suddenly overcome.

"Baron, I don't think—" she began.

"Call me Korbinian."

"Korbinian—"

"Shh…." Korbinian pressed a fingertip to Babette's lips. "No uncertainty," he said, leaning in close. "If you wish for me to stop, tell me to stop. But do not tell me what others would think."

Babette smiled and closed her eyes, tilting her head upward to meet him.

"Why would I tell you to stop?" she asked softly.

She felt Korbinian's hand caress her hair as their lips brushed. The warmth of anticipation filled her as she suddenly hungered for Korbinian. In that instant, she wanted nothing more than to be enfolded into him, like one spirit that would never part.

"Babette!"

Her father's shout shattered the moment, and Babette turned away.

"Damn it!" she cursed under her breath.

Why did Father have to arrived at such a moment?

She looked at Korbinian and then down the hallway. Her father was not yet in sight. She heard him calling from the direction of the stairs. It would only be a few moments before he arrived and found them!

"What is—" Korbinian began.

"My father!" Babette said.

"Your father?" Korbinian seemed perplexed rather than concerned. "Why has he come down here?"

Babette looked at him in astonishment. How could such a clever man be so stupid?

"It's his house!" she answered.

Korbinian tilted his head, and a smile slowly crossed his lips.

"You are Babette *Varanus?*" he asked.

"You didn't know?"

How could he not have known?

Korbinian ran his fingertips along Babette's cheek.

"I had no idea," he said. He looked toward the passage. Father's shouts were drawing nearer. "I think I should go before you are seen with me."

Babette caught his hand and asked, "When will I see you again?"

Korbinian did not answer. Instead, he slid his fingers through Babette's hair and drew her to him. His mouth met hers in a kiss of desperation and passion that Babette had never dreamed was possible. She felt herself fading away again, lost on a sea of scents and sensations until there was nothing left but the two of them.

A moment later Korbinian broke away and released her. Babette's head swam, but all she saw were Korbinian's gray eyes looking into her own.

"Soon, *liebchen*," he said. "Very soon."

With that, Korbinian bowed, stepped out the door, and vanished into the night.

Babette leaned against the wall, the haze of delight still encompassing her. She only half saw her father as he rounded the corner.

"Babette!" Father cried. "There you are!"

"Hello Father," Babette said with a sigh.

"Where have you been for the past half hour?" Father asked. "Alfonse des Louveteaux has been looking for you! The quadrille is about to begin! What have you been doing?"

"I was only getting some air," Babette said. She looked at the bowl. "And eating strawberries."

CHAPTER FOUR

From the moment she awoke the next day, Babette could think of little but Korbinian and the kiss they had shared. The very thought of him made her dizzy. Everywhere she turned, everything she saw reminded her of him. She was bewildered by it all, disarmed by the very strangeness of being so elated. She had never felt that way before. It would have frightened her had it not been so pleasant.

Still, though delightful, the experience made it frightfully difficult for her to concentrate upon her Latin grammar, which would surely make Grandfather cross. Babette rose from her chair in the upstairs library and sighed, partly in delight but mostly in frustration. She crossed to the window and stood there, bathed in the warm afternoon sunlight. The sensation reminded her of him.

How very peculiar, she thought, that sunlight could remind a person of another person. It did not seem at all sensible or scientific. Had Korbinian been there, she was certain he would have had something interesting to say about it.

I've done it again!

Babette put her hands to her temples and shook her head. How could every little thing she saw, heard, felt, and smelled possibly remind her of him? It was too impossible to make sense of it!

As she stood at the window, she chanced a look out onto the grounds. To her astonishment, she saw a man not unlike Korbinian riding up the drive on a dappled gray stallion. Babette sighed and turned away, covering her face with her hands.

Now she was seeing things! It was dreadful!

She turned back to the window, determined to put her mind at ease, and saw that her eyes had not deceived her. Indeed, it was Korbinian walking up to the front steps as bold as brass.

Babette bolted for the door. She had to try the handle twice before she managed to open it.

What was Korbinian doing here, now of all times? Surely someone would see him!

She raced out into the passage and ran for the stairs. She heard Korbinian knocking on the front door. What was she to do?

She reached the upstairs landing in time to see a footman answer the door. She wanted to cry out, but that would only make things more difficult. She squared her shoulders and was about to descend and sort the matter out when her grandfather stepped into the foyer, walking stick in hand.

Babette clapped a hand over her mouth to keep from crying out and crouched as low as she could to avoid notice.

Surely something dreadful was about to happen.

William Varanus did not expect to encounter anyone as he departed for his afternoon walk, certainly not the young stranger of German extraction who had danced with his granddaughter the night before. But there the young man was, standing in the doorway in riding coat and breeches and a vest of an audaciously sharp green, acting for all the world as if there was nothing peculiar about his arrival.

"And what is this Vatel?" William asked the footman.

"Apologies, sir," Vatel said. "This...person only just arrived. I was about to show him into the drawing room to await Monsieur James."

"Thank you Vatel, I will handle this."

"Very good, sir," Vatel said and withdrew a few paces.

William turned to the young man in the doorway and sized him up. He was tall, as William recalled. He smelled decent enough. There was the scent of horse, naturally, and some traces of cologne but at least neither was overpowering. The boy's own scent was healthy and robust.

"Who are you?" William asked, direct as always. "What is your business?"

The young man bowed and introduced himself:

"I am Korbinian Alexander Albrecht Freiherr von Fuchsburg. Am I right to think that I am addressing William Varanus?"

"You are," William said. "And your business?"

"My business, sir," Korbinian said, "is with you. It concerns your granddaughter, Mademoiselle Babette."

Really...? William thought. *Interesting. Most interesting.*

"If the matter concerns my granddaughter," he said, "then surely you wish to speak to my son James, her father."

Korbinian appeared confused for a moment but quickly rallied. He exhaled in a soft laugh and met William's stern gaze.

"*Nein,*" he said. "Forgive me sir, but I have made inquiries about the town—else I would have attended you sooner. I am given to understand that it is you sir who is the master of the house, not your son. And so I have come to speak to you."

Clever boy.

"Regarding my granddaughter?" William asked.

"Yes," Korbinian replied. "As I have said."

"So you have."

Korbinian took a breath and said, "Sir, I would prefer if we discussed this matter in private. It is of a delicate and most important nature."

"Is it?" William asked.

"It is," Korbinian said, his gaze never wavering.

William chuckled. Toying with the boy was amusing, but only as a passing distraction. His walk beckoned and he was in no mood for further delays. Then again, if he suspected the boy's purpose correctly…

William tapped the foyer floor with the end of his stick and said, "I am just about to depart on my afternoon stroll in the gardens. It will take precisely thirty minutes."

He checked his watch and frowned at the delay.

"Twenty-seven minutes," he corrected. "You may accompany me, Baron von Fuchsburg, and you have the duration of my walk to present me with your business and convince me of its worth. Do you understand?"

"Most clearly, sir," Korbinian said. "Thank you."

William looked at his watch again.

"Twenty-six minutes. Come along, we will walk briskly."

A quicker pace during the conversation would be a good test of the boy's lungs.

As soon as the front door closed, Babette broke from hiding and ran to the nearest window. She watched Grandfather and Korbinian walk briskly across the drive toward the gardens at the side of the house. Grandfather's manner was relaxed, though purposeful, which Babette took to be a good sign. Korbinian kept pace easily, and his stride was marked by great confidence.

Babette watched them silently, wondering what words passed between them. As they walked out of the window's line of sight, she moved to the next and the next, following them with her eyes until they had vanished into the gardens.

Babette placed her fingertips against the glass and stood at the window in silence, her mind awhirl.

"Now then," William said, as he savored the fresh air, "what is this business of yours, Baron von Fuchsburg?"

Korbinian cleared his throat with a cough and raised his chin.

"Sir, I wish your permission to marry your granddaughter."

As William had suspected. And to think, they had only met the night before. Ah, the impetuousness of youth.

"My granddaughter?" William asked.

"Yes, sir."

"Have you met my granddaughter?"

"*Ja*," Korbinian said. He gave William a purposeful look. "You know that I have, sir. You saw us dancing at your family's ball last night."

William hid a smile. *Clever boy.*

"So I did," he said. "And after one dance you have decided to marry her?"

Korbinian fell silent for a moment before he answered:

"We also spoke, she and I, for no less than twenty minutes, on a great many topics of mutual interest. I was impressed by her intelligence, forthrightness, and wit."

"And those are qualities you regard as ideal in a wife?" William asked.

"I do, sir. She is a rare woman, your granddaughter. Any man would be honored to wed her."

William smiled. "And why do you believe that you are worthy of that honor?"

Korbinian drew himself up.

"Because, sir, I am Korbinian von Fuchsburg," he said, speaking as if it was the only logical answer. He paused. "And because I love her."

Love, William thought. *A manifestation of the foolishness of youth.*

"Tell me of Fuchsburg," William said, pretending not to recognize the name. "What property and wealth does your title entail? Or are you a baron in name only?"

"The Barons von Fuchsburg are old nobility from the days of the Holy Roman Empire. Napoleon sought to erase us. The Prussians sought to absorb us. But we are still here, still masters in our homeland."

"Your property?" William repeated.

"The Barony of Fuchsburg controls thirty thousand acres of land," Korbinian said, "two towns facing one another across the Rhine, the oldest university in the German-speaking lands, and the finest vineyards in all of Europe. I have more than enough wealth to ensure your granddaughter's comfort and happiness, whatever her whims and desires."

Korbinian looked at William intensely and continued:

"She will want for nothing, I assure you. Each day, when she wakes, she will view the majesty of the Rhine from her tower in the castle. She will be attended by the most dutiful servants—"

William almost scoffed, but he kept his thoughts private. Babette hated being fussed over by the servants.

"—She will never lack intelligent conversation," Korbinian said. "Her sitting room will be graced by none but the finest minds in all the world, I promise you sir. Artists, philosophers, scientists, and scholars shall be at her beck and call, there to delight her mind and senses whenever she desires it!"

William held up a hand to silence him, taken aback by the statement. Few men would have known to speak of introducing his granddaughter to scientists and scholars before they spoke of kings and courtiers.

"Why would my granddaughter have any interest in such things?" William demanded, sounding angry. "Clearly you do not know her."

Korbinian kept his head high and gave William an accusing look.

"You are mistaken, sir," he said. "When she and I spoke, we spoke of nothing but the Classics, philosophy, and matters of substance. She delighted in them, as a foolish girl might delight in dresses and jewels." He looked William directly in the eye and said, "If you think otherwise, then you do not know truly your granddaughter."

William was amused enough at the boy's challenge to indulge it a few moments before adjusting his stance and intensifying his glare. Korbinian was only human and he looked away, but he resisted the predator's gaze longer than most men could have.

The boy was proving most interesting, William thought. Most interesting indeed.

He stopped at the edge of the apple orchard and looked out across the sea of trees. Small leaves and buds were beginning to form on the branches. Soon they would be in bloom.

"You are an interesting man, Baron von Fuchsburg," he said. "And I will admit that you possess a better understanding of my granddaughter than do most men."

Certainly a better understand of her than her own father possesses, he thought.

"You will grant your consent?" Korbinian asked.

"Do not be hasty," William said, resuming his walk. "You and Babette have known one another for but a single day. I would not trust either of you to make a wise decision on this point within the span of twenty-four hours. I must think of my granddaughter, you understand."

"She will be provided for—" Korbinian began.

"*I* can provide for her," William said, interrupting him. "I wish to be assured of her happiness."

"As do I, sir," Korbinian said, with such vigor and earnestness that William almost laughed aloud.

"What of your relations, Baron?" William asked. "Your father?"

"My father is dead, sir."

"Dead?" William raised his eyes at this. "And how did he come to die?"

"Asia, sir," Korbinian said.

"Asia is a place," William said, "not a cause of death."

"When I came of age," Korbinian said, "my parents went on an expedition into Persia, leaving me and my sister alone so that we could come to understand our duties. While in Asia, my parents came to be at war with one of the local khans over some matter that does not concern me and, therefore, of which I am ignorant. The khan killed my father moments before his own death."

"How did the khan die?"

Korbinian smiled proudly and said, "My mother stabbed him through with my father's sword and threw him from the top of the tallest tower of his palace. I am informed by my mother that the same fate was a form of execution used by the khan on his subjects for many years, so it met with the general approval of the populace."

"Really?" William asked. He made his voice sound doubtful, but if what the boy said was even partly true, it spoke very highly of his lineage....

"I swear upon the name of Our Lord, it is true," Korbinian said.

"Yes, best not to bring Him into this," William said. He and God had not been on speaking terms for as long as he could remember. Swearing upon the name of Christ only annoyed him. But Korbinian was young; he could be forgiven for it. "And where is your mother now?"

"She remains in Asia," Korbinian said. "She took the kingdom by right of conquest and now rules as khan."

William chuckled. The boy was telling stories, of course, but at least he was creative. James would never have understood why that was a good thing, but William did.

"You mentioned a sister," he said.

"Yes," Korbinian said, "my sister Ilse. She is unmarried, but she entertains suitors from the finest families in Europe."

"Is she your elder or younger?"

"She is my twin, sir," Korbinian replied.

William nodded but said nothing, considering various points in his head. At length he spoke again:

"Baron von Fuchsburg, you have impressed me today. But you must understand that I cannot give consent for my granddaughter to marry a man that she scarcely knows."

"Then give me leave to court her," Korbinian said. "I beg you, sir. My mind is like fire since I met her. My thoughts are aflame. I think of nothing but her."

"Wait a week's time," William said, "and see how hotly your thoughts burn then. Better still, a month."

"This is not mere desire, sir!" Korbinian cried. "You may doubt me sir, but I am driven by love, not by some base fantasy!"

William recognized the passion in Korbinian's eyes and voice. At the very least, the boy thought he was sincere in his emotions.

"You have lodgings in the village?" William asked.

"I do," Korbinian said. "And in Paris. I was meant to spend the spring there, meeting eligible young women. Now I wish for none of them but your granddaughter."

"Remain in the village," William said. "Wait for my reply."

"I would wait an eternity, so long as it may lead to my seeing her again," Korbinian said.

William looked at him and nodded.

"I do believe you would," he said. "Thankfully for the both of us, my answer will not be an eternity in coming."

Babette's future did not have the time for eternities.

"No! Absolutely not! I forbid it!"

James's cries assailed William's ears like the protestations of a small child in want of a toy.

"James," William said, smiling at his son in his best patriarchal manner, "how can you say such a thing? You 'forbid it.' What nonsense. Surely you are as concerned for Babette's education as I am."

"No, no, no," James continued, for once in his life talking over his father's voice. "I will not allow this! The social season is about to begin! Babette *must* be in Paris!"

They stood in the downstairs library, William freshly returned from his walk. James wore an informal day suit and a velvet *robe de chambre*, as he always did the day following a gathering.

William folded his hands and looked at his son sternly.

"James," he said, "stop this foolishness at once."

"Foolishness?" James cried, turning pale. "I seek to defend my daughter's happiness against this madcap scheme of yours, and you call it *foolishness?*"

"Babette has a restless mind," William said. "This has become quite clear to me. She is tossed about by the mad currents of intellect, swept from one new idea to the next."

"All the more reason for her to be married! Why, her mother—"

"Babette is nothing like her mother, James," William said flatly. "She will not be content with dresses and bows, Society and gossip! She delights in the intellect. If she is to have a contented home life, she must either be paired with a husband of intellect who is willing to indulge her, or she must be taught how to indulge the needs of her own keen mind without failing in her duties as a wife and a woman of means."

James turned to walk away, then turned back toward William. He spun about in place a few times in this manner, cutting a ludicrous figure as he did so.

"This is all so incredible!" he cried. "I cannot believe this! Babette is no *philosophe*, Father. She wants what all young women want."

"And what is that?" William demanded. "Marriage? Children? Parties, dresses, and miniature dogs?" He grabbed James by the arm and shook him, not violently but firmly enough to capture his son's attention. "No James, she does not. Your daughter would like nothing more than to live the life of a monk: spiritual, contemplative, and chaste. *Childless*," he added, putting great emphasis on the word.

James sank into a nearby chair as if he had been struck down.

"Oh God..." he moaned. "You're right, of course, Father. Where did we go wrong? If only her mother were here...."

William rather suspected that Babette's mother would only have made things worse. He could scarcely imagine the horror of her and James both fussing Babette to death. It was the sort of thing that drove sane people to suicide or murder.

"Forget her mother, James," William said. "It is up to us to manage this. The only solution is to teach Babette how to compromise between her love of intellect and her duties as a woman. By the grace of God, I have realized this now and not later. Babette is still young. She is sixteen. A year's delay in her courtship will make no great difference."

"A year?"

"A year," William repeated. "A year for her to be tutored in science, art, and philosophy. A year for her to prove that she can still maintain her place in Society in spite of her studies."

"*Studies?*" James cried. "You make it sound like she is to be sent to a university!"

Yes, William thought, *what a horror that would be.*

"I think this is all a dreadful mistake," James said. "We should be restraining Babette, punishing her for these foolish lapses, not indulging them! What will the neighbors say?"

"If all goes according to plan, they shall have nothing to comment on," William said. "Whereas, if we do nothing and simply ignore the problem, the neighbors—indeed, all of France—will have a great deal to speak of."

"But we leave for Paris at the end of the week!"

"Indeed we do," William said. "Babette will be introduced into Society. She will be presented to the Emperor and Empress. She will attend the major balls and functions this year. But in between, we will retire to this house where she will be allowed to indulge her intellect. I have even selected a tutor for her."

"But—"

William grabbed his son by the shoulders and shook him.

"James, don't you see? If we do nothing, Babette's own natural instincts will lead her into scandal! Already she ignores protocol, she dismisses social position, she despises fashion, and she is given to wandering off to the library when guests are present! Do you think she will stop all that once she is married?"

James looked down at his hands. After a long while, he finally murmured, "No…."

"There is but one solution, James," William said. "The one that I have proposed. You know as well as I that it is the only means of preventing an eventual scandal."

"But what of Paris?" James asked. "How can we hope to meet all of our social requirements while remaining here in the country?"

"James, my boy," William said, "all things are possible in this modern age."

"I'm not riding on one of those railroad machines!"

"Of course not," William said, smiling.

"And we will attend all of the season's social functions?" James asked.

"All the *important* ones, yes," William said. The list was very short in his estimation.

James looked away, his expression conveying his many doubts and great uncertainty.

"What of this tutor?" he asked.

"Most suitable," William said. "Most suitable."

"But will Babette like him?" James asked. "You remember the disaster with Monsieur Laurant…?"

"I have interviewed him myself," William said. "I have every confidence that the two of them will get on wonderfully."

CHAPTER FIVE

Paris, France

The next few days were a confused blur for Babette as she was bustled about by Father, driven mad by the fussing of servants packing—including a trunk full of new gowns that she had no interest in wearing—and finally compounded into delirium by the hurried journey south to Paris.

Their rooms in the capital were spacious and charming, but Babette had scarcely enough time to familiarize herself with the surroundings before she was again uprooted, pulled out to visit jewelers and dressmakers for even more adornments—"for later in the season," Father had said. She soon found herself forced into the company of French society and her fellow debutantes, people she had no inclination to like.

She was presented to the Emperor and Empress along with the other girls, a process that somehow managed to be both tedious and brief. The days that followed were filled with balls and luncheons, fine dinners and quiet salons. Day and night it was an unending chorus of music and trite conversation. There were no books.

It was unbearable.

It was nearly two weeks before Babette saw Korbinian again. By that time, she had lost all thought of when she might encounter him next, though he had never left her mind. Far from it: she could scarcely think of anything else as the tedium of high society surrounded her, slowly choking away her will to live. She had not seen him in Paris since their arrival, not once. By the end of the second week, she had all but given up hope.

Which is why, when she saw him at Madame de Saint-Étienne's soiree at the end of the second week, she nearly dropped her glass. For a moment she could not believe her eyes, and she stood there, amid the other guests, and stared across the well-appointed chamber. Was she mad? Was he a figment of her imagination?

But no, as she blinked several times, she realized that her eyes did not deceive her. There stood Korbinian just as she remembered him, clothed in black and scarlet and smiling at a joke only he understood. He met her eyes from across the room and slowly bowed his head. Babette felt the corner of her mouth curl up into a smirk and she nodded slightly.

The cunning devil. He had come there unannounced to surprise her! She was certain of it! But how had he known? Someone must have told him....

She closed her eyes as her mind began to whirl out of control. That was nonsense, of course. No one in Society would miss the chance to be entertained by Madame de Saint-Étienne. Her soirees were almost as official as the presentation to the Empress Eugénie. The social season was not complete without them, informal as they were. Of course Korbinian had guessed she would be there.

Babette took a sip of her wine to settle her nerves. The sight of Korbinian in all his foreign elegance was enough to make her head spin. It would not do to make a fool of herself in front of him. Or in front of the rest of Parisian society...she supposed.

She traded looks with Korbinian across the room for a few minutes, the two of them smiling at their secret communication, of which—she was certain—the rest of the company was wholly ignorant.

She was interrupted as the opulence of Madame de Saint-Étienne appeared from the crowd, dressed in a glittering gown of magnificent proportions, and rushed forward to envelope her with hospitality.

"My dear Mademoiselle Varanus," said Madame de Saint-Étienne, taking Babette's hands for a moment and giving her a warm smile. "How are you?"

"Well, Madame," Babette said.

"I am most pleased that you are here," Madame de Saint-Étienne continued, saying the same thing that she had said to every other guest over the course of the evening. Still, it was a pleasant thing to hear. At least Madame de Saint-Étienne had a spirit to her. There was more substance to her than her baubles and frills, at least if Grandfather was to be believed.

"Your father has been looking for you," she added, her eyes twinkling. "Playing the dutiful chaperone of course, as he always does."

"Yes, I fear we were separated by the crowd," Babette said. "I simply couldn't find him again, so I thought to wait here until he found me."

"Of course you did," Madame de Saint-Étienne said, smiling.

Babette smiled back politely and flicked her eyes in Korbinian's direction, wondering how to engineer a meeting with him among the throng. Their dance at Grandfather's ball had been daring enough. If she approached him here, there would be no end of unwanted gossip. That would make Father fuss more, and that would be insufferable.

But Korbinian was nowhere to be seen. He had vanished as suddenly as he had appeared. Babette felt a twinge of irritation. How dare he disappear before she had deduced a terribly clever way of speaking to him!

She looked back at Madame de Saint-Étienne and nearly cried out in surprise. Korbinian stood a few paces away, carefully maneuvering himself in the direction of Madame de Saint-Étienne's elbow.

The clever scoundrel! Clearly he meant to draw the lady's attention and inspire her to introduce them.

As expected, Madame de Saint-Étienne chanced a look in Korbinian's direction and gave a cry of delight.

"My dear Baron von Fuschburg!" she exclaimed. "So delightful that you could attend. How is your father?"

"Dead," Korbinian replied.

"Oh, what a dreadful thing," Madame de Saint-Étienne said. "Your mother?"

"In Asia."

"Oh, the poor dear! Grief does such peculiar things to a person. And yourself?"

"I am neither dead nor in Asia," Korbinian said.

Babette hid a titter of laughter behind her hand.

Without pause, Madame de Saint-Étienne turned to her. "My dear, have you met the Baron von Fuchsburg?"

"No, I—" Babette began.

"Yes," Korbinian said quickly, "at Monsieur William Varanus's ball a fortnight ago." He turned to Babette and added, "You recall, Mademoiselle, your grandfather introduced us."

Clever scoundrel indeed....

"Yes, of course," Babette said demurely. "What a pleasure, Baron. Have you been in Paris long?"

"Only the week," Korbinian said.

"How odd. I am certain I did not see you at any of the social events until now."

"No," Korbinian said, "I fear that I was otherwise engaged until tonight. But I am pleased to have completed my business. I am now entirely at your service...Madame de Saint-Étienne," he added slyly, turning toward the lady to give the impression that it was she he intended to charm.

Madame de Saint-Étienne smiled at him, then at Babette, and said, "Mademoiselle Varanus, I think I shall go and find your father. He is surely wondering where you are. I am certain you and the Baron can look after one another for a few moments."

"Of course, Madame," Babette said. "*Merci.*"

"Madame, a pleasure," Korbinian said, bowing.

Madame de Saint-Étienne looked at them carefully for a moment, as if to say "behave". Then she spun about and set off through the crowd, cooing in delight at each guest she encountered. It would take her at least a few minutes to find Father, Babette noted.

Good.

"What brings you to Paris, Baron?" Babette asked coyly.

"Why does anyone come to Paris?" Korbinian asked.

"For the culture?"

"To find a wife," Korbinian said.

"A noble aspiration," Babette said. "Every young man should find a wife. It provides a certain stability in his life."

"And do you have a great deal of experience in that regard?" Korbinian asked.

"None at all. My mind is unclouded by the frivolities of such an experience."

They shared a quiet smile at this.

"Really, why did you come?" Babette asked softly.

"To see you, of course," Korbinian said. "Why did you need to ask such a thing?"

"You ought not to speak that way," Babette said, though she was rather pleased that he did.

"Why would you believe me to be a man who does what he ought to do?" Korbinian asked, laughing softly.

"Less belief, Baron, than hope," Babette said. "One hopes that a man such as yourself does what he ought to do."

"Such as?" Korbinian asked.

"To marry, for example," Babette said. "You have come to Paris to find a wife. A man such as you *ought* to find one."

"Perhaps I already have," Korbinian said.

"That would be presumptuous of you," Babette said. "Why, you have been in Paris for less than two weeks. That is insufficient time to find a wife. A proper one at least."

"What makes a proper wife?" Korbinian asked, his eyes twinkling.

Babette thought for a short while and replied, "The ability to stand upright and to communicate by means of language."

"What a curious outlook you have," Korbinian said. "That would seem to be the most fundamental criteria for a human being."

"Clearly you have not been in Society long, nor have you any familiarity with politics."

Babette looked at Korbinian, challenging him to dispute the point with her. Korbinian merely cocked his head at her, working to hide his smile. It would not do to be seen as cheerful in public, Babette reasoned. People might talk.

"I concern myself merely with matters of war…and love," Korbinian said. "Politics and Society are terribly boring to me."

Babette looked into Korbinian's eyes and asked, "War and love? Are the two often in one another's company?"

"Why, they are almost the same thing!" Korbinian replied.

"I do not think," a familiar voice said from over Babette's shoulder, "that war is a suitable topic for a young woman."

Alfonse!

For a moment Babette's expression was clouded with fury and frustration. She quickly calmed herself and turned around, putting on her best polite smile. There stood Alfonse, resplendent as ever, towering over her like a cockerel come to claim mastery over one of his hens.

"Ah, Captain des Louveteaux," Babette said, "a pleasure as always."

"Yes," Alfonse said, "a pleasure Mademoiselle Varanus."

He did not sound very convinced of it himself. Why the devil did he have to keep bothering her when his heart was clearly for another? Everything about his manner announced that he despised her, and yet here he was, *again*, trying to assert his claim on her.

"I do not agree," Korbinian said.

Alfonse snapped his head around and looked at Korbinian.

"You…what?"

"I do not agree," Korbinian repeated. "About war. I think that it is most suitable for young ladies. After all, a young lady will become a bride. Then she will become a mother. She may become the mother of a son. And then one day her son may become a soldier and go off to war. And is it not terrible that the only time a woman may think upon war is when she fears that her son will die in it?" Korbinian shook his head. "Most dreadful, I think."

"I did not ask your opinion, Monsier," Alfonse said, drawing himself up. Tall as Korbinian was, Alfonse still managed to tower over him.

"Baron," Korbinian said.

"What?" Alfonse demanded.

"I am a baron, Monsieur." Korbinian's polite smile was a devious contrast to his commanding tone, which made Babette almost giggle with delight. "You should address me properly."

"Very well, *Baron*," Alfonse growled. "But I am no monsieur either. I am the son of the Count des Louveteaux."

"Ah!" Korbinian cried, clapping his hands in delight. "And is your father yet living?"

"He is!" Alfonse said proudly, his tone indicating that he thought he had evaded some impending comment about his heritage.

"*Wunderbar!*" Korbinian said. "Then one day you will outrank me." He smiled. "But not today."

"Hmph!" Alfonse snorted. "The son of a count—"

"Is still not a baron," Babette finished.

Alfonse turned his eyes upon her, and Babette merely looked back with a smile. She fluttered her eyelashes as innocently as she could manage.

"But you wear the uniform of an officer," Korbinian said, as if trying to make amends for the slight.

"Yes," Alfonse said. "I am a captain in His Imperial Majesty's cavalry."

"That is wonderful," Korbinian said. "You see, I also am a military man."

"Yes, I see," Alfonse said, eyeing Korbinian's uniform. "A lieutenant I presume."

"Colonel," Korbinian corrected.

"*What?*" Alfonse's eyes fairly bulged out of his head.

"As Baron of Fuchsburg, I command the Fuchsburg Regiment of the Prussian Army. I am, of course, a hussar. I find that all brave men are either hussars or dragoons. Which are you?"

Alfonse growled again.

"I am a cuirassier," he said.

"Fine men, the cuirassiers," Korbinian said. "Then again," he added, "wearing that armor does seem rather *cautious*, don't you find?"

Alfonse was in the process of turning bright red. Babette wondered whether he would try to strike Korbinian. That would be an interesting thing to see. Far better than the opera, surely.

"I didn't know they had horses in Fuchsburg," Alfonse said, speaking slowly as he struggled to reign in his temper. "From what I have heard, it is a very wooded land. With mountains."

"Yes," Korbinian said. "And while we are discussing geography, you mustn't forget that rather large river running through it."

"Quite. I only ever hear of your *infantry*. Your *riflemen*."

Alfonse clearly thought this was an insult. Korbinian seemed not to share his view.

"Yes, the *jägers*," he said proudly. "The finest light infantry in all of Europe. They killed a great many Frenchmen during the Wars of Liberation. Of course, that was during my grandfather's time. And did you know, he once shot an officer of the cuirassiers dead in mid-charge?"

"Really?" Babette asked, intrigued. Her excitement at the statement only made Alfonse look angrier, as she had intended.

"Yes," Korbinian said. "With a *windbüchse*—a wind rifle."

"A wind rifle?"

"*Ja*," Korbinian said proudly. "It used compressed air to fire a ball without smoke or noise. When our *jägers* set upon the French from the woods, the Frenchmen could not understand what was happening. They thought that it was witchcraft or the hand of God!"

Alfonse grunted.

"It sounds far-fetched to me," he said. "But if you are an officer of cavalry and your regiment is nothing but infantry—"

"We maintain a squadron of cavalry, of course," Korbinian said. "How else could I be in the hussars? No, you see there is a major in command of the Fuchsburger infantry."

"Your younger brother, no doubt," Alfonse said derisively. "Or a cousin."

"The gamekeeper, actually," Korbinian said. "A fine man with a very good head for tactics. You would enjoy serving under him, C*aptain*."

"Better a captain of noble birth than a peasant major," Alfonse snarled. "And better a common soldier in the Empire of France than master of a third-rate state among the Germans." He turned to Babette and bared his teeth at her. "Mademoiselle Varanus, I will take my leave. We will speak properly soon, and in better company."

With that, the big man turned and left.

Babette looked up at Korbinian, who looked back at her.

"What a peculiar person," Korbinian said. "I did not say anything improper, did I? My French, you understand…"

Babette smiled at him.

"Not at all, Baron," she said. "It was perfect."

Normandy, France

Though the meeting with Korbinian that night was a welcome relief from the tedium of Society, it was to be a single island amid a sea of boredom. As the month progressed, she saw less and less of him. He called at their rooms of course, only to be politely refused by Father. And while he did make an appearance at other engagements, they were few. In the meantime, Alfonse redoubled his efforts to corner Babette and impose his company upon her in Korbinian's absence. At first the challenge of politely rebuffing Alfonse was amusing, but it soon grew wearisome.

Above all, Babette longed for intelligent conversation, and there was little of that to be had.

At the end of the month, at Grandfather's insistence, they departed for a brief respite back in the country, though Father spent the entire trip reminding Babette that their stay at home was only temporary. He phrased his words in the manner of reassurances, when they did quite the opposite. Without Korbinian at hand, Paris was simply intolerable.

Babette felt a sense of calm come over her when the towers of the house came into view over the trees. She leaned out of the coach window and felt the warm sun on her face. She heard birds chirping and the scurrying of small animals in the brush as the driver turned onto the path leading up to the house. Even the clop-clop of the horses soothed her. Home was home: it would always comfort her.

As they neared the house, Babette saw a figure dressed in a riding coat, standing in front of the fountain at the center of the circular drive, waiting for them. Her heart leapt. Even at a distance, she knew it was Korbinian.

The coach had scarcely come to a stop before she flung open the door and leaped out. She was grateful that Grandfather had allowed her to change into the simpler, straighter garments she wore at home before they departed. In one of the new dresses, with their wide skirts and heaps of lace, she might have stumbled or even broken her neck on landing.

But she kept her grace as she alighted, and she approached Korbinian with as much poise as she could muster in the excitement. He in turn beamed down at her, making no effort to conceal his delight. He bowed and she curtseyed in reply, and for a little while, they simply stood there enjoying their reunion.

"Good day, Baron," Babette said at length. "What brings you here? I thought you would be in Paris."

"I find Paris to be rather tedious," Korbinian replied. "I found some relief in the company of scholars during my visit, but a young man is often looked at oddly when he prefers the company of books and bookworms to that of fashionable young ladies. I thought the country air would do me good. I see that you have had much the same revelation."

"My grandfather's idea," Babette said. "He considers it unhealthy to spend all of summer in a metropolis. Apparently, we shall be dividing our time between the country and the city."

"He is a wise man, your grandfather. A very wise man indeed."

Babette smiled and tilted her head, regarding Korbinian with great suspicion. She knew that he was up to something.

"You still have not told me why you are *here*," she said.

"Did your grandfather not tell you?" Korbinian asked.

Grandfather? What did he have to do with all of this?

"No," Babette said, "he most certainly did not."

She looked over her shoulder and saw Father and Grandfather standing by the carriage, deep in conversation. Father did not seem at all pleased, while Grandfather had the look of the cat that stole the cream.

"What didn't he tell me?" she asked, turning back to Korbinian.

The Baron flashed a devious smile and said, "Your grandfather has engaged me as your tutor for the summer."

Babette raised her head and stared at him, astonished. A tutor? For what reason? She didn't need a tutor, certainly not after the last one they had tried to impose upon her. Although it did have the felicitous coincidence of allowing her and Korbinian to spend a great deal of time—

Oh I see… she thought. She looked over her shoulder at Grandfather. She could have sworn that he winked at her.

"Well then, Baron," she said, "it seems we shall be spending a great deal of time together. For my studies."

"We shall indeed," Korbinian said. "I know all the things that a young lady ought to learn. Art, history, mathematics, the Classics, Latin and Greek, natural philosophy, riding, shooting…."

"I already know how to ride, Baron," Babette said, "and to shoot."

"Then I shall teach you to do both together," Korbinian said.

"What a curious view you have regarding the things a young lady ought to learn."

"I am from Fuchsburg," Korbinian said. "We are more enlightened there."

"I'm certain you are, Baron," Babette said.

"Now then," Korbinian said, "I am your tutor, not a baron. Call me Korbinian if it pleases you."

Babette resisted the temptation of the offer. Instead, she drew herself up and fixed him with an admonishing look.

"I most certainly shall not," she said. "Your Christian name is far too familiar. I shall call you Master von Fuchsburg."

"Meister von Fuchsburg," Korbinian said, rendering the title in German. "Yes, I like that. If only it were true."

"If I can call you neither baron nor master, how are you to be addressed, Monsieur? Colonel, perhaps?"

Korbinian laughed and replied, "I hardly think that colonels are qualified to teach anyone anything, much less Latin and Greek to young ladies."

Babette thought for a moment.

"Then I shall call you Monsieur von Fuchsburg," she said with great finality. "And you shall address me as Mademoiselle Varanus."

"I think that is most suitable," Korbinian said. "And now, I have taken the liberty of asking the servants to prepare a luncheon basket. You must be very hungry after your journey."

"I am slightly peckish, yes," Babette admitted.

"*Sehr gut!*" Korbinian clapped his hands. "Then we shall eat, begin your first lesson, and enjoy this beautiful weather all at the same time."

"Monsieur von Fuchsburg," Babette said, "that strikes me as an excellent idea."

William had known that James would be cross to learn of the plan, but his son's reaction was more comical than anything else. As they stood and watched Babette and the Baron von Fuchsburg converse, he quietly explained the details to James, working hard to conceal a smile as James's expression clouded with indignation.

"You never said that *he* would be the tutor!"

"It seemed unnecessary at the time," William replied, his voice soothing. He knew how to manage his son when this sort of foolishness took him. James simply lacked his father's broadness of vision, or indeed, any sense of vision at all.

"Is he even qualified?" James asked, his tone indicating that he expected an answer in the contrary.

"He is very well educated, yes," William said. "It will allow me to test just how he and Babette get along, and what they have in common to speak about."

"Why…?" James asked.

"Because," William said, as he watched Babette and Korbinian retire into the house, "I have given the Baron von Fuchsburg leave to court her."

Three, two, one… he counted silently.

"Father!" James cried as if on cue. "How can you do such a thing? He is completely unsuitable!"

"We don't know that yet, James," William said. "Indeed, he is so far the single most suitable man who has ever shown an interest in your daughter. That is something to be thankful for."

"Suitable? He's not even French! Good God, he's not even *English!*"

William growled a little and replied, "Do not mention your heritage with such distain, my son. And do not think less of a man because he comes from east of the Rhine. I have made inquiries. The Baron von Fuchsburg comes from an old and distinguished line of nobility. His father was Spanish, also of good family. The Baron is a hussar and commands a regiment of mixed infantry, cavalry, and artillery for the Prussian Army."

"That speaks little of him," James said. "His rank is *inherited!* I doubt that his gallantry has ever been tried!"

"Inherited it may be," William said, "but from what I understand, he gave a very good account of himself during the recent war in Italy. Very noble and brave. The equal of any man on either side, I have heard it said."

James quickly changed the subject, as he often did when William countered a poorly-argued point:

"Alfonse des Louveteaux has also served. In Italy, and in the Crimea before that."

"Alfonse des Louveteaux has no sincere interest in Babette," William said. "None at all."

"His father suggests otherwise—" James began.

"His father suggests a great many things," William interrupted, "very little of which is of any consequence. I am well acquainted with the family, James, as you will recall. I have known them since before you were born, and I have watched Alfonse grow from a child to a…man. There is only one woman for whom Alfonse des Louveteaux has any honest affection, and that is Claire de Mirabeau. Not Babette. Anyone else will be a possession to him, *at best*. And if you believe otherwise, James, you are a fool."

James looked at him in anger but held his tongue. Finally, he said, "If people learn that Babette is being courted by a stranger, by a German and a hussar, there will be talk!"

"You needn't put so much concern in idle gossip," William said.

After all, like any good Scion he knew that the best way to stop wagging tongues was to snap the necks they were attached to. William had arranged such things in the past to ebb the power of his own scandal. If Society took it upon itself to speak ill of Babette, he would attend to that as well. It was not at all unthinkable for a talkative noblewoman to be found murdered for her jewels, and scandals quickly changed their focus when the gentlemen whispering them turned up dead in the beds of harlots.

But James did not—could not—understand such things, and that made reassuring him tiresome.

"Idle gossip?" he demanded. "Father, this is Babette's reputation we are speaking of!"

"I would rather they talk about Babette being courted by a well-bred German than about her being courted by *no one at all!*" William snapped. He took a breath to regain his composure and placed a hand on his son's shoulder. "James," he said, "I know that you want what is best for Babette. But you must understand, I do as well. And I know how to do that. Have I not always steered this family on the best course?"

James slowly nodded, and said, "You have, Father. You have."

"Then trust me, James. Babette is not her mother. She is by nature a difficult girl to find a match for. Be happy that we seem to have found one and see where the summer takes us. At worst, there is always the good Captain des Louveteaux. His interest will never wane, so long as his father lives. I can assure you of that."

"If you say so, Father," James said, smiling hopefully. He seemed overly pleased at the possibility of that contingency.

William smiled back, but it was a lie. He would never allow his flesh and blood to be mated with the likes of a des Louveteaux.

Never.

CHAPTER SIX

Summer, 1861

Babette flew across the park, past the line of trees, astride her chestnut horse as it galloped onward, obeying her direction without hesitation. Caught in the wind, her hair streamed out behind her. She had lost her hat amid the chase and cared too much for the thrill of pursuit to stop to retrieve it.

Her vision had gone crimson like the color of her riding habit. She might have thought it was odd, but in the thrill of the moment, it seemed perfectly natural. The deer was no longer in sight, though she swore she could both hear and smell it. It was afraid. Elegantly afraid. It had fled for the trees in the first minutes of the chase and now lurked there—if a fleeing thing could be said to lurk—seeking an escape that would not come.

It was already dead and she knew it.

That realization formed a warm tingling on Babette's tongue. It made her hungry. Eager.

In a rush of leaves and brush, the deer burst from the trees and tried to cut across Babette's path. Korbinian emerged a moment later atop his dappled gray, driving the deer into her path.

"Shoot!" Korbinian shouted.

Babette reached for the carbine in the scabbard in front of her saddle. It did not come free. She pulled harder, growling in frustration. Ahead of her, the deer continued running. Babette nudged her horse after it as she continued to tug on the carbine. She leaned forward, pulling with all her might. The back of the horse struck her in the chest twice, knocking the breath from her.

The wind was too fast, too hot for her to breathe. Suddenly she was suffocating.

No matter. Either the deer would die or she would die. She would not give up her prey.

Finally the carbine came free. The jerk of motion nearly knocked her from the saddle, but she grabbed her horse's mane and held on hard.

Righting herself, Babette banked her horse to the side and reined it in. The creature whinnied at being denied the chase, but it obeyed. Ahead, the deer kept running, no doubt entertaining some illusionary hope of escape.

Babette raised the carbine and fired, just as Korbinian had taught her. The deer jerked, stumbled, and fell, pierced in the chest. Babette kicked her horse and hurried across the field to where the deer lay.

It was not dead—far from it, indeed. It thrashed about, trying to stand again that it might yet escape. Babette tilted her head and watched it with a sort of dread interest. How strange to see the weaker animal struggling for survival. How cold and detached the sensation, far removed from the delicious bloodlust of the chase.

Korbinian rode up alongside her and drew his rifle. It was a peculiar repeating weapon from America, a "Volcanic" as he called it. Babette watched as Korbinian took aim at the hapless deer and shot it twice through the head.

"The chase always begins in cruelty," he said, "but ends in mercy."

Babette felt the hint of a smile creep upon the corner of her mouth.

"As in love," she said.

Korbinian took her gloved hand and pressed it to his lips.

"*Ja*," he said, "but in the hunt, it is the prey who suffers cruelty and is relieved by mercy. In love, it is the hunter."

"A gentleman should not speak of love so freely," Babette said as she withdrew her hand. She reached up and touched her wild hair. "My hat is gone. I must retrieve it."

"Leave it. I prefer your hair as you are: free and spirited."

Korbinian caught her wrist and pulled it toward him. Babette gave a token resistance before allowing him to take her hand. She sighed as he pressed his soft lips to the underside of her wrist, just where the sleeve and glove met. Babette closed her eyes and allowed the sensation to enfold her senses. Soon there was nothing in the world but her wrist and Korbinian's gentle kisses.

At length, Babette finally found the strength to pull away.

"My hat," she said, opening her eyes.

She thought that Korbinian would be angry with her, as men were when they did not get their way. Instead, he smiled at her with his mysterious, knowing expression and said:

"Fetch it, then."

Babette turned her horse and retraced their path along the park. After a few minutes, she found the hat where it lay discarded among the grass, black upon green. She dismounted to claim it and walked back to Korbinian, leading her horse by the reins.

When she returned, she found Korbinian stripped to his shirt and vest, his sleeves rolled up to reveal long, graceful arms. He had his knives and tools spread out upon a blanket of leather on the ground and was already in the midst of butchering. Babette caught the scent of fresh blood and smiled, not knowing why. They had hunted together for the past three months, and each time it was the same: they chased, they killed, and then Korbinian prepared the carcass. Three months ago, Babette had only occasionally tasted venison. Now she scarcely knew how to go without it.

Korbinian looked up from his work and regarded her. He had blood on his hands and forearms.

"Come," he said, motioning to her.

"No," Babette replied. "I think I shall sit awhile and read my Schiller."

"No, no, come here," Korbinian said. "I want to show you something."

"Very well," Babette said.

She knew what to expect. Since they had started hunting together privately, Korbinian had taken it upon himself to demonstrate the finer points of skinning and butchering to Babette. He seemed to delight in it, just as he delighted in showing her how to shoot or to read German.

She knelt beside him and folded her hands in her lap.

"Another lesson?" she asked.

"Yes," Korbinian said. "I have taught you anatomy. Now it is time for you to put what you know into practice."

"With a deer?" Babette asked.

"The animal is not so unlike a man in body," Korbinian said. "A pig is closest, but the deer shall suffice."

"I find this all very questionable," Babette replied.

"Here, remove your coat," Korbinian said. "I will show you."

Babette did as instructed and took the added step of rolling up her sleeves. There would be a great deal of blood involved.

Korbinian knelt behind her and placed his hands upon hers. Babette smiled to herself at the sensation of his touch. The deliciousness of his scent—stronger now from the sweat and vigor of the chase—tickled her nose, tempting her toward follies that she would not allow herself to indulge.

"Take the knife," Korbinian said, pressing it into her hand. He had already cut back the hide from the top flank of the deer. "Begin cutting here."

Babette allowed Korbinian to guide her in cutting a long slab of meat from the flank.

"There," Korbinian said. "You have a good hand. Steady. But I knew that from the way you write your letters."

"You are too kind, Monsieur von Fuchsburg," Babette said.

She leaned back and turned her head to look at him. They shared a smile. Korbinian gently tilted her chin up and kissed her. Babette closed her eyes and leaned back into him, feeling his chest against her shoulders.

When Korbinian drew away again, Babette's eyes fluttered open and she said, dreamily, "I think you ought not to have done that, Monsieur von Fuchsburg."

Korbinian placed one finger against her lips, painting them with a smear of blood. The taste of it was delicious.

"I disagree," he said. "A fitting reward for a fine cut."

"A kiss for a cut?" Babette asked. "That seems a dangerous trade."

"Dangerous, but fair," Korbinian said.

Babette grinned at him and gently sliced off another slab of meat. The smell of heated blood mingling with Korbinian's scent made her confused and heady. She closed her eyes and savored the sensation of the knife sliding through flesh. It was such a strange experience to find violence so sensual.

Father would never have approved.

Babette removed the next slab of meat and held it up for Korbinian to see.

"A good cut?" she asked.

"Perfect," Korbinian said, kissing her.

Babette dropped the knife and took Korbinian's face in her hands, holding him close to her as their mouths pressed together. Amid the blood and excitement, she hungered for his touch and his kiss as she had never hungered before.

Korbinian took her in his arms and pulled her close to his chest. They pulled at each other, practically devouring one another in a fury of passion and desire.

Without thought of what she was doing, Babette tore Korbinan's vest from his body, sending the buttons flying into the grass. His fine shirt beneath came untucked as they tumbled about in the soft, sweet smelling grass. She felt his warm hands caress her body, gently undoing the mother of pearl buttons down the back of her blouse. In reply she strained against the confines of her corset, yearning to feel the touch of Korbinian's fingers against her skin. She felt hot and alive. All sense of reason vanished into a sweet burning haze.

They had held each other many times over the past three months and kissed more often than Babette could count, but this was different. She had delighted in Korbinian—in his touch, his smile, his kiss. Now she yearned for him in a way that she could not describe.

She pulled herself up and away from Korbinian, breaking their kiss abruptly as she pushed him back against the grass. He fell gracefully on his back, his hands ever so gently resting on her hips. His gray eyes stared intently into hers for a moment, a charming half-smile playing about his lips. Babette shifted slightly, the rustling of her skirt enveloping them. She moved atop him and kissed him while his hands caressed her shoulders and arms. She ran her hands through his black hair and down to his soft shirt.

After a moment's hesitation, she tore open his shirt to expose his smooth, pale chest. So elegant. So beautiful. She ran her fingers against his warm skin.

Korbinian grabbed Babette's throat, making her gasp in surprise. His grip tightened and he pulled her to him until their lips met again. Korbinian ran his fingers through her hair, tossing it wildly about her face. Babette smiled and laughed softly. She kissed him, biting his lip and drawing blood. She savored the taste of it.

Korbinian took her hand in his and gently pressed her fingers to his lips, kissing each fingertip in turn.

"*Liebchen*," he whispered, his voice heavy with desire.

"Korbinian—" Babette breathed.

"Babette, my love," Korbinian said, brushing back the hair behind Babette's ear. "You are like fire. You are the heat that has drawn me in from the cold."

He kissed her palm and wrist tenderly, making Babette gasp with delight.

"Ah, my love, my love!" Korbinian cried, as he held her close, his hands caressing her tightly corseted waist. "Since first we met I have desired you with all my being, with my very soul!"

"Your words, Korbinian," Babette said, "they are my words to you!"

"*Liebchen!*"

Korbinian held Babette tighter still and kissed her fiercely. Babette held him in turn, feeling the lean muscles of his back rippling beneath his shirt.

"Free me," Babette whispered, pulling off her blouse. Together, she and Korbinian tore at her clothes until she was reduced to skirts and corset. She tugged at the corset but it held fast.

"Allow me," Korbinian said.

He drew one of the knives and cut the laces along Babette's back in a single, smooth stroke. The corset fell to the ground, and a shiver of delight flowed through Babette. Free from the confines of her stays, she clutched Korbinian with renewed vigor, yearning to feel his touch upon her skin.

"We are as one," Korbinian said, kissing her neck with gentle lips. "Now…and forever."

* * * *

William was in the back hallway, on his way from the library to the stairs, when he scented blood. It was not fresh—an hour or two old perhaps—and it was faint. But it was there.

He turned and saw Babette and Korbinian standing near the side door. Some effort had been put into straightening their clothes, but lost buttons and torn laces could not be covered up.

They were damp as well. They had washed themselves in the river before returning. They had been hunting and must have butchered their kill. The thought made William smile a little.

And there was something else as well....

William stopped his pondering. Babette and Korbinian stood still as stone, looking at him with apprehension, like mice caught by a cat. Ready to run.

William looked both ways along the corridor and saw that they were alone. He nodded toward the servants' stairs.

"Be quick," he said.

He allowed Korbinian to pass but caught Babette by the arm when she tried to follow. Korbinian looked back at them, but William matched his eyes for a moment and forced the young man to relent and withdraw without comment.

William turned back to Babette and asked, "Do you love him?"

"I do, Grandfather," Babette said, looking up at him in earnest. "With all my heart."

"Good," William said. He released her and patted her hand. "Go, make yourself presentable for dinner."

Babette smiled and said, "Yes, Grandfather," before hurrying off toward the stairs.

William smiled and stroked his beard. All was progressing to his satisfaction. Over the previous months, he had seen Babette and Korbinian drawing ever closer to one another, sharing heat and desire, passion and accord. Any lingering doubts about either of them were fading away.

Now there remained but one person left to convince, the most critical to arranging Babette's marriage:

Her father.

CHAPTER SEVEN

Autumn, 1861

The arrival of autumn came as a relief to Babette. It meant the end of the social season, and with it the end of their regular trips back and forth between home and Paris, which she could not help but regard as an unnecessary interruption of her time with Korbinian. Each trip to the metropolis had done little but bore her and force her and Korbinian to restrain their natural impulses beneath the chains of decorum.

Which was not to say that it had not been enjoyable smiling at one another across the ballrooms and parlors, sharing a private joke at a distance amid the ignorant masses of the *elite*. But there were only so many times she could watch Korbinian snicker at the follies of their peers without giving in to the desire to kiss him. In Paris, the temptation had been unbearable.

But safely returned to Grandfather's estate, Babette lost no time in taking advantage of every moment to be spent with Korbinian. Her studies had been repeatedly interrupted by the trips to the city, and now she threw herself back into them with abandon. The changing of the season renewed the discussion on the nature and qualities of plants, while the arrival of the harvest invoked great excitement in Korbinian, who took it as an excuse to discuss different harvest celebrations across Europe. From there, the lessons quickly began to embrace the study of folklore. Babette was certain that Father would not approve.

With the air still pleasant but free of the oppressive summer heat, they spent more and more time walking the grounds, especially the forest that dominated one side of the property beyond the gardens and orchards. Korbinian loved this part of the estate the most, he often told her. The romance of those deep woods reminded him of his home, and he often spoke at length of it and of the many delights that Babette would find there when they were married.

Marriage was a point on which neither of them had any doubts.

"I feel," Korbinian said, as they strolled through the forest arm in arm, "that we must make an expedition to Mont Blanc. I am given to understand that the primeval horror of the view is most inspiring."

Babette sighed at him and rested her head against his shoulder. She could not have done so in company, but there among the ancient trees, they were free to profess love and affection, whether in triumphant oaths or quiet gestures.

"You have been reading Shelley again," Babette said.

"And what if I have?" Korbinian asked. He raised Babette's hand to his lips and kissed it. "Herr Shelley is a fine poet. He stirs the soul with his words, even if they are English."

"Oh, what nonsense!" Babette scoffed at the very idea.

Korbinian caught her by the chin and turned her face toward him.

"You do not agree, *liebchen?*" he asked in his usual charming way.

Babette looked into his eyes and smiled.

"You may call it a 'philosophical dispute' if you like," she said, "but I assure you that I do not agree with you. Nor can you convince me otherwise."

"Is that so?" Korbinian asked as he leaned in to kiss her.

"It is," Babette whispered as she closed her eyes and inhaled with anticipation.

As her lips brushed his, Babette heard a noise in the trees. She pulled away and turned sharply. Her eyes darted about as she searched for the source of the sound. Korbinian, surprised at the abrupt change, placed a hand upon the back of her neck and gently stroked her hair.

"What is it, my love?" he asked softly.

What a question! Could it be possible he had not heard the sound? But no, surely not. It had been so loud and clear to Babette's ears.

There it is again, she thought. *Closer this time.*

"Something's approaching," she said.

Korbinian listened carefully and said, "I hear nothing."

"Nevertheless, it is there," Babette said.

She finally fixed on the sound's direction and pointed.

Korbinian drew his pistol and held her close at his side.

"What is it?" he asked.

"I do not know," Babette said, clutching his arm.

She heard the sound again, closer and louder, accompanied by snorting and growling. This time Korbinian heard it too. He swung his revolver around and aimed it into the brush.

"Whatever it is," he said, "I will kill it."

"With a pistol?" Babette asked.

Such beautiful arrogance. What a typical hussar.

The brush and branches a dozen feet away split apart in a torrent of leaves and splinters. A dark figure lurched through the opening, knocking aside a sapling and uprooting it in the process. At first Babette thought the creature to be a bear, for its massive, hunched body was covered in coarse brown fur. But its head was of an improper shape—too broad of jaw, flat of snout, and sharp of brow—quite unlike any of the skulls Babette had seen in Grandfather's study.

The creature lumbered forward, walking on its knuckles like an ape. It studied Babette with pale eyes for a moment and sniffed the air. Satisfied by something, it turned its gaze toward Korbinian, and its mouth split open to reveal pointed teeth, ivory amid hungry red.

"*Gott in Himmel!*" Korbinian cried.

He fired his revolver at the beast, but the beast showed no reaction, not even a hint of pain. It continued its advance with slow, measured steps. Korbinian fired again and again until his weapon was empty, but the beast merely grunted.

To Babette, it almost sounded like guttural laughter. With each shot the beast seemed to smile.

The beast lunged forward into the last two shots, taking them as easily as pebbles thrown by a child. First it struck Babette, backhanding her in the chest and flinging her away. The force of the blow made everything go black. Time vanished and, for what seemed like ages, Babette forgot who and where she was.

The first sensation she recognized was the hard discomfort of the ground digging into her back. Babette forced her eyes open and raised her head. Scarcely moments had passed since she had been struck, though it felt like it had been ages.

"*Liebchen*, flee!" Korbinian shouted.

Babette looked and saw him draw a knife and lash out at the beast. The beast grunted and knocked the weapon away.

Babette forced herself up on her elbows, every movement making her body shudder. Perhaps if she ran, she could get far enough away before the beast had finished killing and consuming Korbinian. Certainly that was what he hoped. But Babette would be damned if she left the man she loved to be eaten while she fled like a coward.

Claire de Mirabeau might do such a thing, but not a Varanus.

The beast drew back its paw and slashed Korbinian across the chest. Its claws, like knives, tore through the layers of Korbinian's coat, waistcoat, and shirt with ease. Korbinian cried out in pain and stumbled. A moment later he fell in a heap on the ground.

"No!" Babette shouted. She reached out toward her beloved as he collapsed.

The beast turned toward her and looked at her curiously. The expression in its eyes was both intense and thoughtful, and it made her shiver. A beast in want of reason should not have known such understanding.

The beast raised its claws, still dripping with Korbinian's blood, and licked them clean with its thick tongue. The sight made Babette cry out again, and she struggled to rise. She could not find the breath to move, and her body rebelled. She fell backward into the dirt once more. The beast chuffed at her. It sounded like a laugh.

Babette watched as Korbinian began to crawl toward his knife. It was a futile effort, but the refusal to succumb made Babette giddy for a moment.

She forced herself to her feet, aching with every movement. The beast had turned away from her and now loomed over Korbinian, watching him as if amused by his futile attempt to escape.

Babette looked about for a weapon. The pistol was empty—not that it had done any good—and the beast was between her and the knife. Her eyes fell upon the uprooted sapling that the beast had torn from the ground.

It was an unlikely chance, but it was the only one that Babette could see.

She stumbled over to the sapling and picked it up. The young tree was heavy and unwieldy, but under the heat of the moment, she found that she lifted it with ease. Babette spun around and saw the beast hunched over Korbinian, pinning his arms down with its massive forepaws.

She hefted the sapling and ran for the beast. If the pistol's bullets and the knife had been unable to stop it, a blow to the body with a glorified cudgel would be no better.

Find someplace vulnerable... Babette thought.

The eyes.

Babette raised the sapling into the air as best she could and brought it down on the beast's head with all her might. She had been aiming for the bridge of the beast's snout, but instead she connected with the top of its brow. Her makeshift club struck and bounced off, making her stumble back a pace.

But it had had an effect. The force of the blow made the beast lurch, though it showed no sign of pain. Instead, it looked up, having suddenly forgotten Korbinian, and patted the top of its head with one massive forepaw. Slowly it turned toward Babette and snarled at her.

Babette swung the sapling again and struck the beast full in the face with its roots. The beast let out a snarl of pain and jerked away, lashing out at the sapling with its claws. Babette was thrown off balance and fell to her knees, but the beast withdrew a few paces as it rubbed its eyes with the heel of its forepaw.

Hand, Babette realized. The beast's forepaw was like a hand, fingers and all. Good God, what sort of creature was this?

She picked herself up again and raised the sapling. With a roar that rose from her toes and into her belly, she charged at the beast and swung again, throwing all her weight into the blow.

The beast reached out with one hand and snatched the sapling in midair. With a single, easy movement, it tore the weapon from Babette's grasp and flung it away. Babette fell onto her side and threw up an arm to shield herself, expecting the beast's next blow to be on her.

When nothing came, she opened her eyes and saw the beast looming over her, watching her. It sniffed at her and grunted. For a moment it seemed to shake its head.

What can be the meaning of this? Babette thought. Why had it not killed her?

The beast chuffed. One massive hand took her by the shoulder and shoved her aside. Babette rose again as quickly as she fell. Grabbing the beast by the arm, she pulled herself ahead of it and flung herself upon Korbinian. The beast drew up short and snorted angrily at her. It reached for her again, but she pulled away from it, all the while keeping herself between it and Korbinian.

The barking of dogs rose in the distance. The beast raised its nose and sniffed the air. Grunting, it looked into Babette's eyes. Babette stared back and saw something there she never thought an animal could know: frustration.

The beast turned and thundered back into the brush.

Babette lay there, gasping for breath for a few moments. She could scarcely comprehend what had just happened, what she had just seen.

What the deuce...?

Another thought came to her:

Korbinian!

Babette turned and looked down at Korbinian. His eyes were closed, but he was breathing. Babette touched his cheek, and his eyelids fluttered open.

"Babette..." he murmured.

"Hush," Babette said.

She pulled the tattered edges of Korbinian's clothing away from his bloody chest. She gasped at the sight of the wounds left by the beast's claws. Korbinian's pale skin was awash with blood, the old mass drying and dark amid the flowing crimson.

"*Liebchen...*" Korbinian said, reaching out for her.

Babette pushed his hand away impatiently.

"Be still, my love!" she said. "For God's sake, be still."

What could she do? The claws had not cut deep—Korbinian's ribs were still intact—but the blood was endless. She would have to staunch the flow of it. Only then could she even begin to think about moving him. That would be a dreadful risk, but she could not leave him there, not in his state.

But what to use for bandages? All their clothes were covered in dirt, and dirt seemed the last thing that should be going inside one's body.

But of course, she realized, not all of their clothing had been soiled during the fight.

Babette grabbed Korbinian's knife from where it had fallen and wiped it off on the cleanest part of her sleeve. She hiked up her skirt and began cutting her petticoats into pieces as quickly as she could manage. For the first time in her life, she had found a practical use for the damnable things.

She packed a bunch of fabric pieces together into a mass and placed it against Korbinian's chest. She pushed on it as hard as she could, just as it had been described to her during their many lessons on medicine. To think that now she the student had to perform on her teacher.

Or that his life depended on how well she had learned.

Babette bit her lip, but the grim realization only hardened her resolve. Korbinian would not die because of her.

The sound of dogs was louder now. Babette turned toward it and saw a pair of hounds, straining at their leashes, leading a figure in rough clothing through the trees.

"Gustave!" Babette shouted, recognizing the figure as her grandfather's game warden.

"Mademoiselle?" Gustave said. He hurried to her and knelt, looking at Korbinian in shock. "What has happened? I heard a shot and thought it was poachers."

"There is no time!" Babette said. "Lift his chest for me."

Gustave set his shotgun down and looped the dogs' leads around a branch. The animals were incensed, and they snarled and barked in the direction that the beast had fled.

Without a word, Gustave took Korbinian by the shoulders and raised his upper body. Babette cut longer strips of cloth from what remained of her petticoats and wrapped them around Korbinian's chest, binding the wound tightly. They would not be good for long, but at least the makeshift bandages would last until he could be returned to the house.

"Gustave," Babette said, "you must return to the house. Tell them that there has been an animal attack. Fetch men, fetch a cart, and have them send for a doctor at once!"

"But Mademoiselle, I cannot leave you—" Gustave began.

"And I cannot leave *him!*" Babette snapped. "The dogs will protect me. Give me your shotgun if you think they are not enough."

Gustave picked up the shotgun and hesitated. Babette snatched it from him and set it on her lap.

"Now go!" she shouted.

Gustave bowed his head, stood, and raced off in the direction of the house.

Babette's head swam from the excitement. In the sudden calm, she felt herself falling into a swoon, and she knelt with her head down for a moment to steady herself.

"Babette, my love?" she heard Korbinian ask weakly.

She turned to him and looked into his eyes, smiling bravely. She could not lose him. It would be the death of her, she knew that now.

Touching his cheek, she said, "Be strong, my dearest. You must be strong. Help is coming. But you must keep your eyes open."

Korbinian took her hand and pressed it to his lips.

"I could never look away from you, *liebchen*," he said softly. "So long as you are here, I will never close my eyes."

There was such pain and such determination in his voice that Babette felt tears wet her eyes.

"*Liebchen*," Korbinian said, gasping for breath, "my love for you is such that I cannot describe it. I could die now content in knowing that you are safe."

"*You will not die!*" Babette cried. "I forbid it!"

Korbinian smiled at her and took her hand. He kissed it gently and said, "Mademoiselle Babette Varanus, I have but one thing to ask of you."

"What?" Babette asked.

Why had Korbinian suddenly used her proper name for the first time in months?

"If I live," Korbinian said, struggling with his words, "I wish that you would give to me the greatest happiness that a man can ever know."

He looked into her eyes and clutched her hand tightly.

"Babette, my darling, will you consent to be my wife?"

Babette's breath caught in her throat. Such a thing had always been understood between them, but it was an unspoken understanding. Now, to hear the question asked in full....

She wept freely with joy and kissed him. She could hardly speak, but there was only one word she needed to say—indeed, only one word she *could* say.

"Yes!"

CHAPTER EIGHT

William found James in the parlor, playing a sentimental tune on the pianoforte. He watched his son in silence from the doorway, listening to the music as James, enraptured by his work, failed even to notice his approach, much less stop playing.

I should despise him, William thought. And it was true. James was so weak, so fragile, so sensitive.

So unforgivably human.

That alone was crime enough in the eyes of most Scions on the Continent, which was compounded further by his softness of spirit, his lack of will, and his foolishness. It was a miracle that he had fathered Babette, especially in light of his late wife who had been worse even than he.

But even so, William could only look upon his son with pity, perhaps even with love. James was like a pup that could not grow up.

"James," William said, stepping into the parlor and approaching the pianoforte, "I would like to speak to you."

James looked up in surprise and said, "Of course, Father, what troubles you?"

William sat in a nearby chair and folded his hands.

"James," he said, "we must speak seriously about Babette."

"What about Babette?" James asked, paling slightly. "Has there been talk?"

Bloody fool, William thought, *fussing over what the neighbors think of us.*

"Of course not, James. Do you not recall? She was a perfect young lady in Paris. Indeed, she and the Baron von Fuchsburg were the pinnacle of elegance and propriety."

"Yes, that is true," James said, smiling. "Her mother would have been so very proud...."

William cleared his throat and said, "Of course she would have been. But to the matter at hand. We cannot deny that there is a great affection forming between Babette and von Fuchsburg."

Evidently James *could* deny it, for he raised a finger in protest.

"Now just a moment—" he began.

"James," William said, interrupting his son, "denying the fact will not change it. Let us acknowledge the truth of the matter."

James hesitated and finally nodded.

"Very well, I will acknowledge that Babette has formed an *infatuation* with the Baron. But what of it?"

"It is not infatuation, James," William said. "It is love. Of that I am certain."

"Love?" James demanded. "Father, how can you say such a thing?"

"How can you deny it?" William asked. "One needs merely to watch them for an hour to see the way that they look at one another, speak to one another, even sit in silence with one another. It is love, James. And I feel quite certain that should we deny them, the result will be disastrous."

"You exaggerate, Father."

"I do not," William said. "And James, you cannot deny it."

James shifted uncomfortably and looked toward the windows.

"Why do you come to me about this?" he asked.

"Because, James," William said, "I suspect that one day very soon, young Korbinian will ask for Babette's hand in marriage. And you and I will give the union our blessing."

"I will do no such thing!" James cried. "What a horrible notion!"

"To grant your daughter leave to marry the man she loves?"

"He's a *German!* People will talk!"

"Better German than English, I suspect," William said with a chuckle. "And I do not doubt that his refined lineage will outweigh any concerns regarding his lack of French blood."

"It's precisely his lineage that will be discussed! There are such rumors about the von Fuchsburgs."

"I would still rather people talk about Babette marrying a von Fuchsburg than about her not being married at all."

"Surely it will not come to that," James said. "In time—"

"Who else is there that she will marry?" William asked sternly.

James was a weak creature. With enough pressure he would succumb. It was just a matter of force and reason.

"Well, Alfonse des Louveteaux—"

"She despises him," William said. "And he holds no love for her either."

"Nonsense," James said. "Why, Louis—"

"Alfonse loves only his cousin, Claire, whatever his father might say about it. Do not be deceived, James. Louis des Louveteaux has only his own interest at heart: not his son's, not ours, and certainly not Babette's. I can see quite plainly now that the only man she is likely to be happy with is the Baron von Fuchsburg. And her happiness is sufficient for me. You do want her to be happy, don't you?"

James's face took on a pained and indecisive expression at the suggestion. William smiled inwardly. He had chosen the correct piece of leverage. Whatever his faults, James truly did love his daughter.

"Of course, Father, but are you *certain* that von Fuchsburg will make her happy?"

"He already does," William said.

There was a commotion in the hall, and William stood and turned toward it, ready to admonish whichever of the servants had seen fit to disturb them. He saw the footman Vatel in the doorway. The man's face was ashen.

"Vatel, what is it?" William demanded.

"It is Mademoiselle Varanus, sir," Vatel said. "And the Baron von Fuchsburg."

"What of them?"

"There has been an attack, sir."

"Good God!" James cried, rising from his seat. "Babette!"

William waved his son into silence and asked, "What happened? Who is hurt?"

"An animal of some sort attacked them in the forest," Vatel said. "Only the Baron was injured, but Mademoiselle Varanus refused to leave his side."

James gasped and cried, "She's not still out there, is she?"

"She is, Monsieur," Vatel said. "Gustave, who found them, said that she sent him back to bring help and a cart."

"And a doctor," William said. "Make it so, Vatel. *Now!*"

"It will be done, sir."

"Did Gustave say what kind of animal attacked them?" William asked.

Vatel thought for a moment before replying, "You may wish to ask him yourself, sir, but I believe he said 'a bear.' He only caught a fleeting glance."

William felt the blood rising in him. An attack in the woods? Along the border of Louis des Louveteaux's property? By a bear? And only Korbinian was injured?

"Vatel, have the carriage sent for Doctor Artois at once," William said. "And tell the groom to saddle my horse."

William did not wait to be shown into the des Louveteaux house. As soon as the footman had opened the door for him, he shoved the man to one side and stormed into the opulent foyer. He took a moment to look around for any sign of the family and another moment to frown disdainfully at the gaudy surroundings. The des Louveteaux had never recovered from the shock of the Revolution, and even now they surrounded themselves with the worst aesthetic crimes of the *Ancien Régime*.

"Monsieur, I must insist—" the footman began.

William grabbed him by the collar and forced him to his knees.

"Where is Louis?" he demanded.

"I…I…" the footman stammered.

"*Where?*"

"William?" Louis's voice came from the direction of the upstairs landing.

William looked up and saw Louis descending the stairs. The man's stance was one of caution, his expression innocent, but the look in his eyes said everything.

He knows. As I suspected.

"William, what is the meaning of this?" Louis asked, reaching the ground floor. "You are, of course, always welcome in my home, but to come unannounced? And to manhandle my servants? What madness—"

"I know what was done, Louis," William said. Thankfully all of Louis's servants were inducted into the cult, and William was at liberty to speak freely. "Not an hour ago my granddaughter and her tutor were set upon by a beast in the woods shared by our lands. A beast that assaulted only von Fuchsburg. A beast that my gamekeeper described as being 'like a bear.'"

"William, you cannot possibly believe that I had anything to do with this," Louis said. "There *are* beasts about. Do not forget, we cultivate them so that we may hunt them when we grow old and weary of stag and fox. Who am I to say who is attacked by one?"

"Do not trifle with me, Louis," William said. "Do you have any sense of the scale of this affront? You have meddled in my family's affairs time and again, and this time you have gone beyond the pale!"

Louis tried to lay a hand on William's arm, but William pushed him away with a sharp growl.

"Where is he?" William asked.

"Who?"

"You damn well know who!" William snarled. "Your trained hound! Your grandfather's illegitimate whelp! The only creature that would have savaged my granddaughter's tutor while leaving her unharmed." He raised his finger and held it before Louis's eyes. "I know what you are about. You know that Babette has no interest in your son, so you seek to kill off the only young man in her life!"

"William, how dare—" Louis began.

"Let me tell you, Louis des Louveteaux, your plot is of no avail! Even were he the only man in all of Europe, Babette would never consent to marry your son! And were it not for your meddling, he would seek no claim on her either!"

"William, I insist that you leave *at once!*" Louis barked. "Or else I shall bring complaint against your trespass on my territory!"

William only half heard Louis. A scent had caught his attention, and he sniffed at the air. It was blood. The boy's blood, if he was not mistaken.

Where was it coming from?

William pushed Louis away and advanced deeper into the house, past the parlor and the dinning room. With every step, the smell of blood grew stronger. And with every step, Louis struggled to deter him.

"I have had enough of this foolishness, William," he said, grabbing at William's arm. "Leave at once!"

William swatted him away. Louis grabbed for him again, this time with a serious grasp. William spun about and growled, baring his teeth in challenge. It was an unthinkable thing to do in another Scion's home, and Louis drew back from the very shock of William's sacrilege.

At the back of the house, William flung open the door to the servants' passage. In the half-light, he saw Gustave's 'beast' just as he had expected: a tremendous mass of fur and muscle, not quite badger, or wolf, or bear, that glowered back at him with pale blue eyes. A pair of servants struggling to wash the creature in the cramped space turned and stared wide-eyed at William.

"Good day, Gérard," William said.

The beast snorted and bobbed its head in a nod.

William turned to Louis and said, "Perhaps next time you should hide him in the carriage house."

"I frighten horses," the beast growled.

Louis made a noise.

"Be quiet, Gérard," he told the beast.

"The scent of the boy's blood is still on him, Louis," William said. "No more of your lies. You sent Gérard to kill him."

Louis hesitated but finally spoke:

"The boy is human. There are no protocols against such a thing."

"As my granddaughter's tutor, he is a member of my household," William said. "That is an affront in itself. What is more, the crime was committed on my land. These are grounds for war, Louis."

Louis laughed at his words.

"You would not dare. My family alone outmatches yours. Your allies are few and mine are many."

"My cousins in England may have exiled me," William said, "but if it comes to war, they will defend their blood. I am certain that they should be overjoyed to expand their lands into Normandy and beyond."

"A gamble," Louis said.

"Yes," William said, "but one that the elders will take seriously when I bring it before them along with my complaint against you for your abhorrent trespass against my estate."

"You wouldn't dare," Louis said.

"Good day, Louis," William said, turning and walking back toward the foyer.

"Wait!" Louis snapped.

William did not stop.

"Wait!" Louis repeated, hurrying after him. "What is it you want?"

William smiled a little. Those were hard words for Louis to say.

In the foyer, William turned toward Louis and said, "You will withdraw your suit toward my granddaughter. Your son will no longer court her, you will relinquish your claim before the elders, and you will stop your damnable attempts to convince my son of the union's wisdom. You and yours will leave my family alone. Do this, and I will be silent. Do not, and by our great ancestor, I will bring every shame and fury down upon your head. Are we clear?"

Louis worked his mouth without speaking for a minute, while William looked at him in silence.

"Very well," Louis said, "so agreed."

"Good," William said with a smile. He snapped his fingers at the footman and motioned for him to open the door.

"But William," Louis continued, "understand that this matter between us is not finished."

"Such matters never are, Louis," William said. "Not until death."

Babette had never prayed before in her life. Not properly. She had been forced to attend church, of course. It was extremely important to Father, as it had been to Mother while she had lived. But each time Babette bowed her head, each time she said her rosary, it was a lie perpetrated to deceive those who could not accept the truth: that there was no God, just like Grandfather said.

But as she sat at Korbinian's side, holding his hand tightly while Doctor Artois struggled to stitch closed his chest, she found herself offering a few silent words of supplication to the Almighty for Korbinian's safety.

Just in case.

Korbinian, in the throws of a brief period of lucidity, fluttered his eyelids open and smiled at her. A moment later, he gasped in pain at the next tug of the thread and clenched his eyes shut.

"There," the gray-haired Doctor Artois said as he snipped the thread. "The wounds are clean and closed now." He motioned to Vatel, who stood nearby. "Come, help me bandage him."

"Will he…will he live, Doctor?" Babette asked.

Artois shrugged, sympathetically and with sincere uncertainty.

"Who can say?" he asked. "He is in God's hands now. But," he added, "the Baron is young and healthy. Strong. I believe that he has as much chance as any man in his place."

Babette squeezed Korbinian's hand and felt him squeeze back.

"*Liebchen*…?" he asked.

Babette looked down and touched his cheek.

"I am here," she said.

"Good," Korbinian said, smiling weakly. He patted the table on which he lay. "Is this a table?"

"Yes," Babette said, laughing, relieved that he was strong enough to ask such a silly question. "You are in the dining room. It was too difficult to carry you up the stairs."

"Have I bled all over the Persian carpet?" Korbinian asked.

"No," Babette said.

What a fool he was to worry about such things.

"Where is he?" came Grandfather's bellowing voice from the hallway. A moment later, he appeared in the doorway, hat in hand. He looked upon the assembled and ran a hand through his mane of hair.

"Doctor," he said to Artois, exchanging a nod, "thank you for coming."

"It is my pleasure, as always, Monsieur Varanus," Artois said as he cleaned Korbinian's blood from his hands in a small basin of water. Drying them, he added, "Mademoiselle Varanus was of great assistance to me in keeping the Baron awake during the procedure."

Babette smiled proudly and was rewarded with an approving nod from Grandfather.

"Where is James?" Grandfather asked.

Everyone else in the room exchanged awkward looks.

"Father had to lay down in the morning room after the great strain of worry," Babette said.

In fact, Father had fainted at the first sight of Korbinian. Or perhaps it had been Babette, unharmed but also covered in blood, that had caused him to be overcome. Knowing Father, that was the more likely.

"Will he live?" Grandfather asked, motioning to Korbinian.

Artois laughed a little and said, "That is the question of the hour. I believe that he will. The Baron von Fuchsburg is a strong young man. But for that to happen, he must be allowed to rest."

Babette rose and joined them.

"Can we move him from the table?" she asked.

The hard wood surface must be of great discomfort to him.

"Yes, I am finished here," Artois said. "If Gustave and Vatel would be good enough to prepare the stretcher, let us move the good Baron to someplace more comfortable. But he must remain on this floor until he can walk. He will be too difficult to carry upstairs without aggravating the wound."

Grandfather looked at Babette, who still held Korbinian's hand tightly.

"Gustave, Vatel, do as the good doctor asks. Put him on the *chaise longue* in the library. That should be comfortable enough. And once he is well enough to sit up, there will be plenty to occupy him while he convalesces."

The library? Babette smiled. *Then I shall have every pretext to see him.*

She looked at her grandfather, wondering if he understood that implication.

Grandfather caught her gaze and smiled at her. Babette knew the look.

He knew. And he approved.

"Babette, what are you doing here at this hour?"

Babette looked up from her book and laid it in her lap. She saw Father standing a few paces inside the library door, wearing his dressing gown and cap. He was ready to retire.

What time was it?

Babette glanced toward the clock on the mantelpiece. It was near midnight.

"Babette?" Father said again. "Babette, do you hear me?"

"I am reading, Father," Babette said, smiling. "Plutarch."

"Ah, yes," Father said. "You and your Greeks." He shook his head. "But why are you reading at this hour?"

Babette patted Korbinian as he lay on the *chaise longue* next to her chair.

"I am watching over the Baron through the night. Doctor Artois felt that we should not leave him alone."

Father frowned and said, "Surely one of the servants—"

"Father," Babette said, "the Baron von Fuchsburg risked his life protecting me from the beast that attacked us. It would be dreadful and callous of me not to sit the first watch."

Father sighed but nodded.

"I suppose that much is true," he said. "You are such a good young woman. So dedicated. So much like your mother."

"Thank you, Father."

"Well…" Father said, clearing his throat. "I suppose I shall retire."

"Goodnight, Father," Babette said.

Father hesitated in the doorway.

"I am so very glad that you were not killed today," he said.

"I know, Father," Babette said. She smiled at him, strangely touched by the sentiment in his voice.

He was truly afraid that I had been hurt, she thought.

"Well, goodnight, Babette," Father said.

"Goodnight."

Babette watched her father depart the library and close the door behind him. She picked up her book and resumed her reading. After a moment, she felt a hand upon her leg.

"*Liebchen?*" Korbinian asked amid a wide yawn.

Babette took his hand and squeezed it.

"I am here, my dearest," she said. "I am here."

"Good." Korbinian yawned again. "I am very tired."

Babette smiled. She leaned over and kissed him gently. Brushing the hair away from his face, she said:

"Rest then, my love. And I will be here when you wake."

Korbinian regarded her with heavy eyes, a smile playing delicately about his lips.

"Always?" he asked.

"Always."

CHAPTER NINE

Winter, 1861

Babette lowered her book and gazed off into the cold sunlight outside. The remainder of autumn had passed by with Korbinian confined to bed—his bed, thankfully, once he had been able to hobble upstairs with Vatel's aid—and now winter had gripped the land with its chilled fingers. The orchards were bare, the trees skeletal.

Babette had not ridden in weeks, not that she had planned to do much riding in any event. She had lost track of how much time she had spent at Korbinian's bedside. Almost every waking hour had been devoted to watching over him. Babette simply found that she could not trust anyone else with the task.

A bird landed on the branch of a tree outside and fluttered its wings. Babette watched it in silence. How terrible it must be for the poor creature to be alone in the cold. How had it come to be there without others of its kind?

At her side, Korbinian shifted in his bed and slowly blinked. He had been sleeping a great deal since the attack, but his eyes were as bright as ever. He looked up at her and smiled.

"Ah, my dearest," he said, "as ever, you are the morning star, greeting me with your radiance each time I awaken."

He took her hand and held it against his lips. Babette sighed and smiled.

How lovely life was.

"I have been asleep for how long?" Korbinian asked.

"Today?" Babette glanced at the clock. "Ten hours."

It seemed longer. But of course, Babette had lost proper track of time over the days. All that mattered was Korbinian.

"I have been too long in bed," Korbinian said, sitting up with Babette's assistance. "I must not be so idle."

"Shh, shh," Babette said, placing one hand upon Korbinian's chest and pushing him back against the pillows. "You must rest."

"I have rested for weeks," Korbinian said, frowning. "I grow tired of it."

Babette rested her chin on her hand and smiled quietly.

"And I have watched over you as you rested every day," she said. "Do you grow tired of my company? For I can easily depart and leave you in peace...all on your own."

That would get a rise out of him.

Korbinian laughed and touched her cheek with his soft fingertips.

"Hush, my darling," he said. "I have treasured every moment we have spent together. But surely, our time would be better spent out and about."

"In the bitter cold?" Babette asked, giggling.

Korbinian held his head high and said, "Amid winter's monstrous majesty."

"Monstrously cold majesty," Babette corrected.

Korbinian smiled at her.

"The cold is one thing that makes us human. Who but man braves the worst of winter? Animals seek shelter in their dens when the earth is frozen and the land wrapped in snow. But man braves the cold without complaint. It is part of his mastery over nature."

"I believe," Babette said, "that man's greatest mastery over nature is his ability to build houses, to create shelter where there is none."

She smiled and tilted her head, looking out of the window through the corner of her eye. She could almost feel the sharpness of winter's chill on her face.

"We honor the greatness of civilization," she said, "by sitting here and staying warm."

Korbinian smiled at her and took her chin between thumb and forefinger.

"That is not at all adventurous of us," Korbinian said.

Babette took Korbinian's hand and lifted it to her lips. She gently kissed his fingertips and said:

"Nonsense. We can be far more adventurous, and comfortable, if we stay here."

Korbinian stroked her cheek with his free hand and murmured, "Well, that sounds very sensible of you."

"Grandfather has always said that I am the sensible one in the family," Babette said.

She ran her fingers along Korbinian's chest, across the soft bandages. They were clean and dry, though they had not been changed in a day. It was a good sign. Korbinian was recovering quickly. Soon there would be no excuse for her to insist on his remaining abed, nor any excuse for her to wait up by his bedside.

Best to take advantage of the time that they had.

She leaned over and kissed his lips gently. Korbinian ran his fingers through her hair and pulled her sharply to him. Babette gasped with delight as she tumbled onto the bed.

Giggling, she rested her head on his shoulder and murmured, "It seems your recovery was unexpectedly swift."

Korbinian undid the buttons on Babette's cuff and slid his fingertips along the length of her wrist, making her gasp with delight.

"I have had a good nurse," Korbinian said. "One who encouraged me to improve quickly."

"I see," Babette said, touching Korbinian's lips with her finger. "And have you improved?"

Korbinian took her finger between his teeth and bit gently. Babette felt his hand brush along her back down to her waist. She took Korbinian's head in her hands and kissed him with vigor, all but devouring him. Her head swam and she was lost in the scent and taste of him.

She felt Korbinian pull up her skirts and reach beneath them. His hand caressed her thigh, making her sigh. She kissed him again with even greater fervor. Korbinian took her by the back of the neck and held her, desiring her, possessing her. Babette grabbed his arm and thrust it away.

How dare he? she demanded silently, delighted all the same.

She kissed the soft flesh at Korbinian's collar and bit his shoulder, drawing blood. Korbinian snarled and laughed. He grabbed her by the throat and flung her onto the bed beside him. He rose to his knees, looming over her, and Babette grabbed him by the arms, pulling him down to her.

Their lips met again, and Babette found herself lost in the rush of passion.

"*Liebchen! Liebchen!*" Korbinian cried as he kissed her.

In desperation Babette tore at her clothes, struggling to be free of them so that she could feel Korbinian's touch on every inch of her skin. Her petticoat fell away. Her coat tumbled to the floor. The accursed corset remained in place. She seldom thought about it, but now…

"Allow me," Korbinian whispered in her ear.

With his expert fingers, he undid the offending garment and slipped it from Babette's body. The corset fell to the floor, unwanted and unnecessary. Korbinian's fingers traced Babette's bosom as he kissed her throat.

Babette gasped in delight and felt her senses fall away one after another into the delicious chaos of the moment.

* * * *

William sat at the window of his study, sipping tea and admiring the frigid weather outside. He liked nothing better than to watch nature in its native state. What a waste it was in the modern age for men to gird wild places with fences and hedges. To make a display of wealth or exaltation was one thing, and of course, cities had their place as centers of the economy, but William often felt that humanity had lost something when it had presumed to tame the wild. Man was an animal in search of his place in a world to which he no longer belonged.

William took a sip of his tea—black, with bergamot oil and fresh bull's blood. Perhaps it was only his old age speaking. As a young man, he had enjoyed much that civilization had to offer, but he could not deny that with each passing year, the urge to escape the comforts of society grew stronger and stronger.

Perhaps I should have a grotto constructed on the grounds, he thought. *I could spend my days as a hermit.*

He laughed aloud at the thought.

"Grandfather?"

William looked over his shoulder. He saw Babette standing a few paces away. Her clothes and hair were disheveled, though William could see that she had taken pains to look otherwise. He knew what she had been doing. Her father would not have approved, but William knew that it was for the best.

"Yes, Babette?" he asked, smiling warmly at her.

"Why are you laughing?" Babette asked.

This made William chuckle, but he reined in his amusement.

"Just the quiet thoughts of an old man," he said. "How is your patient?"

Babette's expression brightened.

"He is much recovered," she said.

"Then soon he shall no longer be confined to bed," William said. "You will be at liberty to resume your studies, which have been much neglected."

"That is simply not so, Grandfather," Babette protested. "During Korbinian's convalescence, he instructed me in many matters of importance."

"Of course he did." William took another sip of his tea and asked, "How is your German grammar?"

"Well, Grandfather. Korbinian was most impressed. He said that my command of his native tongue was nothing short of incredible."

"Good," William said, nodding in approval. "And your arithmetic?"

Babette laughed.

"What *use* do I, a well-bred young lady, have for *arithmetic?*"

William chuckled and motioned for Babette to join him in an empty chair. As he poured her a cup of tea, he replied:

"Babette, you must realize by now that, as your father's sole surviving heir, you are to inherit the entirety of my estate once both I and your father have passed on. While I have come to regard the Baron von Fuchsburg favorably, it is my wish that only my blood relations shall control my company. My properties, my ships, my warehouses, my goods, they will all fall into your hands—perhaps sooner than expected if your father continues to display his blatant disinterest in the business once I am gone."

"Grandfather, you musn't speak of—"

William held up a hand to silence his granddaughter.

"Babette, do not interrupt me with idle nonsense," he said. "Let us speak plainly. You are far more sensible than your father. Even without a proper education in figures, you are a capable administrator. After all," he added with a wry smile, "you were the one who properly organized the library. That is no small feat."

"Hardly comparable to managing a business," Babette said. "If you will pardon my frankness, a librarian does not a skilled businessman make."

"But of course," William said. "Which is why I insist that you be properly instructed in matters of business and accounting."

"Well," Babette said, smiling somewhat smugly, "I *can* balance a ledger."

"A step above your father," William said. "But can you tell me the going rate for American cotton?"

"Should I?" Babette asked, sipping her tea coyly. "Have not the United States become immaterial to the cotton market now that they are at war with one another?"

William concealed a smile.

"Why should that be?" he asked.

Babette sighed. She saw through his game.

"Because, Grandfather," she said, "cotton is produced by the states in rebellion. The navy is controlled by the loyalists. The loyalists will never allow the rebels to export it."

Babette drank what remained of her tea in a single, hungry gulp and concluded:

"No, for the duration of the conflict, the United States are irrelevant to the topic of cotton exports, and I doubt very much that the rest of the continent will produce sufficient crops to compensate for it. The Americas are no longer viable. If you wish my advice, look to Egypt or India. And I would even suggest taking advantage of the growing shortage to drive up the price. Stockpile, allow your competitors to exhaust their supply, and dominate the market."

William laughed aloud in delight. Babette looked at him, her expression torn between confusion and offense.

"What is so amusing, Grandfather?" she asked.

"I have already begun, six months ago."

Babette blushed, suddenly embarrassed. Her expression grew clouded and she demanded, "Then why did you ask me such a question?"

William smiled for a moment, admiring her in all of her indignant anger. She was indeed a Varanus.

He patted Babette on the knee and said:

"To remind me of how proud I am of my granddaughter."

Babette was silent for a time, her anger slowly fading and a smile of realization forming on her lips.

"I am happy to please you, Grandfather," she finally said.

"I do mean that, Babette," William said, taking her hand in both of his. "I am so very proud of you. More proud, I think, than I have been of any member of my family."

Babette looked away.

"But surely," she said, "Father—"

"I love your father, Babette," William said, "but I cannot be proud of him. You understand that. He is not a Varanus."

"I know," Babette said. "You have always been more of a father to me, Grandfather."

William nodded but said nothing. Silence drifted over them, and for a time they sat together, looking out into the frozen land beyond the window.

At length, William cleared his throat and spoke:

"Has young Korbinian proposed marriage to you yet?"

Babette went pale and snapped her head around to look at him.

"I…what?" she asked.

"Has young Korbinian proposed marriage to you yet?" William repeated. "You need not be coy about the matter with me. I know that the two of you are very much in love. You have shown great affection to one another. Marriage is the next logical step. So I ask again, has he proposed marriage?"

Babette blushed a bright pink and quickly hid her face behind one hand.

Perhaps not the sort of thing a young woman wishes to discuss with her grandfather, William thought, which was a pity for Babette, as she had no choice in the matter. William needed to know in order to plan his next steps.

"Has he?" he asked.

Babette sighed and replied, "Yes, yes he has."

"And have you accepted."

"I have."

"And has your father been informed?" William asked.

This made Babette blush all the more.

"No," she admitted. "It is a difficult subject to broach with Father. I know that he wishes me to marry Alfonse."

"Yes, well," William said, "that will not happen so long as both you and your father remain under my roof. You need have no fear of that. But as for the Baron von Fuchsburg, I would advise him to seek your father's approval for the union at once."

"What if Father refuses?" Babette asked.

William smiled and patted her hand.

"Leave your father to me."

CHAPTER TEN

Christmas Eve, 1861

Grandfather was as good as his word.

How he had done it, Babette could not say, but when Korbinian went to her father to request Babette's hand in marriage, James gave it willingly. With reluctance and reservation, of course, but willingly all the same. It occurred to Babette that Father's change of heart was impossibly sudden. Whatever Grandfather had said, he must have been working on Father for weeks beforehand to enact such an astounding change. Babette was certain of it. How like Grandfather to make a promise after he had already carried it out.

Still, Babette reflected, looking out over the sea of guests in the ballroom, all that mattered was that it had been done. She leaned on the balcony railing and watched the crowd milling about, dancing, chatting, and celebrating a joyful Noël. The Varanus family's annual Christmas Eve Fête was the toast of Normandy, and invitations were coveted throughout France. Only the best were allowed in, and every guest room in the house had been filled by visitors from as far as the Riviera. The feasting and dancing were tremendous and delightful, but Babette knew—and delighted in—the secret special purpose behind this year's celebration.

She smiled as Korbinian joined her at the railing. He wore his hussar's uniform, just as he had the night they met. He was so very handsome in it, she thought. And now, with Father's blessing, he was hers.

Soon to be hers, of course. But near enough. Nothing could stand in their way now.

Babette felt Korbinian place a hand on her hip, and she leaned against him for a moment. Smiling at him, she said:

"Hello my love. Good of you to join us."

"I was preparing myself," Korbinian said. "Beauty does not happen with a snap of the fingers, you know. A man must attend to his appearance before he graces the public."

"There is little excuse," Babette said. "You did not have to put on a crinoline."

Korbinian scoffed at the counter:

"Well, that is what servants are for."

Babette fluttered her eyelashes at him and turned away.

"What a poor soldier you must make," she said, laughing, "if you require a manservant to dress."

"I did not say that *I* required a servant," Korbinian answered, placing one hand to his chest as if wounded. "I keep a servant so that he may be employed, just as I keep a cook, a groom, a gamekeeper, and all the rest. It is as much an act of charity as it is one of convenience."

Babette rolled her eyes.

"Yes, of course it is," she said. "You are the very *soul* of generosity."

"I have always believed this to be true," Korbinian said. "Come," he added, taking her hand, "let us dance."

Babette snapped open her fan and placed it before her face in a display of modesty.

"So soon?" she asked. "We have only just arrived."

"From our respective chambers," Korbinian said, pulling her closer.

"I am exhausted from a long journey down the corridor," Babette said, leaning back against the railing in a mock faint and fanning herself. "Modern travel is so tiring."

"And dangerous," Korbinian said, smirking, "what with all these brigands lurking in the pantry nowadays."

"It must be the economy."

Korbinian leaned in close and whispered in Babette's ear, "I know just the thing to relieve your exhaustion."

"And what is that?" Babette asked, looking at him slyly out of the corner of her eye. "If it is your customary remedy, then we shall surely be missed. One cannot vanish from a party for the better part of an hour these days without *someone* noticing."

A slow smile crossed Korbinian's lips, and he looked away for a moment.

"I think," he said, "that in such a situation we must confine ourselves to dancing until the throng has departed, and we are free to pursue more aesthetic diversions."

He offered Babette his arm, which she took gracefully.

"I find your suggestion to be most agreeable," she said. "Dancing is a poor substitute, of course, but I daresay it will prove an agreeable *apéritif* for the diversions to come."

Korbinian chuckled and said:

"Come, let us whet our appetites for the feast."

* * * *

William surveyed his guests from the landing of the staircase that wove its way up to the second floor gallery overlooking the ballroom. It had been a specific construction, built during renovations with the express purpose of giving him a stage from which to address his guests.

He saw James at the foot of the stairs and motioned for his son to join him. James politely excused himself from his conversation with a visiting Gascon gentleman of limited significance and joined William.

"Is it time?" James asked.

"It is," William said. "Now, where is the couple of the hour?"

"Dancing," James said, "as they have been all night."

From his tone, William knew he did not approve.

"Well, they are in love," William said. "Protocol be damned tonight. This is my ball, and I say that my granddaughter may dance with whomever she pleases as many times as she likes."

"Yes, of course," James said. He did not sound convinced. "Father," he added, after a short pause, "tell me...."

What now? William thought in irritation. James was using the tone he always preferred when he wanted an answer of agreement but did not want to ask for it.

"Are we doing the right thing?" James continued.

William sighed and said, "Yes, James, we are. We are allowing Babette to marry the man she loves. A man who, you will recall, loves her in return. A man, moreover, who is of noble birth and of sufficient means to care for her in the manner to which she is accustomed without any assistance from us. What better service could we do her?"

"Yes, but, is it right?" James asked.

He was trying to wheedle his way out of his earlier agreement. William was not about to let that happen.

"He has asked," William said. "She has consented. You and I have both given the union our blessing. Now is not the time to question what has been done, James."

As expected, James withdrew from the fight and attempted another path.

"Well, of course," he said, nodding. "I mean, not the marriage itself. But is tonight the right time to announce it? Would it not be better to wait until the New Year?"

"No James," William said, "it would not. Tonight we have some of the finest people in all the country present. I think now is the *ideal* time for such an announcement."

James sighed.

"Yes, of course," he said. "Shall I have them sent for now?"
William considered the question and smiled.
"No, James, I think we can allow them one more dance."

When Babette and Korbinian had joined them on the landing, William motioned to the orchestra for silence. The guests turned toward their host in expectation as a hush drifted across the room. William gave an almost imperceptible nod to his butler, Proust, who began directing the serving staff to give each guest a glass of champagne. William accepted his own glass from Proust directly and cleared his throat with an almost imperceptible growl.

"My Lords and Ladies, Messieurs and Mesdames, dear friends," he said, his voice carrying to the four corners of the ballroom, "it is, as ever, a pleasure and an honor to welcome you into my home. It warms my heart to see so many persons of grace and distinction at this humble little *soirée* of mine year after year."

This elicited a chorus of good-natured laughter, as it had intended. Like all of his official gatherings, the Christmas party was practically a feature of the calendar year in France. The idea that anyone below the status of count would willingly pass up an invitation was a joke in itself. The devoutly religious objected, of course, but anyone who could not or would not attend if asked was discretely left off the invitation list.

"My family and I hope that tomorrow you will join us for mass in the village church as we celebrate the birth of our Lord—"

A necessary concession. Though William cared little for the trappings of religion, one could not celebrate Christmas Eve with music and drink only to ignore the demands of the faith on Christmas Day.

"—but in the meantime, let us revel and delight in good company and good cheer!"

There were soft words of assent from the crowd.

"Customarily I would offer a toast now," William continued, "but tonight I have a very important announcement to make on behalf of my family. As you all know, my dear granddaughter Babette Varanus had her first introduction into Society this year. Words cannot describe the pride that my son and I have felt. I only wish that Babette's mother had lived to see this moment."

William's voice caught for a moment in a display of restrained emotion that he did not actually feel. James did feel it, however, and William put a comforting hand on his son's shoulder and paused a moment before continuing. The effect upon the crowd was exactly as he had calculated.

Expressions of sympathy blossomed throughout the room, and more than one respectable lady dabbed at her eyes.

"Fortunately," William said, "fate not only takes but gives. This year a most remarkable young man came into our lives, and I think it is not overly sentimental to say that he and my granddaughter have fallen truly in love with one another.

"I am pleased to say that after months of courtship, the Baron von Fuchsburg has asked for Babette's hand in marriage. She has accepted, and both her father and I have granted our blessing on the union."

There were whispers from the crowd, a few gasps of shock, and the odd disapproving murmur, but to William's pleasure, most of the guests smiled with genuine delight at Babette's good fortune.

Nothing like a fairytale to distract the simple-minded, William thought.

"And so," he said, motioning to Babette and Korbinian, "I give to you Mademoiselle Babette Varanus and Baron Korbinian von Fuchsburg. Let it be known by all that they are officially *affianced.* And it has been decided that their marriage shall take place one year hence on the first day of summer."

William raised his glass in triumph. As he did so, he made a point to catch the eye of Louis des Louveteaux, who could not quite conceal his fury behind an expression of aristocratic serenity.

"To Mademoiselle Varanus and the Baron von Fuchsburg!" William exclaimed, uttering a chorus that was repeated joyfully by the crowd:

"Mademoiselle Varanus and the Baron von Fuchsburg!"

William waited for the guests to resume their revels before descending from his pulpit. He made his way through the crowd, smiling politely at the words of congratulations that greeted him at every turn. He saw Louis and Alfonse des Louveteaux standing together. Louis looked furious, which William took as no surprise. Alfonse had the shamed expression of a dog that had just been berated for losing scent of the game. It made William smile.

"Count des Louveteaux," William said, approaching, "I am so pleased that you could attend. And the good Captain as well."

Louis forced a smile with gritted teeth.

"What a notion," he said. "How could I possibly miss the brightest light of winter? And with this most recent revelation of yours, it seems that congratulations are in order."

"Indeed," Alfonse said. He lowered his voice and added, "It seems the *runt* has found someone foolish enough to take her."

"I will thank you not to speak so of my flesh and blood, child," William said softly, his smile never wavering. "Why don't you go and bugger your cousin in the rose bushes?"

He spoke softly so that only Alfonse and Louis could hear him. More loudly, he added:

"I am so very pleased that you can bear witness to this happy occasion. You are, after all, my closest and dearest neighbors."

"Yes," Louis agreed. "Such a pity your granddaughter did not choose to join herself with my son. We could have combined our estates."

"Alas," William said. "What might have been."

"If you gentlemen will excuse me..." Alfonse said brusquely. He bowed, turned sharply, and walked away.

"Ah, youth," William said. "Still, all's well that ends well."

Louis grimaced and said, "I do not know what you mean."

"Nonsense. The matter is concluded, surely you see that. The will of the elders has been fulfilled."

"Your granddaughter is not married yet," Louis said, "nor has the union borne fruit. The will of the elders remains unfinished."

William eyed Louis suspiciously.

"Surely the matter is inevitable," he said carefully. "And I will remind you what will happen if you attempt to interfere."

Louis held up his hands.

"Nothing of the sort. I am merely reminding you that nothing in life is certain. After all, the Baron is a hussar. They are notoriously unpredictable."

"Do not test me, Louis," William said.

"William," Louis said, smiling, "I wouldn't dream of such a thing. Whatever will be, will be."

There was something in the way Louis said it that made the hairs on the back of William's neck stand on end.

Babette stood with Korbinian near the windows, fanning herself and smiling politely as each and every one of the guests came forward to offer their congratulations. If not for Korbinian's reassuring presence at her side, she would surely have screamed. It was bad enough to be ignored by the majority of Society for most of her life. To suddenly have those same people feign joy at her happiness simply to please her grandfather was an insult beyond toleration.

Finally, the last of the well-wishers finished delivering their mouthful of fawning praise and faded back into the crowd.

"Thank God that is over and done with," Babette said.

Korbinian smiled and raised her hand to his lips.

"Patience, *liebchen*," he murmured. "Soon it will be over, and we will be free to return to more important pursuits."

"Of course," Babette said. "Soon."

She was impatient and disappointed, but nothing could be done. They could not leave without attracting attention—especially now that they had been made the centerpiece of the evening. Babette wanted nothing more than to be held in Korbinian's arms, murmuring words of affection and delight. Instead, she had the French aristocracy standing between her and doing deplorable things to the man she loved.

Society truly was a bore.

Suddenly, a familiar smell assaulted her nose: the stench of perfume and horse.

Alfonse. She knew it was he even before she saw his towering figure moving through the crowd in their direction. Babette felt Korbinian move closer to her. He placed one hand against the small of her back as if to assure her that he was there, and he took a half step forward.

Ever the gallant knight, Babette thought. She had no need of knights, but it was a touching sentiment all the same. She had saved him from one monstrous beast. Now he would do likewise for her.

Whatever his intentions, Alfonse approached with a smile.

"*Bonsoir*, Baron, Mademoiselle Varanus," he said, his voice betraying only a hint of animosity.

"Yourself as well, Captain," Korbinian said.

"Indeed, Captain," Babette said, smiling as sweetly as she could, "it is a delight to have you at my family's *soiree*."

"I understand that congratulations are in order," Alfonse said.

There was something in the way he spoke that made Babette shiver with distain. Though Alfonse made a great show of politeness in his manner and words, something in his tone, in the meaning behind the statement, was extremely offensive.

"Thank you, Captain," Babette said. "How kind of you to say. Indeed, tonight is a night for celebration."

"And I see that the Baron is recovered from his injuries," Alfonse said. "I had heard rumors of an animal attack."

Babette slowly raised one eyebrow. How did he know about that? Grandfather had taken countless precautions to conceal that information.

"Fully recovered," Korbinian said. "I have suffered far worse on the battlefield. A wild animal is nothing to me."

"*Bon.*" Alfonse smiled. "I am pleased that you are well. You see, I had thought of a little amusement that you and I could perform for the guests tonight."

"An amusement?" Babette and Korbinian asked in almost perfect unison.

"Yes, a fencing bout. A display of swordsmanship to delight all in attendance." Alfonse tapped his chest with his hand and then motioned to Korbinian. "You and I are both cavalrymen, trained in combat. I think it would be just the thing to celebrate your engagement."

"Go on…" Korbinian said skeptically.

"Just imagine, a good-natured duel between two rivals for the hand of a beautiful woman." Alfonse bowed his head to Babette. "I think it will be the perfect demonstration that there is no ill will between us. Don't you agree?"

Korbinian hesitated for a short while and exchanged looks with Babette. Finally, he looked back at Alfonse.

"Very well," he said. "Yes, I will do it. It sounds like good fun. When is it to be?"

"Tonight," Alfonse said, "in an hour or two. Before midnight, of course."

"Good," Korbinian said. "It would be wrong to make a display of violence on the day of Christ's birth."

"Yes, wouldn't it?" Alfonse did not sound particularly sincere.

"And the weapons?" Korbinian patted his waist. "I seem to have left my foil in Fuchsburg."

"We will borrow the blades from Monsieur Varanus, or failing that, a servant can bring them from my family's estate. Had we known about the engagement before tonight, the bout could have been planned more efficiently, but we shall make due."

"Has my grandfather agreed to this?" Babette asked.

It sounded quite unlikely.

Alfonse gave a toothy smile and said, "But of course."

"Out of the question," William said. "A duel? Tonight, in the midst of the ball? Nonsense, utter nonsense."

"But William—" Louis began.

"No," William said, "I will not hear of it. I say again, *nonsense*."

Louis spread his hands and smiled. William found the manner of the smile most displeasing.

"William," Louis said, "consider this a final resolution between our two families. I would like proof that the boy is a worthy match. If he performs well in combat against Alfonse, I will deem it so."

"And?" William asked.

"And I will withdraw my suit," Louis said. "I will announce before the elders and our whole assembly that I have reconsidered my position and that I see no reason to interfere with your family's affairs."

Is that so? William wondered. How difficult it was to accept Louis's words with any confidence. Still, what was the alternative?

"And if I refuse?"

"Then it will be war between us," Louis said. After a moment he laughed and slapped William on the shoulder. "No, no, I jest! But truthfully, William, this is the one chance your young baron has to prove that he is a worthy substitute for a Scion. Too long have we been at odds. Let us set aside this animosity for the sake of our families and our race."

"I am disinclined to agree, Louis," William said, "especially in light of recent events. Need I remind you of your lapdog's trespass against my rights of territory?"

Louis laughed again and shook his head.

"No, William, no," he said, "that will not do at all. You see, I have spoken to my cousins. They are united in their support of my family. If this conflict continues between us, I cannot say with any certainty what might happen."

Of course not, William thought. *You conniving fiend, what is your game?*

"So this is our one chance to make peace?" he asked. "Our one chance to avert war?"

"To avert a war that has been long in coming, William," Louis said. "You cannot deny this."

"Perhaps." William considered his options. "If I agree to this, you will leave my family in peace?"

"I will consider all current disputes between us settled," Louis replied. "If some other point of conflict should arise in the future—which I truly hope it will not—we shall attend to it then. But your granddaughter? Her marriage? Settled, once and for all."

William took a deep breath and nodded, reluctantly. Peace with the Scions of France was something he desperately needed at such a time. He could not afford to war against his own kind, least of all when they were many and organized.

"Very well," he said. "One match."

"*Bon*," Louis said, smiling. "Your guests will enjoy it, I assure you."

CHAPTER ELEVEN

Korbinian tested the weight of his sword. A little heavy in the hilt, but he could manage. The real trick would be adjusting to a thrusting blade once more. He had practiced only sabre since the war in Italy two years ago. Foil was useless on horseback.

"It is good," he said.

"As is mine," Alfonse said as he held his own blade up to the light to inspect it.

"I see that they are edged and tipped."

Alfonse laughed and asked, "What of it? Do you fear to be cut?"

"No," Korbinian said, laughing. "But I would be loath to draw your blood in the presence of all these fine folk."

Alfonse snorted but said no more.

Korbinian removed his dolman and handed it to one of the servants. Both he and Alfonse were to fight in shirt sleeves, which would, no doubt, properly delight and sensationalize the audience.

He felt Babette take his hand in both of hers. He looked at her and smiled. She was so very beautiful. He could scarcely count the days until they were married and finally joined for all eternity.

"Yes, *liebchen?*" he asked, raising her hands to his lips.

"Be careful my love," Babette said. "Alfonse is a strong swordsman."

Korbinian laughed. What a silly thing to say. And how unlike her to show fear.

"I also am skilled with the blade," he said. "And this is but a demonstration. I face no danger."

"I know that," Babette said. "But something troubles me, I know not what. Promise me that you will take care."

Korbinian smiled and looked into her eyes.

"I will take care," he said earnestly. "I swear it."

"Come," Alfonse said, interrupting them. "Let us begin. Much longer and it will be Christmas."

Korbinian grinned at him and said, "Then hurry we must."

He walked to the center of the room and stood, his back straight and his chin raised. Alfonse joined him and adopted a similar pose, thrusting his chest out in an effort to surpass Korbinian's stance. The result was comical, and Korbinian smiled in an effort not to laugh.

The crowd drew back in a circle around them, amid hushed words of excitement. Across the ballroom, William Varanus climbed the stairs to his pulpit-landing and addressed his guests:

"My Lords and Ladies, Messieurs and Mesdames," he said, his voice booming throughout the room, "Christmas Day is almost upon us, but before we all retire for some pious reflection—"

The guests laughed at this, and Korbinian found himself chuckling. Christmas Day would be spent recovering from the evening, not in prayer. However, William continued as if nothing he said was in the least bit odd:

"—I am honored to present you with a display of martial prowess. The Baron von Fuchsburg, soon to be my son-in-law, and our own Captain des Louveteaux have agreed to give us a mock duel. They will show us the same technique by which young men do battle and by which they settle matters of honor."

He extended his hand to indicate Korbinian and Alfonse. Korbinian took the opportunity to flash a smile, visible to the crowd but directed toward Babette.

William continued, "The rules are simple. Touches to the torso only. Three touches wins the match. I and my good neighbor the Count des Louveteaux will judge. Between the two of us, I am certain we can make a fair count of it."

The guests laughed again. The humor was not lost on Korbinian. He was William's champion; Alfonse was Louis's. The two judges would keep a fair count only because the one would argue with the other.

"Baron, Captain," William said, "are you ready?"

Korbinian and Alfonse nodded to one another and Korbinian answered:

"We are, Monsieur."

"Then take your places," William said.

Korbinian took his place across from Alfonse, and the two men exchanged salutes. Korbinian moved with elegance and precision, and he gave his blade an extra flourish mid-salute when he saw Babette watching. He eyed Alfonse.

Too much force in the arm, Korbinian thought, watching Alfonse salute. *He is used to a heavier sword to hack his enemies. He will not know finesse*.

That realization made Korbinian smile.

"Begin!" William commanded.

Korbinian fell back into a fencing stance and began moving without hesitation. The footwork came to him unbidden, as if he had ended his lessons only the day before. He and Alfonse touched swords and the gentle dance began.

Korbinian quickly lost track of things as the old rhythm came to him. His sword tapped the steel of Alfonse's weapon, and Alfonse responded in kind. They wove about, advancing, withdrawing, circling.

Judging that Alfonse was a little uncertain with his blade, Korbinian gave a few precise but unimportant half-thrusts. Alfonse deflected them easily, as Korbinian expected, but each attempt at a riposte was countered by a flick of Korbinian's wrist.

He is clumsy, Korbinian thought, flashing a brief half-smile. *Forceful, yes, but without finesse—*

His thoughts were interrupted as Alfonse made a quick lunge and chopped downward with the length of his blade. Korbinian caught the blade with his own and flicked it away. Without a thought, Korbinian made his own lunge and tapped Alfonse's side with the tip of his sword.

"A touch!" William proclaimed. "Do you concur?" he asked Louis.

Louis gritted his teeth for a moment but answered with a nod. The crowd applauded and then fell silent.

The match resumed. Korbinian saw anger in Alfonse's eyes. The man was ashamed at having lost first blood, even if no blood was drawn. Alfonse redoubled his efforts, and Korbinian was forced to withdraw beneath a flurry of blows. Alfonse made all efforts to pursue, but Korbinian had no difficulty disengaging.

Still, Alfonse was not finished. He continued to press in, slashing and thrusting ferociously. Korbinian's wrist flicked back and forth, countering each blow. Under the onslaught, his arm began to tire. Alfonse was strong, and each strike that Korbinian met made his blade shake. Korbinian tried one of his exquisite ripostes, but this time Alfonse countered and knocked his blade away.

Korbinian snapped his sword back in time to feel Alfonse's blade cut him across the ribs. It stung and drew blood. Korbinian exhaled and raised his hands.

"A touch!" Alfonse proudly proclaimed.

"And the first to draw blood," Louis said, although his words could not conceal the insult of his son's blow landing second.

Korbinian and Alfonse resumed their places.

"You bleed," Alfonse said, grinning. "What do you say to that?"

Korbinian shrugged and replied, "I suppose if you swing at the air enough times you are bound to hit something eventually."

This evoked a titter of laughter from the crowd and made Alfonse scowl.

"The question is," Korbinian said, "can you score another?"

At this, Alfonse snarled and lunged with his sword. Korbinian had not expected the taunt to work so well, and he stepped sideways to avoid the attack. He brought his sword around and thrust at Alfonse's chest. Alfonse managed to parry, but only just. Korbinian circled Alfonse's flank and attacked again. Again it was countered, and Korbinian bounded back a pace in case of a riposte.

But Alfonse's parry had been late, and he had over-swung to block Korbinian's sword.

He's not used to fighting without his breastplate, Korbinian realized. *When he fights, he is weighed down. Now he moves with greater ease than he is familiar with.*

Korbinian recovered from the parry and lunged again, stretching out his arm to its full length and leaning in to make up the distance. He knew that if Alfonse managed to counter and attack, he would be exposed and helpless to defend himself.

The tip of his blade stuck Alfonse in the side, drawing blood. Korbinian withdrew and spun in place with a flourish, bowing to the crowd as the ballroom thundered with applause.

"A touch!" he proclaimed.

"A touch indeed," William said. "Two to the Baron, one to the Captain."

"We will soon see that number remedied," Alfonse said.

Korbinian blew a kiss to Babette and turned about to face his opponent.

"I think not," he said, "but you are welcome to try."

Alfonse came at him with even greater fury than before, something that Korbinian had not thought possible. They wove back and forth, steel sliding against steel, feet pounding on the floor as Alfonse lunged again and again, and Korbinian darted away each time with a parry and an attempted riposte. But each time the counterattack was halted by Alfonse's blade.

Something's awoken in him. Korbinian was bewildered at the sudden change. He had seen men enraged before, and they always made easier targets. Now it seemed that Alfonse's anger had empowered him, given him greater coordination and the rhythm of a proper swordsman. Gone were the almost clumsy movements of a man whose own strength was against him. Now Alfonse swung his blade faster and harder than Korbinian could see, and the harder he swung, the more coordinated the strike.

Korbinian's eyes nearly missed when Alfonse's blade swept down toward his head. He caught a glint of metal and threw himself backward. He hit the ground and lay there for a moment. One cheek stung.

He looked up at Babette and saw her covering her mouth with her hands, her eyes wide with horror. The rest of the guests stared at him with similar expressions.

What…?

Korbinian touched the side of his face and felt wetness. He brought his hand away and saw blood on his fingertips. Alfonse had cut his cheek.

He looked up and saw Alfonse standing over him, arms raised in triumph. He sneered at Korbinian before turning to William.

"A touch, I think," he said.

Korbinian looked at William and saw the old man's jaw tighten. William's hands gripped the railing in front of him.

"Hits to the torso only," William finally said, emphasizing each word as if scolding a child who had broken a priceless vase.

Korbinian bounded to his feet and smiled.

"Let it count," he said. He turned toward Babette and looked into her eyes. "I am unharmed," he said, to her more than to anyone else.

This did not seem to be the response Alfonse wanted. He turned on Korbinian and cocked his head, glaring at him.

"Perhaps you should bandage your face," he said, "lest it scar."

"Nonsense!" Korbinian laughed. "I think I ought to have a scar, you know. I am a hussar. We are known to face danger without fear. We certainly don't hide behind breastplates and helmets like men afraid of getting a scratch."

He patted Alfonse on the back and added:

"Perhaps you should give yourself a scar. It might improve your chances with the ladies."

Alfonse leaned toward him so that their faces were barely inches apart.

"I will beat you," he whispered, speaking just loud enough for Korbinian to hear him.

"What of it?" Korbinian asked in the same tone.

This seemed to confuse Alfonse.

"I will *win*," he said, emphasizing the word.

What a fool.

Korbinian smiled and said softly, "I have already won. I have Babette and you do not. And you will never have her. A swordfight does not win a woman's heart."

Alfonse snarled at him. *Rather like a dog*, Korbinian thought. Korbinian made to step away, but Alfonse threw an arm around his shoulders and held him fast.

"Then I will kill her," Alfonse whispered "so that neither of us will have her."

Korbinian stared at him. It was a dreadful thing to jest about. But there in Alfonse's eyes he saw a glimmer of sincerity that made his stomach turn cold and hollow.

Alfonse turned away and took up his position. Korbinian hesitated for a moment, shaken by what Alfonse had said. When he resumed his stance, it was with a pounding heart. He glanced toward Babette and saw her smile back at him.

Could it be true? Surely not!

Korbinian looked back into Alfonse's eyes and saw the horrible look there, hidden behind the man's jovial smile.

"Now for the final round," William said. "And remember, *torso only*."

"Of course, Monsieur," Alfonse said with a laugh.

"Yes, of course," Korbinian said.

This time he waited for Alfonse to come at him. The bigger man obliged him without hesitation, charging in with little finesse and tremendous enthusiasm. Korbinian knew what to expect this time. He brought his weapon up, trapped Alfonse's sword, and stepped in close until the two of them stared eye-to-eye through their crossed blades.

"You lie," Korbinian said before thrusting Alfonse away.

They traded a few more blows before Alfonse brought them back into speaking distance.

"Do I?" Alfonse asked in the same hushed tone as before. "Do you recall the beast that attacked you in the woods?"

Korbinian broke the hold and pushed Alfonse away. He withdrew a step and waited at the defense, his mind whirring.

How did Alfonse know about that? The sickness in Korbinian's stomach began to grow.

Alfonse moved it close again and again their swords crossed at the hilt.

"I know," Alfonse said, as if reading his mind, "because I sent it. A family pet. I gave it Babette's scent and dispatched it after her. It would have killed her if you hadn't interfered."

They broke again, and this time Korbinian made a retaliatory jab. Alfonse knocked his sword away, startled. After a moment he laughed.

Korbinian circled Alfonse at close distance, and they continued to speak quietly:

"What you suggest is impossible," Korbinian said. "It was a bear."

"Have you seen trained bears?" Alfonse asked, tapping his sword against Korbinian's. "They are very obedient. And hungry. But as the animal has failed me, I will use men next time."

So saying, Alfonse lunged for Korbinian's chest. Korbinian knocked the sword aside, and the two of them traded back and forth with a quick series of attacks and counters.

"If you hurt her..." Korbinian said.

He felt his temper rising as it had never done before outside of battle. How dare the pompous inbred barbarian threaten his beloved Babette? *How dare he?*

Alfonse took one long step inward and brought his sword down hard. Korbinian caught the attack with his own blade just above the guard and stood, struggling against the pressure of Alfonse's tremendous strength that pressed downward upon him.

"I will not merely 'hurt' her, boy," Alfonse said. "I will *kill her*. And who can say? Perhaps I'll ravish her first. Let her experience a man instead of a boy."

Korbinian tried to say something, but all he could manage were snarls. The sickness in his belly had been replaced with burning rage that infected every last inch of his body. He felt hot sweat upon his brow, shivers along his back, and pounding in his head that sounded out one word over and over again:

Kill! Kill! Kill!

"The only way to save her," Alfonse said, pressing down harder and harder, "is to break the engagement and flee back to your dunghill on the Rhine."

Kill! Kill! Kill!

Korbinian felt his strength failing him. The force of Alfonse's titanic body was unlike that of any opponent he had fought before. He glanced sideways and saw Babette staring at them, her fists clenched tightly before her. Their eyes met and for a moment Korbinian felt that they were alone, just the two of them together as they would be—as they *must* be—for all eternity.

"I know another way," he said.

"What?" Alfonse asked.

Korbinian dropped his guard and pushed hard on Alfonse's sword, guiding it and all the strength behind it to the side. He twisted away in the opposite direction and spun around. The blood pounded in his head harder than ever. Now all he could see was the man who dared intend his beloved Babette harm.

The man who had to die.

Korbinian watched Alfonse stumble as his sword hit the floor. Alfonse hurriedly turned in place and raised his weapon, bellowing in rage at Korbinian's evasion.

In a single smooth movement, Korbinian advanced a pace and thrust his sword into Alfonse's chest just below the ribs. Alfonse let out a gasp, stumbled, and collapsed to his knees. He dropped his sword and clutched at his bleeding belly. He looked at the blood staining his hands and slowly raised his head to meet Korbinian's eyes.

For the first time since he had met the man, Korbinian saw fear—genuine fear—in Alfonse's face.

You who would be a murderer, Korbinian thought, *learn what it is to die.*

"No!" he heard Louis cry. He looked and saw the man clutching his hands, mouth agape with horror. All of the guests had similar expressions.

Korbinian turned toward William. William's eyes were furious but he seemed neither angry nor horrified. Instead, his mouth was set with a narrow smile, one of satisfaction.

"A touch!" Korbinian cried, holding his bloody sword aloft. "*A touch!*"

Let Alfonse please himself with scars and threats. The men of Fuchsburg did not resort to such pettiness.

They killed.

Giddy and lightheaded, Korbinian turned to face Babette. Her hands were clutched before her face, her mouth was agape and speechless, and tears streamed down her cheeks. But the expression on her beautiful face was so like her grandfather's: free of horror and filled only with satisfaction.

Korbinian kept his sword raised high in triumph, and he extended his hand toward his beloved.

Somewhere in the distance, a clock struck midnight.

He had shed his enemy's blood and saved the woman he loved, and all before Christmas.

Babette was certain her heart would burst from her chest. Throughout the entire fight, she had held her breath with anticipation, which had only grown worse and worse as the fighting became more violent. Now that her champion, her beloved, her Korbinian had arisen victorious, all of the dread that had filled her turned to joy. Her heart beat harder and faster than it had ever before.

He was hers and he was alive.

Grandfather's guests were all silent, and a hush had fallen over the room. What was wrong with them, Babette wondered. Did they not see how joyous this moment was? Alfonse had tried to murder her beloved, and her beloved had struck him down.

Now was a time for celebration!

Korbinian stood before her, hand outstretched, calling her to him. She took a step toward him, and another, and another—one step for each chime of the clock as it struck twelve. Everything felt very slow. Each step was heavy and uncertain, like in the dull haze of a dream.

The chimes of the clock reached twelve and faded into silence. A shiver ran down Babette's spine.

Something was wrong.

Babette's eyes snapped toward where Alfonse lay on the ground in a pool of blood. She saw him roll onto his side and slowly rise.

Impossible!

She stared in silence, struggling to make any kind of sound as Alfonse stood and raised his sword.

She saw Alfonse draw back his arm to strike.

"NO!" she screamed.

Korbinian's face clouded in confusion. He stared at her with questioning eyes.

A moment later, Alfonse let out a roar and thrust his sword through Korbinian's chest. Korbinian staggered but for a moment he still stared at Babette, as if silently pleading for her to explain what had happened. He slowly looked down at the tip of Alfonse's blade, which extended from his chest.

Behind him, Alfonse laughed aloud, blood bubbling into his mouth as he did. He pulled his sword free, slipped on his own blood, and fell to the floor.

Korbinian sank to his knees with a gasp. His sword slipped from his fingers and clattered against the ground.

"Korbinian!" Babette cried, her voice finally returning to her.

She ran to him and knelt beside him. She clutched him to her, heedless of the blood that stained her gown.

"No, no, no, no!" she cried.

She cradled Korbinian's head in her lap and stroked his hair, sobbing in spite of herself. She looked up at the sea of blank faces looking down at them and shouted:

"Someone fetch a doctor!"

No one moved.

Babette felt Korbinian's hand brush her cheek. She looked down at him, gazing into his eyes.

"*Liebchen*," Korbinian said, smiling at her. There was blood upon his lips.

Babette tried to speak, but all she could manage were stammers and sobs.

This couldn't be happening, not now!

"*Liebchen*," Korbinian repeated.

"Yes?" Babette asked, tears stinging her cheeks.

"Do not cry," Korbinian said. He coughed and spat blood. "Why do you cry?"

"Because I cannot lose you!" Babette cried. "Because you are my heart! My soul!" She looked up in despair and said, "Because I cannot bear to be without you."

Korbinian took her hand and pressed it to his lips.

"But *liebchen*," he said, "you will never be without me. Ours is a love that can never die. Not even God Himself can stand between us."

Babette looked at him from behind the tears that filled her eyes. How beautiful he was. How perfect. Even the blood—oh, God, the blood!—even it could not mar the dying Adonis.

"Do not weep for me," Korbinian said, his voice now little more than a hoarse whisper. "I can die well knowing that you are safe now, knowing that the fiend dies with me. And when I fall into that unending sleep, let my dreams be only of you."

"My love—" Babette began.

"Kiss me, *liebchen*," Korbinian said. "Let me taste your lips once more."

Without hesitation, Babette pressed her lips against Korbinian's. It was a kiss more fervent, more desperate than any they had shared before. Babette clung to that kiss, praying for it all to be a terrible dream from which she could awaken.

When I open my eyes, she told herself, *Korbinian will be there at my side. And I will tell him of all this. And we will laugh.*

But it was not a dream.

She felt Korbinian's strength fading, and she drew back to look at him. The light in his eyes shone but weakly. Babette could see the glimmer of life fading as she gazed upon him.

"Remember, *liebchen*," Korbinian whispered, "I will always love you."

So saying, Korbinian fell silent and died.

Babette clutched him to her, sobbing aloud, crying out to God, to Grandfather, to anyone to intercede and undo the loss of half her soul.

But no one, neither God nor Grandfather, answered.

CHAPTER TWELVE

Winter, 1862

William took a last look at the letter in his hand and placed it gently back on his desk. He wanted to crumple it into a ball and throw it across the room, but that would accomplish nothing. Instead, he sat at his desk and folded his hands in his lap.

Breathe.

James, resting on the settee, looked up at him with expectant eyes.

"News?" he asked.

"News," William said. He scowled for a moment before elaborating:

"The letter is from an associate of mine in Paris. Society is filled with stories of the duel."

He did not mention that the stories being told were both disparaging and wildly inaccurate. Somehow they all agreed that, far from Alfonse committing murder after being stabbed, Korbinian's death was entirely his own fault. He had, the rumors said, impaled himself upon Alfonse's blade while attempting cold-blooded murder.

Damning nonsense, William thought, scowling again. Louis's reach was not surprising, but he had not anticipated the speed with which the slander spread. At least his own rumormongers had kept his family safe from the worst of the scandal. If the letter was to be believed, the name "Varanus" only arose amid words of pity for the victims of the Rhine-lander's shameful ruse.

"What a disaster!" James cried.

"The scandal is manageable," William said, irritated by his son's outburst. "We are seen as innocent."

"Not the scandal! The Baron's death!"

"I thought you disliked him," William said.

"I did not approve of him," James said, "but Babette truly loved him, and now the man she loves is dead. My daughter is in pain, and there is nothing I can do to comfort her."

William sighed and selected pen and paper from his desk. He began writing a reply to his man in Paris.

"It is a tragedy, yes," he said, "but Babette will recover. Life is filled with sorrow. We know that better than anyone, James."

As he said this he looked at James, but his son looked away.

"She will recover in time, once she has been allowed to grieve."

"Then why have you instructed the servants never to leave her alone?" James asked. "Why can't they leave her in peace?"

William looked up from his writing and said, "Because, James, if she is left alone, I greatly fear she may attempt to kill herself."

The look on James's face almost made William regret his words.

"*What?*" James covered his mouth with his hand. "Father, you must not say such things!"

As if speaking the truth would invite it to happen, William thought.

"She is fragile now, James," he said. "More fragile than she has ever been in her life. A part of her has been torn away, never to return. You and I both know what it is to suffer that, and both of us were older than she is now when we experienced it."

"What do we do?" James asked.

"We give her time, James," William said. "We give her time. Eventually her pain will lessen, and she will learn to love another."

Whether that other would be at all worthy of her was quite another matter.

"What concerns me more," he continued, "is this sudden illness she has contracted in the wake of the incident."

"Yes, of course," James said. "What do you think it is? No one else seems to have succumbed, thank God."

"I have my suspicions," William said. "But when Doctor Artois has finished inspecting her, we will know for certain."

James nodded and said, "Yes, of course," in a particularly unconvincing manner. After a short pause, he added, "What are we to do about the scandal?"

"It will dissipate in time, of its own accord," William said. "The important thing is for us to remove ourselves from the public eye. Babette especially. If Society does not see her, it will grow tired of the stories about her."

"Withdraw Babette from Society?" James asked, his mouth open and his eyes wide. "No, no, no, no.... We cannot!"

"James, listen to me—"

"She has only just been introduced!"

"James!" William snapped, silencing his son. Lowering his tone, he continued, "She is still just sixteen. One year at this stage is manageable. We will keep her at home for the coming year. We will claim that she is in mourning. There will be talk, of course, but the whispers will be less severe than if she were present to have them exchanged behind her back. We will wait a year, and by then I suspect the trouble will have passed."

His confidence was sincere. It would require money and some careful manipulation, but William had no doubt that in a year's time he could deal with the problem.

"Out of Society for a year," James said, his voice sounding hollow and forlorn. "Poor Babette."

"I suspect she will persevere," William said.

He finished his letter with a flourish and signed his name. Looking back toward James, he saw Vatel standing in the doorway with Doctor Artois behind him.

"Doctor Artois for you, Monsieur," Vatel said.

"Thank you, Vatel. That will be all," William said. He beckoned to Artois. "Doctor, come in. Have a seat. Join us in a glass of port?"

"Yes, thank you," Artois said, crossing the room with his slow, shuffling steps. He eased into an empty chair by William and accepted the glass he was offered.

William poured glasses for himself and James as well and took a drink of the port.

"How is my granddaughter, Doctor?" he asked. "What is the sickness?"

Artois took a deep breath and exhaled slowly.

"Monsieur Varanus," he said, "I fear I must bring you news of a most delicate nature."

William gritted his teeth. *I knew it*, he thought.

"Gentlemen," Artois continued, "Mademoiselle Varanus is...with child."

James dropped his glass. It struck the carpet with a dull 'thunk', spilling its contents.

"Good God!"

William was almost astonished at James's astonishment. Surely the possibility came as no surprise? But no, James's own courtship had been almost painfully chaste. Of course he never suspected that Babette and Korbinian had been at one another before their wedding day.

"How long has she been so, Doctor?" William asked.

"Not long," Artois said. "A month. Perhaps a month and a half. Not more."

"How is she otherwise?"

"She is in perfect health, Monsieur," Artois said. "Indeed, I suspect that she will weather her condition admirably."

"Good," William said.

Artois finished his port with a long sip and stood, his old limbs moving slowly.

"Well, Messieurs," he said, "I should depart. My thanks for the wine."

"Thank you for coming, Doctor," William said, as he and James both rose.

"It is nothing, Monsieur Varanus," Artois said with a wave of his hand. "For your family, anything."

"Good of you to say so," William said, smiling. "And of course, you will not breathe a word of this to anyone."

"*Bien sur*," Artois said. "I will take it to my grave if you do not tell me otherwise. Good evening gentlemen."

Artois bowed, which William answered with a nod. The old doctor showed himself out of the room. When he had gone, William sat and motioned for James to do the same.

"Well," he said.

"With child," James said. "Babette is *with child*."

"So it would seem."

"*His* child," James said. His voice sounded hollow.

"Don't be foolish, James," William said. "Had he lived, the Baron von Fuchsburg would have made a wonderful father. Alas, now we must take steps to deal with the problem."

"How?" James asked.

How indeed?

"We must leave the country," William said.

"What?" James demanded, aghast.

"The Mediterranean I think." William was scarcely listening to James as he thought aloud. "Italy. Yes, Italy. Venice. I will send a letter to Niccolo first thing in the morning."

"Venice, but—" James began.

William held up a hand for a moment, then placed it on James's shoulder.

"James, my boy," he said, "we have no choice. The only way to conceal the pregnancy will be to have Babette away from the rest of Society. We will explain a general absence under the guise that she is in mourning for her dead fiancé. Then, as soon as arrangements are made, we will relocate to a villa in the Italian countryside. 'For her education,' we will say. Once she gives birth, I will make arrangements for the child, and we can give Babette a proper educational tour of the Mediterranean to confirm the pretense."

James laughed weakly. It sounded as if he wanted to weep.

"You make it sound so simple, Father," he said.

"It is, James," William said, smiling at his son. "By week's end it will all be in hand."

"But will people believe us?"

William chuckled at the question.

"James, the first thing you must learn about people is that they prefer big lies over small ones and outlandish stories over the truth. Which is the more outrageous? That a young woman became pregnant by her fiancé? Or that the newest blossom of French Society was so enamored of the mad and murderous Baron von Fuchsburg that, even having seen his crime firsthand, she mourned him for a year?"

James was silent for a moment.

"I know which sounds more likely," he said, sighing. "And I know which sounds more interesting."

"And which will have the longer lifespan of gossip?" William asked. "Especially when there is no child?"

James nodded slowly and said, "I take your point, Father. I take your point."

Venice, Italy

A month later, William stood on the *Ponte di Rialto*, admiring the Grand Canal. He took a deep breath and scowled, his nose assaulted by the stench of salt and fish. Venice was so beautiful; what a pity it was on the water.

Bloody salt water, he thought. Not that any of the people around him noticed, accustomed as they were to the unnatural scents of the lagoon. *That is why mankind never achieves its potential: it eats far too much fish.*

"Something troubling you, my friend?" asked the gentleman standing at his side. The man was about William's age, willowy of build, with dark hair and beautiful features, almost like a woman. He rested a closed lace fan against one cheek.

"Of course not, Niccolo," William said, forcing a smile.

Niccolo smiled back and wagged a finger.

"You cannot hide anything from me, William," he said. "What is it? My beautiful city disagrees with you?"

"The salt air is what disagrees with me," William said. "I shall never understand how you tolerate it."

"Oh, William!" Niccolo laughed. "It is a good, healthy smell. You will learn to love it."

"Not bloody likely."

"But how can this be?" Niccolo asked. "You arrived by boat."

"Kindly do not remind me," William said. "At least now I stand on solid ground."

Niccolo laughed again and slapped William's arm in delight.

"Oh, how I have missed you my friend," he said. "It has been far too long. I had almost forgotten how *finicky* you are."

William chuckled. Coming from anyone else, the statement would have gravely offended him. But from Niccolo, it was endearing.

"Come," Niccolo said, "let us walk and speak while your family is settled in at my house. Your letter was…ambiguous. For good reason, I assume."

"For very good reason," William said.

Niccolo raised his eyebrows and gave a lengthy "Ahhh."

"Let us walk," he said. "You should see the *Piazza San Marco* while you are in the city. It is a wonder to see."

"Of course," William said, falling into step beside Niccolo. Behind them, two young men who shared Niccolo's dark hair and beautiful features slipped from their positions in the crowd and began following about a dozen paces back.

"I see your hounds are at the ready," William said. It was reassuring to see.

Niccolo made a "tush" noise and tapped William's arm with his fan.

"Do not speak of my nephews in such a way. They are good boys, and they will keep us safe from any who might seek to do us harm."

"Is that likely?" William asked.

Niccolo spread his hands and asked, "Who can say? Perhaps yes, perhaps no. This is *Venezia*: anything can happen."

"I thought that was Paris," William said.

Niccolo's eyes flashed with anger.

"Do not speak to me of Paris, my friend!" he cried. "They have but a river; we have a lagoon! There is no comparison."

William laughed and threw an arm about Niccolo's shoulders.

"I have missed your company, Niccolo," he said. "By God, I have missed it."

Niccolo merely chuckled. They walked on for a few minutes more, meandering rather indirectly toward St. Mark's Square. At length, Niccolo spoke again:

"Now then, William, tell me of your troubles. What has brought you to my fair city?"

"Do you recall the young man I mentioned in my letters?" William asked. "The Baron von Fuchsburg?"

"Yes," Niccolo said. "Courting your granddaughter as I recall."

"He was murdered," William said.

"Good God!" Niccolo exclaimed, placing his fan across his heart.

"On Christmas Day—"

"Sacrilege!"

"By his rival for Babette's hand—"

Niccolo shrugged in grudging understanding and said, "Such are the ways of the heart."

"In the middle of my party," William finished.

"What dreadful manners," Niccolo said. "I tell you, William, the young people are simply unbelievable in their lack of shame. Truly."

Niccolo snapped open his fan to mark the point.

"I knew you would understand, Niccolo," William said.

"Who was the rival?" Niccolo asked.

"Are you familiar with Alfonse des Louveteaux? Son of the Count des Louveteaux?"

"Eh." Niccolo rolled his eyes. "I have heard rumors. And I know the father well: an utter bore. But, of course, you know that. He is your neighbor, is he not?"

"Sharp as ever, Niccolo," William said.

"Oh, William, you say the kindest things." Niccolo patted William on the arm and continued, "Now, I think I know why you have come. Let us be to business. How many members of the family do you want killed? Alfonse, of course. No charge."

"Um—" William began.

"The father? I will do it at cost."

"Niccolo, I didn't—"

But Niccolo continued on as if not hearing:

"The next five men in line for the title? Half price."

"Niccolo," William said, "I can hardly ask your men to kill off seven prominent members of one of the most respected families in France."

For a moment Niccolo looked hurt.

"William, how can you say such a thing? This is my stock and trade. We Pavones have murdered lords and generals for the crowned heads of Europe. A few Frenchmen on behalf of my dear friend is nothing."

"I do not need them killed, Niccolo," William said. "Revenge is the least of my concerns now. For the moment there is a more important matter."

"Yes?" Niccolo asked.

"My granddaughter," William said, lowering his voice to a hushed whisper, "is with child."

"My word," Niccolo said. "The father?"

"Her late fiancé." William cleared his throat. "I hope you will not judge her too poorly for her mistake."

"Nonsense," Niccolo said. "I am a Pavone. We understand these things. Whither the heart commands…"

"Thank you, Niccolo," William said. "Of course, what this means is that we must have a quiet, secluded place for Babette to stay, at least until the beginning of autumn."

Someplace where she would not be disturbed until the pregnancy had run its course.

"I quite understand," Niccolo said. "Staying in the city is out of the question. Things are too busy here." He snapped his fingers. "Ah, I have it. We will take you to our villa in the countryside. No one will disturb you there. It will be a long, peaceful spring and summer."

"Servants?" William asked. Aside from his and James's valets and Babette's maid, all of his household had remained behind in Normandy.

"The house is fully maintained," Niccolo said. "And they are all discrete. My family employs only the best. We settle for nothing less than complete loyalty."

"Very sensible," William said.

They passed into the *Piazza San Marco*. William looked up at the glorious facade and smiled. Venice truly was a beautiful city. He could almost forgive it the salty air.

"Thank you, Niccolo," he said. "You are a true friend."

"It is nothing, William," Niccolo told him. "What are friends for?" He motioned toward the basilica. "It is beautiful, is it not? And the Doge's Palace?"

"Yes," William said, "and all the rest. A magnificent city, Niccolo. I see why you love it so much."

Niccolo smiled proudly, as if William had just complimented his child.

"You will learn to love it as well, William."

"Perhaps," William said. "If only there were not so much damned water."

"Oh, William, you are not a romantic. A city without the sea is a city without a soul."

William chuckled and said, "No, Niccolo, a city without the sea is a city without the stench of salt, and that is a most beautiful thing."

Niccolo shook his head.

"William, how ever did you manage to construct one of the most successful shipping businesses in Europe?"

"By hiring men with a less refined sense of smell," William replied.

CHAPTER THIRTEEN

Spring, 1862
Veneto, Italy

Despite her initial misgivings, Babette found Italy to be a pleasant surprise. It was warmer than she had expected for the time of year, which proved delightful, and it gave her a much-needed opportunity to practice her Italian. And above all, she took great pleasure in the realization that being "in mourning" meant that she would not be forced to suffer the constant intrusions of Society.

The solitude proved more important than expected. While her impulses for death had faded away within a few weeks of the abhorrent incident—only to be briefly revived on the boat ride to Venice, which had made her unbearably seasick—the agony of loss remained with no signs of abating. Not that Babette had any wish for her grief to leave. For some time it seemed the only fragment of Korbinian left with her. All of his things had been dispatched back to Fuchsburg, including his body, which had been sealed in a lead casket for the journey. Now nothing remained with her but sorrow. Sorrow and the child growing within her.

Babette was not certain at first how to react to this revelation. She was afraid, of course: afraid of the unknown, apprehensive of an experience she understood only through Grandfather's books. Worse, she found herself haunted by the uncertainty of what she would face once the truth of the matter came out. Grandfather was taking admirable steps to conceal her condition, but one could not hide a child in an Italian villa forever.

Could one?

This question troubled Babette endlessly as the days turned into weeks, and the weeks slowly began to progress into months. With the passage of time, her condition worsened. She scarcely noticed at first, distracted as she was with an endless mountain of books. Reading was the only thing that kept her mind from straying back to her sorrow and anger. And as she spent most of her time sitting, she only noticed the changes at first when departing the library for meals or bed. But soon they had compounded themselves so tremendously that nothing could block out the discomfort, the illness, the fatigue, and the many other inconveniences. She could scarcely understand how other women bore them enough to propagate the species. In her estimation, the extinction of the human race was a preferable alternative, and she told Grandfather so on more than one occasion.

Summer, 1862

As spring collapsed into the dawning of summer and Babette found herself increasingly short of both breath and patience, a new curiosity arrived to further complicate her bothersome situation. One day—a Thursday, if she recalled correctly—Grandfather came to her in the reading room.

Babette looked up from her book and saw Grandfather as he stepped through the doorway. More importantly, she noticed the woman standing behind him: a tall blonde with exquisite features, dressed in a rich gown of blue that matched her eyes.

Babette gasped at the sight of her. She looked exactly like Korbinian, save for the color of her hair. It was as if Korbinian had dragged himself from the grave, put on a dress, and transformed himself into a woman.

Just to haunt me, Babette thought. It was the sort of thing he would do. Or would have done.

Babette blinked away a tear and slowly rose from her seat.

"Stay, stay," Grandfather said, extending a hand to stop her. "You must not exhaust yourself in your condition."

That was all anyone talked about these days: her "condition." Like she was sick with consumption.

"Babette," Grandfather continued, motioning the strange woman forward, "we have a special guest whom I would like to introduce to you. This is Elisabeth von Fuchsburg, sister of dear departed Korbinian."

Babette stiffened. What was Korbinian's sister doing here?

Despite Babette's misgivings, the woman approached with a charming smile and extended one gloved hand to her.

"Please, call me Ilse," she said. "You must be Babette. My late brother wrote often of you in his letters. Indeed, he wrote of little other than his great esteem and affection for you."

Babette smiled back, but the compliment made her feel peculiar. Korbinian had spoken of his sister only rarely, as if he were eager to keep her hidden.

"It is a pleasure to meet you, Mademoiselle von Fuchsburg," Babeete said. "Shall you be staying with us long?"

"Oh yes," Ilse said. "Why, with Monsieur Varanus's kind permission, I will be staying until after my nephew is born. Mother and Father passed on several years ago. Now, with Korbinian gone, his child is the only family I have left. And you, of course," she added, squeezing Babette's hand tightly. "Though I understand that my brother was murdered before you could be married, I should like to look upon you as my sister. Would that be all right?"

What a peculiar person.

"Yes, I expect so," Babette said, looking at Grandfather for guidance. He merely smiled encouragingly in response.

"May I join you?" Ilse asked, indicating a nearby chair.

Babette wanted to say no, but she looked at Grandfather and saw him nod. Babette took a deep breath and smiled at Ilse.

"Of course," she said. "I was only reading. I would adore some... company."

It took a moment to force out the last word, but Babette could not bring herself to be rude to a guest of Grandfather's, least of all Korbinian's sister.

Ilse sat and folded her hands in her lap.

"Well, I think I shall leave you two to become acquainted," Grandfather said. "Enjoy yourselves."

Babette looked at him and saw the sentiment in his eyes: *behave yourself.* Having made his point to her, he turned and left.

Babette placed her book on a nearby table and turned to Ilse.

"Well, you must tell me all about yourself," she said. "I fear that Korbinian spoke little of you."

"Oh?" Ilse asked, her eyes fluttering for a moment. "I expect he intended for us to meet one another in person when you joined us in Fuchsburg after the marriage."

"Yes, of course," Babette said. "I should like to see Fuchsburg someday. Korbinian spoke of *it* often."

"Oh, but you will see it," Ilse said, her smile broader than before. "You and the child will be spending a great deal of time there. Fuchsburg is the only place for my brother's child to be brought up. Don't you agree?"

Babette bit her tongue and simply smiled in reply.

Ilse proved to be a constant feature in the villa. With each passing day Babette hoped that she would leave, and each day Ilse demonstrated her disinterest in departure. The woman was pleasant enough, but something about her charm and politeness set Babette's teeth grinding. Ilse was like a German Claire de Mirabeau, all smiles and no substance. She talked endlessly of Society but had nothing of any interest to converse about.

Time and time again, Babette tried to introduce a subject of merit—whether the Classics, philosophy, or politics—and time and time again, Ilse steered the conversation back to something trivial.

And the worsening of Babette's condition did not make Ilse any easier to bear.

One day late in summer, Babette finally lost her patience. As Ilse sat with her in the drawing room, prattling away about the latest Paris fashions that they were both missing, Babette turned to her and said:

"Fräulein von Fuchsburg, I have no interest whatsoever in Mister Worth's latest creations, and if you continue to prattle on about *fashion,* I will be forced to beat you senseless with a croquet mallet!"

Ilse blinked a few times and slowly set down her cup and saucer.

"My goodness," she said, taking a deep breath. "I never imagined that you possessed such a distain for fashion. Perhaps I should have…"

"Are you incapable of sustaining a conversation of any significance?" Babette demanded, rising to her feet. "All you can speak of is fashion or marriage or the south of France! Have you no concept of a wider world?"

"I hear that Saint Petersburg is quite majestic," Ilse said innocently.

Damned harebrained fool!

Babette began shaking in anger. She looked at Ilse, expecting shock and instead saw a pleasant smile.

She's taunting me.

Ilse rose and took her by the hand.

"Now Babette," she said, "you must not upset yourself so in your condition. It must be the heat. I told your grandfather that you ought not to be so far south. You should have come to Fuchsburg straight away. The climate is much healthier, and it will be most difficult to travel once the child is born."

It was the same thing she had been repeating for months at every opportunity.

"Ilse," Babette said, "as I have told you no less than fifty times since our first meeting, I have no intention of raising my child in Fuchsburg!"

As she shouted, releasing months of frustration, she felt a sharp pain in her abdomen. It lasted just a short time but then came again. Her entire body quivered, and her knees suddenly grew weak. She sank to the floor, unable to stand. Her legs were wet. The pain came again.

"Ilse, I would be much obliged if you would call for my grandfather. I think something is very wrong."

* * * *

William stood on the outside terrace and watched the morning sun. It was going to be a beautiful day.

James and Niccolo stood beside him. Niccolo held a lit cigar, which he smoked with relish. James looked positively ashen. The contrast made William chuckle.

"William," Niccolo said, "you will soon be a great-grandfather. How exciting."

"The thrill of a lifetime," William said flatly. "I imagine it is rather like having a grandchild, only with far less responsibility."

"Father, you mustn't say such things," James said, clutching his hands. "Not even in jest. This is Babette's child we are speaking of."

"Yes, of course, James." William stroked his beard thoughtfully. "Of course, all this does bring up an important topic we have not yet discussed. What to do about the child."

James turned and stared at him, mouth agape.

"What to do? Father, you and I both know how to raise a child. We will employ the best nurses, the best governesses, and the best tutors."

"That is not quite what I meant," William said. "What I meant is that Babette is unmarried. She *cannot* be a mother. A widow with child is a tragedy, but an unwed mother is a scandal of unimaginable proportions. We cannot subject her to that."

James frowned deeply and let out a sigh.

"I will be the father," he said.

"James, I think you may be mistaken about the nature of the problem," William said.

"Nonsense," James replied, "we have already concealed Babette's pregnancy. We shall simply say that the child is mine, not hers."

Niccolo let out a laugh. William understood his amusement. *Bloody fool!* James had no idea what he was talking about.

"James, as noble as it is for you to fall upon your sword for you daughter, who precisely is supposed to be the mother of the child?"

"What?" James asked.

"*Madonna!*" Niccolo exclaimed, rolling his eyes. "James, your father means that you cannot be the father of a child without there being a mother."

"Yes, of course," James said, suddenly flustered. "Well, a serving girl perhaps."

"They will not accept it," William said. "They will know it would be concealed. And besides, no one would ever believe that you were capable of a tryst with a serving girl. No, James, I fear that would only work if your late wife were still with us."

William noticed a familiar scent approach from behind them. He looked over his shoulder and saw one of the servants in the doorway.

"What is it, Giovanni?" William asked.

"Pardon, *Signore*, but the doctor has finished," Giovanni said. "Your granddaughter has given birth to a healthy boy."

William clapped his hands and said:

"Wonderful news! Niccolo, put that dreadful thing out, there's a good man. This is a time for celebration, not for fouling the air with the smoke of that American weed!"

Niccolo chuckled but did not put out the cigar.

"James," William said, "why don't you go along ahead and see to Babette. Niccolo and I have one or two matters of finance to discuss."

James hesitated, his face becoming pale.

"I, uh…" he began. He turned to Giovanni and asked, "Is there much blood?"

"Yes, some," Giovanni said, "but the doctor says she is well."

James grew paler.

"I think I shall wait in the parlor until the linens have been changed," he said.

"Yes, James, I think that would be best," William said. "Giovanni, fetch him some brandy, there's a good fellow."

When they had gone, Niccolo exhaled a long series of smoke rings and asked, "Your son is afraid of blood?"

"Alas, yes," William said. "Babette's birth was complicated. Her mother bled to death while resting afterward. James was the one who found the body. He has been *sensitive* ever since."

"Poor man," Niccolo said.

"He will persevere," William replied. "In the meantime, I have a more serious problem to attend to."

"Yes," Niccolo said, "how to conceal a child."

"Alas," William said, "the list of options is rather short."

When he entered Babette's bedchamber, William saw that Giovanni had understated the amount of blood. The bedclothes were drenched in it. For a moment, William had recollections of Babette's poor mother.

Thank God James had elected not to enter. No doubt, he would have fainted.

William saw Babette lying in bed, propped up by a mound of pillows. She looked exhausted, but her expression was rapturous as she held the newborn child in her arms. One of the serving maids hovered about at the bedside, but it was unlikely Babette would allow her to do anything with the child.

William turned to the doctor, who was busy washing his hands in a basin of water.

"How is my granddaughter?" William asked.

"Surprisingly well," the doctor said. "And the child is healthy. Fine lungs as well, I can tell you."

"I see a great deal of blood."

The doctor nodded and said, "She experienced significant hemorrhaging toward the end. I was afraid for her safety, but it appears to have healed of its own accord."

"Remarkable."

"As you say." The doctor nodded. "By rights she should be dead, but she is well. I do not understand, but I am most relieved."

William hid a smile. Perhaps there was more Scion in Babette than anyone had given her credit for.

"Babette and the child are well," William said. "That is all that matters to me. Now, if you will both excuse us, I would like to sit with my granddaughter."

"Of course," the doctor said, bowing his head.

As the doctor and the maid slipped out the door, William sat in a chair by the bed. With one hand, he gently stroked Babette's hair. She looked up at him and smiled, then looked back down at the child.

"A beautiful baby," William said.

"Yes," Babette murmured, her voice so filled with delight that William felt a tear come to his eye. "He will look just like his father."

"You are sure?"

Babette smiled and said, "I know it."

"What will you name him?" William asked.

"Alistair," Babette said. "His name is Alistair Korbinian."

William smiled and took a deep breath. Babette was so precious to him, more precious even than his son. She was like him in thought and temperament, and her son would, no doubt, grow up to be a man worthy of his Scion lineage.

It made William feel an honest twinge of guilt at the realization that he would have to take the child from her. Babette would be devastated, but unwed the child would be the ruination of her.

It would be the ruination of them all.

* * * *

Autumn, 1862

Babette knew nothing of her grandfather's thoughts, and he was not quick to act upon them in any event. As summer drew on and faded into autumn, she spent almost every waking moment with little Alistair. She doted on him, reading aloud to him for hours on end from her favorite books, reciting Plutarch and Tacitus, Newton and Leibniz, Voltaire and Goethe as if they were children's stories or works of poetry. To her delight, Alistair listened in rapture, staring up at her with his big violet eyes and gurgling with excitement whenever Babette found it necessary to emphasize a particular passage.

For the first time since Korbinian's death, life was perfect again.

Then, one day in late autumn, Babette awoke to silence. She had become so accustomed to Alistair's periodic disturbances that the lack of noise unsettled her far more than any hungry or frightened cries. She rose from bed in an instant. It was early morning, and she saw the first strains of daylight warming the sky.

Alistair should have been hungry again. Why was there no noise?

Clutching her nightshirt about her, Babette rushed to the bassinet that stood only a few paces away from her bed. She threw back the blanket, fearing the worst, and saw nothing.

The bassinet was empty.

What was happening?

Babette rushed to the door and flung it open. The villa was quiet. No one stirred. But Grandfather would be awake. He would know what to do! Had Alistair been kidnapped? But no, that was nonsense. Perhaps Father had decided to hold Alistair for a time, to let her sleep properly. Grandfather had tried that once a month before, and Babette had berated him for it.

She rushed along the upstairs passage and into Grandfather's study. She saw him and Father sitting in chairs by the window. As she entered, they looked toward her. Grandfather's grave expression made Babette's heart stop with dread.

No!

"Where is Alistair?" Babette demanded.

Grandfather and Father exchanged looks. Grandfather rose, his mouth set in a deep frown.

"Babette," he said, "I fear we have dreadful news."

"No!" Babette cried.

"Alistair has…passed away," Grandfather said.

"I'm so sorry, Babette," Father said, standing and rushing to her, tears in his eyes.

"No! No!"

Babette looked from one to the other, waiting—begging—for them to reveal their cruel deception and to produce Alistair, alive and well, from some place of hiding.

"I found him so in the small hours," Grandfather said, "as I came in to check on the two of you. He must have passed in the night."

"It's not possible…" Babette said.

"I am sorry, my dear," Grandfather said. "I am so very sorry. But there is nothing to be done."

Babette sank to her knees, gasping for breath. It felt as if a hideous weight was pressing down upon her shoulders, collapsing her body into itself. Her head swam and lights danced before her eyes.

"No, no," she repeated.

Father knelt beside her and enfolded her in his arms.

"Oh, Babette," he said, weeping. "Oh, my dear Babette."

"Let me see him," Babette said, her voice little more than a hoarse whisper.

"I don't think that would be wise," Grandfather said. "It would only upset you further. But we plan to hold the burial for him tomorrow."

"Let me see him!" Babette shouted, struggling against her father. "Let me see him!"

They did not, of course. In the end, Babette had to be restrained—for her own good, Grandfather said, though she hardly agreed with that statement. One of the servants brought a cup of medicine that the doctor had left, and she was forced to drink it. It tasted vile, and it made her head spin. Unable to resist further, she was carried back to bed.

The rest of the day passed in a fog. When she finally regained her senses, Babette saw that it was evening. The sunlight was rapidly fading. She stood shakily and went immediately to the bassinet, hoping that it had all been a terrible dream.

But the bassinet was empty, just as she remembered.

Alistair was dead. Babette felt tears brimming in her eyes. It was like Korbinian's death all over again. He had been returned to her through their child, and now their child was dead.

She stumbled to the door but found it locked. She needed comfort, reassurance, but all she found was silence.

Alone, she thought, as her body shook and the tears rolled down her cheeks. *I am all alone*.

Forever.

Slowly she walked out to the balcony and stared off into the darkening sky. The world that she had delighted in only a day before now looked hideous to her. The birds' evening songs made a mockery of her sorrow. The rolling hills beyond the villa walls were like barrow mounds for a dead earth.

In that moment, wracked with sorrow, heavy with loss, and still confused by the medicine's poison, Babette saw nothing left for her. All that she loved was gone. She was a woman of reason, and she saw only one reasonable solution to her pain.

With uncertain movements but with unhesitant thoughts, Babette climbed onto the railing of the balcony. She looked down upon the stone courtyard beneath her. It was difficult to gauge the distance in her muddled state, but she was certain that the fall would kill her—if not at once, then within a few hours. She could bear the pain of a slow death. What she could not bear was the pain of a long life.

"Korbinian," she whispered, "Alistair, I am coming."

She opened her arms to the dying sun and stepped out into oblivion.

"*Liebchen*."

That voice…

"*Liebchen*."

But it was not possible.

"*Liebchen*, you must wake up."

Babette slowly forced one eye open. As she did so, she felt a rush of agony flow through her. She lay on the paving stones of the villa courtyard, drenched in her own blood. Something was broken, several somethings, in fact.

But she was alive, and to her horror she felt not the slow ebb into death but an insurmountable rush of life. Her body felt as if it were aflame, weightless, filled with vigor, as it never had been before. Her will to live had returned, forced upon her from some primeval source buried deep within her.

But the voice…

Babette tilted her head and looked up. It was painful to move, but she did not care.

She saw Korbinian, dressed in his uniform as he had been that terrible night. He knelt before her and looked down upon her tenderly, his eyes alight with passion just as she remembered them.

"Babette, my love," he said, "come, we must get you inside."

"But…" Babette stammered. "But you are dead."

"Did I not say that I would always love you?" Korbinian asked. "Death cannot keep us apart."

"But how?"

"It does not matter," Korbinian said. "What matters is that you are hurt. Give me your hand; we must get you inside."

Babette reached out and took Korbinian's hand. She expected him to vanish at her touch, like a phantom from a dream, but she felt his strong, warm grasp, his smooth skin, his gentle fingers.

"Now we will never be apart," Korbinian said. "Never."

CHAPTER FOURTEEN

William peered into his cup of brandy for a short time.

"You say my granddaughter threw herself from her balcony?" he asked Giovanni, who stood nearby.

"Yes, sir."

"And she then—let me see if I have this right," William said. "She then crawled from the courtyard into the foyer before collapsing? Where she was found by one of the serving maids?"

Giovanni nodded and repeated, "Yes, sir."

William lowered his glass and leaned forward.

"She *crawled?*" he asked, sharply emphasizing the word.

"Yes."

It seemed impossible. A grown man should not have been able to move after such a fall, certainly not a tiny young woman like Babette.

Her Scion breeding finally made manifest, William thought, almost smiling. *It must be.*

"Where is she now?"

"In her bedroom, resting," Giovanni said. "The doctor has been sent for."

"Where is my son?" William asked. "Has he been told?"

"He is with her while she rests, *Signore*."

William nodded.

"Inform me when the doctor arrives," he said. "You may leave."

Giovanni bowed and backed out of the study.

William sipped the brandy and mulled over a few disparate thoughts. He had anticipated an attempted suicide, but the medicine they had given her ought to have kept her asleep until morning. That her body had recovered from it in half the expected time was as remarkable as her surviving the fall.

The Blood breeds true.

It was a pleasant thought, and it made William laugh. They had, all of them, been wrong about her. Babette was not a runt; she was as true-blooded as he was, certainly more than her father. It meant that she would survive the ordeal.

It also meant that William had been right to deal with the child. The scandal Babette would have faced was nothing compared to the violence that Alfonse would inflict upon both mother and son if he knew that Babette was more than a runt to be dismissed. To lose a human was an irritation, but no worse than a dog wandering off to a different master. But to be rejected by a Scion of lesser lineage was a humiliation. And the line between humiliation and fury was quickly crossed.

No, he had certainly been right to do it.

The next day, after the child's funeral, William went straight up to Babette's room. He had seen her briefly the night before, just after the attempted suicide, but Babette had been delirious and in poor condition for conversation. It had gone without saying that she would not join them for the burial.

It was just as well. James had been sufficiently distraught. William did not need a sorrowful mother there as well.

Babette was awake and alert when he arrived. She looked up at him and smiled. She seemed strangely happy for a woman who had attempted to kill herself only a day before.

"Hello, Grandfather," Babette said.

"Babette, how are you feeling?" William asked, sitting by the bed. "You gave us all a fright yesterday."

"Well, it is rather painful," Babette said. "I fear my legs may be broken. And my ribs."

She placed her fingers against her chest and pressed inward. She winced in pain and stopped.

"Yes, the ribs as well."

"That sort of thing does come from a fall upon hard stone," William said. "What in Heaven's name possessed you to do such a thing?"

Babette thought for a moment and gazed off toward the window. She slowly looked back and said:

"Primarily grief. Grief and that abysmal tonic you gave to me. You can scarcely blame me under the circumstances."

"Perhaps," William said. "You seem quite recovered."

"Nearly dying changes one's perspective on life," Babette said.

That was probably true.

"I shall have to take your word for it," William said.

"That would seem best," Babette said to Grandfather. "It would be most unfortunate if you were to come within any proximity to death. I would be upset. Don't you agree?"

She looked to Korbinian, who sat in bed next to her. She smiled at him. How marvelous to have him back. It was so marvelous, in fact, that she did not allow herself to ponder the impossibility of his appearance. He could not be a ghost because ghosts did not exist. And he could not be an hallucination because that would mean she was mad, and she was not mad.

"You know that he cannot see me," Korbinian said to her, touching her cheek with his fingertips. "Only you can."

Grandfather raised an eyebrow at Babette, and she quickly looked back at him.

"I certainly agree," he said. "I seem to have developed a singular distaste for death in my old age."

"Did you bury Alistair?" Babette asked. She glanced toward Korbinian, preparing to explain whom she meant.

Korbinian held a finger over his lips and motioned toward Grandfather.

"I know," he said. "Our son. Talk to your grandfather. He will become suspicious if you continue to look at me."

"Yes, we buried him by the chapel," William said. "Niccolo was very generous to allow it." He leaned forward and folded his hands. "Babette, listen to me. We must not speak of Alistair again, certainly not in the presence of others. If someone were to learn that you had a child out of wedlock—"

"But, Grandfather!" Babette exclaimed.

How could he speak of such things the very same day that her child had been cast away into the ground? And to say "out of wedlock" like Alistair had been the product of some sordid tryst! She and Korbinian were in love. If he had not been murdered, Alistair would have been born in wedlock. They would have been forced to perform the marriage a year early and postpone the christening for a few months to conceal Alistair's true date of birth, but that was not the same as him being born out of wedlock.

"*Liebchen*," Korbinian said, leaning in front of her and meeting her eyes with his, "he is right. I am dead and so is our son. You cannot allow your future to be dragged into the grave with us."

Babette took a breath and said, "I'm sorry, Grandfather. You are right. We will not speak of Alistair again."

Grandfather blinked a few times and sat back.

"Good," he said. "Very good."

"Where is my sister?" Korbinian mused aloud.

"Yes, where is she?" Babette asked. She quickly added, "Mademoiselle von Fuchsburg that is. Did she attend the funeral?"

"No, no," Grandfather said quickly. "She departed early this morning. The grief of her nephew's death was too much for her."

Babette looked at Korbinian. Korbinian shrugged.

"It does sound like something she would do," he said.

"And what do you intend for the family?" Babette asked Grandfather. "Are we to return to France?"

Korbinian looked at her and asked, "With both of your legs broken?"

Grandfather smiled and shook his head.

"I think travel is out of the question for a little while now. The fact that you survived gives me great hope for your recovery, but it will be some time in coming."

"And when I can walk again?" Babette asked.

"*If* you can walk again," Korbinian said.

"Well…" Grandfather said. "We are already in the Mediterranean, the heart of classical antiquity. I think it would be very instructive for you—indeed, for all of us—to travel for a while. I have always felt that a young woman of culture and distinction should visit Rome, Athens, and Vienna as well as Paris if she is to appreciate art and culture. Perhaps we shall even have time for a few weeks in Constantinople."

"Oh yes, let us," Korbinian said, clapping his hands together. "Vienna is so very beautiful. As is Constantinople. And Rome is…nearby."

Babette smiled and said, "I think that would be most agreeable, Grandfather. Most agreeable indeed."

Winter and Spring, 1863

The speed of her recovery took Babette by surprise, just as it seemed to do for everyone else in the household. As it was, the pain of Babette's injuries faded into a sort of dull tickle by the end of the second week, though her ribs still ached from time to time and she was quite unable to stand. More curious, by the end of the first month, Babette found that she *could* stand after a fashion. Five weeks into her convalescence, she could even hobble about so long as she clung to the furniture, as she discovered when her lady's maid, quite foolishly, moved the book she had been reading to the far side of the room while she was sleeping.

After that, Grandfather came to her and explained quite pointedly that Babette was to remain in bed without complaint until three months had passed. She was above all never to speak of her swift recovery to anyone, not even Father. Babette knew not what to make of these strange instructions, but she complied without complaint. For several days, she and Korbinian conversed in whispers, musing over the source of her unexpected recovery and Grandfather's concealment of it. Babette assumed it had something to do with the strict—and rather eccentric—diet of beef and milk pudding that Grandfather had given her to eat. Korbinian supposed it to be the Italian water. Why Grandfather insisted that they keep the marked improvement a secret was beyond both of them.

Still, it gave Babette ample time to read and chat with Korbinian, who was her constant companion. He made far better conversation than anyone in the house save for Grandfather, even if no one else could see or hear him. People were peculiar that way.

The memory of Alistair never ceased to haunt her, least of all in her dreams. Every few nights, she would wake in a cold sweat with her lost child's name upon her lips. Thank God that each time Korbinian was there to comfort her. Without him, she suspected she would have gone mad.

The visions were not confined to sleep, however, and Babette found her mind always turning back to her son when she left it unoccupied. Even the most innocent of sights found some way to twist back to Alistair: the sunshine, a flower, even the violet-blue of the sky just before sunrise and just after sunset that so perfectly matched his eyes. Daydreams held nothing but Alistair. A casual glance toward an empty chair would produce him like a phantom from the shadows. The light filtering through the window somehow formed his face. It was unbearable.

Instead, Babette threw herself into books, a pastime she and Korbinian gladly shared. It allowed them to associate without the awkwardness of conversing aloud, which always led to questions when they were overheard. She read endlessly from rising to retiring, and on as many subjects as she could set her mind to. The only books she rejected out of hand were those that she had read to Alistair. They were too painful even to look at.

Finally, as the months wore on, Grandfather permitted her to make her recovery public—gradually, of course. It almost made Babette laugh when, in keeping with the charade, she was forced to hobble around on Father's arm long after her legs had healed. And of course, each step of the way Father fussed over her like a mother hen.

But in the end, Grandfather proved to be as good as his word. With the coming of spring, when the doctor was finally permitted to see Babette again and to declare her well, Grandfather announced his intentions for the future. One evening over supper—the first time that Babette was permitted, or rather forced, downstairs to eat with the family—he stated almost casually:

"Now that winter has passed and we are all in good health again, I think we ought to take Babette on a proper tour of the Mediterranean. You agree, of course, don't you James?"

Father balked openly at this, the expression on his face such that Babette exchanged looks with Korbinian, who stood unnoticed by the sideboard.

"The Mediterranean?" Father demanded. "Are you mad? What about the Season? We must return to Paris!"

"Paris?" Grandfather asked. "Nonsense. Babette has only just recovered from her fall. Is that not right, Babette?"

Babette looked back at them and quickly nodded.

"Oh, yes, quite so," she said. "I couldn't even think of dancing."

"I don't know," Korbinian said with a smirk. "You waltzed beautifully last night."

Thank God no one else could hear him. Even after death he was still so damned incorrigible.

"In any event, I should be quite wasted on Society for at least the remainder of the year," Babette continued. "And I quite agree with Grandfather on this point. It would be most unfortunate for my education if we were to miss such an opportunity. After all, Father, how many times have you said that I simply must visit the places of Antiquity before I am married?"

"Well, um," Father said, stammering in confusion. "Not once that I recall—"

"Precisely," Babette said. "And why haven't you?"

"Well, I—"

"We are in Italy," Babette said, "and yet you have no intention of visiting Rome? What manner of Catholics are we?"

"Now Babette, you must understand—"

"Your daughter is correct, James," Grandfather said. "We should make a pilgrimage while the destination is so close."

Father looked confused.

"Would not a proper pilgrimage entail the Holy Land?" he asked.

"Well, I suppose, time permitting…" Grandfather said.

Father frowned and said, "That's not quite what I meant."

"Father," Babette said, "I feel that Grandfather is right. It would be a shame for us to depart this antique land without first seeing the wonders of the ancient world."

"But—" Father protested.

"Good," Grandfather said, "we are agreed. I knew you would understand, James. After all, we are doing this for Babette."

* * * *

Spring and Summer, 1863
The Mediterranean

After a few more weeks at the villa and another in Venice—during which time Grandfather complained about the salt air endlessly when he thought no one was listening—Babette and the family made their way to Rome. Babette found the experience exhilarating. While Father insisted upon tiresome gatherings with the Roman elite, Babette had ample opportunity to slip away during the afternoons to visit the old ruins. She found the ancient city to be properly romantic, although Korbinian insisted that it was merely Babette's love of the Classics misleading her better judgment. Rome, he said, was nothing but a relic of a dead age. Babette was inclined to disagree, and the two of them had great fun arguing the point as they strolled along the Tiber.

Departing Rome, they turned northward, spending a month in Tuscany—where Babette quickly developed a great affection for Florence—and another two months touring the cities of the north before returning to Venice, which had been Babette's favorite in spite of its fish and sea air. Next, they traveled down the Adriatic, stopping along the Dalmatian coast, until turning east and finally arriving in Greece.

The country was in a state of excitement when they landed. A new king—a Dane apparently—had been proclaimed that very spring, though he had not yet arrived. The knowledge of King George's heritage proved to be most amusing to Grandfather, who from time to time joked about their being distant relatives to the Greek Crown. He also mused aloud to Babette, wondering somewhat curiously what sort of beard the king would grow when he was older. Babette understood none of it, and Korbinian was of no help.

During her stay in Greece, Babette fell in love with the blue Aegean. Time and again, she forced Father or Grandfather to escort her on a boating expedition to one of the countless islands dotting the sea. She inspected the relics of the ancient world with great delight, forcing even Korbinian to acknowledge that there might be something to her love of Antiquity.

There was one singular incident that stayed with Babette throughout their journey. Once, while visiting an abandoned monastery in the mountains—one of the oldest in Greece, Grandfather said—Babette came across a most peculiar sight. She found a marble statue that she felt certain predated the coming of Christ, which had somehow been kept clean and fresh. Korbinian suggested its care was the work of nearby villagers, although the closest settlement was an hour's walk away. The statue, which had been made with all the finesse of the Classical period, depicted a monstrous figure: a hunched, wolfish beast that stood upon two legs like an ape. It reminded Babette of the beast that had attacked her and Korbinian in France, a point with which Korbinian readily agreed. Most curious of all, when Babette pointed it out to Grandfather, he went pale for a moment and then, after consulting the sun, declared it time for them to depart. Nothing more was said about the incident, and whenever Babette tried to broach the subject again, Grandfather found an opportunity to change the subject.

The stay in Greece proved too short for Babette's liking, but soon Grandfather insisted that they relocate to a land "less polluted by proximity to the ocean." That meant the Hapsburg lands: the Danube, Buda-Pest, and Vienna.

CHAPTER FIFTEEN

Vienna, Austria

Babette found much in Vienna to please her. It was a beautiful city that still held the majesty of the *Ancien Régime*. Above all she favored the Imperial Library, which she visited in Grandfather's company as often as possible—at least three times a week, she insisted. There she devoured books like macarons, delighting in the touch and smell of the old texts as well as the knowledge they contained.

One day a message came for Grandfather just as they were leaving for the library. Babette watched in silence as Grandfather read the letter in the carriage and saw a scowl cross his face.

Whatever could be the matter, she wondered.

But Grandfather said nothing about it. He simply tucked the letter into his pocket and smiled at her.

When they arrived, he helped her down from the carriage but did not follow.

"Grandfather?" Babette asked. "Are you coming?"

"I have something that I must attend to urgently," Grandfather said. "I will return as soon as I am able. You go ahead. Herr Raab will look after you until I return. If anyone questions your presence there without me, refer them to him."

Babette thought to protest, but she knew the look in Grandfather's eyes. There was something he was not telling her and for a very good reason. Best not to make a fuss about it.

"Of course, Grandfather," she said, bowing her head. "I will wait for you in the *Prunksaal*."

She made her way inside, smiling pleasantly at the now-familiar faces of the staff. Most of the men kept their Germanic stuffiness, but two of them smiled back and even exchanged brief pleasantries.

In the *Prunksaal*—the domed central hall of the library—Babette saw old bearded Herr Raab standing by one of the hall's many statues. He was speaking to a tall, slender man who stood in the fading shadows by the bookshelves. The second man, who looked to be the same age as Babette, was black of hair, regal in features, and dressed like a gentleman. As Babette approached, he looked toward her with eyes blue like ice.

"Ah, Fräulein Varanus!" Herr Raab exclaimed, catching sight of her. "I will be just a moment."

Herr Raab exchanged a few more words with the mysterious gentleman and bowed to him. The gentleman merely inclined his head in acknowledgement but otherwise showed no reaction.

Herr Raab turned to Babette and bowed.

"Fräulein Varanus, a pleasure as always to see you," he said. "And what do you wish to read today, hmm?"

"An odd request, Herr Raab," Babette said. "I am looking for a book that I have seen referenced twice before in later works. I believe a copy is held in the collection here."

"*Ja, ja*, of course," Herr Raab said. "And the name?"

"It is called the *Codex Hermeticum*," Babette said.

Curiously, though the mysterious dark-haired gentleman stood too far away to have heard her, Babette noticed him raise an eyebrow and snap his gaze in her direction when she spoke the name. Babette looked back at him, raising her own eyebrow curiously. She saw a smile slowly cross the man's face, and he looked away.

"Did you say the *Codex Hermeticum?*" Herr Raab asked, scratching his head. "Are you certain you do not mean the *Corpus Hermeticum?*"

Babette had known it would be a cause for confusion. Sighing, she said:

"No, Herr Raab, not Ficino's *Corpus*. The *Codex Hermeticum*. I am quite certain that a copy is to be found here in the *Hofbibliothek*."

Herr Raab gave a wheezing laugh and said, "It is most peculiar that you ask this. Lord Shashavani has just requested the same book, and he also insists that we have it, though I do not recall it. Of course, if I do find it, I will have to give it to him first. Perhaps there is something else you would prefer to read…?"

"If I may interject," said the stranger.

Babette nearly jumped in surprise. He had approached in perfect silence without her notice and now stood directly behind her and Herr Raab.

"Oh, my God," Herr Raab exclaimed, as taken by surprise as Babette had been. "I do beg your pardon, my lord, you startled me."

"It is no matter," the stranger said, speaking quite matter-of-factly. "But if I may interject, once you find the book, I will be pleased to share it with…Fräulein Varanus was it?"

"Yes," Babette said, looking back at him without hesitation. "And who might you be, sir?"

The stranger smiled and waved Herr Raab away with the words, "Find the book. It is in the library, perhaps right in front of your eyes. All you must do is look."

"Of course, my lord," Herr Raab said before bowing and quickly departing.

"I repeat," Babette said, "and who might you be, sir?"

The stranger smiled and bowed his head.

"I am Iosef Shashavani," he said.

"I believe that is Lord Shashavani, if I heard Herr Raab correctly," Babette said.

Iosef smiled faintly and replied, "It is so. But I have little interest in such formality. After all, knowledge cares nothing for titles, only for intellect."

Babette felt Korbinian appear at her elbow. He whispered in her ear, "How very sensible of him."

Babette smiled a little and glanced at him. How nice of Korbinian to say what she had been thinking.

"Are you in the habit of offering to share books with strange young women?" Babette asked.

"Indeed, no," Iosef said. "I prefer to read alone. But I make an exception for anyone who can name an obscure grimoire such as the *Codex Hermeticum* with neither prompting nor hesitation. Tell me, what is your interest?"

This gave Babette pause. Truth be told, she had no greater purpose than her own curiosity. And Iosef had the look of one who might take offense at a dilettante.

She saw Korbinian approach Iosef and inspect him carefully. Iosef, like everyone else, gave no indication of noticing him.

Korbinian turned about to face Babette and said, "Tell him."

Babette looked at Korbinian curiously for a moment before turning her eyes to Iosef.

"My interest is nothing but my own curiosity," she said. "I have no greater purpose than simply to know. Shameful, I realize, but—"

"Not at all," Iosef said. "Knowledge is a virtue of its own, although there comes a time when we must apply what we have learned. What use is knowledge if it does not change the world?"

"You do not believe in knowledge for its own sake?" Babette asked.

"Knowledge is a tool, not a purpose," Iosef replied. "Information acquired but not applied is like medicine that the doctor withholds from the sick. To learn is admirable, but in the end it is pointless."

"But knowledge may be amassed," Babette said. "It may be recorded and stored."

"All flesh dies," Iosef said. "All material decays. The scholar and the text alike will one day turn to dust. Knowledge is not eternal."

"I cannot accept that, sir," Babette said. "Knowledge does not *die*. And truth exists whether we know it or not. Gravity existed long before Galileo or Newton. And I think it is worthwhile that we understand it."

"Why?" Iosef asked, smiling slightly. "What good is a knowledge of physics if we do not use it to build, maintain, or destroy?"

"I think I understand you, sir," Babette said. "You would claim that knowledge for its own sake is arrogance, that it exists only to gratify the scholar, with no greater significance than one's private delight. But if that is so, then knowledge becomes nothing more than cheap drink."

Iosef flashed another smile, though it was brief. But he did seem entertained by her words, which pleased Babette. He was the first scholar she had ever encountered who had seen fit to argue against the primacy of knowledge.

"Nonsense," Iosef said. "Knowledge unused is far worse than alcohol."

"Oh?" Babette asked. "How do you suppose that?"

"Because," Iosef said, "as they each imbibe their respective vice while contributing nothing to society, the scholar becomes arrogant, the drunk ashamed. And shame is something they should both feel."

"I think I understand your meaning, sir," Babette said, "if you will pardon the presumption."

Iosef spread his hands toward her and said, "By all means."

"They are both tools for progress," Babette said. "Drink comforts the working man as his labors keep society alive, and how can we begrudge him that when his labors are so much harder than ours?"

"Indeed, we cannot," Iosef said.

"Drink is only shameful when it becomes a purpose unto itself."

"And knowledge?" Iosef asked.

"Well, knowledge inspires the artist, instructs the builder, guides the ruler, and makes possible the engineer. Society cannot advance without knowledge; but I suppose that if knowledge sits unused, then it has as much benefit as if it had never existed in the first place."

"My argument exactly," Iosef said. "And do you agree with it, having stated it so eloquently?"

Babette considered this for a short while, mulling the points over. It made sense, but…

"There is one thing that I would dispute with you," she said. "Where is the moral imperative to be of use to society? I am intelligent and resourceful, of good family, and possessed of means, as are you sir. Why shouldn't we indulge our predilection for knowledge in the same way that the rich man indulges in wine and women? Where is my obligation to improve the world? If I can afford my *tour d'ivoire,* why should I not sit in it, high among the birds, and laugh at those who cannot assail me?"

Iosef smiled again, and again it was brief. It seemed to Babette that he was unused to offering expressions of humor. It was quite intriguing, actually.

"Is this a regular pastime of yours?" he asked. "Do you make a habit of sitting in an ivory tower, laughing at peasants?"

"No," Babette said, smiling back. "I fear I may have exaggerated when I said that I could afford one. The price of ivory is remarkable these days, and towers are very tall."

"What a peculiar turn of phrase," Iosef mused. "'Ivory tower.' Apt, I suppose, but peculiar. How very French."

"Thank you," Babette said, "but I fear I borrowed it from someone. Still, I ask again, why should I not indulge my liberty to be of no use to society?"

"There is no moral imperative," Iosef said. "Indeed, many of the greatest members of society are of no use whatsoever."

Babette giggled at this and covered her mouth.

"Well said," Korbinian agreed.

However, Iosef showed no sign of humor and merely continued:

"But the state of humanity does not improve when those of means and privilege do nothing but indulge their own interests. Wealth must become patronage. Power must effect change. Knowledge must guide activity. If they do not, we must languish in stagnation. And things that are stagnant die."

"How grim," Korbinian whispered in Babette's ear. "I like him, but he seems so very *serious!*"

Babette was inclined to agree and not unfavorably.

"Ah," Iosef said abruptly, interrupting Babette's thoughts. He nodded in the direction of Herr Raab, who was approaching from the far side of the hall with an old tome in his hands. "I see that the good Herr Raab has found our book."

"As you told him, he would," Babette said.

"Indeed."

"Now, Fräulein Varanus," Iosef said to Babette as she sat at a reading table, "if you will bear with me for just a few minutes, I will be content to leave the book entirely in your hands."

"Oh, yes?" Babette asked, surprised. She patted the top of the heavy *Codex* with one hand. "I was not aware one could read a book of this size in a few minutes."

Iosef sat at the other side of the corner from her and gently opened the book.

"That is correct," he said. "However, I am only interested in a few particular pages."

He removed a pencil and a leather-bound journal from his coat pocket. Without a word, he consulted a set of notes—written, Babette noticed, in a script that she had never seen before—and turned to a few select pages in the *Codex*. Babette watched as Iosef peered at the blank corners of the pages and gently brushed them with his fingertips.

"How peculiar," Korbinian said. He leaned over Babette and brushed her hair as he studied Iosef. "What a curious fellow. I wonder what he is doing."

Babette looked at Korbinian, admonishing him with her eyes.

"What?" Korbinian asked, spreading his hands. "Oh very well, I will stop distracting you and your new friend."

He walked to the far end of the table and sat, folding his arms.

"But tell me honestly," he said, "aren't you a little bit curious? Clearly he is looking for something. What can it be?"

"What are you looking for?" Babette asked.

"What do you mean?" Iosef asked, without looking up.

"You are clearly looking for something that is not there," Babette said. "Hidden writing?" A thought came to her. "No, you are touching the page. It is something tangible. A watermark perhaps? Or an emboss?"

Iosef looked up.

"Indeed," he said. He sounded surprised. "How did you determine that?"

"Quite easily," Babette said. "You are inspecting blank portions of the pages. What you seek is clearly concealed."

Iosef studied her for a little while.

"What I seek," he finally said, "are images hidden within the pages themselves. It is said that light reveals them."

"Simple enough," Babette said. "Place the book in the sunlight and hold up each page. What you seek shall be revealed amid an aura of glory."

At the far end of the table, Korbinian rested his head upon his hand and asked, "Do you suppose, my love, that he has already thought of that?"

"Shhh!" Babette told Korbinian.

"What was that?" Iosef asked.

"I beg your pardon, sir," Babette said. "I sneezed."

"Of course."

"I suppose," Babette said, "that you already thought of the sunlight."

Iosef nodded.

"But should we not at least try it?" Babette asked.

"Unfortunately, the sun and I are on difficult terms," Iosef said.

"How do you mean?"

"I am very sensitive to sunlight," Iosef said. "It is a common condition among those of my house. We suffer sunburn very easily."

"Even from a beam of sunlight filtering through a window?" Babette asked.

She had never heard of such a thing. In truth, the idea fascinated her in a way that, she acknowledged, was probably not normal.

"It may be difficult to believe, but yes," Iosef said. "I could fetch gloves and a veil, but that seems unnecessary now that I have an assistant."

He smiled and motioned to Babette.

Korbinian laughed loudly and clapped his hands together.

"Oh, *liebchen*," he said, "I think we both knew that he was about to say that."

"Well, it seems the least I can do to thank you for sharing the book," Babette said, now thoroughly curious about the book's hidden contents.

She carried the book further down the table to where it was crossed by a beam of light from one of the windows. Turning the book sideways, she raised the first page and stared at it. Backed by the sunlight, the page became translucent, and Babette saw a collection of strange marks and sigils that she did not recognize.

"Oh," she said.

"I take that to mean that you see something," Iosef said, "which is very good, as this is the third copy of the *Codex* that I have inspected."

"The first two were the wrong copies?" Babette asked.

"Indeed, and much to my frustration," Iosef said. "The Vatican was the most surprising and the most disappointing." He looked off into the distance for a moment and murmured, "I truly believed it would have been there, but it was not."

"What a shame," Babette said. "At least your search is finally at an end."

"Oh, it is but beginning," Iosef said. He slid his journal and pencil across the table to Babette. "If you would be so kind, please copy the images you see as precisely as you can."

Babette took up the pencil and looked at Iosef.

"I am puzzled, Lord Shashavani," she said. "You have no reason to trust me. Why allow me to see all of this?"

Iosef looked amused for a moment.

"The images in the *Codex* will mean nothing to you," he said. "Even if they do, it does not matter to me. The contents of the journal are no secret I wish to conceal. Read it, if you like."

"Thank you, but no," Babette said. "I suspect its contents would mean no more to me than these sigils."

"Rather the point, I think," Korbinian said.

Babette began copying the images as precisely as she could.

"Tell me, sir," she said, "where are you from? I do not recognize your accent."

"I am from Georgia," Iosef said. "Whereas you, Fräulein, are from France, the north of France, if I am correct. You are also very accustomed to speaking English. I recognize both strains in your accent."

Babette smiled a little and said, "Most impressive, sir."

"I do my best."

Babette moved to the next page and continued, "Georgia, you say. That is in Russia, is it not?"

"For the time being," Iosef replied. "It is a recent condition of geography."

"What is your land like?"

Iosef took a deep breath and looked off into the distance.

"It is very beautiful," he said. "Words cannot do it justice. But perhaps you will visit it someday."

"That has the sound of an invitation," Korbinian said.

"Perhaps I shall," Babette said.

As she spoke, she had no idea how correct she was.

William removed his hat as he entered the coffee house and sniffed at the air cautiously. He disliked coffee as a rule. It was too pungent an odor for his liking, and its smell was too stale and bitter besides. And, as a well-bred Englishman, he knew that tea was a far more civilized drink.

He spotted Niccolo immediately. The Venetian sat on his own at a table in the back, nursing a cup of the bean poison as only a Continental could. William approached his friend and sat down without a word.

"William, wonderful to see you," Niccolo said. "Coffee?"

"I would rather die," William said, but he smiled nonetheless.

"I see you received my letter."

"Yes," William said. "What is this about, Niccolo? I should be minding my granddaughter at the *Hofbibliothek*. Why am I here, in this place, which smells of *that?*"

This last question was directed at the cup in front of Niccolo.

"Oh, William." Niccolo laughed. "I shall never understand your peculiar tastes. But as to the business, it concerns your granddaughter. And it is most serious."

"I know it must be serious to have brought you here to Vienna," William said.

Niccolo raised his hands quickly and said, "Actually, I am here for another matter entirely, but I am glad that we are in the same city. I prefer to tell you myself."

"Well, what is it?" William asked, growing impatient.

"Word from my spies in France," Niccolo said. "The des Louveteaux have been busy in your absence."

"I know this," William said. His own spies had told him as much. "I am aware of their slander toward Babette's late fiancé."

"And you are aware that Alfonse des Louveteaux remains unmarried?" Niccolo asked. "That he has yet to begin courting another young lady?"

"Not courting?"

William let out a breath and frowned. That was unlike Alfonse and most unlike his father. He had hoped that in Babette's absence they would turn their eyes to another. But if they had not, it could only mean one thing.

"Alfonse is waiting for Babette to return," he said. "He still intends to marry her."

"That is what I suspect," Niccolo said. "Can he achieve it?"

"He can try," William said. "The des Louveteaux have a great deal of influence. Babette will not want him, but the des Louveteaux will apply all the pressure they can. And unfortunately, her father thinks highly of them. He believes that Alfonse is a good match."

Niccolo put his cup down in shock, spilling some of the coffee onto the table.

"Is your son a fool?" he asked. After a moment's consideration, he answered his own question, "Yes, yes he is."

"He is a man of Society," William said. "He believes their lies."

Niccolo leaned forward and said, "William, my friend, I urge you, let me kill them."

"Niccolo—"

"The whole family! Free of charge! I will do it myself!" Niccolo gripped William's hand tightly. "Only do not let them bring this ruination upon your house!"

"Would that I could, Niccolo," William said. "And I thank you for the offer, my dear, dear friend. But I cannot. There are considerations that I dare not speak of."

Niccolo sighed. "As you wish, William. But you are too soft on them. Men like the des Louveteaux understand nothing but power. If they believe they hold power over you, they will squeeze you until you are dry. You must break them, William. You must show them who is the boss."

"In due time, Niccolo," William said. "Believe me, I understand this better than you know."

Niccolo frowned and drank his coffee.

"Then what will you do, William, if you will not kill them?" he asked.

William considered the question for a long time. Finally, he said, half to himself, half to Niccolo:

"I must keep her away from France. The longer Alfonse cannot court her, the more likely he is to give up and pursue another."

That was the answer. Babette had to stay abroad without raising suspicions. And thankfully, Babette's well-known predilections gave William the one most ideal excuse he needed. With another woman it might have raised suspicions as well as eyebrows, but with Babette the response would be scandal rather than suspicion.

He would send her to school.

CHAPTER SIXTEEN

One day, not longer after her encounter with Lord Shashavani, Babette was summoned to the room in their hotel suite that Grandfather had appointed as his office. It was spacious and opulent, like everything in the hotel, with a pleasant window view of the avenue below. Babette had seen it only once before, when they first arrived in Vienna—Grandfather was very particular about the sanctity of his private space—but she immediately felt at home amid the towering bookshelves.

Babette entered cautiously, first rapping her knuckles against the half-open door to announce her arrival. She saw Grandfather seated at his desk, which had been neatly organized in spite of several noticeable stacks of paper. With the volume of correspondence that Grandfather received, a lesser man might well have succumbed to the onslaught and allowed the paperwork to transform into a disorganized heap. But Grandfather demanded too much structure in his life to allow such a thing to happen.

"You sent for me, Grandfather?" Babette asked, unconsciously bowing her head to him for a moment.

"Yes, yes," Grandfather said, setting aside some papers. "Come in my dear. Close the door behind you, there's a good girl."

Babette did as she was bidden and looked about for a seat. The first chair she turned toward was already occupied by Korbinian, so she pulled another chair up from the far corner of the room and sat in it. Grandfather looked at her curiously but did not comment.

"Ah, Babette," Grandfather said, "you look quite lovely today. Quite lovely indeed."

"Thank you," Babette said, blushing a little. Grandfather was seldom free with his compliments.

"I told you that the green was a good choice this morning," Korbinian told her. "And to think, you were actually considering that monstrosity in mauve."

Babette shot Korbinian a look to silence him, though she felt herself smiling. He was such a charming rogue, in death as in life.

"I trust you have been enjoying our stay in Vienna," Grandfather said.

"Oh yes, Grandfather." Babette nodded quickly. "The whole excursion has been a great satisfaction to me. I scarcely want it to end."

Grandfather frowned deeply and said, "Yes, I know. Alas, end it must, and soon. I fear that I have left matters of business in the hands of my Parisian agents for long enough. Much longer and they might begin to damage the company. Managers, as you know, cannot be trusted to manage anything."

"That is a shame, Grandfather," Babette said. "But perhaps I might be permitted to remain here only a little longer? I am certain that my presence in France would be quite unnecessary at least until spring."

"Oh, Babette," Grandfather said, laughing loudly. "Oh, you incorrigible child. No, I fear that for you to remain on this extended holiday would soon raise suspicions. After all, you cannot expect Society to take seriously the claim that you are still in mourning for a man that you had not even married."

"Such callous words," Korbinian said. "Oh, how they wound me!"

Babette covered her mouth with her hand for a moment and hissed a "shhh!" in Korbinian's direction.

"Yes, of course, shhhsh me," Korbinian said, throwing up his hands in mock despair. "Why should anyone care what the dead man has to say?"

"I suppose that is true, Grandfather," Babette said. "But whatever Society thinks, I do still love him."

"And mourn him," Korbinian reminded her.

"And mourn him," Babette said quickly. Good of Korbinian to remember that. From time to time, Babette forgot that to all the world save her he was dead and gone.

"Beg his forgiveness," Korbinian said.

Babette eyed Korbinian dubiously and said, "Grandfather, I beg your forgiveness—"

"But," Korbinian said.

"But—" Babette repeated.

"You have no wish to be thrown back into the mire of courtship," Korbinian finished. "Do you?"

Ah, so that was what he was getting at. Suddenly it made sense.

"But I have no wish to be thrown back into the mire of courtship," Babette said, "least of all where I can be stalked like game by the likes of Alfonse des Louveteaux." After a moment, she quickly added, "I do hope you will forgive my candor, Grandfather; it is just that you are the one person who I think will understand my distain for that which I am asked to do."

Grandfather nodded slowly and said, "Yes, Babette, I understand. That is why I have asked you here today, without your father. You see, I suspected as much, and I have no wish to force you back into 'the mire of courtship', as you so charmingly put it."

"Thank you, Grandfather," Babette said.

"But," Grandfather continued, his voice becoming stern, "if you are to be exempted from your appointed lot in life, there must be a good reason. You cannot simply return to Normandy and live out your life as a spinster. I would never hear the end of it." He paused for a short while and then said, very seriously, "Babette, I have decided that you are to go to school. Does this agree with you?"

"School?" Babette asked.

"Yes," Grandfather said, "to a university for a proper education. I have always known that your path is one of the mind. It was folly for your father to have pushed you along a more material course. Does this please you?"

Babette struggled to speak. Suddenly her tongue was limp in her mouth, making her choke on her own words. School? A university? She had never before dared to dream of such a thing! As Father was fond of saying, it simply wasn't done. Was it even possible? Legal?

"Well good heavens, child," Grandfather said, "say something."

Korbinian rose and walked to her. He knelt behind her and whispered in her ear:

"You must say something, *liebchen*, lest he think that he has offended you."

"Yes!" Babette finally exclaimed, her hands clutched tightly together in excitement. "My God, Grandfather, yes! I should like nothing better! But is it legal?"

Grandfather laughed loudly at this.

"It is certainly not *illegal*," he said. "No, it is merely a matter of finding a university that will accept women, and while that number is quite small, I have taken the liberty of conducting a search. I believe Zurich would be an ideal choice."

"Zurich?" Babette asked.

"You could go to Fuchsburg," Korbinian said. "We've had women there for centuries."

"What about Fuchsburg?" Babette asked. "I have always wanted to go."

"Yes, well...." Grandfather cleared his throat loudly. "I feel that Zurich is the better choice. Fuchsburg would no doubt bring about all manner of painful memories. Zurich is also much further from Normandy. I doubt you want dear Alfonse showing up to court you in the midst of a lecture."

Babette opened her mouth to speak but thought better of it. For whatever reason, Grandfather's mind was clearly made up. The offer of attending university was too incredible to jeopardize over a triviality.

"You are right," she said. "Zurich sounds wonderful. And they will admit me?"

"They have been allowing women to attend lectures for more than ten years now. I have no concerns." Grandfather's eye twinkled mischievously. "Besides which, I am acquainted with one or two members of the faculty. It will be quite simple to arrange, I assure you."

"I suppose I shall be expected to return home between terms," Babette said, already disappointed at the prospect.

"No, no," Grandfather said, dismissing the notion like a silly dream. "I don't think that would do at all. You must be attentive to your studies, Babette. No, you will remain in Zurich, or perhaps you can visit the Pavones in Venice. But I will not allow you to wile away your time on the trivialities of the country life. If you are to be educated, then it must be the entirety of your attention."

Babette smiled to herself but quickly thought better of it and looked at Grandfather with a serious expression.

"Surely you and Father will want me to visit," she said.

"No," Grandfather said abruptly. "Your father and I shall visit you. The brisk mountain air will do wonders for our health."

"Brisk mountain air?" Korbinian asked.

"Grandfather," Babette said, "Zurich is below the Alps."

Grandfather did not hesitate with his reply:

"Better still. I find that mountain air is a trifle too thin for my comfort."

"You are serious, Grandfather?" Babette asked.

It was all too impossible to believe.

"Oh yes," Grandfather said, looking very grave. "And it's dreadfully cold up in the mountains as well. Horrible for one's health."

"No, I mean about school," Babette said. "You truly mean to let me go."

"I do," Grandfather said with a broad smile. "I have known for quite some time that your lot is not that of a Society woman. You would not be satisfied with a man of great standing and little intellect. Perhaps if you are among men of learning, you will find someone you are willing to marry. At least, that is what I will tell your father. For myself, I only want you to be happy."

Babette rose from her chair and threw her arms around Grandfather's neck.

"Thank you, Grandfather!" she cried. "Thank you! Thank you!"

* * * *

Zurich, Switzerland

Babette found much to please her in Zurich: the beautiful old city, the fresh air, and the majesty of the Alps rising over the lake. And above all, she delighted in the peace and quiet. Removed from the madness of Society, from Father's endless fussing and interference, life became remarkable pleasant. In the days before her time at the university began, Babette spent hours strolling along the lakeside with Korbinian. They spoke endlessly, suddenly free of the constraints of the household. Grandfather had, of course, furnished servants for her—a local husband and wife to look after the house and a pleasant Venetian girl provided by the Pavones to serve as her maid—but they all had the good sense to leave her in peace.

Surprisingly, school was just as she had expected. Education was nothing new to her, but the structure was quite changed from the governesses and tutors who had instructed her in her youth. She found many of her lectures informative but tedious, and except for the rare ray of light, her fellow students were nothing but a pack of self-important fools. Korbinian often reminded her that her view may have been skewed by the tendency of the young men to dismiss her as something less than a proper scholar. Babette disagreed.

At first her studies were in philosophy, like the few other women allowed to sit lectures with the men. This occupied her for a time, but soon she found her interests tending toward more practical topics. Four months into her studies, she began insinuating herself into the faculty of medicine. It was difficult at first, but with a combination of charm, intellect, and relentlessness, she finally managed to crack their resistance.

When Grandfather visited her the following summer, she was able to report to him the good news as he joined her for tea in her house's small sitting room.

"Grandfather," she said, as she added the cream to her tea, "I have decided to become a doctor."

Grandfather paused in the midst of drinking. He slowly lowered his cup and looked at her, blinking a few times.

"A doctor?" he asked.

"Yes, Grandfather."

Grandfather shrugged and asked, "Do they allow women to study medicine here?"

"Doctor Höffner has already agreed to let me attend his lectures this year," Babette replied, "provided that I agree to spend time as a nurse in the hospital in the meanwhile. And what is more, provided I make a good show of it, he has agreed to speak to the rest of the faculty on my behalf."

"That is wonderful news, Babette," Grandfather said. "I am most pleased."

"You approve?" Babette asked, very much surprised. She had not expected such a response.

Grandfather thought about the question for a short while.

"Well," he finally said, "it is unorthodox, certainly, but I have never been overly enamored by orthodoxy. Doing what has always been done is no way to run a business. Why should it be the standard for our lives?"

"Do you think Father will approve?" Babette asked.

"No," Grandfather said, "but leave him to me." He took a sip of tea and added, "In fact, if it would be of any use to you, I would be most happy to speak to the faculty as well, to give clear demonstration of my approval. Perhaps a financial incentive as well."

"Thank you, Grandfather!" Babette exclaimed. "Words cannot describe how grateful I am!"

Grandfather smiled warmly at her. He set down his teacup and took her hand in both of his.

"Babette," he said, "you are the dearest thing in the world to me. You are the daughter I never had. Your happiness is paramount, and it makes perfect sense to me that you would prefer a life of scholarship. If you wish to become a doctor, I shall do everything in my power to ensure it."

"Thank you, Grandfather," Babette said, squeezing his hand.

"Now," Grandfather said, "you are aware that this will be a difficult road for you. Even if you can achieve a full doctoral degree, your colleagues will not be very favorable toward a female among their order. If you work at all, you are likely to be relegated to the status of a glorified nurse. I suspect your best hope will be a position at some children's hospital."

"Relegation as a doctor will suit me far better than exaltation as a wife," Babette said.

"I know." Grandfather picked up his cup again and took a drink. "And I shall explain it to your father. In the meantime, let us plan for the future. Will the faculty grant you a doctoral degree for medicine?"

Babette sighed and said:

"I don't know. I have cause to doubt it. I know that the male students will be up in arms over my merely attending lectures and—God willing—dissections. But what alternative is there?"

"Remember, child, we are thinking in two or three years' time," Grandfather said. "Pursue a degree of some sort here, and in the meantime, I will see what can be done to arrange doctoral studies for you.

Perhaps Paris. There are progressive forces at work in France. The possibility of women's education is becoming more and more promising. I understand that the Empress Eugénie is favorably disposed toward the idea. And I myself am not unknown at court."

Babette felt Korbinian appear behind her and place a hand on her shoulder.

"What he means," he whispered, "is that as one of the men bankrolling the French economy, the Emperor and Empress have good cause to regard him as a dear friend to France."

"Speaking of which, what news from France?" Babette asked.

"Well, you are missed, of course," Grandfather said. "But you may be pleased to hear that Alfonse, though still pining for you, has begun to cast his eye elsewhere. I suspect you will no longer have to worry about his attempts at courtship should you return home in a few years' time."

"That is most welcome news," Babette said, smiling with sincere joy. "I wish him every good fortune in the pursuit of his new conquest."

Grandfather smiled back, his eyes twinkling, and said, "Don't we all, child. Don't we all."

Paris, France

Babette's time in Zurich passed in the blinking of an eye. Her studies occupied most of her waking hours, for she embraced them with the utmost determination. What little time she had left was devoted to her work at the hospital. By the time of her graduation, none of the medical faculty could doubt her qualifications.

But it was not Babette's intention to practice medicine in Switzerland, as much as she came to enjoy the country. Her home was France, and she was determined to be accredited there. Fortunately, Grandfather had done his work in her absence. Supported by both the Empress and the Dean of the Faculty of Medicine, she entered the University of Paris. There she pursued her studies with just as much fervor as she had in Zurich, filling her free time with private research, medical observation, and experiments. Some of her work she endeavored to publish, but several of her more esoteric studies she reserved for her own purposes.

Throughout it all, Babette maintained a lengthy, if intermittent, correspondence with the peculiar gentleman she had met in Vienna. Iosef Shashavani proved most eloquent and attentive in correspondence, and together, over hundreds of miles, they conversed about her rather incredible choice of career.

But graduation brought its own frustrations. Though graduating with honors, Babette found few institutions eager to accept her. Many of her colleagues proved immediately disparaging, and even those who hailed her as a beacon of progress, expressed their naïve certainty that, as a woman, her ideal role in medicine would be in attending to children or to the concerns of her own sex. Babette's wish to become a surgeon, her dreams of advancing the frontiers of science like Galen or van Wesel immediately floundered.

Soon, however, like the enabling hand of God, war came again to Europe, and suddenly a path opened to her.

CHAPTER SEVENTEEN

Autumn, 1870
Sedan, France

"Lescot! How many times must I tell you, *do not* put lint in my patients' wounds! It is most *unhygienic!*"

Babette shouted in the narrow confines of the surgery, enraged by her assistant's inability to follow instructions. Fortunately, she had the presence of mind to keep her voice in the lower tone that she had used for the past month. Being a man was not too difficult once one got the hang of things, but sometimes the little things were there to trip one up.

"I'm sorry, Doctor Sauvage," Lescot said, drawing his hands back from the wounded man on the table. "I'm sorry, but that is the appropriate technique."

"It is primitive and foolish," Babette said. "You must clean the wound with the alcohol solution that *I have already prepared!*"

She grabbed a bottle of the stuff from a nearby stand and waved it under Lescot's nose.

"And having done that," she continued, "you must not pack the wound with fibers acquired from God knows where! You must bind the wound tightly with multiple layers of bandages—"

"And the final bandage must be treated with alcohol or carbolic acid, I know, Doctor!" Lescot cried.

Babette stopped herself mid-rant. She had admonished the poor man in such a way ever since the first casualties had come in from the front. Now, of course, the front had moved far closer to them than anyone could have expected. If the stories were true, the Prussians and their allies were at the very gates of Sedan. Babette did not know the truth of it: she had scarcely left the hospital all week.

She took a deep breath. The bindings over her breasts were making her chest ache again. It was always worse when she shouted. Given the stupidity she regularly encountered, shouting was one of her main occupations apart from surgery.

"Prepare the bandages for me," she said, as she treated the patient's wound with her tonic.

"Yes, Doctor," Lescot said.

The patient—a soldier injured early that morning—bit back a cry of pain.

“Easy there,” Babette said as gruffly as she could manage. “Just a few minutes more and you’ll be ready to convalesce until the Germans knock on the door.”

“Do you really think the Germans can win over us?” Lescot asked, passing Babette the bandages.

“Ask me at the end of the day,” Babette said, binding the wound. After she was done, she said, “There. Summon the stretcher bearers to remove this man and send in the next patient.”

She wiped her bloody hands on the worn frock coat that she wore for operations. It was caked with old blood, like any good surgeon’s coat should be. She washed her hands in a nearby basin of water—by now dirty with blood. Her block of soap was little more than a sliver and obtaining a new one would be difficult work. Her colleagues saw it all as one of the ridiculous rituals of “Mad Doctor Sauvage”, rather like the refusal to pack wounds with lint and her obsession with sterilization.

Behind her, Lescot helped the stretcher-bearers carry the soldier out of the surgery and then called for the next patient.

“Let us through!” someone shouted from outside.

There was a commotion and a pair of cuirassiers forced their way past Lescot, bearing a third man similarly uniformed between them.

“Officers!” cried Lescot. “You cannot come in here! There are other patients—”

One of the cuirassiers pushed him out of the away. They helped the man between them to the table and set him down. His breastplate had been perforated by bullets in five places, and sword wounds marked his arms and legs. Still, for all his injuries the wounded cuirassier seemed more angry than afraid. Snarling, he raised his head.

It was Alfonse.

Babette caught her breath and turned away, quickly busying herself with her bandages. One of the cuirassiers grabbed her by the shoulder and turned her around.

“My captain has been wounded,” he said. “Badly.”

“Very badly, by the look of him,” Babette said.

“Help him!” the cuirassier shouted. “Now!”

“There are other patients as badly wounded throughout the hospital,” Babette said. “You cannot drag him in here ahead of them.”

“This man is the son of the Count des Louveteaux,” the cuirassier said. “He is worth more than a dozen of those peasants out there. Now attend to him!”

Babette looked back at Alfonse and saw him staring up at her, his eyes narrowed. Babette’s disguise had been largely confined to shorn hair and a change of clothes. She had originally planned for a false moustache, but the risk of discovery was too great. In expression and bearing, she looked little like her old self—she had even fooled one of her professors from Paris—but if Alfonse recognized her....

She saw him sniff the air, and his eyes widened for a moment.

He knows! Babette thought.

"Hush, *liebchen*," Korbinian whispered in her ear. He had been remarkably silent all morning, perhaps wishing not to distract her on such a busy day. But now he was there beside her, murmuring, "Do not react or else he will know that his suspicions are correct. Carry on as though nothing is amiss."

"Take off his cuirass," Babette said, selecting a probe and a pair of long forceps to deal with the bullets.

The cuirassiers did as instructed, hauling off Alfonse's breastplate. It clattered onto the floor, and one of them kicked it off into the corner.

"Leave us," Alfonse said.

"What?" Lescot asked, looking at Babette.

"I dislike a crowded room," Alfonse said. "Everyone but the doctor, leave at once."

"Doctor Sauvage—" Lescot began.

"Go," Babette said. "Find me more bandages."

Lescot hesitated for a moment. He looked at Alfonse, who growled. Lescot went pale and backed away a step.

"I'll...I'll do as you ask, Doctor," he said before rushing out the door.

"Christophe, Marais," Alfonse said to the two cuirassiers, "wait outside and do not let anyone in until I say so."

The cuirassiers exchanged looks but quickly saluted with a sharp "Yes Captain." So saying, they withdrew and silence filled the room.

Babette looked at Alfonse who looked back at her in turn.

"The Liston knife is on the table," Korbinian said softly, brushing a hand through her hair. "Remember that."

"Well, Doctor?" Alfonse asked.

"Well?" Babette echoed.

"Shall we begin? Or do you intend for me to bleed to death?"

Babette shook her head to clear it. *Keep calm*, she told herself.

"Remove your jacket and shirt and lie down," she said. "This will be painful."

"No more so than I have already endured, I suspect," Alfonse said, doing as instructed.

Babette picked up her tools and examined Alfonse. She was surprised by what she saw. The sword wounds she found to be shallow and clean. They had already begun to clot, and there seemed little need to tend to them now. The bullet wounds were equally remarkable. Careful testing with the probe found that all five of the bullets were intact. The wounds were shallow—the effects of Alfonse's armor, Babette could only assume—and no bones had been broken. She removed the bullets as quickly as she could and washed the wounds with alcohol.

Alfonse suffered through it all without a sound. He simply stared at her with an unwavering gaze.

Babette said nothing as she bandaged Alfonse. With the bullets gone, the flow of blood began to slow. The wounds would soon clot and scab over. Babette had seen nothing like it before. In another set of circumstances, she would have loved to perform a study of Alfonse's physiology.

"Neatly done," Alfonse said, looking down at himself. "How far you have come, little runt."

Babette kept her expression inscrutable.

"I do not understand you, Captain," she said.

"Come now, Babette," Alfonse replied, "let us speak plainly."

Babette put a hand to Alfonse's forehead and said, "You do not *feel* feverish. Perhaps an injury to your head?"

Alfonse grabbed her by the wrist.

"Do not play games, Babette!" he snarled. "I know who you are."

Babette tried to pull away, but Alfonse's grip was far too strong. Snarling, Alfonse thrust his other hand into Babette's coat. Though her breasts were bound, still there was something there to be found. A disgusting leer crossed Alfonse's face.

"Just as I thought," he said. "You're hiding a great surprise, 'Doctor Sauvage.'" He grabbed her firmly by the chin and forced her to look at him. "You are Babette Varanus. It has been years since last I laid eyes on you. What strange fate has brought us together again."

No point in pretending. Just make him leave.

"What do you want, Alfonse?" Babette demanded.

Alfonse chuckled.

"What do I want?" he said. "Oh, where to begin?"

The hand at Babette's chin moved to her throat, and Alfonse pushed her down against the bloody surgical table.

"Do you know, I was meant to marry my cousin Claire?" Alfonse asked. "Ever since we were children, it was understood. And then… you."

"Me?" Babette asked.

She looked toward the closed door out of the corner of her eye. Where was Lescot?

"My father wished me to marry you," Alfonse said. "Why is beyond me. You are such a pathetic thing, unworthy of me."

At this, Babette felt her hackles rise. How dare that inbred dolt call her unworthy? She was a Varanus. What was a des Louveteaux to a Varanus?

"The satyr to Hyperion," Korbinian said as he loomed above them, gazing into Babette's eyes from behind Alfonse's shoulder. "A dung beetle to a king."

"But my father sent me after you like a dog after a rancid bone," Alfonse continued. "You. The runt. And then you had the audacity to refuse me. You took up with a *German*."

Babette felt Alfonse's grip tighten about her throat.

"I had to kill him," Alfonse said. "I had to kill him to get rid of him."

What?

Babette looked up at Korbinian. She saw him as he had been the very night of his death, his chest covered in blood. Blood trickled from the corners of his mouth and stained his lips as he spoke:

"You always knew he murdered me, *liebchen*. An accident? Self-defense? Lies. Murder. Murder by the blade."

Murder by the blade.

Korbinian pointed toward something on the table. Babette tried to look but Alfonse's grip held her fast. Still, groping blindly, Babette found what Korbinian wished her to find.

The Liston knife.

"And then you left," Alfonse said. "You *left!* You should have been mine, as my father insisted, but you ran away. And my father insisted that I wait. *That I wait!* By the time he finally accepted that you would not return, Claire had been married to another. She should have been mine, but she isn't, and because of you. *You!* The runt!"

Alfonse climbed atop Babette, choking her even harder until stars erupted before her eyes. Her head swam, the world lost its clarity, and finally there was nothing left but her and Korbinian and Alfonse and the knife.

"But I think," Alfonse said, "that if I fuck you like the bitch you are, then perhaps you can earn my forgiveness, one pathetic yelp at a time."

Snarling, Alfonse tore open Babette's coat and then her vest, buttons flying in all directions. He bared his teeth at her behind a hideous smile and licked her face with his tongue, like a cat lapping up milk from a saucer.

"Make me believe you enjoy this," he whispered, "or I'll kill you like I killed the German." He looked into her eyes and said, "And like the German, no one will care."

Babette looked back at Korbinian. He was drenched in blood. His face was pale just as it had been moments before his death. Babette saw him mouth a single word, a word that Babette heard herself cry aloud as crimson flooded her vision:

"Die!"

She stabbed Alfonse in the soft flesh between throat and shoulder, making him howl in pain. She stabbed again and again, each time repeating the word.

"Die! Die! Die!"

The Liston knife lodged in Alfonse's flesh, and Babette could not pull it free.

Alfonse began screaming. With a strength she did not recall possessing, Babette flung him off of her. The big man struck the ground, blood gushing everywhere.

Babette saw Korbinian offering her his hand. She took it, and he helped her off the table.

She looked into his eyes and said, "I love you."

Korbinian touched her cheek with his hand and said, "I know."

She took Korbinian's face in her hands and kissed his bloody mouth, just as she had done so many years ago as he lay dying, the victim of Alfonse's barbarity. But now things had changed. Now it was Alfonse who would die.

Murder by the blade.

Babette turned toward Alfonse, who sat on the ground howling, struggling to pull the knife free. As if in a dream, Babette reached down and drew the blade from his flesh with a sharp tug, releasing another gout of blood.

She heard shouts from outside and the sound of fists hammering on the door.

"Finish it, *liebchen*," Korbinian said.

Babette took Alfonse by the chin and forced his head back. He grabbed at her feebly, but the sudden loss of blood had rendered him impotent.

The door burst open behind her. The cuirassiers rushed into the room, Lescot close behind them.

Babette placed the Liston knife against Alfonse's throat.

"A life for a life," she said, and began to cut.

One of the cuirassiers grabbed her from behind, pulling her away from Alfonse before she could make more than a token slash. She kicked the cuirassier in the knee with her heel, making him loosen his hold. She twisted around in his grasp and tore his throat apart with the knife.

The second cuirassier lunged at her as his comrade fell. Babette ducked beneath his arms and stabbed him in the leg. The man dropped to one knee, and Babette struck him hard across the face.

"Run, *liebchen!* Run!" Korbinian shouted.

Babette ran for the door, the bloody knife still clutched in her hand. Lescot cowered away from her as she ran past, but he was of no interest to her.

She ran through the hospital, past the beleaguered staff and teeming masses of wounded. She hesitated for a moment. There were so many patients. They needed her.

But she heard Korbinian's voice in her ear:

"Run, *liebchen!* Run!"

And so she ran, out into the streets, which were choked with soldiers. She forced her way through the living and stumbled over the dying and the dead, who lay unwanted in the gutters of Sedan. The air was filled with cries, an incoherent chorus singing an ode to the doom of France.

The end had come, heralded by the thunder of the Prussian guns that shattered the sky and shook the ground.

It was the end of the battle, the end of France, and the end of the life that Babette had known. Now there was no going back. Only the road forward lay open to her.

CHAPTER EIGHTEEN

Babette fled west from Sedan. She followed the road but stayed off it to avoid notice. She passed Glaire, about a mile away from Sedan, and continued on to the Meuse. She paused on the shore and took stock of her situation. Across the river and to the south were German soldiers. There would be no escape in either direction.

The north was no better. The river merely looped around and continued back toward Sedan. And besides, that way lay either the French, who would by now be hunting Alfonse's murderer, or more Germans who had dislodged the French.

Perhaps if she swam downstream, she could bypass the soldiers on both sides and make her escape…

Babette took off her boots, securing them around her neck, plunged into the cold water, and made her way south. She silently thanked God that Grandfather had taught her how to swim as a child. Like him she loved the water, so long as it was not the sea.

Finally, near where the river bent west toward Donchery, she came ashore. She lay on the bank for a few minutes to catch her breath. She was astounded by her good fortune so far, but she would eventually be found by someone. She toyed with the idea of hiding until nightfall, but that would be hours, and the longer she waited the greater the chance of being caught.

She put on her wet boots, stood, and turned south, intending to make a run past the German lines. Instead of open country, she saw a pair of men on horseback watching her from a dozen or so feet away. Babette gasped and dropped to the ground, hoping that they had not seen her.

"This will not help, you know," Korbinian said from where he lay on the grass beside her. "They must have seen you."

"Shhh!" Babette hissed.

"They can't hear me," Korbinian reminded her. He stood up and waved to the men, neither of whom reacted. Turning back to Babette, he said, "They can't even see me."

"I know," Babette said.

"And they are coming this way. Yes, they have seen you. No point in pretending."

Korbinian extended his hand and helped Babette to her feet. Babette brushed herself off and waited while the two riders approached.

One was dressed in a leather riding coat that he wore closed over what appeared to be civilian clothes. His hair was dark, he wore a neatly trimmed moustache, and he bore a rifle in a side scabbard by his saddle. The second rider wore black: clothes, gloves, cloak and hat, and a voluminous black veil that covered his face.

The first rider called out to Babette in French. His voice was crisp and strong, though he spoke with a strong accent that Babette could not place.

"You there, approach please. Who are you, and how do you come to be swimming in a river at such a time as this?"

Babette cleared her throat and said:

"I am Hercule Sauvage. Doctor Hercule Sauvage. And you? This is the middle of a war."

"You did not answer my second question," the rider said.

His companion held up a hand to silence him and climbed down from his horse. The man crossed to Babette and studied her intently from behind his veil. After a moment he spoke:

"No," he said, his voice strangely familiar, "you are Babette Varanus. Doctor Babette Varanus, formerly of Zurich, now of Paris."

"How…?" Babette asked. "Who…?"

The man lifted his veil and swept it back across the top of his hat. Babette gasped aloud. It was Iosef, who was young and beautiful, just as Babette remembered him, uncannily so, in fact. He wore spectacles with tinted lenses to protect his eyes from the sun, and he seemed scarcely older than when Babette had first met him in Vienna.

"Lord Shashavani!" Babette cried.

Iosef smiled for a moment and removed his sunglasses.

"Hello, Doctor," he said. "How do you come to cross the Meuse in this manner?"

"There were complications in Sedan," Babette said. "I was forced to leave with all possible haste."

"So I have heard," Iosef said. "Still, swimming down a river is quite an extreme solution."

"There were Germans everywhere else," Babette said.

"There are Germans here as well," Iosef replied. "We were watching the artillery fire on Sedan from atop that hill yonder, and there were a number of Germans present. But we grew tired of the display and thought it better to admire the serenity of the Meuse on our way back to Donchery."

Babette looked at him in surprise and asked, "What were you doing with the Germans?"

"We were in the German states when the war broke out," Iosef answered. "I received permission from the King of Prussia to accompany their armies as a foreign observer. Luka and I have been with them since the summer."

"Luka?" Babette asked.

Iosef motioned to the man in the leather coat, who politely bowed his head.

"My manservant, Luka," he said. "Tell me, Doctor Varanus, how do you come to be here, in the midst of a battle, dressed in the manner of a man? I realize that things are strange in this land, but I was not aware that the French disguised their women as men as a tactic of war."

"Very droll, my lord," Babette said.

Iosef's eyes twinkled but he replied, "That was not a joke."

"A pity," Babette said, hiding a smile. "In fact, I am dressed as a man because, as you may have surmised, I have been pretending to be one."

"Ah," Iosef said. "The mysterious Doctor Sauvage, am I correct?"

"The very same."

"I seem to recall reading a number of rather clever articles by Doctor Sauvage over these past few years," Iosef said. "Indeed, there was even a monograph about...what was it?"

He tapped his fingertips together, deep in thought.

"Blood transfusion, my lord," Luka said.

"Blood transfusion," Iosef said, nodding. "That was it."

"I recall the subject, my lord," Luka said, removing a long smoking pipe from his pocket and packing it with tobacco, "because you remarked upon its insights to me on no less than three occasions."

Iosef replaced his sunglasses and said, "That will be all, Luka."

"Very good, my lord," Luka replied, lighting his pipe. Though his voice was devoid of emotion, Babette could not help but think that the two men were sharing in some mutual joke. But why else would they speak to one another in French, if not for her to hear?

"Tell me," Iosef said to Babette, "why have you invented this Doctor Sauvage?"

Babette laughed and replied:

"Because, alas, it is remarkably difficult for a woman to be allowed any responsibility in medicine not pertaining to children, their production, or the means thereof. Blood transfusion is, evidently, out of the question."

"It would seem a most uncivilized thing to do, transferring the blood of one creature into another," Iosef said. "Most uncivilized."

At this, Luka suddenly coughed and exhaled a great quantity of smoke. He cleared his throat loudly and said something to Iosef in a language that Babette did not understand. Iosef said something in reply, and the two men chuckled.

"Is there a reason why you pretend to be Doctor Sauvage now?" Iosef asked.

"For the same reason that I invented him," Babette said. "You see, when war was declared, I decided I wished to serve my country as a doctor and to make a study of battlefield injury firsthand. Shockingly, the military was not interested in the assistance of a woman surgeon."

"Shocking," Iosef said rather flatly. Evidently he was no more shocked by it than she had been. "Tell me, Doctor, where are you bound?"

"Normandy," Babette replied.

"But you reside in Paris, do you not?"

"I do," Babette said. "But the estate of my grandfather is in Normandy, and I wish to return there, especially in light of recent events."

"Yes, the ancestral home of one's forefathers," Iosef said, gazing off across the river. "I know its call. Very well, Luka and I shall escort you." He looked back at her and added, "With your permission, of course."

"Escort me?" Babette asked. "Why?"

"The countryside is dangerous for travelers alone," Iosef said, "whatever the land. And now, in a time of confusion such as this, I would be even more concerned about dangers on the road."

"You are traveling with the Germans," Babette said. "Why would you offer such a thing?"

Iosef shrugged and answered, "I find Prussians very tedious."

"The Württembergers were pleasant, my lord," Luka said.

"Yes, the Württembergers were pleasant," Iosef agreed.

"But the Prussians were tedious."

"Yes, Luka," Iosef said, "as I have said."

"Very good, my lord," Luka said. "Very good."

A quiet smile passed between them briefly. Another private joke it seemed.

"Very well," Babette said, "traveling companions would be most welcome. And especially one that I know and feel instinctively that I can trust as a gentleman."

"The power of correspondence is truly remarkable," Iosef said. "Like an alchemist's elixir, it transforms near strangers into fast friends."

"As if 'twere lead into gold," Babette replied.

"Tell me," Iosef said, "as far as anyone is aware, Babette Varanus is still residing in Paris. Is that correct?"

"Well yes," Babette said. "I suppose she never left."

"Then we shall go first to Paris," Iosef said, "and you shall travel with us as Doctor Sauvage until we reach it. In Paris you will become

Doctor Varanus again, quit your lodgings—or at least make it known that you are departing them for a time—and together we shall all go to Normandy. I do expect the hospitality of your family when we arrive, at least until we can arrange transportation back to Georgia."

"The hospitality of the Varanuses is a thing of legend in these parts," Babette said. "You will not be disappointed."

Iosef flashed a smile.

"Good," he said. "Then I think it would be best if we departed at once." He turned to his manservant and said, "Luka, take Doctor Varanus to Donchery. Some of your dear friends the Württembergers may be there, along with the Prussians. I will consult von Bismark and von Moltke for leave to depart. I think I have seen all that I need to see. Sedan's surrender is inevitable."

"You would not prefer to disappear without warning, my lord?" Luka asked. It was surely in jest, but his tone was as flat as Iosef's.

"I think not," Iosef said. "The Prussian Army is not noted for its enjoyment of surprises."

"What if they refuse to give you leave?" Babette asked.

"I would not worry about such a thing," Iosef said. "I have been noted as a persuasive man in my time." He looked to Luka. "You have your papers, Luka?"

"The ones signed by the Prime Minister?" Luka asked.

"No, Luka," Iosef said, "the ones signed by the Patriarch."

Luka exhaled a puff of smoke and said, "Oh dear, my lord, I fear I left those at home. I only have the papers we obtained in Berlin."

"Then you must make due, Luka," Iosef said, "and pray to God that these Germans know who Otto von Bismark is."

Donchery, France

As fate would have it, they did not depart for Paris until the following morning. Babette went with Luka into Donchery. The Prussian troops let them pass once Luka showed them his papers. In any event, it seemed that most of the troops in town recognized him. He was rather distinctive, and his master doubly so.

Luka obtained some fresh clothing for Babette—men's clothing of course, as it was necessary to keep up that pretense. When Iosef joined them a short while later, he explained that they would be obliged to wait until the next day before leaving. It was a necessary measure to allay any suspicions on the part of the Prussians.

Not that this seemed much of a worry to Babette, for she immediately noticed that Iosef had a most remarkable rapport with their new hosts. That evening, once Babette had washed and dressed, Iosef introduced her to Prime Minister von Bismark and King Wilhelm of Prussia, along with several other Germans of distinction and an American named Sheridan. It was all rather a blur, but Babette clearly remembered her encounter with Bismark. Iosef had introduced her as an Alsatian by the name of Gustave, a patriot who had been jailed in Sedan for openly advocating the return of her—"his"—homeland to the Germanic bosom. Freed from confinement by the artillery bombardment—"like a hand of God from on high," Iosef said—"Gustave" had fled toward the Prussians in the hope of sanctuary and subsequently encountered Iosef and his manservant. No longer safe in France, Iosef meant to take "Gustave" with him when he departed, first to England and eventually back to Russia via the Baltic.

Far-fetched as the story was, Iosef delivered it with his usual placidity, as if discussing nothing more important than last year's vegetable marrows. And though Babette could tell that the Prime Minister was a man of intelligence, he seemed to accept the tale without reservation. He spoke at some length to Iosef in German, discussing the likely reaction of Russia to recent events, but he said little to Babette.

After a modest dinner, Iosef was summoned by King Wilhelm to discuss matters pertaining to their two countries—which in Iosef's case was understood to mean Russia. Babette was shown to their lodgings by Luka and promptly retired, exhausted by the day's events.

When she awoke the next morning, Babette found that Iosef had already risen, having returned while she slept. Luka had procured a horse and saddle for her. He did not explain where they came from, and Babette did not ask, though she suspected they had once belonged to one of the many dead at Sedan.

They set out early on the road to Paris. Whatever Iosef had said to the Prime Minister and the King during his private meetings with them, it had done the trick: aside from being asked for their papers, they were neither halted nor detained by the troops.

As they left Donchery, Babette spotted von Bismark and the Emperor of France sitting together at a rather nondescript cottage. What words passed between them she did not know, nor did she have any interest in knowing, but she suspected it dealt with terms of surrender. The Empire was finished, that much was clear from the haggard expression on the Emperor's face.

They traveled southwest at a quick pace and reached Paris in less than a week. News of Sedan had already preceded them—indeed, upon arrival they received confirmation of Sedan's surrender on the same day they had departed. Paris was in an uproar, filled with a patriotic fervor that swept throughout the populace in a manner that Babette had never seen before. The Empire had been overthrown in a bloodless *coup,* and a republic had been declared. The old France was gone and in its place was something new and fragile, a glimmer of the first republic standing like a sandcastle in the path of the Prussian tidal wave. Word had it that the new government had rejected Prussia's demands and that the fighting would soon resume. It would not be long, Babette knew, before the Prussians and their allies converged on Paris. When they arrived, the city was the last place Babette wanted to be.

In Paris, Babette threw off the identity of Hercule Sauvage, changed into her old clothes—which she had not worn in months—and was once again Babette Varanus. She emerged from her "seclusion" quite dramatically, going so far as to admonish one of her neighbors for playing his violin too loudly. The softness of her arrival and the drama of her departure, she hoped, would ensure that no connection whatsoever would be drawn between her and Doctor Sauvage.

She emptied the bank account left for her by Grandfather. Most of her funds were held in trust, but she liquidated the monthly allowance that she had access to and immediately paid off her landlady and secured a carriage. While Luka helped her pack her things, Iosef disappeared into the depths of the city. He said nothing about his business, and Babette sensed that there was no point in asking.

Iosef returned in the small hours of the morning, but he seemed not in the least bit fatigued and insisted on their immediate departure. Babette was inclined to agree. They packed the carriage with their assorted belongings and left the city for Normandy.

They finally arrived at Grandfather's estate a few days later. In an instant, Babette was at peace. All the madness and chaos of recent events faded away at the sight of the neatly trimmed trees flanking the drive leading up to the house. As Luka turned the carriage down the drive, Babette exhaled and allowed the calmness of the ordered landscape to fill her.

She was home.

CHAPTER NINETEEN

Normandy, France

Babette paused at the front door, uncertain of how to proceed. It had been nearly ten years since she had been home. Grandfather's house felt strange, like an idea of comfort rather than comfort itself. Just the sight of the old familiar place summoned up memories. Was it right to destroy them with an infusion of reality?

The question was answered for her as the door opened to reveal Vatel, a little older than she remembered but still in good health. He stared at her in silence for a moment before smiling in delight.

"Mademoiselle Varanus, welcome back," he said. "We spied your carriage approaching down the drive. The Messieurs Varanus await you in the parlor."

"Thank you, Vatel," Babette said.

"And may I inquire as to the identities of your companions? Monsier Varanus will be most eager to meet them."

Meaning that Grandfather was extremely suspicious of her unannounced arrival in the company of strangers.

Iosef took a step forward and addressed Vatel:

"You may inform the master of the house that Prince Iosef Shashavani has come to call on him."

Vatel's eyes widened ever so slightly.

"Of course, my lord," he said. "Please, follow me."

"Very good," Iosef said. "My manservant Luka will attend to the carriage."

"As you wish, my lord," Vatel said.

Babette followed Vatel into the house with Iosef at her side. They entered the parlor, and she saw Father and Grandfather seated by the window. They both rose to their feet in an instant as she entered.

"Prince Shashavani and Mademoiselle Varanus, Messieurs," Vatel said.

"Thank you, Vatel, that will be all," Grandfather said, without missing a beat. "Babette, Prince Shashavani, please join us. It seems we have much to speak about."

Babette took a seat in a nearby chair. Iosef did likewise, tactfully choosing one that was not directly adjacent to her. This was just as well,

Babette noted, for the chair beside her was already occupied by Korbinian, who smiled at her and kissed her hand without a word.

"Well," Father said, "this is unexpected."

"That would be a word for it," Grandfather said.

"We have never entertained royalty in this house before," Father added.

Iosef smiled and said, "It is not quite so exciting as you may think. In Russia, a prince is much like a duke in France."

"I am familiar," Grandfather said. "Nevertheless, it is a great honor. How do you come to be in France? Or indeed, in the company of my granddaughter?"

"He rescued me, Grandfather," Babette said, "in Sedan."

"*Sedan!*" Father exclaimed. "What were you doing in Sedan?"

"Being rescued by Prince Shashavani, evidently," Grandfather said. He cleared his throat. "Babette, I think that your father would very much like to speak with you in private, to hear about all the things you have been doing since we last visited you in Paris. And in the meantime, Your Lordship," he said to Iosef, "I wonder if you might join me for an afternoon stroll in the garden? There are one or two things of a horticultural nature that I should like to present to you."

Damn it all, Grandfather was going to meddle!

"Grandfather, I—" Babette began.

"I would be delighted to do so, Monsieur Varanus," Iosef said. "I am a keen follower of horticulture myself."

Grandfather smiled, showing his teeth, and said, "Good."

"You must forgive Vatel," William said, as he led Iosef through the gardens—now largely bare or withering with the onset of autumn. "I fear he is not experienced with the nobility of Russia. We ought to address you as Your Illustriousness, am I correct?"

Iosef flashed a short smile, which quickly faded. For a young man, he seemed remarkably serious.

"Indeed," Iosef said, "that would be an acceptable translation. Still, I feel no need to stand on ceremony if you will join me in ignoring it. Lord Shashavani shall suffice."

"Tell me, Lord Shashavani," William said, "if you will pardon my curiosity, what part of Russia are you from? And how do you come to be in France at such a time as this?"

"I am from Georgia, in the Caucuses," Iosef said. "The House of Shashavani holds a great estate in Svaneti, in the highlands of that country."

"Babette has spoken of you many times," William said. "You and she have corresponded at length, have you not?"

"We have," Iosef said, "for several years, since she and I first met in Vienna."

"She has spoken very highly of you," William said.

Babette certainly had and at great length when William had been alone with her. Babette had been far less conversant when James was about, not that William blamed her. James would have thought the correspondence improper.

Iosef bowed his head slightly and said, "I am honored to receive her praise. Your granddaughter is a remarkable young woman. She was so when first I met her, and she has become all the more remarkable since."

"I have always thought so," William said, measuring his tone carefully. "I have always said that she possesses the mind of the scholar."

"A scholar," Iosef said. He seemed to agree, though there was no emotion in his tone. "A doctor now. She is learned, intelligent, and driven. You and her father have good cause to be proud."

"That is an unexpected view," William said. "My neighbors in Society seem rather skeptical about the prospect of a lady doctor."

"I have spoken about medicine at length with your granddaughter," Iosef said. "I have also spoken with many doctors in my time. I can say without fear of contradiction that Doctor Varanus surpasses, or one day will surpass, the great majority of them."

Flattery?

"You truly believe so?" William asked.

"I do," Iosef said. "We Shashavani have a great love of knowledge. We are taught to appreciate the wise among us, whoever they may be and wherever they may come from."

How very eccentric, William thought.

Aloud, he said:

"Well, it is very kind of you to speak so highly of my granddaughter and her aspirations."

"Indeed," Iosef said, "Doctor Varanus is the reason I am in France."

"How so?" William asked.

Iosef motioned to his clothing. His veil was drawn back onto his hat so that he and William could speak face to face, but the rest of his body remained shrouded.

"We Shashavani suffer from a hereditary condition," Iosef said. "We suffer pronounced sensitivity to sunlight."

"My sympathies," William said.

"It is of no matter," Iosef said. "My family has borne our condition for hundreds of years. We are accustomed to it by now. However, I have decided that it is time to find a cure. It will not vanish of its own accord, and with the progress of science in this marvelous modern age, I thought that perhaps the medical profession here in the West might be able to discover a cure. And, knowing that my dear friend had become a doctor, I naturally made a point to visit France and seek her opinion."

"Well, my condolences that your visit coincided with this beastly outbreak of war," William said. "It is most unfortunate. France is far more tolerable when there are fewer Germans about in the countryside."

"So I imagine," Iosef said. "Tell me, Monsieur, have they penetrated this far west?"

"No, thankfully," William said.

He hardly expected them to do so, of course. There was little in Normandy to interest the Prussians. Once Paris capitulated, they would have what they wanted.

"You must stay, of course," he added, "until it comes time for you to depart France. Unless you have pressing business elsewhere...."

"No," Iosef said. "You are most kind. Luka and I will stay until we depart for England."

"Wonderful," William said. "I will have rooms made up for you. Now, if you will come with me, let me show you the apple orchard. It's far more beautiful during the spring, but I think the order of it will interest you."

He motioned for Iosef to follow him and walked off toward the woods, new plots and plans spinning in his head.

To Babette's surprise, Grandfather took to the idea of Iosef staying rather well. Even Father came round to it, though it took a great deal of persuading. The official story, Grandfather informed her, was that Iosef had come seeking her medical opinion on his family's unfortunate condition. Not that the neighbors were particularly nosy, what with the war and all, but Grandfather insisted upon contingency plans.

Word soon arrived that Paris was under siege, darkening the local mood further. People were sullen and angry, furious at the ongoing offense to French honor. Several times Grandfather went down into town to speak about the sanctity of France and the need for strength and courage in the days to come. As he explained to Babette, however the war ended, it would end with France intact. The last thing a person could dare to be at such a time was an enemy of the nation. When peace finally came, the public would want someone to blame for the shame of defeat, and Grandfather had no intention of letting the shadow of suspicion fall upon his family.

At the house, life passed quietly. Babette spent much of her time either in study or out riding on the grounds. Most days Iosef joined her, though he went about covered during the daytime. Outdoors this was a matter of course, but even inside this was necessary for the house was bathed in light from the broad windows most hours of the day. While the story about medical treatment was a ruse, Babette did engage in a little study of possible causes. The topic intrigued her, but she made little progress. Still, she enjoyed the challenge that it set for her.

One evening, Babette awoke to the sound of someone gently knocking on her door. She rose, curious at the disturbance, and put on her dressing gown. The night was clear and the moon was near to full. Moonlight drifted in through the window, casting the room in delicate silver.

Babette opened the door and saw Iosef, fully dressed, standing in the hallway. He smiled at her pleasantly and bowed his head, as though there was nothing peculiar about his arrival.

"Good *evening*, my lord," Babette said.

"Good evening, Doctor," Iosef said in reply.

"Can I help you in some way?" Babette asked, arms folded across her chest.

"Yes," Iosef replied. "I wonder if you would care to join me for a stroll."

A stroll?

"It is the middle of the night," Babette said.

"Indeed," Iosef said, "and the moon is so lovely." He extended his hand. "Shall we?"

Babette paused for a moment, considering the decision. It was a terrible idea to accept the offer. Though she had corresponded with Iosef for years, in truth she hardly knew him. Father would go mad if he found out.

Babette took Iosef's hand and smiled.

"I would be delighted, my lord."

She followed Iosef out into the night. The air was cold with winter's approach, but she did not mind it. Indeed, there was something refreshing about the chill, like a dive into icy water early in the morning.

“We should remove ourselves from the house,” Iosef said, “lest we are seen.”

“And what if we are?” Babette asked.

“It might be perceived that we are embarking on an illicit tryst,” Iosef replied.

“We aren’t?” Babette asked, surprised at the statement.

Korbinian kissed her on the cheek and asked, “Disappointed?”

Babette ignored him.

“No,” Iosef said. For a moment he almost seemed to smirk. “No, we have something very important to discuss. But we should do so away from prying eyes. I believe the far side of the orchard will suffice.”

Babette raised an eyebrow.

“That is something of a walk for such a late hour,” she said, “and somewhat dark, even in the moonlight.”

Iosef looked toward the sky, which made the pale light do something rather magnificent with his profile. Babette took a moment to admire him on principle.

“He really is a beautiful man, isn’t he?” Korbinian asked. “Of course, not quite as beautiful as I am, but….”

Babette smiled and murmured, “Hush.”

“I find it quite easy to see,” Iosef said, looking back at her, “but then again, there are different considerations in my case.”

“What considerations?” Babette asked.

“That is precisely what I wish to speak to you about,” Iosef said. “Shall we go to the orchard?”

Babette laughed and said, “As you will recall, it is something of a walk. And besides, I have no shoes.”

“That is a simple matter to settle,” Iosef said.

Before Babette knew what was happening, Iosef swept her up in his arms. She let out a startled cry but quickly covered her mouth with her hands lest she wake the house.

“My lord?” she whispered.

“Remember to breathe,” Iosef said.

Without another word, he took off through the garden. Taken quite by surprise, Babette threw her arms around his neck to steady herself. She regained her senses after a few moments, and she began to look about, watching as the rose bushes flew past. The line of the orchard appeared out of the darkness and moved steadily toward them.

A few moments later, the trees were all around them. The moonlight filtered in through the branches, painting the ground in a spiderweb of silver and black.

Iosef stopped at the far end of the orchard, where it met the open grounds, and set Babette down.

Babette swayed a little as she regained her balance. Her head swam from the thrill of the run.

"That was incredible!" she exclaimed. "How did you manage that?"

"It was nothing," Iosef said. "A horse could have managed the same, and much faster."

"Yes," Babette agreed, "but you, my lord, are not a horse. You are a man, and men do not run a mile and a half on uneven ground, *in the dark*, while carrying well-bred young ladies, in but a handful of minutes without stumbling once."

"When you put it that way, it does sound rather flattering," Iosef said.

Babette listened carefully for a moment. Something about him bothered her, something to do with sound.

Breathing.

"You're scarcely breathing," Babette said. "You should be gasping for air after a run like that."

"Indeed," Iosef said.

Babette reached out with one hand and placed it against Iosef's chest. His body felt cool to the touch.

"My God," Babette said with a gasp. "You should be hot and short of breath. But you're as cold as the night air. You scarcely breathe. And your heart! I can't even feel it beating."

"You find this impressive?" Iosef asked.

"Astounding!" Babette exclaimed. "How is this possible?"

"This is as nothing," Iosef said. "I can rest submerged in icy water for hours with neither pain nor fatigue. I could have carried you at a run around the entire circumference of your Grandfather's estate without tiring. Here in the moonlight, I can see as clear as day. I can hear your heart beating, each breath that escapes your lips, and, just as clearly, the rustling of the trees that ring the grounds."

"How is that possible?" Babette asked. Surely it could not be true. "This is part of your family condition, isn't it?"

Iosef smiled for a moment and said, "Very good."

Babette looked into his blue eyes, which glinted in the dim light like those of a cat.

"What are you?" she asked.

"'What,'" Iosef said, smiling more broadly than Babette had seen before. "Now that is a very perceptive question."

"And you have given me a very evasive answer," Babette said.

Iosef nodded. "Yes, I have." He paused. "Tell me, Doctor, are you familiar with the concept of the vampire?"

"What, Polidori and such nonsense?" Babette asked. "The drinking of blood and the ravishing of women?"

"Not quite," Iosef said, "but it is a place to start."

"I know that the tales come from among the Slavs," Babette said. "Something to do with corpses raised from the dead."

Iosef looked at her, seemingly astonished at her method of summation.

"As I understand it!" Babette protested. "I do not make a habit of studying Serbian folklore. There are far more important things to occupy my time. Or do you mean to tell me that you are a 'vampire?'"

"In a manner of speaking, yes," Iosef said. "The vampire is a conjecture derived from truth. The folk tales were first created by men who saw but did not understand, then passed down to men who had not even seen, generation upon generation until what remained was awash in ignorance and superstition. And worse, now here in the West, your Polidori and Byron and *Varney the Vampire* have transformed the myths into cheap amusements, all but devoid of truth."

"So your kind is the origin of the vampire?" Babette asked. "But surely, Georgia is not a Slavic land."

"Indeed it is not," Iosef said, "and there is good reason why the myth has arisen elsewhere. You see, we Shashavani are careful to conceal our nature from prying eyes. We are scholars as well as kings and warriors. We seek understanding, a task that becomes remarkably difficult when ignorant peasants try to burn your house down. But, alas, from time to time there have been some among our order who become seduced by power. Those who lack the will to withstand such temptation are exiled. Some settled in the Balkans, some on the Magyar plain, and still others in the shadow of the Carpathians. And I fear they have inspired some rather disreputable views on our order."

"In that case, have you brought me here to tear open my throat and drink my blood?" Babette asked. "I inquire," she added, "because it is rather cold tonight, and I would prefer to get such things out of the way."

Iosef tilted his head back and laughed loudly.

"No, no, my dear Doctor Varanus," he said, "I have no intention of drinking your blood. For one thing, it would not satisfy me. You eat far too little, and it has been too long since your last meal in any case."

"Do you mean to tell me that for a vampire blood is not blood?" Babette asked.

"In a manner of speaking." Iosef paused for a moment, evidently measuring his words. "We do drink blood, but it is for sustenance, just as we eat meat for sustenance. The better fed our meal, the more it sustains us. But as we age, all forms of food become less and less important. I can last at least thrice as long as a healthy man without eating. It is as if I am sustained by the world itself."

"You mean that seriously," Babette said, studying him. "You truly mean that." She shook her head. "I can scarcely believe what I am hearing."

"And yet, it is true," Iosef said.

"How old are you?" Babette asked. "Honestly."

"Quite old, at least by mortal reckoning," Iosef said. "I was born in 1705."

"You look very young for your age," Babette said.

Iosef smiled a little at the comment.

"I was made immortal at the age of eighteen," he said. "Once one is inducted into the order, one remains...*unchanging*."

"Remarkable," Babette said. "Most remarkable. Of course, I would prefer proof of all this, to satisfy my scientific curiosity."

"I can do more than that," Iosef replied. "You see, doctor, I came to France seeking you. You are without a doubt one of the most remarkable people I have ever met. You are intelligent, driven, and perceptive beyond your years. I have been seeking a scholar to act as my apprentice, to be inducted into the Shashavani order. I have searched for nearly one hundred years, and I have finally found you."

"Is that an offer of immortality?" Babette asked.

"Immortality, health, youth, tirelessness," Iosef said. "You will never need to sleep, you will scarcely need to rest, your meals will be simple and few, and you will have eternity to devote to the pursuit of knowledge. What do you say to that?"

Babette laughed and said, "I would be a fool to refuse. What is the catch?"

"You will have to return with me to Georgia," Iosef said.

"Done," Babette said without hesitation.

"You must swear to devote your life to knowledge, to never indulge excess, and always to know that you are a custodian of mankind, not its master."

"I have already devoted myself to knowledge," Babette answered, "and I have little patience for mankind whatsoever, master or otherwise." She rubbed her arms briskly. "Now, if you don't intend to ravish me or drink my blood or transform into Lord Byron, could we go back inside? It's rather cold."

Iosef paused for a moment and raised one hand as if feeling the air. Finally he said:

"Ah yes, it is cold, isn't it? I often forget about temperature."

CHAPTER TWENTY

Winter, 1870

After that night, there was for Babette no doubt that she would soon go to Georgia. The only question was how to arrange Father's consent. Grandfather would be easy to win over—indeed, as the days wore on, Babette saw him quickly grow to like Iosef. But Father would be stubborn.

The most reasonable tactic, Babette decided, would be to marry. There was no need to ask Korbinian's permission—indeed, he was the one who suggested it one morning as they lay together in bed watching the sunrise. "The ideal means of escape," he put it. Babette voiced the idea to Iosef that very afternoon. She expected an answer in the negative—who heard of a woman proposing marriage to a man?—but after a few moment's of silent contemplation, Iosef readily agreed.

From that point on, their combined efforts were put toward ensuring that Iosef's offer of courtship was cast upon fertile ground. Grandfather was only too happy to agree—surprisingly eager, in fact, Babette noted—but Father proved just short of intractable. While he gave his consent to the courtship with some reluctance, behind closed doors Babette heard him arguing the point with Grandfather. "Married to a Russian?" was the repeated refrain, to which Grandfather was always heard to answer, "At least he isn't German this time."

Such nonsense.

But as winter came upon them, Father finally gave his consent. Babette suspected he had been worn down by the relentlessness of Grandfather's petitions.

The Christmas *fête* was a somber affair that year, quite understandable under the circumstances. Paris was still under siege and, in spite of spirited fighting by the French, the Germans continued to press deeper into France. French reverses against the enemy were soon undone, and the situation was grim. For the first time in years, the attendance was limited to locals—travel was simply impossible. But even war could not stifle the great winter event of the north, and the elite of Normandy came to pay their respects to the family of Varanus and to reassure one another that the war would soon end, and in France's favor. It was a naïve sentiment but a pleasant one.

For Babette, Christmas brought a twinge of sorrow, as it had for nearly ten years. The anniversary of Korbinian's death always reminded her of that horrid night; and worse, when Korbinian appeared to her, reassuring her that he was still with her, her thoughts turned like clockwork to the memory of their lost child. Each year she readied herself for the inevitable memory, and each year she found herself unprepared. She kept her pain concealed from everyone—everyone except Korbinian, from whom she could never keep anything hidden—and withstood it in silence, consoling herself with quiet study until it finally passed.

Winter, 1871

With the New Year came defeat, and with it shame. At the end of January, 1871, Paris finally fell to the Prussians, and soon after the government capitulated. No one with any sense could be surprised at the outcome, as Grandfather remarked privately to Babette. The war had been lost at Sedan. The resistance of Paris and the French armies in the countryside had done little but delay a foregone conclusion. But anger was not an emotion guided by sense, and the bitter resentment felt by the French people came as no surprise to Babette. Indeed, she felt it as well, if only on principle.

To think that the *Prussians* of all people had led the coalition to defeat France, and this time without requiring the aid of England! It was a slap in the face to both sides of Babette's heritage. Korbinian also had several choice things to say about the Prussians being allowed to lead anything. The words "horrid" and "boorish" were oft repeated at the dinner table along with several other comments on the newly proclaimed Kaiser's ancestry that made Babette glad that no one but she could hear him.

Still, there were more pressing matters of a domestic nature to attend to. As winter broke into spring, Father's reluctance finally broke as well. He began to speak of Iosef in fond tones, reluctantly at first, but soon in casual conversation. Babette even overheard him remark to Grandfather on Iosef's "suitability as a husband" for her. It was a remarkable change brought about, as far as Babette could tell, by nothing so much as hours of polite conversation and carefully chosen words by Iosef. There was even talk of announcing the formal engagement at the start of the Season—something to lift all their spirits.

* * * *

Spring, 1871

One particularly crisp and clear morning in March, Babette went for a walk in the woods with Iosef. Luka joined them, as he always did, following several paces behind them and carrying a loaded shotgun that he rested against his shoulder. He looked like a gamekeeper. All he needed was a lead of dogs.

Babette wore the uppers of one of her riding habits—the one in tones of green—with a pair of matching bloomers. Father was scandalized of course, but no amount of complaining would sway her. In the privacy of the estate, who was to know? And of course, Iosef was enough of a sight in his black shroud and hat. Anyone who came upon them would be quite distracted by him and surely never notice her pantaloons.

A shiver of apprehension came over Babette. She smelled something strange in the wind. She stopped and looked around the wood. They had entered a small clearing of sorts. After a moment, Babette recognized it as the place where she and Korbinian had been attacked by the beast so many years before. She had not intended to stray so close to the des Louveteaux's lands.

Iosef held up a hand.

"Horses," he said.

He was silent for a moment more. Babette could almost swear she saw his ear twitch. Iosef slowly pointed in the direction of the neighboring estate. Behind him, Luka lifted his shotgun from his shoulder and moved to one side so that they would not be in his line of fire should he be forced to use it.

Babette found it most charitable of him.

"How many?" Babette asked Iosef. He was right about the horses. She could smell them now.

"Three," Iosef said. "One very large. And men with them." He paused and his lips draw back in a wide grin. "And blood."

Blood? Babette wonder.

"Shall we depart?" Iosef asked. As ever, his tone was without emotion.

"No," Babette said. "Let us see who they are and what their business may be."

After a minute or so, the three horsemen came into view through the trees. They were men, large and well built, dressed in warm coats and riding breeches. But it was the third man alone who most captured Babette's attention.

"*Alfonse?*" Babette whispered in shock.

It was not possible!

And yet, there he sat, astride a massive black charger in a thick woolen coat. His neck was swathed in bandages, which extended below the collar of his shirt. He turned his head to look at her, and a sick smile crossed his face. His movements were slow and stiff, but he was very much alive.

"Good day, Mademoiselle Varanus," Alfonse said, bowing slightly at the waist. "It has been too long."

"How is this possible?" Babette demanded. "I killed you!"

"You tried," Alfonse said. "A lesser man might have succumbed, but a des Louveteaux is above the frailties of lesser men. The likes of you can never kill me."

"I cut your throat!"

"Part of it," Alfonse said. "It might have been fatal if not for your assistant. But, by the grace of God, he was a fair surgeon. That young man saved my life at Sedan. And after that, Nature did the rest."

Alfonse's gaze fell upon Iosef, and his expression clouded for a moment. He seemed uncertain about Iosef, almost fearful. He sniffed the air and scowled for a second or two before quickly resuming his attitude of arrogant cheer.

"And who is this?" he asked.

"A friend of the family," Iosef replied. "Who are you?"

"I am Captain Alfonse des Louveteaux," Alfonse replied, "son of the Count des Louveteaux. And you?"

Iosef slowly removed his sunglasses and met Alfonse's eyes.

"I am Prince Iosef Shashavani," Iosef said, "of the Russian Empire."

Alfonse fell silent for a moment, his eyes widening again. It made Babette smile to see him so disarmed.

"A Russian?" Alfonse finally asked with a little laugh. "I fought many of your countrymen in the Crimea."

"Indeed," Iosef said. "Though I fear they were none of my family, else you would not be alive to speak with me."

"Bold words," Alfonse said.

"And true," Iosef answered.

Alfonse looked to Babette and said, "First a German, now a Russian. The company you keep is so peculiar, Mademoiselle Varanus. What happened to your love of Frenchmen?"

"It was soured by you," Babette replied.

Alfonse laughed bitterly.

"You are such a willful thing," he said. "You still have not learned your place, not after all these years."

Such an arrogant man. Babette shook her head. Such a foul creature.

"My place is what I choose it to be," she said, "and you are not a part of it."

"You are a fool to think it," Alfonse said. "You are the child of shopkeepers. It was an honor for you to receive my attentions, and you had the audacity to refuse them."

"They were not to my taste," Babette said. "I prefer more civilized meat than yours."

"Such arrogance from a woman with nothing but money to her name." Alfonse snarled at her. "No wonder that no respectable man would have you."

Self-important fool! Babette bared her teeth at him.

"I think you should leave now," she said. "This is my grandfather's land. You are not welcome here."

"It was curious, you know," Alfonse said, "seeing you in Sedan after so many years away. At first I thought little of it, distracted as I was by my injuries and the shelling of the Prussians. But after you tried to murder me—"

"After I *defended myself* from you," Babette said.

"—it made me think," Alfonse continued. "Why were you there, disguised as a man? What was your purpose?"

"My patriotic duty," Babette replied. "Not that it is any concern of yours."

"But I disagree," Alfonse said. "Your kind has no love of country. Why should you sacrifice anything for France, you, the daughter of merchants and peddlers? No, I think you had another purpose. You insinuated yourself among us, like a flea in the hairs of a dog."

"What a charming and not at all informative thing to say," Babette said.

"It all came to me when you tried to murder me," Alfonse said. "You, the daughter of an Englishman, the fiancé of a German. You somehow happened to be at Sedan, in disguise, when the Prussians and their ilk encircled us. There is but one explanation."

"And what is that?" Babette asked.

"You are a spy," Alfonse said. "A spy for the Germans."

The statement was so absurd, Babette had to laugh aloud.

"What?" she asked. "Nonsense!"

"You blame France for the death of your fiancé," Alfonse said.

"I blame *you* for it," Babette said. "*You* were responsible!"

"You betrayed France to its enemies for petty revenge," Alfonse said. "You truly are English. You have all the perfidy of your ancestors."

"I did no such thing!" Babette snapped.

How dare he suggest it? The inbred swine!

“Whether you are a spy or not matters little,” Alfonse said. “At a time like this, the people of France will want someone to blame for our defeat. They will thank me for giving you to them.”

This made Babette pause. He was right about that. Already the people were angry at their shame—she was angry! To give them a scapegoat....

“You have no proof of your lies,” she said.

“I have the word of your assistant and one of my soldiers,” Alfonse said. “The one you didn’t kill. And my own testimony. As a war hero and the son of a great family, I think that will count for much. And the people will be eager to believe what I say.”

“Why?” Babette asked.

“For this!” Alfonse snarled, pointing to the bandages at his throat. “And because you cost me my cousin.”

Iosef coughed softly to interrupt him and took a step forward.

“As the Doctor has said, you should leave,” he told Alfonse.

One of Alfonse’s men turned his horse into Iosef’s path. He extended his riding crop and patted Iosef on the cheek with it.

“Stay out of this,” he said. “This is between the Captain and the whore.”

“You should not address the Doctor in such a way,” Iosef said. “Apologize to her.”

Alfonse laughed at him and demanded, “Why should my man do anything of the kind? You are far from Russia, good prince. You are in the woods with no one around to help you. Do you think that a servant with a fowling piece frightens us?”

Alfonse motioned with his hand, and his second companion drew a large revolver and leveled it not at Luka but at Iosef. Luka exchanged looks with Iosef and slowly lowered his shotgun.

“No,” Iosef said. “But neither am I frightened by three French peasants who seek to ape their betters.”

“How dare you!” shouted the man with the riding crop.

He raised the crop and brought it down on Iosef’s head. Babette felt her breath catch, and she lunged to Iosef’s defense, knowing that she would be too late.

A moment before the crop connected, Iosef thrust his hand upward and grabbed the man by the wrist. There was a single moment in which the man was held there, half suspended out of the saddle, caught effortlessly in mid swing by Iosef. Iosef met the man’s eyes and smiled.

Having made his point, Iosef stepped sideways and pulled the man from the saddle. The man hit the ground in a heap, and Iosef placed his foot across the man’s throat.

“Apologize,” Iosef repeated.

The man on the ground snarled defiantly and spat at Iosef. Iosef shrugged and applied a little more pressure until the man began choking for air.

"Pardon! Pardon!" the man cried, gagging.

Nearby, Luka took advantage of the confusion and raised his shotgun again, leveling it at Alfonse's head. Babette saw him glance at the man with the pistol, arching an eyebrow as if to offer a challenge.

"Full of surprises," Alfonse said. "What company you keep, Mademoiselle Varanus."

"I say again, you should leave," Babette said. "I will not repeat myself."

She nodded at Iosef, who released the man on the ground and hauled him to his feet with one hand.

"Very well," Alfonse said. "We shall go. But I warn you, Mademoiselle Varanus, you will hear from the police very soon. When I deliver you to them as a traitor to France, I will be showered with praise. And you, bitch, will be put in your place."

"You shouldn't talk so much, Captain des Louveteaux," Babette said. "It is bad for your wound. As a medical practitioner, I advise rest, clean water, copious amounts of silence."

"Will that make me feel better, Doctor?" Alfonse asked dismissively.

"It will certainly make your company more tolerable," Babette said.

William poured himself a glass of brandy and took a drink. He slowly turned to face Babette and Iosef, who sat away from the window. They were in William's study. He had drawn the curtains when they entered, leaving the room lit only by the gaslights.

"Tell me again," William said.

"Alfonse discovered me in Sedan," Babette said. "He…assaulted me. I defended myself."

"You tried to kill him," William said.

"I defended myself," Babette repeated. She took a deep breath. "Unfortunately, I was prevented from finishing him."

"And now he has threatened to accuse you of espionage," William said.

"Yes," Babette answered.

William drained his glass and refilled it. This was a disaster.

Joining a military hospital disguised as a man? Good God, Babette, what were you thinking?

"Lord Shashavani, what do you make of all this?" William asked. "Of our little family disaster."

"Having met Captain des Louveteaux," Iosef replied, "I think it is a pity he did not die."

William chuckled a little at this.

A pity indeed.

"I suppose you feel that our family troubles are no concern of yours," William said.

"I feel quite the opposite, in fact," Iosef said. "After all, if Doctor Varanus and I am to be married, this concerns me as well."

Babette looked at him and smiled quizzically.

"After all this, you still wish to marry me?" she asked.

It was a question that William had as well.

"More so than ever," Iosef said. "The only thing regrettable about your actions is that you were interrupted before you could finish him. There are men in this world who ought to die, and he is one of them."

Babette smiled at him, then looked back at William.

"What are we to do, Grandfather?" she asked. "Will the police believe him?"

"They might," William said. "These are uncertain times, and the des Louveteaux have influence. The courts may just be inclined to seek a sacrificial lamb for the shame of Sedan." He thought for a moment and made up his mind. "Alas, it is a risk we cannot take."

"Grandfather?" Babette asked.

"You must leave the country," William said, "at least for a few years, until the shock of defeat has passed and things are more settled."

Babette stared at him, wide-eyed.

"You cannot mean that, Grandfather!" she cried.

"I do," William said. "We must take precautions."

"If I leave now, will it not appear that I am fleeing?" Babette asked. "It would be an admission of guilt!"

"After the police become involved, perhaps," William said. "But if we act quickly, we can preempt Alfonse's plot."

"If I am not here, I will be accused and tried *in absentia!*"

"Better than being accused, tried, and punished in person," William said. He turned to Iosef. "Lord Shashavani, what is your commitment to my granddaughter? You say you still wish to marry her?"

"I do," Iosef replied. "If asked, I would marry her today."

"You intend to take her to Georgia, correct?"

"Yes," Iosef said.

"Good," William said. "You will leave first thing tomorrow."

"Grandfather, you cannot be serious," Babette said. "You want me to leave now? Just like that?"

"I know that this is difficult, Babette, but it must be done. I cannot risk your safety to the whims of public opinion. You will leave the country at once, and I will contact you when it is safe to return."

Babette was silent for a time. Finally, she nodded.

"As you wish, Grandfather," she said. "As you wish."

CHAPTER TWENTY-ONE

Svaneti, Georgia

They departed at first light, as Grandfather instructed. Babette was inclined to agree with his decision, and anyway there was no arguing with him. It was a tearful goodby—particularly for Father—but although Babette felt a sense of remorse at leaving her childhood home behind, she was filled with a sense of hope. She realized that all her life she had been searching for a change, something to release her from the constraints and frustrations that had been, all too clearly, thrust upon her. Studying abroad and becoming a doctor was supposed to have been that change, but she had found that the boundaries of her sex were drawn just as boldly by the intellectuals as by Society.

Not that she harbored any pre-conceived illusions about Iosef and the life that he offered her—if, indeed, he spoke the truth. Babette would know that once they arrived in Georgia. But there was something wonderfully final about leaving home in such a definite way. She had been cast into the wild, and this time she did not have to worry about the lambs constantly trying to call her back into the flock. It was a realization that warmed her as much as it caused her apprehension. Now, for the first time in her life, the only way she could go was forward.

Grandfather had somehow secured them passage on a ship bound for Lisbon. It was a miraculous thing to have managed in less than a day, but Grandfather was the sort of man who purchased miracles daily with the anticipation of future rewards.

They remained in Portugal for two weeks before departing for the Mediterranean. They stopped briefly in Italy, again in Greece, enjoyed a brief visit to Istanbul—which Babette found to be most charming—and finally reached Georgia via the Black Sea port of Poti.

Babette fell in love with Georgia the moment she laid eyes on it. The land was lush and fertile, a beautiful green but touched with a gilded tint as if golden. Iosef made for the mountains almost immediately. They traveled by horse, winding their way up into what seemed the remotest, most majestic part of the whole world. They passed small villages protected by ancient stone towers, like something from a medieval fairytale. Babette saw lush forests, open fields, vineyards, and gorges blanketed with mist and shadow.

They traveled into the mountains, which were still touched with snow in places. The air was fresh and pleasant. Far from feeling the exhaustion of the road, the further they traveled the more invigorated Babette felt. She remarked about this to Iosef. This made him smile, though he did not say why.

The journey took several days, especially once they began traveling the rough highland roads. At the villages they passed, Iosef would stop and speak to the people in a language that Babette could not understand—but one, her ear told her, that Iosef had not used with the Georgians of the lowlands. Though quiet at first—doubtless suspicious of strangers—the villagers displayed tremendous hospitality. They ate good, honest food each night and listened to the beautiful songs of the highland people. The Svans, Iosef called them.

Finally, on the fifth day, they passed into a broad valley ringed with trees and surrounded by the high walls of the mountains. From their raised vantage point at the mouth of the pass, Babette could see several villages dotted about the vale, and at its center, alongside a clear rushing river, she saw a great castle.

The sight of the castle made her stop and stare with wonder, for it was unlike anything she had ever seen. It was a relic of an ancient world left standing in defiance of time. It had high, straight walls and many towers, all constructed in strong, simple geometric shapes, like the village towers. Everything was heavy and reinforced, leaving Babette with no doubt that the building had withstood the might of armies in ages past. But it was beautiful as well as strong, with many windows in the upper reaches and vantage points. The brutal shape of the walls was smoothed by an array of embellishments in the Byzantine style, with domes and arches and mosaics of multi-colored brick.

"It is beautiful, is it not?" Iosef asked, looking out over the valley. "I have traveled the world for many years, but I have never found a place as beautiful as this."

"Never?" Babette asked. She could believe it. The majesty of the mountain valley was breathtaking.

"Never," Iosef said. "Though I did find Iceland to be most remarkable."

What a peculiar thing to say.

Babette looked at him and raised an eyebrow.

"Iceland?" she asked, somewhat incredulously.

"Have you ever been there?" Iosef asked.

"No," Babette admitted.

"You must," Iosef said.

Babette was about to reply when she sensed movement above them. Looking up, she saw a pair of towers overlooking the pass, their masonry built directly into the rock. They were nearly invisible, even when viewed from only a dozen or so paces away. It was a clever trick to be sure.

Babette saw a trio of men standing on a wide balcony beside the tower. They were armed with rifles, and they all wore chokhas—long coats closed in front, akin to a cassock, with pouches for holding ammunition sewn across the chest. Babette had seen other Georgians wearing such garments during their journey. One of the men raised his hand and called down in Iosef's unfamiliar tongue. It was Luka who answered, calling back and motioning to Babette as well as to Iosef. Babette could not deduce the content of the exchange, but at the end, all three watchmen laughed with joy and bowed low to Iosef. Iosef nodded in reply and smiled at Babette.

"What are they saying?" Babette asked.

"The watchmen have inquired after your identity," Iosef said. "You see, visitors are not common these days."

"What has Luka told them?"

"Only that you are a Frenchwoman and my new student." Iosef smiled at her. "The watchmen are most excited. We have not inducted a foreigner into the order for a very long time."

"Oh?" Babette asked.

"Indeed. Until now, I was the last."

"You? A foreigner?" Babette studied Iosef carefully. "But I thought you were Georgian."

"I am," Iosef said with a chuckle. "But I am not a Svan." He motioned to Luka to continue on and said, "Come, let us make haste to the castle. It is nearly dusk, and Sophio will be expecting us."

"Sophio?" Babette asked.

"The head of our order," Iosef said, "my teacher, and my wife."

"You did not tell me you had a wife," Babette said, as she followed Iosef into the front hall of the castle.

"It did not seem pertinent at the time," Iosef replied. Now free of the oppressive sun, he removed his hat and sunglasses and handed them to Luka. "One does not often discuss wives with young ladies that one intends to marry. It often misleads the conversation."

"I take it we are not to be married," Babette said.

"A difficult question," Iosef replied. "In the eyes of the Church, I am already married. In the eyes of the Law, I am already dead. And the dead cannot be married."

"Can't they?" Babette asked.

"Indeed," Iosef said. "Or else widows who remarry become polygamous. And I think that is illegal."

Babette stared at him. "You *think* it is illegal?"

"It has been some time since I cared about the laws of mortal men," Iosef replied.

Babette followed him along the hall, past ancient mosaics and finely woven tapestries, statues and furniture, and gilded adornments. They passed through a side corridor lined with portraits. Babette looked up at the faces cast in oil paint that looked down upon her from on high. The images were old, none younger than a hundred years old, and many of them dating back to the Renaissance.

Beyond the corridor lay a great hall adorned in polished marble. Its vaulted ceiling rose three stories to a glorious dome covered by intricate mosaics. Balconies and galleries looked out into the chamber from above.

At the far end of the chamber stood a high dais, which bore a great throne of polished wood, surrounded by brocade carpets and upholstered in padded silk. On the throne sat a vision of unearthly beauty: a woman, black of hair and fair in complexion, with dark eyes that seemed to demand possession of all that her gaze fell upon. She wore a gown and headdress of black and white, decked with jewels and pearls and golden thread.

The woman looked at Babette as she and Iosef approached, and Babette, try as she might, could not bring herself to meet the woman's eyes. She struggled with each step as she felt her vigor falter, and she cast her gaze toward the floor in frustration.

"Do not speak until she gives you leave," Iosef whispered. "Answer her questions truthfully, but do not say what has not been asked. Do you understand?"

"Yes," Babette replied.

A dozen paces from the dais, Iosef stopped and knelt. Babette followed his example, still unable to look upon the mysterious woman. The harder she tried, the more impossible it became, and the more it angered her.

The woman spoke something in Iosef's tongue and Iosef rose. He responded in a long statement that seemed so eloquent and descriptive that Babette wished all the more that she understood the words. The woman smiled coldly and nodded her head.

Iosef turned to Babette and said in French, "My lady Sophio, *Eristavi* of the House of Shashavani, has deigned for us to speak in your native tongue."

"I am most grateful, my lady," Babette said. She quickly caught herself and fell silent.

"Iosef, my beloved," Sophio said, seeming to ignore Babette's interruption, "who is this one that you have brought before me? This creature of the outside world cursed by ignorance and death?"

She spoke French easily, though accented. But the manner in which she spoke, the way in which the words were pronounced, seemed archaic to Babette. It was as if Sophio were speaking French for the first time since the days of the *Ancien Régime*.

"She is a sojourner among the living, my love," Iosef replied. "One who looks but cannot see. One who lives yet fears. One who will fade and die."

"And why have you brought this one here?" Sophio asked. "Why have you brought death among the living?"

"Though born under the shadow of death, this one seeks the path of life," Iosef said. "She has been born into ignorance but wishes to embrace the light of wisdom."

"The gift of life is not to be granted lightly," Sophio said.

"I believe that she is worthy, beloved," Iosef answered. "She is wise beyond her years, strong and upright, and moral. She will bring honor to the House of Shashavani."

"And you, supplicant?" Sophio asked. "Do you come before me of your own accord?"

Babette suddenly found that she could look up again and did so.

"I do, my lady," she said.

"And do you reject ignorance and superstition?" Sophio asked, her tone indicating a degree of skepticism. "Do you embrace knowledge as the greatest glory of mankind?"

"I do, my lady," Babette said firmly.

"Very well." Sophio looked back at Iosef. "She is in your custody, husband. Let her be observed for the passage of a moon. If she proves of quality, you may take her as an apprentice and give her the cup."

"I thank you, mistress," Iosef said. "I shall attend to her as if she were my own."

"You must be weary from your long journey, husband," Sophio said. "Have the supplicant taken to her new quarters."

"Yes, my love," Iosef said, bowing.

He motioned to Babette to follow him, turned, and withdrew.

Sophio raised a hand and called after him, "Before you depart, husband, tell me: what of the outside world? What news from Europe?"

Iosef halted and turned back.

"The Germanies have united, my love," he said. "They have defeated France in open war, and the French Empire has collapsed. It is a remarkable redress of the balance of power in Europe."

"Is that so?" Sophio asked. "So the Holy Roman Empire has remade itself. Remarkable." She stared off into the distance, looking at nothing in particular—or so it seemed to Babette. "I wonder what effect this shall have on Russia."

"Who can say, my love?" Iosef asked. "Who can say?"

Sophio was silent for a time. She stared off into the distance without speaking for several minutes, as if watching something of great significance. Babette knew better than to break the silence, but she glanced at Iosef uncertainly, hoping that he might give her some sign of what to do. He looked back at her out of the corner of his eye and slowly, almost imperceptibly, shook his head. Babette looked back at Sophio and waited in silence.

Finally, after almost five minutes, Sophio looked back at Iosef and replied:

"We must be cautious, husband. You recall the betrayal of the Russians."

"I do," Iosef replied.

"They covet all the world," Sophio said, "like the Mongols of old. You recall the invasion of the Khans?"

Iosef cleared his throat and said, "You will remember, beloved, that was before my time."

This seemed to surprise Sophio for a moment.

"Oh," she finally said. "Yes, of course. No matter. Svaneti has never been conquered. The lands of Shashava have never been conquered."

"Indeed, my love," Iosef said.

Sophio slowly nodded. "When time permits, husband, send men into the west to investigate these newly united Germanies."

"As you wish."

"You say that they defeated France?" Sophio asked.

"They did," Iosef said.

"Then perhaps they will be strong enough to break the Tsars," Sophio said. "See to it."

Iosef placed his hands together and bowed deeply.

"As you command, my love," he said.

"That will be all, husband," Sophio said, waving him away with a flick of her hand. "Take the supplicant. Let her be studied."

"Yes, beloved," Iosef said, bowing again.

He looked at Babette and nodded very slightly. Babette quickly bowed as he did. Without another word, Iosef backed away a few paces, turned, and walked back toward the door, head high. Babette mimicked his movements perfectly and followed him out of the hall.

In the adjoining corridor, Iosef turned to her and gave her a very serious look.

"My mistress approves," he said.

"Why did you not tell me of her?" Babette asked.

Iosef seemed surprised at the question.

"It was unnecessary," he said. "Come, you must be tired, and you need fresh clothing. I will have Luka show you to your new chambers."

"I dem—" Babette caught herself. "I *request* an explanation."

"And you shall have one," Iosef said. "Soon. Once you are settled and night has fallen, I will show you the grounds and explain many things to you, some that you did not even know needed explaining."

Babette very nearly gasped aloud when Luka opened the door to her new quarters. The set of rooms, located on the second floor of the house, were decked in rich brocades and layers of silk. Woven carpets, similar to those that she had seen in Sophio's audience hall, covered the floor. The furnishings were of various woods, mostly Lebanese cedar but also mahogany and teak—no doubt imported from India ages ago.

The first room was a parlor, with pillows and sofas set around in a semi-circle. Babette picked her way across and investigated the two adjoining rooms. One was a study, with shelves of books, empty tables, and a desk of Persian design. On the opposite side of the parlor, Babette found the bedroom, an enclosed chamber with a canopy bed draped in thick red fabric. Beyond it lay an alcove for washing, which was effectively dominated by a large pool built directly into the stonework. It had already been filled with hot water and rose pedals, filling the air with a pleasant vapor. All three rooms had windows that looked out onto the grounds to the north, and each window was swathed in curtains and augmented by ornate shutters.

"My God," Babette breathed. "It's—"

"Very beautiful," Korbinian murmured in her ear. Babette felt him wrap his arms around her waist.

"Lord Shashavani hopes that it is satisfactory," Luka said. He crossed the room and carefully closed the shutters. "It would be best if you kept these closed during daylight hours," he added. "It is a good habit to develop, even before it becomes necessary."

"Yes, of course," Babette said.

Was she to become like Iosef, she wondered, unaccustomed to the touch of sunlight? Not that it wasn't a fair exchange of course, but she did wonder.

"I will leave you now," Luka said. "As you see, a bath has already been drawn for you. You may wash at your leisure. In a short while Ekaterine will come to keep you company."

"Ekaterine?" Babette asked. "Who is Ekaterine?"

"She is the woman who is coming to keep you company," Luka replied.

"I. . . ." Babette stopped before protesting. She could tell that it would not earn her an explanation. "Thank you, Luka," she said. "That will be all."

"Very good, Mademoiselle Varanus," Luka said. He bowed to her and backed out of the room, closing the doors as he did so.

"What a peculiar state we find ourselves in," Korbinian said.

"Most peculiar," Babette agreed. She smiled as Korbinian took her in his arms, and she rested her head on his shoulder.

"And how horrid of them to offer you a warm bath and a maid to wait on you," Korbinian added. He leaned down and kissed the top of her head. "What ever shall you do in the face of such barbarism?"

"Oh hush," Babette said. "It is a good thing no one else can hear you. I fear you would offend our hosts with your tactless prattle."

"A very good thing indeed," Korbinian said, kissing Babette's neck and making her sigh happily. Korbinian began unbuttoning her coat with his gentle fingers. "Now then, let us get you out of these traveling clothes and into that bath."

Babette did not realize when she fell asleep in the bath. After the long days of travel, the heat of the water and the rose-scented steam went right to her head. One moment she lay there in the water, held in Korbinian's arms. In the next, she opened her eyes to see a young woman peering in past the curtain.

"Who—" Babette began.

"Your pardon, Mademoiselle," the woman said in French. She spoke somewhat uncertainly and with a thick accent. "I am Ekaterine. I have brought clothes. They are on your bed. While you become ready, I will be in the other room."

With that, the mysterious woman withdrew and vanished behind the curtain.

Babette looked at Korbinian and whispered, "What do you make of this?"

"She is a rather pretty girl," Korbinian said.

"You are of no use," Babette told him.

Korbinian stroked her cheek gently. "That's not true," he whispered, kissing her.

Babette smiled and purred.

"Perhaps you have a few uses," she said.

Korbinian rose elegantly from the pool and extended his hand toward her. He should have been wet, with rivulets of water coursing down the length of his smooth, sculpted body. But he was bone dry. Not a single droplet from the pool clung to him, and the surface was still about his waist.

Babette smiled at him and sighed. "I should not keep the girl waiting."

"She might wonder why you are talking to yourself," Korbinian said.

"Hush!"

Babette took Korbinian's hand and stood. She selected a towel from a pedestal by the pool.

"Allow me," Korbinian said, taking it from her.

Babette smiled and raised her arms.

"As you wish," she said.

After being gently toweled dry by Korbinian, Babette returned to the bedchamber. Her clothes were gone, but in their place she found a long robe of crimson wool laid out for her on the bed. She touched it with her fingertips and found the fabric to be of the utmost softness, like cashmere. It was too large for her, she found, especially in the train and the sleeves, but it was comfortable all the same. The robe buttoned closed at the shoulder for modesty and was belted about the waist with an embroidered girdle of gold and rich blue.

Babette found Ekaterine in the adjoining room, waiting patiently on one of the sofas. She stood as Babette entered and bowed her head politely but with dignity and very little deference. This surprised Babette, for she had first taken the girl to be a servant. But there was nothing servile in her attitude.

"Good evening, Mademoiselle," Ekaterine said, smiling and motioning for Babette to join her.

"You speak French?" Babette asked, unsure of what else to say.

"Yes," Ekaterine said. She looked more than a little embarrassed at the question. "But I speak the French only a little."

"Is there another language you would prefer to speak in?" Babette asked, before she realized how foolish the question was.

Not German or English, surely, she silently chided herself. *Nor Italian. It is enough of a miracle that we have one language in common.*

"Russian?" Ekaterine asked. She gave a wide, genuine smile, expressing her knowledge that it would not be so. "Or Persian? I know that you understand neither Svan nor Georgian. Luka has said so."

"Alas," Babette said, "but you are right. I am ignorant on all four counts."

"Then the French must suffice," Ekaterine said. "I shall endeavor to become more accustomed to it. And at the same time, you shall learn Svan. Lord Shashavani has said so."

How thoughtful of him to consult my opinion, Babette thought. But it was true: if she were to reside there, she would have to learn the language—or both languages, as it seemed.

"I trust you will help me with my lessons," Babette said.

"It will give me great pleasure," Ekaterine said. "I most enjoy to teach."

"Tell me," Babette said, "where are my clothes?"

"They have been taken to be cleaned," Ekaterine replied. "You cannot have thought about wearing them again, not after bathing. They were—I beg your pardon—filthy."

It seemed very painful for her to speak in such a manner, though whether it was the French or the criticism that bothered her, Babette could not tell.

"You do not like the robe?" Ekaterine asked.

"It is a wonderful robe," Babette said, "but it is also quite large."

"Too large, you mean," Korbinian said.

Babette glanced at the doorway of the bedchamber where he stood, still nude. She watched as he crossed the room with a haughty stride and threw himself down upon the sofa behind Ekaterine. Resting his chin on one hand, he fluttered his eyes at Babette, almost daring her to respond to him.

Babette was very careful to ignore him, difficult as that proved to be.

"However," she said, "I would still prefer my own clothes."

"New clothes, yes?" Ekaterine asked. "Tomorrow I will bring the tailors to measure you for new dresses. Like mine." She drew her hand down in front of her, indicating her own dress, which resembled a chokha in pale green worn over a broad skirt and a high-necked tunic. "You will like it. Most comfortable. Not like the clothes you brought."

"If you mean my corsets, I happen to be rather fond of them," Babette said.

Ekaterine look horrified for a moment, her eyes going wide and the blood draining from her face. She quickly forced a smile and took Babette's hand in both of hers.

"New clothes," she said with a firm nod. "Most comfortable."

Babette sighed and said, "If you insist."

Perhaps the tailors could make new copies of the clothes she had brought. That would be very welcome.

"Where is Lord Shashavani?" she asked.

"He is in study," Ekaterine said. "But he has asked that you meet him on the northern terrace one hour after sundown. I will bring you. But first, you must eat. The servants are coming with food."

"Can I not see him now?" Babette asked.

Ekaterine shook her head and said, "No, certainly not. Lord Shashavani is very busy. Whenever he returns from the outside, he insists that he be told of all things that transpired while he was away. He will be occupied until nightfall. And besides, he gave me instructions that you are to be washed, fed, and clothed before attending him. Hospitality, you understand."

"How insufferably hospitable of him," Babette said. She sat on the sofa beside Korbinian and sighed. "Very well, I will eat first. And you, Ekaterine, must tell me all about yourself."

CHAPTER TWENTY-TWO

Babette found Iosef waiting for her on the northern terrace one hour after sunset, just as Ekaterine had said. The night was cold, and Babette wore a thick fur mantle over the scarlet robe and a hat pulled tightly over her ears. She saw Iosef standing near the edge of the terrace, looking out across the valley. He wore a chokha of black over a high-necked white shirt.

The moon was full and high, and it shone against his face in brilliant silver as he turned toward her.

"Good evening, Varanus," he said. "I am pleased to hear that you are settling in well."

"I find the accommodations agreeable, yes," Babette said.

"And Ekaterine?" Iosef asked.

"Very pleasant," Babette said. "Though I must confess, I do not understand her role in things here. She attended to me, but she is not a maidservant, is she?"

Iosef almost seemed inclined to laugh. Certainly, his eyes twinkled with amusement, though his countenance remained emotionless.

"No, she is not," he said. "She is… Well, she is like Luka."

"And is he not a servant?" Babette asked. It was a question that had puzzled her for some time.

"Abroad, we refer to him as my valet," Iosef said. "But he is not. It would be more accurate to say that he is the Tariel to my Avtandil… though I suspect that is a reference you are not familiar with."

"I fear not," Babette said.

"Call him the Oliver to my Roland," Iosef said. "He is as my brother."

"And Ekaterine is to be as my sister?" Babette asked skeptically.

"No," Iosef answered, "she is to keep you company until you join me on the northern terrace one hour after sunset. But I do think that you two will find much that you have in common, not least of which is your mutual understanding of a language. As a Frenchwoman now residing in Svaneti, I think the significance of that is clear."

Babette folded her arms and said, "Your point is taken, my lord."

"Good," Iosef said. He offered his hand. "Come, join me."

Babette walked to the edge of the terrace without hesitation and looked out. At such a height, the drop was tremendous. Thankfully, the most terrifying part of the view—the vastness of the walls and spires below them—was concealed in the blackness of night, revealed only by the flickering of lanterns from some of the windows. Otherwise, the castle was dark and silent.

"You should have told me about your wife," Babette said after a lengthy pause.

"I disagree," Iosef said. "To tell you about Sophio would have served no purpose, and if your family had learned the truth, it would have made your journey here impossible. The most prudent course of action was the one that I followed."

"You lied to me," Babette said.

"Again, no," Iosef replied. "Ever since our first meeting in Vienna, I have told you nothing but the truth. I have kept information from you, certainly, but I have never lied. And whenever I have kept something from you, it has been for a purpose. I do not arbitrarily seek to deceive you, Varanus."

Varanus. He kept calling her by her surname, whether or not he addressed her by her title of doctor. It was unusual, but not unpleasant.

Babette shook her head and reminded herself of the topic at hand. How dare he distract her in such a way?

"Lord Shashavani—"

"Iosef."

"*Lord Shashavani*," Babette repeated, more forcefully, "I will confess that I am cross with you at this moment. You have placed me in a most difficult position."

Iosef chuckled with genuine amusement.

"Have I?" he asked. "I have offered you a safe haven here in my country. I have granted you impenetrable asylum from the man who would do you harm. I have offered you the possibility of immortality and far more freedom than you could ever hope to enjoy in your homeland. What is this difficulty of which you speak?"

Babette frowned, displeased at Iosef's evasions.

"I came here with the intention of marrying you," she said, "only to find that you are already married."

"Nonsense," Iosef said, "you came here to accept the gift of immortality so that you might continue your work for all eternity. The topic of marriage was always a means to that end for you. Unless I am tremendously mistaken."

Babette set her lips in a frown. He was right about that. How dare he be right at such a time?

"Do you love her?" she finally asked.

"Does that matter?" Iosef asked. "You love a dead man. Who are we to judge one another?"

"How did you—" Babette began.

She heard Korbinian clearing his throat from behind her. She glanced over her shoulder and saw him—clothed again—standing a few paces away.

"The Russian is an intelligent man, *liebchen*," he said. "Your affection for my memory is no great secret. He spent the entire winter with you in France. Of course he knows about it."

Babette turned back to Iosef and folded her arms. Even sheltered by the furs, the chill of the night made her shiver. How Iosef managed to stand there, lightly dressed and bareheaded, was a mystery to her. It had something to do with his condition, no doubt.

"Why did you not tell me about your wife while we were in France?"

"And risk your father or grandfather discovering that fact?" Iosef asked. "No, that would have been foolish. Your purpose in coming here was clear from the outset, and it should not be confused by the subject of marriage."

"You are not the master of your own house," Babette countered.

"It is not my house," Iosef said. "It is Shashava's, and Sophio is the Vicar of Shashava. Until he returns, she rules in his stead. But that has nothing to do with us. As Christ says, 'render unto Caesar those things which are Caesar's.' So long as you respect Sophio's position and do not interfere with her, you will be free to pursue your work as you see fit."

"And what if I desire to become embroiled in politics?" Babette asked. She did not, but the question was worth the asking.

"But you do not," Iosef said. "You wish only to work, to pursue your research free from interference. And that is something that I have placed within your grasp."

He turned away and looked back out across the valley toward the northern mountains.

"Do not be mistaken, Doctor Varanus," he said. "If you wish to leave, I will dispatch you for home first thing tomorrow. You are not a prisoner here. You have not yet taken an oath in Shashava's name. Until that time, you are free to leave whenever you choose. But consider, where would you go?"

Babette frowned with great displeasure. He was right about that. She *could* go anywhere, thanks to Grandfather's money. Not back to France, of course, but to the new Germany or to Italy or to England. Perhaps even to America. But none of it would satisfy her. Only the offer of immortality that Iosef held before her piqued her interest. Besides, where could she go that she would be judged for her intellect rather than for her sex?

Iosef, seeming to understand her thoughts, added:

"There is no other part of the world that will afford you the liberty that you deserve. Here in the valley, you are the equal of any man, both in custom and in law. Beyond the lands of the Shashavani, you will always be a woman first and a doctor second—and a most distant second. What I offer you is not merely eternity. I offer you those rights and dignities that Nature has bestowed on you but that Man has abrogated."

"Is Georgia so miraculous a place that the laws of men and women do not exist here?" Babette asked.

Iosef laughed and said, "No. Georgia is no different than the rest of the world. And you will find that the Svans, for all their admirable qualities, are as beholden to tradition as any people living. But in this valley, governed by the laws of Shashava, we reside in a place guided by wisdom rather than folly. The mortals among us, the villagers and farmers, live in accordance with many of the traditions of their Svan brethren. But all those who have taken the oath are regarded as equals by nature, divided only by their accomplishments. Sophio serves as the Vicar of Shashava because she is the oldest and wisest among us, with centuries of experience to guide her. The fact that she is a woman matters for nothing."

"Admirable," Babette said, "but you will forgive my skepticism. How can the world be so different here? Am I to believe that I will be judged equal in my own right? Or do men deign to treat me so for their own amusement?"

I will not tolerate that, she thought, looking into Iosef's blue eyes with a firm, almost angry stare.

Iosef did not flinch in replying:

"No, the world is different here. Members of our order have studied the origins of such divisions between the sexes and their conclusions vary; but the view shared by many of us is that men have always ruled first by simple virtue of strength and, later, by virtue of familiarity. Man may overpower woman; therefore, man has always ruled woman. And man, feeling perhaps somewhat guilty for the mistreatment of his mother, daughters, and sisters, places such commandments into the mouth of God to justify his conduct.

"But you must understand, Varanus, there is no such distinction among the Shashavani—indeed there cannot be. Even the frailest woman of our order is more powerful than a strong mortal man. And we grow stronger with age, regardless of what we were when we languished in the shadow of death. If we were governed by the law of might, the old would tyrannize the young, and Great Shashava would have dominated his accolytes like the god-kings of old. But Shashava, guided by wisdom, rejected strength as the source of authority. If anyone has deigned to grant equality, it was he. And he granted it to all who came after him in equal measure."

"Most intriguing," Babette said, "though I doubt it will catch on. Men 'languishing in the shadow of death,' as you put it, do so enjoy their tyranny."

"If only we could change the world," Iosef said, chuckling. "But we can only guide humanity, watch and safeguard it. The follies of mankind must change because people understand that their ways are foolish, not because they are made to change. An enlightened dictatorship lasts only as long as the dictator is enlightened, while an enlightened society remains so generation upon generation of its own accord."

Babette looked at Iosef very seriously and said, "I do understand the wisdom in that, my lord. But speaking as a woman who has endeavored to achieve a purpose in life greater than that of child-bearer, believe me when I say that there are times when an enlightened dictatorship would be a most welcome instrument of change."

"I can understand that sentiment," Iosef said. He tilted his head and looked at her, suddenly concerned. "You shudder. Why?"

"I am shivering," Babette said, "because it is cold."

"Ah yes," Iosef said. He looked toward the pale moon and spread his hands. "Cold. Again, I have forgotten."

"With so much to think about, surely minor details such as food and temperature fall by the wayside," Babette said, not entirely—though mostly—sarcastically.

If Iosef realized the sarcasm in the statement—how could he not?—he gave no indication of it. Certainly, he did not seem offended. Instead, he placed one hand on the small of Babette's back and motioned toward the doors.

"Let us go inside where it is warm," he said. "I will show you the library. You will like it, I think."

To this, Babette replied, "I will like anything, my lord, that is warmer than here."

There were several libraries in the house, Babette soon discovered, each with their own purpose: astrological subjects in the library by the observatory, martial topics in the reading room of the armory, and so forth. It was a realization that delighted her immensely. But when one spoke of "the library", Iosef told her, one always meant the common library at the center of the castle. The reason for this became immediately apparent to Babette once they arrived.

She entered through a door on the fourth floor and instantly felt her breath escape her in a gasp. She stood on a broad balcony of polished wood, ancient and smooth after ages of wear. All around her rose shelves of books five stories tall, filling a space as great as the *Grande Salle* of the Paris Opera beneath the watchful eye of a single massive dome. Balconies circled the room, each ten feet above the one below it, while walkways crisscrossed the space at intervals, connecting the balconies and accessing more shelves set in the middle of the room. Staircases rose at the corners, joining each level in an endless circuit of steps.

Babette walked to the balcony and leaned out, rising on tiptoe to improve the angle of her view. She felt dizzy at the sight, but strangely elated as well. Perhaps a dozen men and women in chokhas, robes, and gowns were busy on the ground floor, carrying books from the shelves to tables or reading chairs. She saw a few more on the various balconies, perusing the tomes in search of their night's reading.

"Magnificent," she said, when she finally found her breath again.

Iosef joined her at the railing, arms folded.

"It is," he said. "It is more than a thousand years old, but it is still as sturdy as the day it was completed. Much of the wood is more recent of course—it is replaced regularly to circumvent age and rot—but the carpenters always match the shape and color with such precision that you would not know the wood was new by looking at it."

"A thousand years old?" Babette blinked as she looked at Iosef. Tilting her head upward, she studied the dome for a little while before turning back to him. "I find that rather incredulous. The size of that dome is tremendous for a thing so old, and especially one constructed of stone."

"True," Iosef said, "but it is not without precedent. The architects took many lessons from the building of Hagia Sophia in Constantinople."

"Construction must have been difficult this high in the mountains," Babette said.

"Yes, it must have been," Iosef agreed. "It is my understanding that the construction of the library, indeed of the entire castle, was a formidable undertaking. Of course, that was before my time."

"Like the Mongol hordes," Babette said.

"Indeed."

"When precisely was your time?" Babette asked.

"A century and a half ago," Iosef replied. "Not terribly long ago in the scheme of history, but enough to grant me perspective from which to observe things. Once one has outlived the shadow of death, things become much clearer."

"You said you were a foreigner," Babette said. "Not a Svan."

"That is correct."

"How did you come to be here?" Babette asked.

"You wish to hear the story?" Iosef asked.

"I do," Babette said, most sincerely. She was intrigued by Iosef. He was normally so reluctant to speak about himself.

"Very well," Iosef said. "Come."

He motioned for her to follow him and began walking along the balcony. Babette hurried after him and fell into step beside him, which took a little effort at first given the great difference in their respective strides. Finally, Babette found a tolerable pace of a step and a half to each of Iosef's.

"I was born at the dawn of the 18th Century," Iosef said, "the third son of a third son. My father was the child of a Georgian nobleman from the lowlands, but left with no prospects for inheritance, he took up his sword and traveled north to Russia in search of fortune and glory."

"I take it he found them," Babette said.

"Indeed," Iosef replied. He did not seem particularly concerned by the interruption. "My father became an officer in the service of Peter the Great and served with great distinction during the taking of Azov and in the war against Sweden. He took a Russian wife and set about producing my elder brothers and me in quick succession."

"Quick succession?" Babette asked.

For a moment, Iosef seemed almost to smile.

"Very quick," he said. "By all accounts, my parents were *very* fond of one another and very healthy as well. Both of my elder brothers survived to adulthood, more's the pity."

They reached one of the staircases, and Iosef led Babette down to the floor below.

"When I came of age," he continued, "I joined the Russian Army as an officer of cavalry. My commander was, in a word, a fool. In two words, an arrogant fool. When war broke out against Persia, we were sent as envoys to the Shashavani to beg their aid. Georgia and Armenia had already readied men to the cause, but the heirs of Shashava, despite pledges of support, were notably absent. I was sent because of my heritage and my knowledge of Georgian and because my low rank made me expendable if the Svans proved hostile."

"Did they?" Babette asked.

"Not the Svans, no," Iosef said. "Sophio." He paused and turned toward her. "Upon arriving in the valley, we were greeted with great hospitality. And we were not killed on sight, despite arriving armed and without warning, which I now realize was utterly foolish.

"Sophio proved a model host," he continued. "She invited us in, had our horses stabled and our men fed. She ordered that a feast be laid out for us as emissaries of the 'King of the Rhos.' Alas, my commander proved boorish and impatient. In the midst of dinner, he had the audacity to demand words with Sophio's lord and master—as, surely, no woman could rule. Upon learning that Sophio was indeed the highest authority in the valley, my commander ordered her to provide him with soldiers and arms to be ready for departure under his command within a week."

"I would have killed him," Babette said.

"She did," Iosef replied. "There in the hall, before everyone, she tore his head from his shoulders and ordered the body thrown to the wolves for the offense. The men, loyal to their commander, attacked Sophio. It was a bloodbath."

"But Sophio is alive—" Babette began. She caught herself, understanding. "Oh."

"The guards of the house were on hand to protect her, but they were an added consideration. Most of the soldiers were slaughtered by Sophio's hand alone."

"How did you survive?" Babette asked.

"It was surprisingly simple," Iosef said, turning down the next flight of stairs. "I neither fought nor fled. While the other men were cut down in the fighting or killed as they ran in fear, I finished my dinner."

"You *what?*" Babette stared at him, shocked beyond measure.

"It was a very good dinner," Iosef said, "and I never had much affection for my captain. I suspect he was similar in thought and conduct to your Captain des Louveteaux."

"Well," Babette said, "that does put things in a different light. But what of your men?"

"If I could have stopped them, I would have," Iosef told her. "But they did not listen when I ordered them to hold. Any fool could see the only likely outcome—she *had* just torn a man's head from his body—but still they attacked her. So I sat there and finished my dinner. I expected to be killed along with them, but Sophio apparently noticed the difference between the men attacking her and the man sitting quietly at her table."

"So she spared you," Babette said rather than asked.

Iosef nodded. "After my dinner and her slaughter had both finished, we sat and spoke for a long time. We discussed many things, and by the time she retired at dawn, she had, apparently, decided to keep me."

"Your marriage," Babette said.

"It was legitimate," Iosef replied. "Although I do wonder what the Church would make of it if the Patriarch knew that my wife was a thousand years old at the time. Since then, we have maintained a careful genealogy of succession to keep up the illusion, and whenever I travel abroad, I do so in the guise of my descendants."

"How did you explain the deaths of the men?" Babette asked.

"A rock fall," Iosef replied. "And as the sole survivor, I was in the perfect position to corroborate the claim. I rejoined the Army, bringing with me the coveted Shashavani troops, and together we served, admirably I feel, at Rasht and Baku in '23. After the victory, I returned to Svaneti to marry Sophio and, after my observance, I was inducted into the order. And the rest is a story for another day."

He led her to the final set of stairs, and they descended to the ground floor.

"What is this 'observance' that you mention?" Babette asked. "Sophio spoke of it as well, but no one has explained it."

"It is simple," Iosef said. "During your observance, you are observed. Members of the house watch you, study you as you go about your daily life. We determine from your conduct and habits whether you are to be inducted into the order. It is of great importance, though in practice it seldom prevents a supplicant from joining our ranks. The instincts of our members are sufficiently honed that only rarely does the observance result in a rejection."

"Good," Babette said. "I would be most displeased to have come all this way for nothing."

"Hardly nothing, I think," Iosef said. "After all, you shall enjoy our hospitality whether your pass your observance or not. And the view of the Caucasus is a sight unique in all the world."

"Yes, your mountains are both majestic and beautiful," Babette agreed, "but I also have a special distain for boats. They do not agree with me."

Iosef smiled a little out of the corner of his mouth and said, "Believe me, Varanus, by the time your month of observance has passed, you will see things to warrant a hundred journeys upon stormy seas."

CHAPTER TWENTY-THREE

Iosef's words proved true. Within days of her arrival, Babette had seen more incredible things than she could count. The sun rising over the Caucasus was the first sight that greeted her the following morning. It was the most beautiful that the sun had ever looked to her.

The month of observance passed quickly. Babette saw little of Iosef and all but nothing of Sophio. Ekaterine was her constant companion, serving as her guide and translator. The language barrier was immense from the outset. Few of the Shashavani spoke French, German, or English, and those that did used archaic vocabulary and had accents determined as much by time as by geography. It seemed that none of them save Iosef, Luka, and Ekaterine had spoken French to a native speaker in less than two hundred years.

Babette spent her days traveling the length and breadth of the valley, exploring the strange new land and its wonders. In the evening, she joined Iosef in the library, though he often left her to her own purposes once he had seen her settled in. The Shashavani archives were sufficient to hold her attention night after night.

The contents of the great library so enraptured her that Babette lost all track of time. She did not even notice the ending of the month of observance until Iosef met her in the library that night.

"Good evening, Varanus," he said. "It is time."

"Time?" Babette asked. Then, with understanding, she asked, "Has it been a month already?"

"It has," Iosef said.

"Am I to be presented to Sophio for approval?"

Iosef shook his head and said, "There is no need. She and I have already met with the other masters of the order to discuss our views on your observance."

There was a pause.

"And?" Babette asked. "With what result?"

"It was as I believed," Iosef replied. "You were approved with but a few reservations on Sophio's part, and she has agreed to trust my discretion in this matter."

"So I am to be inducted into your order?" Babette asked.

"Yes, if you wish it," Iosef said. "You have been granted leave to become one of the Shashavani."

Babette smiled and held her head a little higher, pleased to hear this. It was not every day that one was approved to become one of a cult of vampires. Then again, she had no idea what she was to do next.

She cleared her throat and said conspiratorially, "It may surprise you to know this, my lord, but I have never before become a Shashavani. How does one go about this?"

"One begins," Iosef told her, "by following me."

Without another word, he turned and went out of the library. Babette quickly fell in behind him, hurrying to keep up with his long stride. She followed him through the corridors and down into the deep parts of the castle, through basements and sub-basements, past storerooms and darkened crypts, until they finally arrived in a bleak stone chamber occupied by nothing but a solitary altar carved from a single block of stone that sat in the center of the room. It was decorated with delicate carvings and words written in a language that Babette could not understand.

"Not quite what I was expecting," Babette said.

"Patience," Iosef told her.

He crossed to the altar, knelt, and gave it a firm shove. Under concerted effort, it slowly slid back, revealing a set of stone steps that descended deeper into the earth.

"Oh my," Babette said.

Iosef stood and nodded at the altar.

"It is a precaution," he said. "Only the Shashavani have the strength to open it. Now come. You must be told the story of Shashava before you can choose whether to take the oath."

"I follow, my lord," Babette said.

She watched Iosef take a lantern from a hook on the wall and followed him into the dark hole. The steps descended for a dozen feet or more before the tight passage finally opened up into a proper tunnel with smooth walls covered in mosaics and worn paintings. The images were of various things: mostly, it seemed, kings and queens and scholars, with the occasional warrior or fantastic beast. Babette noticed a gentle slope in the floor, taking them still downward as the tunnel turned, progressed, and turned again, slowly forming a great spiral.

"What is this place?" Babette asked.

"It is ancient," Iosef said. "It was built, the stories say, at Shashava's command when he first arrived in this land, although some tales say that these crypts were made by the ones who came before him—whoever they may be."

"Remarkable," Babette said.

Iosef finally stopped at the foot of a mural, which depicted in icon-style a man dressed in simple robes. His hair was long and plaited, his hands upraised in a gesture of peace. As Babette gazed into the eyes of the man in the mural, she came to the singular conclusion that they were looking back at her, which was, of course, impossible.

She turned to Iosef.

"This is Great Shashava," Iosef said, "the founder of our order. The mural was completed after his departure, of course. During his time among us, Shashava forbade images to be made of himself."

"Departure?" Babette asked.

"I will come to that later," Iosef said. He turned and continued further along the passage saying, "First, I must speak of Shashava himself. We know very little about him, I fear. And the records are conflicted. Some say that he was a prince in Babylon, others that he was a king in Persia. Still others suggest that he was the sole survivor of a great empire that ruled Asia when China was young. We may never know the certain truth. The more devout among us have even suggested that he was the son of Christ, or even Christ himself. They point to his name as if it were prophecy: Shashava, Shahanshah-va, the King of Kings. But as romantic as that belief is, they are wrong."

"Why is that?" Babette asked.

"Because I have read the writings of those who were closest to him," Iosef said. "Shashava predated Christ by centuries, if not millennia. His true age is unknown. Our records of him begin when he first arrived in Svaneti more than a thousand years ago, though they remain fragmented until he issued the first great calling."

"Why did he come here?" Babette asked. "I do not mean to offend your homeland, but surely..."

"We believe that he had been searching the world for something," Iosef said. "Something that he found in Svaneti, in this valley, in these very caves. The secret to our kind."

He paused before continuing:

"You must understand that, while Shashava first gave us the cup of life, he never partook of it. Shashava was immortal long before the first Shashavani. I—and others—believe that he was searching for a means to bring immortality to others."

"So that he would not be alone?" Babette asked.

"No one can say," Iosef told her. "But that answer seems as good as any. Regardless of his reasons, when he came to Svaneti, he was met as an outsider. The local people held him in suspicion, but he soon impressed many of them with his piety, wisdom, and skill at arms. He eventually discovered this valley and settled it, claiming it as his own. Many people from throughout the region came to follow his banner. He even drew them from beyond Georgia, as you shall see. There were those who complained about his great authority. Kings and chieftains resisted their people seeking to join him, and many at first tried to wage war upon Shashava and his community. But each time, they were met and defeated. And through it all, Shashava was wise and magnanimous, never seeking to control anything but this valley."

Iosef stopped her again in front of another mural, this one depicting three men, all richly dressed. One bore the appearance of a scholar, another a king, and the third seemed to Babette to be a holy man.

"These are The Three as we have come to call them," he said. "They were among the first to join Shashava and to take the cup of life, and they became his closest companions until his departure. You will find many references to them when you study the history of our order. But in brief, here they are."

He pointed toward the scholar and said:

"This is Konstantine, sometimes called Michael. He was a Georgian, possibly a Svan, who spent time among the Byzantines and the Arabs studying the writings of the ancient world. He was noted as a scientist of sorts and as a healer. I think you would find much in common with him."

Iosef next pointed to the king.

"This is Valdemar called Vladimir, also known as Oleg, whom the Greeks called the Well-Born. That may well be the greatest testament to his quality, for he was born a chieftain among the pagan Rus, and yet he is remembered as a wise and cultured king. It is said that he devoted his life to the study of rulership and good governance."

Iosef pointed toward the final image, the one of the holy man, saying:

"Lastly, my favorite. Marduk we call him, or sometimes Mordacai, though I am certain neither of those was his name. We know little about him. Like Shashava, he came 'from the south', but whether that means Persia or Arabia or India, no one can say. We know that he was a holy man, but we know nothing of his faith. He was a mystic, a magus perhaps, but even his own writings are cryptic when they speak of his origins."

Iosef turned and continued down the passage.

"The Three represent the tripartite aspects of our order: science, leadership, and philosophy. There were others, of course, but The Three were closest to Shashava."

He led her to another mural on a wall only a few feet away. The man depicted here looked different from the others. He was girded for war, much like Valdemar, but his face lacked the serenity of Shashava or The Three. They had all been as sainted and calm in their expressions as could be conveyed by the medium and the wear of age. This new man was neither saintly nor peaceful. His was the face of a warrior, a killer, and Babette shuddered to look upon the image.

"This is Basileios the Accursed," Iosef said. "Accursed for reasons that I shall soon describe. He was a Byzantine general brought from Constantinople by Shashava for his knowledge of war. By all accounts, he was a great warrior and a natural leader, though Marduk writes often of Basileios's great pride as well.

"There were others of course, but none remain. Some were killed over the course of time, others were exiled, and some left on great sojourns from which they never returned. The oldest Shashavani who is still with us is Sophio. She was but a child when Shashava came to these lands, and she is likewise the only member of her generation who remains."

"Why is that?" Babette asked. "If you are immortal, why are the oldest members of your order missing?"

"A wise question," Iosef said. "Walk with me further, and I shall explain."

Babette followed him to the end of the passage. They were now deep in the earth, a place that knew neither day nor night. Iosef led her through a narrow doorway and into a cavern some two dozen feet tall and nearly as wide. The walls were mostly smooth, but they were formed by the very stone of the earth. The hand of man had done little more than wear away at the walls that nature itself had carved.

Iosef closed the lantern and set it aside. In the absence of firelight, the room was illuminated by a weird blue glow, something unnatural and unwholesome that crawled along the walls in spidery veins and clustered in shining masses in the cracks and crevices.

Fungus, Babette realized as she inspected one of the clusters. *Glowing fungus*.

She felt sick to her stomach and quickly drew away.

In the half-light of the cavern, Iosef spoke again:

"For centuries Great Shashava held court in this very castle, upon the throne now occupied by Sophio. He was part king, part priest, part teacher. Under his rule, this valley became a haven for knowledge. Our brothers and sisters went forth into the world, returning with stories, manuscripts, and artifacts from the furthest reaches of Europe, Asia, and Africa. Had we known of the Americas at that time, our scholars would have journeyed there as well."

Iosef began walking the length of the chamber with careful steps. Babette quickly followed him, casting an uncertain eye toward the shimmering walls. The fungus intrigued her, but it also made her shiver. She could not understand why.

"We did our best to refrain from mortal affairs," Iosef continued, "though I fear our order did become embroiled in some matters. When

David the Builder united Georgia at the turn of the twelfth century, our soldiers marched with him. There were other times as well when we worked openly, but for the most part, we kept our involvement confined to the shadows, content to watch and guide while we amassed our coveted storehouses of knowledge.

"Throughout this time, Shashava would periodically depart on sojourns to the far parts of the world. He always went alone and never spoke of where he went or what he had seen. He commonly left for a year or two, and never more than a decade, though his departures became longer and more frequent as time passed. The only time that he remained here consistently was during the reign of Queen Tamar who, the records say, visited Shashava to seek his council whenever she journeyed to Svaneti. Then, after Tamar's death in 1213, Shashava departed again and did not return. The Three were too busy with their studies and their students to rule, and Basileios became the Vicar of Shashava.

"When the Mongol hordes arrived in 1220, our soldiers rode out with the Georgians to meet them. We recognized the invaders for who they were, and this confused us. Our scholars knew the Mongols as a fractured people. Now they were united in a single great army. Even The Three knew not what to make of it. There was talk of direct intervention, of killing their generals by night and fracturing them again, but we hesitated. And because we hesitated, Georgia burned."

Iosef stopped midway across the chamber and turned toward Babette.

"We were still undecided when the Mongols returned in 1236, and by then it was too late to save Georgia. But we did what we could in the aftermath. When the Mongols ravaged the lowlands—during the invasion and in retaliation for the revolts and rebellions that followed it—we opened our gates to their victims. The displaced, the orphaned, the landless, all were welcomed into the valley. It was an act of kindness, certainly, and I believe there may have been some plan to train them for a war of liberation. But that task seems to have fallen to Basileios, and he had a different plan for them.

"I must emphasize, Varanus, that for the Shashavani, life is a constant battle against temptation. We know the same appetites as mortals, though they are…*changed*…in a manner that I cannot describe. And with our greater physical prowess, the ease with which we might indulge ourselves feeds our baser instincts. So it was with Basileios."

"What happened?" Babette asked breathlessly.

"During his reign, Basileios gathered a cohort around him filled by those Shashavani whose lusts outmatched their discipline. In other days they would have been exiled, but under his reign they were indulged.

With The Three distracted by their studies, Basileios and his ilk slaughtered and feasted among the refugees, indulging such gluttony and cruelty as I cannot describe.

"Eventually The Three and their acolytes emerged from their cloistered existence and discovered the perversion that Basileios has wrought. In horror, they ordered him into exile for his crimes. He refused. War followed.

"It was long and it was bloody." Iosef sighed at the very thought of it, his expression grave. "Though the majority of our order knew that Basileios's crimes had to be punished, those that followed him were largely men and women skilled in battle. The army that he had trained flocked to his side in great numbers, and The Three and those loyal to Shashava's laws were forced to flee the castle. They fought from hiding for many years, aided by the mortals in the villages. Basileios dared not leave the safety of the castle. When he dispatched warbands into the wilds of the valley to hunt down the loyalists, the men seldom returned."

"How was the stalemate broken?" Babette asked.

"Sophio," Iosef said. "At that time she was the chief librarian of the castle, and when the war broke out, she feigned allegiance to Basileios and remained there. After years of work, she finally lulled him into a state of complacency. One day, while Basileios slept, she entered his chambers and cut his head from his body. Before her act was discovered, she helped The Three enter through a passage in the crypts. After heavy fighting, the castle was finally retaken.

"But in the wake of the civil war, The Three were confronted with grave uncertainty. How could the Shashavani order hold itself free from corruption without Shashava's guidance? If Basileios had been corrupted, any of them could be. And so The Three set off to search the world for Shashava. Like Shashava, they have yet to return."

"Is that why there are so few of your kind?" Babette asked. "The civil war?"

"In part," Iosef said. "Some died, yes. But many others were lost in the time that followed. When The Three left, a council of the eldest was left in charge, instructed to rule by consensus until leadership could be returned. Over the years that followed, new conflicts broke out between these elders. They struggled for supremacy, each claiming the right to be Vicar of Shashava. Camps formed and soon our order had turned upon itself. Many died; many more were sent into exile as their leaders were outmaneuvered. Eventually, Sophio intervened. Once she became the eldest member of the house, she immediately claimed the throne. She called for a return to order and offered amnesty to any who agreed to give up their thirst for power in favor of Shashava's laws. Most of the survivors agreed. Those few who did not were immediately put down."

"How grim," Babette said.

"Indeed," Iosef said. "Unfortunate as well. Some of the greatest minds the world has ever known were lost because of corruption, greed, and folly. It is a lesson to all of us who remain."

"Which brings us to the present, I presume," Babette said.

"Indeed."

Iosef motioned for her to follow again and led her to the far end of the cavern. As they approached, Babette saw a great pool of iridescent water that covered the floor. It was shallow at first, but it soon sloped downward into a flooded pit that had no visible ending. A large metal chalice sat next to the pool, bound to the shore by a length of steel chain bolted into the rock.

Iosef knelt by the pool and filled the chalice with water.

"Now, Varanus," he said, "you must make a choice. You must decide whether you truly wish to take the oath to Shashava and join our order."

"Of course I—" Babette began.

Iosef shook his head and said, "You must listen, Varanus. Hear what I have to tell you first. Haste will not avail you here."

Babette nodded and bowed her head.

"Of course," she said. "What must I consider?"

"When you drink this water, one of three things will happen," Iosef said. "First, you may die."

"*Die?*" Babette exclaimed. "What do you mean die?"

"I mean just that, Varanus," Iosef said. "You may die. The cup of life is not a means to cheat death. Its purpose is far greater than that. To become one of us, you must accept your mortality and confront it."

Babette slowly nodded. That made sense. And what if she died? She would not know it. Would she?

"Is it painful?" she asked.

"No," Iosef said. "In all cases, you will fall into slumber. The only question is whether or not you will awaken."

Babette took a deep breath and said, "Very well, I accept the possibility of death."

"Second," Iosef said, "you may become like Luka or Ekaterine. You will be healthier than you are now, fitter, stronger. You will have little to fear from illness, and you will measure your life not in decades but in centuries. But you will still walk in the shadow of death. In time, you *will* age and die."

"I understand," Babette said. "And third, I become like you?"

"Yes," Iosef said, nodding. "Third, you may become as I am: immortal, unchanging. You will not age from this day forth. You will know power that you cannot yet imagine. But you must never abuse that power for your own ends. You will be tempted as never before, and you must resist it for all eternity. Should you break your oath and indulge the temptation of power, you will be killed. Do you understand?"

"I understand," Babette said.

"Good."

"Will I drink blood?" Babette asked.

"Yes," Iosef said. "You do not have to, but it is far more expedient than other meals. And but a little blood will be like a feast to you."

Babette smiled a little at this thought. Somehow, the idea of blood excited her.

Iosef looked into her eyes and said, "You enjoy the thought of blood."

"No, I—" Babette said quickly.

"You do," Iosef said. "Be cautious, Varanus. That is a temptation you must guard against."

"I understand," Babette said.

"Good," Iosef said. "Know also that for a time the touch of the sun will harm you. It may even kill you. It will be like the touch of fire."

"As it is with you?" Babette asked.

"Worse," Iosef said. "It will lessen over time, as it has with me, but you must be careful."

Babette nodded but said nothing.

Iosef raised the chalice and said, "If you are prepared, you will take the oath. Do you, Babette Varanus, swear upon all that you hold in esteem to uphold the laws of Shashava? To resist temptation and corruption with all your strength? And to devote your life from now until the Day of Judgment to the search for knowledge and the betterment of humanity?"

"I swear it," Babette said.

"And do you swear to preserve our secrets from the uninitiated?" Iosef asked.

"I do."

"Do you swear to respect those who have come before you for their great wisdom and to guide those who will come after you? To conduct yourself with honor at all times and to seek the honor in others?"

Babette hesitated for a moment before replying, "Yes, I swear it."

"Very well then." Iosef pressed the chalice into her hands. "Then drink of the waters of life, Varanus, and may God decide your fate."

Babette took a deep breath and raised the chalice to her lips. The water tasted cool and slightly bitter, but it was not unpleasant. Babette drained the chalice in a single long drink. A tingle like electricity coursed through her body, from her fingertips to her toes. She tried to gasp in pain but no sound escaped her.

She looked at Iosef in confusion and saw him vaguely, as if through a haze. It was as if she were seeing him for the first time. He was so beautiful, so graceful. The chalice dropped from her fingers and struck the stone with a clatter.

Babette reached out slowly and caressed Iosef's face with her fingertips.

So very, very beautiful.

She leaned forward, mouth parted slightly. Their lips brushed and suddenly everything vanished into darkness.

"Come, *liebchen,*" Babette heard Korbinian say, "it is time to wake up."

Babette slowly opened her eyes and looked up at Korbinian. He smiled at her and kissed her tenderly.

"I have missed you," he said.

"Where am I?" Babette asked, slowly sitting up.

She lay on an elegantly upholstered sofa, propped up by a mountain of soft pillows. Her clothes were gone. In their place she found herself clothed in a dressing gown of crimson silk.

Where have my clothes gone? Babette wondered as she swept back her auburn tresses.

"Don't you know where you are?" Korbinian asked.

He spread his hands and indicated the room, which was dimly lit and furnished in dark wood and wallpaper. Babette looked around uncertainly. The place looked so familiar. Indeed, it *smelled* so familiar. Warm, rich, comforting. Like leather and aging paper.

Grandfather's library!

Babette looked back at Korbinian and noticed for the first time that he was naked. Had he always been naked? Surely she would have noticed that!

"Why am I here?" Babette asked, slowly rising from the sofa.

Korbinian caught her by the arms and helped her up. As Babette stood, he pulled her against his chest and held her.

"Why would you not be here?" he asked. "This is your home. Where else would you be, *liebchen?*"

"I..." Babette said. Something was wrong. She was not supposed to be there, but she could not think of where else she would have been. "Georgia," she finally said. "Why am I not in Georgia?"

Korbinian kissed her and laughed.

"Why would you be in Georgia?" he asked. "Surely you would rather be here with me."

Babette rested her head against his chest and closed her eyes. He was so warm.

"Yes, of course," she said. "Only, I feel that I *ought* to be somewhere else. Somewhere…cold."

"Somewhere cold?" Korbinian asked. "No, *liebchen*, that will not do. You are too beautiful to suffer in the cold."

"I suppose," Babette said.

She shook her head. The nagging thought would not leave her. Something was amiss.

"Stay, *liebchen*," Korbinian said as he kissed her hair. "Stay here with me. Do not think of other places without me."

"Yes," Babette whispered.

But the thought was still there, lurking in her mind even as Korbinian held her in his arms. Finally, it became too much to bear, and she pulled away from him. Clutching the dressing gown about her, she turned in circles, looking in every direction for something that would make sense of all this.

"I am not supposed to be here!" she cried, turning back toward Korbinian.

Korbinian was gone. The room was empty, and she was alone.

"Korbinian!" Babette cried. "My love, come back to me!"

"Come back?" she heard him say from behind her. "But *liebchen*, I have never left you."

Babette turned to face him. He stood in the doorway, holding a bundle of cloth in his arms. Babette felt dizzy as she recognized what he held.

The body of their child.

"No!" she cried. "No! Take it away!"

"Away?" Korbinian asked. "But, *liebchen*, this is our child—"

"Our child is dead!" Babette shouted. "Dead! I let him die!"

She fell to her knees and covered her face with her hands. She willed herself not to cry, but the tears came against her orders, stinging her cheeks and staining the silken gown.

"I let you both die!" she cried. "You're both gone, and it is my fault!"

She did not see Korbinian approach, but suddenly he stood above her, still holding Alistair's body in the mass of linen. He knelt before her and smiled as he always did when he looked at her.

"No, *liebchen*," he said. "I will never leave you. And look!" He gently pulled back the edge of the blanket to reveal Alistair, alive and smiling. "Our son lives."

The sight of Alistar made Babette sob all the more as years of loss and guilt flowed from her in a violent rush.

"How can this be?" she asked, even as she smiled and cried at the sight of her living child. "I saw him—"

"Did you see him die?" Korbinian asked.

"No," Babette said. "But—"

"Did you see him buried?" came the next question.

"No," Babette said again. "But surely—"

Korbinian shook his head, still smiling at her.

"You are wrong, *liebchen,*" he said. "Our child lives. It must be so."

Babette clenched her eyes shut and gasped in a mixture of confusion and relief. Alistair alive? Was it possible? But there he was, right in front of her, just as she remembered him.

"Let me hold him," she said, reaching out to take Alistair.

To her surprise, Korbinian turned away, keeping Alistair out of her grasp.

"No, *liebchen,*" he said. "Not yet."

"Why not?" Babette demanded. "He is my son! He is alive! Let me hold him!"

Korbinian looked into her eyes and smiled.

"Soon," he said. "But first you must wake up."

"*What?*" Babette asked.

"Wake up."

Babette opened her eyes with a gasp and sat up in a single startled motion. Her lungs felt tired and empty, and for a moment she seemed to be choking on the very air she tried to breathe. The first few breaths were painful beyond measure. Her head swam, and she could make no sense of the shapes and sounds around her.

After what seemed ages, her senses returned to her. She was sitting in her bedroom in the castle of the Shashavani, clothed in a robe of thick brocade silk. She felt cold, yet warm. There was a pounding in her head that she could not explain.

Was she ill? She looked at her hands. Why did they appear so pale?

"Doctor Varanus?"

Babette looked toward the voice. It was Ekaterine. The woman sat in a chair by the bedside, a leather-bound book in her lap. Babette looked toward it. Through the haze of her vision, she could see the worn lettering on the cover perfectly. She looked at Ekaterine and saw the joy in the woman's eyes, the pulsing of blood at her throat, the quickness of breath in her bosom.

Babette clutched her head and asked, "What has happened?"

Ekaterine rose and laid a hand on her shoulder.

"You are well," she said. "You live."

"How long have I been asleep?" Babette asked.

"Seven days," Ekaterine said. "I am so very proud of you."

"Proud?"

Ekaterine touched her cheek and looked into her eyes.

"You are Shashavani now," she said. "Fully Shashavani, free from the shadow of death forever."

Immortal? Babette's heart leapt with excitement, though the sensation was unlike any she had felt before. Stronger yet softer. Suddenly she realized that she could no longer feel her own heart beating.

"Where is Lord Iosef?" Babette asked. She looked around the room but did not see him. For some reason, she had expected him to be there.

"He was here an hour ago," Ekaterine said. "He has visited your bedside each day of your slumber to be sure that you are well. But I would not let him stay."

"Why not?" Babette asked.

"This is no place for one such as he," Ekaterine said. "Only those Shashavani who still walk in the shadow of death may hold this vigil. It is the law, pronounced by Shashava himself."

Babette nodded in understanding and winced as her head and neck began to throb from the movement.

"I feel so weak," she said, leaning against Ekaterine for support.

"Hush," Ekaterine said. "You are tired and hungry."

She drew a knife from inside her sleeve and made a small cut just below her wrist. It was a shallow wound, but it bled freely. The scent of blood assailed Babette's nose, making her head spin all the more. All other perceptions faded into the haze that clouded her head until she smelled and saw only Ekaterine and the blood.

"Drink," Ekaterine said, placing the wound against Babette's lips.

The taste of blood was more delicious than anything Babette could remember. She drank desperately and felt her strength slowly return, drop-by-drop.

After a short while, Ekaterine pulled her arm away. Babette gasped for air and licked her lips, savoring the taste of the blood that had spilled on them. Ekaterine quickly bound her wrist in a strip of fabric, though Babette scarcely noticed. She felt more fatigued than ever, though at the same time a strange vigor coursed through her body.

"You must rest now," Ekaterine said.

"But I have been resting," Babette said, her voice weak. "For seven days."

Ekaterine placed her hands on Babette's shoulders and pushed her, gently but forcefully, back against the bed. She kissed Babette's forehead and said:

"You were not resting. You were *changing*. Your body is exhausted. You must sleep now so that it can recover."

Babette wanted to protest, but she found she could not. Indeed, she could scarcely move her lips to mumble anything, let alone a coherent complaint.

"Rest," Ekaterine said. "I will watch over you."

Babette tried to say something. She did not know what, only that she made the attempt. A moment later, the darkness took her again.

Alistair is alive, she thought, the last coherent thing she could remember before she slipped back into unconsciousness.

CHAPTER TWENTY-FOUR

After the initial shock, Varanus found it strangely easy to adapt to her new life. Varanus, not Babette, she decided soon after waking. She had never liked her Christian name, and now it seemed unnecessary to keep it. She was a new person, remade by the strange water in that luminescent grotto. She was Doctor Varanus. Varanus Shashavani. Varanus or nothing.

In one sense, little had changed. Most of her waking time was devoted to study, whether reading in the library, discourse with Iosef and the other scholars, or preparing a laboratory in the crypts for her experiments. She slept little. Indeed, as Iosef explained, sleep was now unnecessary: the Shashavani required but a few hours of rest and meditation to stave off the madness of fatigue. Her new nocturnal schedule was not at all unusual. Even before her transformation, she was used to staying awake at her desk through the night and into the sunrise.

But in other, very significant ways, life had changed completely. Sunlight was the most glaring. Her eyes, now incredibly sensitive, found the sun blinding. At even the barest touch of sunlight, her skin became red and angry. Within moments it began to boil. The burns healed quickly after escaping the light, but the experience was nothing less than dreadful. And for Varanus, used to taking regular rides in the afternoon, the transition to nighttime rides proved difficult.

The sharpness of her senses and her ever-increasing fitness were more subtle changes, but they still troubled her. It was months before she became used to hearing conversations a dozen feet away with perfect clarity. The slightest movement across a room caught her eye, and she found herself reading books at a distance when she ought to be reading the ones open before her. She was disturbed from her work by the slightest of sounds and smells. For weeks, even a change in the breeze was enough to distract her.

But the greatest change was blood. From that first night when she drank from Ekaterine, Varanus consumed little else. Other food was edible, indeed pleasant, for with her new senses she could discern each and every note of flavor in whatever she ate. But blood was so much *easier* than solid food. It was more convenient to consume, and her body absorbed it almost immediately. The mess of digestion was gone forever.

Though her first meal had come from Ekaterine, it was not to be a regular occurrence. The Shashavani did not feed from one another, whether "living"—as she and Iosef were—or "in the shadow"—like Ekaterine and Luka. There were servants in the castle whose primary purpose was to provide food, a task for which, Iosef told her, they were held in high regard. Their diet was carefully regulated to ensure both the heartiness and the flavor of their blood.

Meals were taken at one's convenience, which for Varanus meant infrequently. But once a month, on the night of the full moon, the entire assembly of Shashavani gathered in the great hall to dine at Sophio's table. It was a mandatory practice and though she tried, Varanus could not convince Iosef to let her avoid the obligation.

The place of honor was left empty to signify the missing Shashava, but Sophio as the custodian of the house sat at its right hand. Iosef sat beside her and Varanus beside him. The honor of the position was not lost on Varanus, but she still preferred the quiet of a solitary meal. From that vantage point, however, she was able to witness Sophio's dining habits, which proved anything but civil and sometimes scarcely dignified.

The first such occurrence came about three months after Varanus's induction. By then Varanus had fully weaned herself from solid foods and had become comfortable with the extraction of blood—carried out by the use of curious syringe-like devices of great antiquity that drew the blood from the donors in measured quantities and deposited it, still warm, in the goblets of the Shashavani. It was a process that fascinated Varanus, and indeed on that particular occasion, she felt inclined to ask about it.

"My lord," she said to Iosef, in between drinks, "this contraption is incredible. It reminds me of Blundell's device for the transfusing of blood, but these all seem too old to be copies."

"Indeed," Iosef said, "these were constructed almost a hundred years ago, and the design dates back centuries more. Konstantine is said to have created them before the Eleventh Century."

"Remarkable," Varanus said. "I can scarcely imagine how—"

She was interrupted by Sophio, who let out a loud sigh of displeasure and threw her freshly filled goblet over her shoulder, spilling blood across the floor. The chamber, which had been noisy with conversation, was suddenly silent. All eyes turned toward Sophio as the Shashavani watched her apprehensively.

"The flavor of this does not please me," Sophio announced. She flicked her hand at the donor. "Take it away and bring me another."

The donor's face fell in embarrassment and shame. Such a public rejection was, Varanus surmised, both rare and greatly offensive. The steward quickly approached and ushered the poor man away with a few whispered reassurances that Varanus could only just make out.

"My lady," the steward said, "what would please you?"

"Bring me the wine and rosemary," Sophio said. "And a fresh goblet."

The steward hesitated awkwardly for a few moments before clearing his throat and replying, "My lady, the only wine and rosemary at the moment is Giorgi. And you have already partaken of him for three days."

Sophio looked at the steward impatiently.

"Meaning?" she demanded.

The steward hesitated again, this time unable to find any words.

"Meaning, my love," Iosef said, leaning toward Sophio and placing his hand upon hers, "that he must rest before we may drink of him again."

"What nonsense," Sophio said.

"If you drink of him again, he will die," Iosef said.

"And what of that?" Sophio asked.

Varanus saw Iosef's jaw clench tightly in anger, but when he spoke, it was with a calm voice.

"And it will ruin the flavor," he added.

These words seemed to make all the difference. Sophio laughed and waved the steward away.

"You are right, of course, my husband," she said. "What a terrible waste that would be. How glad I am that you are here to remind me of these *details*."

"Details?" Babette thought. *A man's life?*

"Of course, my love," Iosef said. He gently placed his goblet in Sophio's hand. "Come, have some of mine."

"You are too kind," Sophio said, looking deeply into Iosef's eyes. The adoring stare lingered on for nearly a minute, and it made Varanus feel extremely uncomfortable merely from the proximity. Finally, Sophio looked at the Shashavani, who all stared back at her in silence. "Come," she said, "as you were."

In an instant, the feasting and conversation resumed, like water released through an opened tap.

"What is this madness?" Varanus whispered to Iosef.

In reply, Iosef looked at her and slowly shook his head.

"What was that?" Sophio asked, halfheartedly glancing at Varanus.

Varanus froze and her breath caught. Of course, Sophio would hear her question. Varanus herself could have heard Sophio whisper thanks to her newly heightened hearing.

"Nothing, my love," Iosef said. "My apprentice was just asking me about Konstantine."

"Oh good," Sophio said. She looked Varanus in the eyes and said, "Continue," before turning away and engaging one of the scholars across the table in conversation.

Varanus fell silent and looked into her cup. It was as clear as day that Sophio was mad. How could Iosef not see it?

There were more examples of Sophio's madness that followed: forgetfulness, distraction, the changing of languages in mid-sentence seemingly without reason, and above all long hours spent staring off into nothing even when others were present. While Varanus had few direct interactions with Sophio at first, it seemed she could not look upon the great Queen of the Shashavani without at least some minor incident of such unusual behavior. Varanus often overheard Sophio speaking to Iosef of the great crusades she would soon send forth against their enemies—"enemies" meaning anyone from the Russians to the Persians to the Turks.

Once Iosef brought Varanus with him to a conference of state in which Sophio spent twelve hours outlining her plan to recapture the Holy Land from the Saracens in support of a crusade that King Giorgi IV had planned in the Thirteenth Century. Yet Sophio spoke of it as if Girogi IV were still alive and the crusade about to be carried out.

She thinks herself to be Tamar of Georgia, Varanus thought to herself, *when she is really like Mad King George of England!*

When Varanus made mention that the Crusades had ended six hundred years before, she was berated by Sophio for her "ignorance" and barred from attending any council for the rest of her life. While this seemed to irritate Iosef, the peace and quiet were a godsend to Varanus. Then, two years later, she was called before Sophio to answer for the grave offense of ignoring her duty to attend the council with her master Iosef. Sophio seemed to have no recollection of her earlier pronouncement against Varanus's attendance.

And so things went in the House of Shashavani. The other scholars said little and did nothing, though Varanus could see that all but an aged few recognized the insanity. It was all like a confused dream had under the influence of opium. Iosef was the most puzzling. Though he surely knew what was happening, he did nothing to confront Sophio's insane pronouncements. Indeed, he facilitated them, calmly and gently appeasing his lady, while at the same time flattering each mad misconception. Varanus knew not what to make of it.

Fortunately, she was kept far too busy by her studies to leave much time to linger on such thoughts. Throughout the shrouded days and the long nights, Ekaterine was her constant companion. They read together, shared discourse on topics of philosophy and science, and taught one another their languages. While Varanus improved Ekaterine's French and taught her English, German, and a small portion of Italian, Ekaterine reciprocated by instructing Varanus in no less than three languages of Georgia—or, more properly, the languages of the Georgians, the Svans, and the Mingrelians, who, she explained, were all distinct though related peoples.

Varanus delighted in Ekaterine's company far more than she had expected. As the weeks turned into months and then into years, Varanus found herself regarding Ekaterine as something like a sister. She had never had a sister, of course, but it seemed the most apt way of describing things. Ekaterine was always there when she needed someone—most often to help with research but sometimes simply for conversation as well. Though intelligent conversation was abundant in the Shashavani house, she found a particular rapport with Ekaterine that made her preferable to everyone except for Iosef. In time, Varanus felt that she came to understand Iosef's curious relationship with Luka far better than before. Not master and servant but comrades, each distinctly strong and distinctly weak, each relying upon the other, sharing in triumphs and failures, joys and sorrows.

It was from Luka that Varanus learned the arts of war. She knew how to ride and how to hunt, but under Luka's tutelege, she expanded her knowledge to the art of killing men. It was grueling work, and Luka was no easy teacher. He pushed her to her limits, night after night. For almost a year, the main focus of the training was entirely exercise. Varanus was made to run endless circles around the castle, lift and carry heavy weights, swim in the lake in the middle of winter, and hold her body in contorted poses while balancing precariously. She despised the exercises—as much for disrupting her work as for the physical discomfort—but she could not deny that they made her fitter and stronger.

The regimen, Iosef told her one evening, was intended to push her body to its limits constantly, forcing it to attain the superhuman vigor of the Shashavani over the course of years rather than decades or centuries. It was the same process he had used to train himself, and Varanus could not deny its success. She noted on many occasions that Iosef seemed as strong or even stronger than many of the Shashavani who were his elders by hundreds of years. Iosef's endorsement of the regimen was enough to keep Varanus dedicated even when she was at her weakest.

About a year after her arrival, Luka began to train her properly in combat. There was some practice of marksmanship, merely to keep up what Luka called an "already tolerable degree of skill." The main work was on fighting at close quarters, something for which Varanus had little aptitude and no experience. Their first work was wrestling, and Varanus quickly discovered that Luka's skill easily outmatched her growing strength. Even when her physical prowess surpassed his, Luka still managed to beat her almost every time. But with effort, she improved. Next came sword training, then sword and shield, then spear, then axe. By the time Varanus began to work with this last weapon, she was strong enough to lift and swing it one-handed. At long last, Luka taught her to fight with a sword in either hand, a technique that he demonstrated with ease, and Varanus attempted with repeated failures. It was an important lesson that was not lost on her: however useful strength might be, skill and practice were always of paramount importance.

From Iosef she learned how to exist as one of the Shashavani. He taught her to focus, to control her rampant senses, to avoid being blinded by the cacophony of information that bombarded her at every moment. He sought to ease her into the experience of blood drinking, but Varanus found it surprisingly simple to adapt to it. It was as though her body had always craved blood, and she was only now fulfilling its needs.

Iosef also taught her to meditate rather than sleep. This was especially difficult. Varanus was a creature of activity, and she had little interest in sitting quietly for hours on end, reflecting on the world. She simply did not see the point. The nature of the universe would be discovered in the laboratory, not through quiet introspection. But in time, Varanus came to see some *minor* value in the practice as a substitute for sleep. An hour or so of meditation left her feeling as refreshed as a whole night of sleep, and she acknowledged the worth of such a time-saving practice.

Perhaps most importantly, he also taught her to withstand the sun. Every day, save when disrupted by other concerns, he made her sit with him on one of the eastern balconies to greet the sunrise. Precautions were taken, of course—they sat with heavy blankets to shield themselves once the light became too painful, and either Luka or Ekaterine was always on hand to help them escape to the darkness inside—but it was still a nerve-wracking experience each time. The creeping dread of anticipation was often worse than the pain itself as the light of dawn rose over the mountains.

Try as she might, Varanus could never withstand the pain for long. The first time she fled immediately. The shock of the experience was simply too much for even her hardened resolve. With practice she managed to stay for a few seconds, then a few minutes. It did not take long for her to master her fear, but her body did not keep pace with her will. As per Iosef's instructions, she withdrew each time once her flesh began to boil. Iosef always remained after she fled, often for thirty minutes or more. Varanus fled while he remained. The shame of it burned her worse than the light of the sun.

One day, she resolved to match him minute for minute. She would prove to him that she was as strong as he. She waited, breathless, as the sun rose. She braced herself as the first rays washed over her. For a moment the sensation was pleasant and warm, with a faint prickling that delighted as much as it hurt. Then came the pain, exactly as she remembered it. At first it was minor, only a sensation of heat beneath the skin. But soon the sensation grew til it felt like her body had been wrapped around bars of heated iron. Her bones ached, her flesh boiled, her eyes went blind, but still she sat there, gritting her teeth and refusing to succumb.

She forgot when exactly it was that she blacked out. Her next recollection was of opening her eyes to the sight of Iosef's face, palid and sun-scarred. As Varanus watched, the burnt flesh began to smooth out and heal.

"Your eyes have reformed," Iosef said. "Good."

"What happened?" Varanus asked. "Why am I here?"

She lay on the stone floor of the room by the balcony. The doors to the outside were now shut and shielded by heavy curtains.

"You are a fool!" Iosef snapped. "Why did you do such a thing? You could have died! You *would have,* had not Ekaterine pulled you to safety!"

Varanus looked at Ekaterine, who sat in a chair nearby, watching her with a mixture of relief and frustration.

"Thank you, Ekaterine," Varanus said to her.

Ekaterine's mouth was tightly set in anger, but she nodded and said, "Of course."

Iosef took Varanus by the chin and pulled her back to face him with a sharp tug. Babette looked into his pale blue eyes without flinching.

"I know the purpose of this exercise," she said.

"Do you?" Iosef asked. "I think not."

"It is a test of fortitude," Varanus said. "Of determination. You prove yourself my master by suffering the pain for longer than I do."

Iosef exhaled and shook his head at her, for the moment speechless.

"I am not your master," he said. "I am your *teacher!* Is that what you think this is about? A show of strength?"

Varanus felt a sudden shiver of doubt. Could she have been wrong? But surely… Why else would Iosef have made such a show of outlasting her?

"Isn't it?" she asked.

Iosef released her chin and folded his hands. Blackened flakes of flesh tumbled away, revealing newly healed skin beneath.

"No, it is not," he said. "This is not a contest, Varanus. This is training, as much as your time with Luka. It has nothing to do with me."

"I don't understand," Varanus said.

Iosef sighed and said, "Perhaps I should have explained earlier, but I intended for you to have firsthand experience with which to understand this. That has always been our way."

"I have plenty of experience," Varanus said. "Explain it to me now. Please."

"The sun is like poison," Iosef said. "Poison that burns like fire, yes, but poison all the same. And like poison, your body can become accustomed to it. Surely you have seen this yourself. You can now withstand exposure many times as long as you could when you first tried."

"This is true," Varanus said.

She thought for a moment or two, and the comparison came to her. Not only had she learned to withstand the pain, the touch of the sun took longer to reach the same point of severity as before. It was a difference of seconds, but the difference was there.

"I understand," she said. "As with arsenic, a little constant exposure builds resistance."

"Yes," Iosef said. "And if you take more than you can manage, you will still die."

"So we expose ourselves to the sun that we might adapt to it?" Varanus asked.

"Indeed," Iosef said. "It is the only way to venture into the outer world. There are those among us who have not faced the sun in hundreds of years. They react to it just as you do. Whereas I, with my constant limited exposure can withstand the better part of an hour—longer if I am protected."

Varanus sighed. She wanted to berate Iosef for not telling her before, but she understood the reason. In truth, she would not have believed him without experiencing it herself.

"When will I become immune?" she asked.

"Ages," Iosef said. "I have spent more than a hundred years training myself in this manner. But mark my words, Varanus, if you are disciplined and adhere to this practice with dedication and *caution*," he greatly emphasized the word, "you will one day be able to dance freely in the sunlight, just as Sophio does."

Varanus smiled at Iosef and said, "I can assure you, my lord, that once I can walk in the sun with impunity, I will use that ability for something more important than *dancing*."

CHAPTER TWENTY-FIVE

Late Winter, 1887

Fifteen years passed almost without Varanus's notice. Removed from the experience of aging, she now found that each night faded into the next with little to distinguish them. Sheltered from the daytime within the halls of the castle, Varanus quickly lost track of when one day ended and the next began. The daily regimen of greeting the sun lasted only the first five years, at which point Iosef had left the decision to continue in Varanus's own hands. Appreciating the wisdom in the practice, Varanus did her best to maintain it, but over the years the regimen slipped from a daily practice to a weekly one, even monthly during periods of especially focused work. Sometimes entire seasons passed without her notice. Before, she had wondered how The Three had managed not to notice Basileios's excesses for so long. Now she understood.

Over the years, Varanus watched as Sophio's madness grew. While Iosef's constant subservience to such a creature astounded Varanus, she saw that he was the only person who could placate the Queen of the Shashavani. Meanwhile, the other members of the house cloistered themselves in their laboratories and reading rooms, leaving all proper affairs of state unattended. It did not take Varanus long to realize that Iosef was the only thing standing between the house and its collapse.

Then, one day near the first thaw of spring, Varanus received a letter from France. This was not an uncommon occurrence—she had maintained a distant correspondence with both Father and Grandfather over the years—and she thought little of it when Ekaterine brought the letter to her study.

"News from France," Ekaterine said as she entered the room. She crossed to where Varanus sat, nose buried in ancient tomes of medicine.

Varanus looked up from her work and waved her hand, saying, "Read it to me if you please, Ekaterine."

She watched as Korbinian leaned across the table and propped his head on one hand, looking at her with a giddy smile.

"News from home!" he exclaimed. "How exciting! I wonder what it can be."

"It will be nothing of consequence," Varanus told him, forgetting for a moment that they were not alone. "Merely Father fussing about the neighbors or this and that."

Ekaterine paused in the midst of opening the envelope.

"Do you wish me to read it to you or not?" she asked.

Varanus quickly caught herself and glared at Korbinian.

"Please do, Ekaterine," she said. "I am merely predicting the contents."

Ekaterine opened the envelope and removed the letter. Clearing her throat with a delicate cough, she read aloud:

" 'My dearest Babette. It is my most fervent wish that this letter finds you well. I fear that I cannot report similar news of myself. You will notice that your grandfather's Christmas letter has not arrived.' "

Varanus's eyes widened a little. Father was right; it hadn't arrived. Varanus had assumed that it was delayed by the distance, but now…

" 'I fear,' " Ekaterine read, " 'that a great misfortune has befallen our family.' " She quickly stopped and looked at Varanus. "Perhaps you would prefer to read it on your own," she said. "This is clearly of a private nature."

"Continue, Ekaterine," Varanus said. Her stomach clenched, and a shiver ran down her spine. She already knew what it would say.

" 'With a heavy heart,' " Ekaterine read, " 'I must inform you that your grandfather has passed. We were all taken by surprise, for as you will recall, your grandfather was always a model of health. But he was taken quietly in the night late in January. We put his body to rest in the family mausoleum, as he would have wanted.' "

Varanus blinked back a tear. Grandfather dead. She had always known his death would come some day, but she had never really thought about what would happen when it did.

Korbinian knelt beside her and kissed her hand.

"It was his time, *liebchen*," he said to her. "Do not let this sorrow tear you apart. He would have been proud to see you as you are now."

" 'Now it falls to me to make sense of the estate,' " Ekaterine continued. " 'I fear that your grandfather was especially private regarding the business, and you know that I never had a head for such things. In truth, I am completely unprepared for the management of the company, the finances, or indeed any of the tasks his death has placed upon my shoulders. I am so terribly alone, Babette. I know not where to turn. And worse, I myself have taken ill. I am lost, Babette, and I fear I must ask you to return home to help me settle the estate. If you and your husband would consent to come to Normandy at once, I would be eternally—' "

"Enough," Varanus said. She took a breath and forced herself not to cry. Grandfather would not have approved. She was stronger than that.

"I must go to France, Ekaterine," she said. "Will you accompany me?"

Ekaterine laughed and shook her head. She walked to Varanus's side and placed a hand on her shoulder.

"That you should need to ask," she said.

Varanus patted her hand and said, "Thank you. Normandy will be tedious, and I will thank God for some intelligent conversation." Another thought occurred to her, and she laughed a little. "Bring my husband...as if I am incapable of managing Grandfather's affairs."

She knew Father meant no insult, but it was there all the same.

Behind her, the door to the room opened. It was almost silent, but Varanus had no difficulty in hearing the faint rush of air. She turned in her chair and saw Iosef standing in the doorway. He wore a dark gray chokha under a similarly drab-colored greatcoat—clothes normally reserved for the soldiers and hunters who patrolled the valley in winter.

Varanus immediately rose and faced him.

"My lord," she said, "what is it?"

"Make yourself ready, Varanus," Iosef replied. "Then meet me at the stables. You as well, Ekaterine."

"As you wish," Varanus said. She motioned to his clothes and asked, "Why are you dressed so, my lord?"

Even in the depths of winter, they did not suffer from the cold. Why should he bother to wear an overcoat?

Iosef pulled open one side of the coat, revealing rows of pistols and daggers concealed inside.

"We go to hunt," he said.

When Varanus arrived at the stables, she found them busier than she had ever seen them. Grooms hurried about readying the horses and tack while the soldiers—Shashavani who still walked in the shadow of death—readied their weapons and ammunition. They were all dressed like Iosef in warm chokhas and greatcoats, with fur hats pulled down tightly over their ears. From that alone, Varanus knew that the night was frigid, though she no longer felt the cold. She was not concerned, and she came dressed for the occasion in a riding habit of crimson and black, which the household tailors had made following the English style. She was secretly delighted to be able to wear it in the dead of winter.

"Hunting?" she remarked to Ekaterine, who walked at her side bundled tightly in a high-collared coat of sable. "I have seen less preparation of arms for a military campaign!"

She saw Iosef and Luka standing by a table of weapons, and she watched in astonishment as Iosef selected a double-barreled elephant gun and checked its aim. Satisfied, Iosef nodded, and Luka handed him a bandoleer of paper cartridges. From the size of the bullets, the weapon had to be a six bore at least.

"All this to hunt wolves?" she asked Ekaterine.

"You have not seen our wolves," Ekaterine said. She gave Varanus a quick looking over and made a noise. "Your collar is crooked," she said.

"Nonsense," Varanus said, but she allowed Ekaterine to fuss over her for a few moments.

"I have grave misgivings about that hat," Ekaterine added.

"The hat stays," Varanus said sharply. She was quite proud of her lady's top hat, a dozen of which had been imported from France a few years before. "It is the style."

"I fear for the future of France if that is so," Ekaterine said.

Varanus saw Iosef motioning to them, and she led Ekaterine across the room to join him. Without a word, Iosef selected a heavy, twin-barreled howdah pistol and handed it to Varanus along with a pouch of cartridges. Varanus looked at them and tucked them into her coat pockets.

"Tell me, my lord," she said, "why are the men arming for battle? I thought this was to be a hunt."

"It is," Iosef said. "But our quarry is quite unlike anything you have encountered."

"I have encountered wolves before," Varanus said.

"Not like these," Iosef replied. "These creatures have breached the valley many times over the years. There are common wolves in the pack, yes, but they are led by something…else. And unlike ordinary wolves, these will not flee at the sight of men. They will not wait in the wilderness for the weak or the old. They will haunt our villages and assault our people, even in broad daylight. We must find them and break them at once."

"I am intrigued," Varanus said, "but not convinced. Still," she added, "I enjoy a good hunt. Give me a rifle, and it will please me to accompany you."

"You will need more than a mere rifle," Iosef said. "Luka, give her the ten bore."

Luka nodded and selected a smaller elephant gun from the table. It was still a huge weapon compared to the rifles of the soldiers. Varanus took it from him and tested the weight. She could lift it as easily as a pistol, but firing it would be another matter.

"Are these truly necessary?" Varanus asked.

"They are," Iosef said. "Can you manage the weapon?"

"Easily," Varanus said. "I only wonder at using guns intended for big game. Are we hunting wolves or rhinoceroses?"

Iosef smiled a little and said simply, "You will see, Varanus."

Varanus hesitated for a moment.

"My lord," she said, "if I may crave your attention for a moment, there is something I must discuss with you."

"Can it wait until after the hunt?" Iosef asked.

"I would prefer now," Varanus replied. "It is a matter of some urgency."

"Of course," Iosef said. "Luka, if you would be so good, see to it that the horses are ready."

Luka nodded and took the elephant guns from both of them.

Iosef turned back to Varanus and asked, "What is it that concerns you?"

"I have just received a letter from France," Varanus said. "My grandfather has died."

Iosef nodded but said nothing.

"My father begs me to return," Varanus continued, "to help him settle the estate. I ask you permission to leave."

"You have it," Iosef said. "You may leave first thing in the morning, if you wish. Ekaterine will go with you, of course." He looked at Ekaterine, who nodded in agreement. "And I will send Luka as well. He is accustomed to traveling in Europe."

"Thank you, my lord," Varanus said.

"No need," Iosef said. "We Shashavani, of all people, understand the importance of family. You will leave in the morning, but tonight, we must hunt. If the wolves are not broken now, no one in the valley will be safe."

Varanus rode out with the soldiers into the cold, moonlit night. She rode with Iosef at the head of the company, with Luka and Ekaterine following close behind. Before them ran a dozen hounds, tremendous creatures the size of mastiffs with thick fur coats and fearsome jaws. Varanus thought them powerful enough to slaughter the wolves on their own.

The hounds had caught the scent even before leaving the castle grounds, and now they led the hunting party across the fields of snow toward the forest. Varanus understood the urgency of the hunt. The forest was old and thickly wooded. If the wolves were allowed to ensconce themselves among the trees, there would be no getting rid of them.

"Luka!" Iosef shouted as they neared the forest. "Continue on with the dogs! I will take a third of the men and flank our quarry! God willing, you will be able to drive them against us!"

"As you wish, my lord!" Luka answered. "God be with you!"

Iosef sounded his hunting horn and motioned for one of the three groups of riders to follow him. Varanus turned her horse to keep pace while Ekaterine remained with Luka. Varanus and Iosef plunged into the dark forest with their soldiers close behind them.

Varanus rode for what seemed like an age, onward through brush and branches. She heard the barking of the hounds and the howling of the wolves, but she could see neither. Somehow Iosef kept them on course, tracking both their allies and their quarry seemingly by sound alone.

The forest was dark around them, the thick canopy of branches blotting out all but a trickle of moonlight that painted everything in a spider web of silver. In the muddled shadows, Varanus's senses began to play tricks on her. She half fancied that she could smell something unwholesome in the air, that she heard something running all but silently alongside them. Once or twice she even thought that she glimpsed it out of the corner of her eye—a hulking, misshapen thing running along on all fours—but each time she turned to look, there was nothing.

Finally, Iosef held up his hand and called the command to "Halt!"

The riders pulled their horses around and stopped. Varanus did likewise. To her astonishment, she realized that they had somehow passed their prey. The barking of the dogs and the howling of the wolves now came from the same direction, moving steadily toward them.

"Ready yourselves!" Iosef shouted, drawing the elephant gun from a scabbard by his saddle.

Varanus drew her own weapon as the soldiers readied their rifles. They fanned out into a mounted firing line, long and curved to envelope the wolves when they arrived. Varanus braced her gun against her shoulder and waited, stomach knotted with anticipation.

The noise of the wolves and the dogs grew louder and louder until finally the shape of the pack appeared from the darkness before them. The pack of wolves was larger than any Varanus had seen before, larger than any pack that should have been possible in nature. Dozens upon dozens of lean, ferocious wolves, haggard and hungry looking, surged toward them in a wave of teeth and fur.

"Fire!" came Iosef's command.

The soldiers opened fire into the oncoming wolves, shooting round after round with discipline and precision that would have made an English officer proud. The first rank of wolves broke almost immediately, but the next came on, and the one after that. Soon the wolves were all around them, snarling and snapping. The horses reared and kicked, two of them unseating their riders. The hapless men fell screaming into the mass of wolves. More men were grabbed and dragged down by the beasts massed around them.

Her weapon empty, Varanus lashed out at the wolves, swinging the elephant gun like a cudgel. She struck and kicked at the howling mass until she could see only blood and fur and teeth. Suddenly, the hounds appeared from the darkness with Luka's riders behind them and smashed into the wolf pack. The animals went mad, wolves and dogs tearing at one another viciously. The soldiers fired round after round into the wolves as they enveloped the pack.

Varanus's eyes caught movement in the darkness, and she turned to look in its direction. A creature emerged from the shadows, a towering mass of fur and muscle. First, it walked on all fours, but when it stormed into the fray, it did so on its hind legs in a dreadful aping of a man. Jaws split wide in a hideous snarl, the beast lashed out with its claws, tearing man, dog, and horse to pieces with equal impunity. Varanus's breath caught in her throat as the creature turned toward her and fixed her with an unwavering stare.

It was almost identical to the beast that had assaulted her and Korbinian in grandfather's forest twenty-five years ago.

At her side, Iosef fired both barrels of his weapon at the beast. The sound of the weapon was almost deafening, easily heard even over the noise of the fray. Iosef's shoulder shifted backward ever so slightly from the force of the shot, but he showed no sign of pain.

The beast roared as the massive bullets tore into its flesh. It turned to look at Iosef and dropped to all fours, preparing to pounce. Varanus snapped her gun open and shoved a new round into the breech. Rather than waste the time to raise the weapon, she fired from the hip. The shot hit the beast in mid-lunge, just below the collarbone. It was knocked sideways and stumbled, crushing one of the dogs beneath its bulk as it lost its balance. It was up again in an instant, but now, bleeding and doubtless in pain, it seemed to recognize that the tide had turned against it. While neither the rifle bullets of the soldiers nor the teeth of the dogs could do it any real hurt, the shots of the elephant guns had inflicted terrible wounds.

Roaring, the beast turned and dove back into the forest.

"Luka!" Iosef shouted. "Their master flees! I must pursue! Break the wolves now!"

Luka, armed with revolver and sword for close quarters, looked up and nodded.

"As you wish, my lord!" he called back. "God preserve you!"

Iosef turned his horse and gave chase to the beast. Without hesitation, Varanus kicked her horse and headed off in pursuit. The beast in

France had been no isolated phenomenon, and now Iosef went to kill its twin as if nothing were out of place.

Varanus would have her answers, monsters be damned.

She rode after Iosef through the darkened wood, pushing her horse hard to keep up with him. It was not a matter of speed but of maneuver, for though they easily outpaced the beast, it gave them a wild chase, dashing this way and that through the trees. More than once Varanus lost track of it, only to see it run across her path from the opposite direction.

At last, she and Iosef broke out into a clearing. The full moon shone brightly above them, lighting the snow with a bright glow. Varanus pulled her horse to a stop and turned about in the saddle.

Where had the beast gone? They had been close upon its heels for so long, and now it had vanished.

She watched Iosef reload his gun. He looked at her and said:

"You are wondering where our quarry has gone."

"I am," Varanus said.

Iosef sniffed the air and replied, "It is here. Somewhere." He paused. "And another."

"Two?" Varanus asked. She sniffed the air as well, but she smelled little but cold and snow. There was a faint hint of the beast's pungent musk, but it was too weak for her to locate its source. "Are you certain?"

"Completely," Iosef said. "They are hidden in the brush nearby, but I cannot determine where."

"What are we to do?" Varanus asked.

"We must kill them," Iosef said. "If they escape alive, they will return with a new pack in a few years. If we kill them, the valley will be safe for a generation."

"You know this?" Varanus asked.

"Indeed," Iosef said. "This incursion is no isolated occurrence. There have been many such attacks over the years, dating back long before my birth. The archives are filled with accounts of these creatures. Vanquished, they flee, only to return once they have gathered another host of wolves. Slain, the valley is left in peace for decades."

"That would suggest a prolonged maturation period," Varanus said, most intrigued by the idea. "Something comparable to humans, in fact."

"You will have to read Konstantine's treatise on them," Iosef said. "His research is extensive. The volumes are buried somewhere, but I will ask the archivists to find them for you."

"I would greatly appreciate that," Varanus said. She looked around the clearing, searching for the elusive beasts that lurked in the darkness. "What are we to do now?"

"Look at me," Iosef said.

Varanus turned back to him and asked, "Why?"

"The beasts cannot understand us, but they are intelligent." Iosef slid his gun back into its scabbard. "We must lull them into overconfidence. We must make them believe that we think ourselves alone."

"Of course," Varanus said, lowering her own weapon and placing it across her lap. "So that they will attack us."

"Precisely," Iosef said. "They are hunters by nature, and they mistake us for prey. We must cultivate that misconception."

Varanus studied Iosef for a little while, mulling over the germ of an idea. Placed within the context of a lure, certain points that had seemed strange to her now began to make sense.

"My lord," she said, "forgive me for speaking plainly, but you are not really Lady Sophio's sycophant, are you?"

Iosef looked at her curiously for a short time, and Varanus suddenly questioned whether she should have spoken. *Certainly not so candidly*, she decided, inwardly kicking herself. She had grown overly familiar with Iosef over the years. She had forgotten their respective places.

Iosef's laugh interrupted her.

"No, I am not," he said. "But I am flattered to know that you were fooled by it. Sophio's mind is so muddled by now that she is easy to mislead, and those Shashavani who are not with me are too focused on their studies to notice anything that I do. An outsider, however, is a true challenge. It pleases me to have passed that test."

"Why do such a thing?" Varanus asked. "I thought you loved her."

"I do," Iosef replied, "with all my heart. But love is not leaving a person in the grip of madness. I tried for many years to ease Sophio's mind, to bring her back to sanity. But she is too far gone, too enchanted by her own power. I realized long ago that the only way to cure her is to remove her from her throne. And that is the only way to save the House of Shashavani as well."

"You intend to overthrow her?" Varanus asked.

"I do," Iosef said. "You have seen the rest of our order. It is like the time of Basileios: they are too absorbed by their studies to notice the madness that sits upon the throne. All those with the will and charisma to replace her were killed or sent into exile centuries ago. Many are willing to see her removed, but only I am willing to act."

"Then why do you not act?" Varanus asked.

"Sophio is powerful, Varanus," Iosef said. "Far more powerful than I am. And she is no fool. I cannot raise the standard of rebellion before things are ready."

Varanus felt something shift in the wind. She eyed the trees cautiously. She saw nothing, but she sensed movement. The beasts were still there, and they were growing bold.

"She seems like a fool to me," Varanus said. "Forgive me if I speak out of turn, my lord, but her mind has gone from her."

Iosef shook his head and said, "Do not be mistaken about Sophio. Hers is one of the greatest minds the world has ever known, even now in the grip of madness. Indeed, it is her intelligence that has destroyed her sanity. It clouds her perception and overpowers her reason. She is misled by thoughts that are brilliant and yet have no bearing on anything of present concern. She remembers events from a thousand years ago with perfect clarity, but she forgets that they are not taking place today. She is blinded by her very genius."

"And that is the one weakness you can exploit," Varanus said.

"Indeed," Iosef said. He sniffed the air and smiled. "They are coming."

Varanus heard the snapping of branches from opposite sides of the clearing. She saw the trees behind Iosef flung aside as the wounded beast leapt from hiding and made for them. Twisting in the saddle, Varanus looked over her shoulder and saw a second beast, this one unharmed but its fur wet with fresh blood, charging from the darkness in her direction.

"Go to the right!" Iosef shouted. "Ride!"

Varanus turned her horse and kicked it hard. The creature, already frightened by the smell and sound of the beasts, needed little encouragement. It bolted for the trees, and Varanus pulled on the reins to force a turn and keep them in the clearing. She did not fancy her chances with the beast in the depths of the forest.

As she turned, she saw Iosef fire both barrels of his gun into the second beast as it charged him. The force of the recoil made him twist sideways, but he kept his seat. Both shots hit the beast in the chest, causing it to stumble and its charge to falter. It let out a howl and bounded away a few paces only to charge again. Iosef turned his horse and kicked it into a run, circling the clearing opposite to Varanus.

Try as she might, Varanus could not line up a proper shot on the beast pursuing her. Cursing aloud in French, she turned her horse and cut across the clearing toward the creature that pursued Iosef. As she came in range, Varanus fired twice in rapid succession. One shot hit, tearing a chunk of flesh from the beast's leg. It howled and fell as its leg gave way, and it tumbled over as its momentum carried it past its balance.

Varanus turned in the saddle to see if the second beast was still behind her. She saw that it had changed course as well and now rushed to intercept her from the front. Varanus turned to evade and saw the first beast loom up before her.

Damn! Damn! Damn!

Her weapon empty, she lashed out with the butt end and caught the beast on the brow. It was not enough. The beast's claws struck in two great swipes, and Varanus's horse all but disintegrated beneath her. Blood and meat erupted in her face, and fragments of bone tore through her clothes and body like shrapnel.

Varanus was not quite certain if she lost consciousness. Certainly, her fall was muddled and confused, but the impact of striking the frozen ground instantly brought her back around and forced the fog from her mind. She smelled the stench of the beasts clearly now, but she could see nothing. There was a painful weight suspended across her lower body, and she found that she could not feel one of her legs.

What remained of her horse had fallen on top of her. This made her angry. She had raised that horse from a foal. She *liked* that horse.

And why wouldn't her damn eyes open?

Varanus clawed at her face with her hands and felt drying blood everywhere. The gummy mass had caked over her eyelids, sealing them shut. She pulled and scratched until she could finally open them.

She saw the wounded beast looming over her, its jaws split apart in a hideous expression not unlike that of a man's smile. Breath like steam flowed from its mouth and nostrils, carrying with it the stench of old meat.

Varanus drew her howdah pistol and leveled it at the beast's face in a single motion. The beast proved the quicker, and before she could fire, it struck her arm with a heavy sweep of its forepaw. The pistol tumbled out of her grip, and the beast's claws tore her arm and hand to pieces. Varanus let out a cry of pain and rage.

No! she thought, snarling like an animal. *I will not be eaten by the likes of you!*

The beast roared back at her. A moment later, Iosef's elephant gun sounded, and the beast shuddered. Whining in pain, it turned away from Varanus and toward Iosef, who rode atop his horse midway across the clearing, still pursued by the other creature.

The moment's distraction was all that Varanus required. Her right arm was useless—nothing below the elbow would move—but her left still obeyed her. Rolling onto her side, she felt around half-blindly, searching for the howdah pistol that lay somewhere in the snow nearby.

The beast above her, now half-engaged by Iosef, hesitated and took a few stumbling steps toward him. Its mangled leg would not cooperate, however, and it seemed to realize the futility of the effort. Varanus saw it turn back toward her, and her fingers scrabbled in the snow, desperately seeking her weapon.

Damn it, where is it?

Suddenly, she felt the back of her hand brush the smooth wood of the pistol grip. She grabbed it just as the beast turned back toward her. As it dove in for the kill, she shoved the howdah pistol against its throat and pulled both triggers.

The recoil of the shot hit Varanus in the chest, knocking the wind from her. The bullets tore through the soft flesh beneath the beast's skull and burst out the back of its head in a shower of brain and bone. It let out a surprised gasp, little more than a wheeze, and stared into Varanus's eyes. It looked genuinely surprised, far more like a man than an animal. Then the light in its eyes faded, and it collapsed atop her.

Exhausted and bloody, Varanus stared into the sky and tried to block out the pain that filled her body. A shape loomed over her, obscuring the moon.

It was Korbinian.

"Resting, *liebchen?*" he asked.

"I am in agony," Varanus said.

"That is because you should be dead," Korbinian said. He smiled. "I am glad that you are not."

"As am I," Varanus replied.

"Tell me, *liebchen*, what has become of the Russian?" Korbinian asked.

"He is—" Varanus began.

The second beast!

A burst of adrenaline coursed through her body as this realization struck. She quickly sat up and gasped at the pain of movement. Several of her ribs were broken, and she suspected internal bleeding. She turned her head and spat blood.

Definitely internal bleeding.

No matter, she would heal.

Varanus looked across the field and saw Iosef still leading the second beast on a merry chase in the moonlight. But even at that distance, Varanus could tell that his horse was tiring and the beast was not.

I must help him!

Varanus squirmed against the ground, struggling to pull herself free from the mound of bodies that pinned her. One leg was shattered; she could feel as much. The other ached from cracked bones, but it still responded. Kicking violently, she managed to free it from the dead weight of the corpses.

Across the clearing, she saw Iosef kick his feet out of the stirrups and climb atop his saddle, bobbing up and down like a cork upon a stormy sea. Varanus was astonished to see him keep his balance.

Iosef drew a pair of revolvers from beneath his coat and leveled them at the beast pursuing him. As the tree line neared, he leapt into the air and began shooting, emptying the revolvers as quickly as they could fire. The bullets struck the beast and tumbled away, seemingly without impact, but the attack made it look up. Iosef's horse fled into the trees, forgotten.

At the height of his jump, Iosef threw the revolvers aside and drew a pair of long daggers from his belt. He tucked his body into a ball and dove feet-first toward the beast, which rose onto its hind legs and spread its arms and jaws to greet him.

Varanus watched his descent with wide eyes, her breath caught in her throat.

Was Iosef mad? To attack such a creature with *knives* was suicide!

A moment later, Iosef struck the beast full in the chest and brought his daggers down into its flesh. The beast roared and dug its claws deep into Iosef's back. The two of them tumbled into a heap of writhing, bleeding fury.

Certain of Iosef's doom, Varanus kicked at the remains of her horse, which still pinned her other leg. Her bloody boot slipped against the leather of her saddle as she struggled to gain some leverage. Finally it found purchase, and Varanus pushed hard with her good leg. With the burning of broken bones and torn flesh, her dead leg finally slid free from beneath the heap of corpses.

She looked toward Iosef and the second beast, but she could make little of them. Their fight was confused and bloody, and in the poor light, Varanus could not tell which, if either, had the advantage. Neither claws nor teeth nor steel flashed in the moonlight; they were too thickly covered by blood to make any reflection.

Damn him, he will not die! Varanus thought. *My grandfather! My horse! But not my mentor!*

But what could she do to aid him? She could not walk nor could she fire her elephant gun with only one hand. The howdah pistol. It would have to do, though she feared for its accuracy at such a range.

Rolling onto her side, Varanus grabbed the weapon and forced it open. Her pouch of cartridges had spilled all over the ground in her fall, and it took her a moment to find two fresh rounds.

Reloading, she began to crawl across the bloodstained snow toward the fight. She saw vicious wounds on both the beast and Iosef, wounds that cut all the way to the bone in places. One great swipe from the beast tore half of Iosef's beautiful face away, though Varanus counted it a miracle that the blow did not kill him. Iosef, shouting war cries in the Svanish tongue, stabbed and tore at the beast's flesh with no thought for his own safety.

He means to die! Varanus thought. *And to take the beast with him in his death throws!*

She would not have that.

Breathing hard, Varanus crawled closer and closer to the fight, ignoring each ache and shudder that wracked her body. She should be dead by now, but she lived.

Halfway to the fight, Varanus's arm gave out, and she collapsed into the snow. She could crawl no further. Sucking in fresh air, she let out a scream of anger and shoved her dead arm in front of her. At least it could still serve as a gun brace in its crippled state.

Leveling the howdah pistol, Varanus waited until she was certain the beast stood the nearer to her. She saw Iosef fall to the ground, his body torn and bloody and exposed to the bone in many places. The beast reared up and howled in triumph.

"No!" Varanus shouted as she fired.

The howdah pistol bucked in her hand, but her aim was true. Both bullets struck the beast in its lower back, tearing into its thick hide. The beast roared again and turned toward Varanus. Jaws gaping, it snarled at her as if to say, "You are next."

Iosef rose from the ground in a blur of rent and bloody flesh. He grabbed the beast by the jaw and pulled down hard, forcing its head to one side and exposing its neck. He raised his dagger high into the air and plunged it deep into the beast's throat.

Blood sprayed into the air. Iosef had struck the artery. The beast howled and struggled, but Iosef held it fast, kicking its legs out from beneath it to keep it restrained. Hungrily, Iosef pressed his mouth against the geyser of blood and drank deeply. Soon the beast's struggle weakened as it teetered on the edge of unconsciousness. Its claws lashed out for Iosef but found only the dirt and snow beneath it. Finally, its eyes rolled back into its head, and it went still with a feeble whine.

Iosef threw the beast to the ground and stood, suddenly revitalized. He wiped his mouth on the back of his hand and stretched as his flesh began to knit together. His bones reformed and set with audible cracks as he walked toward Varanus. He brushed back his hair with one hand as the skin regrew across his face, leaving neither mark nor scar. By the time he reached Varanus, his body was whole, pale and beautiful in the moonlight, though still wet with blood. His clothes, now little more than tatters, draped about him like the shroud of some gothic king.

"Well done," Varanus," he said, kneeling beside her. "I thank you for your assistance."

"I only returned the favor, my lord," Varanus said weakly.

Iosef gently scooped Varanus into his arms and carried her toward the corpse of the second beast.

"Come," he said. "The creatures have fed recently. Their blood is hearty and strong. Drink of what remains, and you will be whole again."

Now that the fighting was done, Varanus felt the adrenaline ebbing from her. She wanted nothing but to sleep for an eternity. The prospect of drinking from the beast did not appeal to her.

"You have already done so," she said to him, as she rested her head against his shoulder. "Can I not drink of you?"

"You know you cannot, Varanus," Iosef replied. "You know that our blood is poison to each other as it is to mortals. Besides, we are not cannibals, are we?"

"Speak for yourself," Varanus answered weakly.

Iosef laughed at this. Reaching the beast, he set her down beside it and lifted its head for her. It had nearly bled out, but there remained enough blood for the task. Varanus drank from the wound, slowly at first but with increasing eagerness. The richness of the blood was incredible, like venison compared to beef.

As the warmth of life filled her, Varanus felt the ache of her bones reforming, the prickling of new tissue closing her wounds. Soon the exhaustion was gone, and she felt invigorated again.

When her leg had reformed enough for her to stand, Iosef offered her his hand and helped her up.

"You did well tonight, Varanus," he said. "Very well indeed."

"Thank you, my lord," Varanus said. She frowned. "Though I am not pleased about my horse. *And* my hat is gone. Crushed beneath it, I should think."

"A tragedy," Iosef said. "I am certain Ekaterine will mourn its loss with you."

Varanus scoffed and said, "She will insist upon celebration!"

"Indeed," Iosef said.

He whistled loudly, and a minute later his horse appeared from the forest, trotting across the clearing to reach its master. Iosef took it gently by the reins and stroked its head, murmuring to calm it. Once the horse was steady, he swung up into the saddle.

"Come Varanus," he said, offering her his hand. "Let us go home."

"I will gladly go anywhere that a warm bath awaits me," Varanus replied, taking his hand and climbing up behind him.

She wrapped her arms around Iosef's waist and held on as he urged his horse back into the woods in the direction of the dogs. What a night it had been, she thought. Tragedy, violence, sorrow, and blood. And yet, she felt more alive than ever.

But one thought worried her even in the midst of victory. The beast that had attacked her and Korbinian was not some lone anomaly. There were more like it, many more it seemed. And far spread enough to be in both France and in Georgia. What were they? How could specimens have appeared in two such distant places without being recorded by science?

These were questions she would answer, she decided, once the awful business of France was concluded.

CHAPTER TWENTY-SIX

Normandy, France

It was the better part of two weeks before Varanus was able to depart for France. The delay was partly the result of packing and preparations, which included securing passage on a ship and obtaining the appropriate stock of foreign currency for the journey. But this was exacerbated by Sophio, who for eight days refused to allow anyone to depart from the valley on account of her conviction that foreign invaders—either the Mongols or the Turks depending on the day—had occupied the Georgian lowlands and were about to lay siege to Svaneti.

When this latest veil of madness lifted, it was like every such incident that Varanus had seen over the years: Sophio denied any knowledge of it and even berated several of the Shashavani who continued to prepare for war on her prior instructions. Varanus secretly wished that Iosef's rebellion would take place in her absence so that she could return home from her business in France to a household of sanity and order.

Despite this delay, the journey to France passed quickly, seemingly in no time at all as Varanus kept herself locked in her cabin, poring over some research notes with her customary indifference to the passage of day and night. When they finally arrived at their destination, she found Normandy as she remembered it, quaint and rustic.

The Varanus household had not changed either, save for the advancing years of the servants. Old Proust had retired in her absence, but Varanus was pleased to discover that Vatel had been advanced as butler in his place. Cook was the same as she had always been, though older now and with far more wrinkles. Varanus's old lady's maid had been let go after her departure, but Father's and even Grandfather's valets remained in the house.

Varanus knew that the servants were astonished by her continued youth, even now, fifteen years after her departure. Only Vatel said anything, remarking simply that she looked "exceedingly well in light of the passing years," if she would pardon him for saying so.

No one seemed to know what to make of Luka and Ekaterine. This did not surprise Varanus. Though they traveled in the guise of servants, Varanus could not bring herself to treat them as such. Indeed, it was only at Ekaterine's insistence that they took their meals with the household staff instead of with Varanus. It would not do, she said, to appear too out of place. The locals would already regard them as peculiar for being foreign.

It did not surprise Varanus to learn that Father was bedridden. She went to him first thing upon arriving. The man she found was a shadow of himself, which was saying something quite significant as he had always been a shadow of Grandfather. Father simply looked *old*, older even than Grandfather had looked at that age. His hair had passed from gray almost to white, and his face, worn and heavily lined, looked exhausted. It was as though he had given up altogether and was simply waiting for the inevitable end. Grandfather's death was clearly too much for him to bear.

It did not take Varanus long to see that the longed-for end would be soon in coming. Pneumonia, she realized. He must have suffered a severe chill during the winter. And coupled with the shock of Grandfather's death, it had, no doubt, grown unchecked into its present state. Varanus knew by the end of the first night that there would be no saving him. Indeed, it was a miracle that he had lingered on so long.

She felt sorrow at this realization, but it was dulled by a sort of forlorn acceptance. So many had died already: a mother she had never met, siblings taken in infancy or childhood, dearest Korbinian and their Alistair, Grandfather.… One more seemed the inevitable outcome. And Father looked so *tired*. All he seemed to want was peace.

Varanus sat with him as much as she could, though it was strained. They spoke little for there was little to say. What could Varanus tell him of her new life? She had little interest in the affairs of Society, and by now Father had fallen out of touch with it. The one thing that Varanus could discuss for hours on end—medicine—passed Father's understanding like a bird flying over a horse.

So they sat in silence, Varanus watching Father as he tried to sleep. They passed two days in this manner, with Varanus taking her meals in the room and helping him with his—though Father ate almost nothing.

Toward midnight on the second day, Varanus heard Father murmuring something to her. It was the first he had spoken in hours.

"Yes, Father?" Varanus asked.

Father felt for her hand and held it in both of his. Varanus could feel his bones through the skin. The touch made him seem even more withered.

"Babette," Father said. His voice caught in his throat, and he coughed violently. "Babette, I fear it will not be much longer."

"Hush, Father," Varanus said, though she knew it to be true. "Do not say such things."

"I am not afraid," Father said. "Soon I will be with your mother again." He smiled weakly.

"I know, Father," Varanus said. "Shall I fetch the priest?"

"I think so, yes," Father said. "It will please him. I have no doubt that Heaven will receive me, Last Rites or no, but receiving them is a final act of kindness I would like to bestow."

"Of course," Varanus said.

She leaned over and kissed Father's brow. She could almost taste the illness. She blinked away a tear and stood.

"I will return soon," she said.

When she had left, William pushed open a door concealed behind the bookcase and entered the bedroom. He sniffed the air. The room smelled of death, which was only to be expected. In light of recent events, he was grateful for his foresight in having the house riddled with concealed doors and passages. They had always made it easier for the servants to get about without making a sight of themselves in front of company, but having faked his death, it was now important for him to do just the same. He was too old now to remain as a man. The change was too pronounced to hide any longer. But with the hostility of the des Louveteaux still tainting his dealings with the Scions of France, it was important for him to keep a personal eye on the matters of his household.

Babette had returned home, no doubt drawn by news of his alleged death. This gave William pause. He had not expected that, though it did please him.

He approached the bed and looked down at his son.

Poor James, he thought. What a poor, pathetic creature his son had proven to be. Unworthy of his Scion blood, scarcely worthy of being called a man, and yet…

William sighed. He should have despised his son, despised him for his weakness. But he could not. For all of James's adult life, William had borne the knowledge that his son was a failure—a failure as a Scion of course, for no amount of wealth or social standing would ever elevate a human above the status of meat. The others of their race had taunted him time and again for James's frailty, for his humanity. William had suffered it all without complaint.

Now, as his son lay dying, William finally understood why. He had always thought that his toleration of James was a matter of misguided pride. James was *his* son and no one else's. It was for *him* to decide whether James lived or died, and he, William Varanus, chose to allow the runt to live.

But it was not pride that had stayed his hand. It was not pride that had kept him from arranging an accident to settle the matter.

No, it was not pride. It was love. He *loved* his son, whatever his frailties.

William leaned down and kissed James on the forehead, just as he had done when James was a child. James stirred a little, but his eyes remained closed, his breathing shallow and labored.

"James, my boy," William said, "No matter what else you are, you are my son. I love you. And I forgive you for your humanity."

Father was laid to rest later that week. The whole village turned out to share condolences, and several of the neighboring potentates were in attendance as well. It would have been a touching sight, but Varanus could not bring herself to see the display as anything but pageantry. The des Louveteaux were there as well, circling like vultures. No doubt they believed that with Father and Grandfather gone, the family holdings would be easy pickings. Varanus meant to dispel them of that belief.

The day was overcast and dreary, threatening rain at some point in the near future. It felt appropriate to have such dismal weather for an equally dismal occasion. And it was a godsend to Varanus, for the concealed sun, combined with the heavy veil that mourning allowed her to wear, left her free to walk about in daytime without fear of injury or public distress.

All of the servants were in attendance, dressed in somber black with matching gloves. Luka kept back from the crowd, watching everyone for signs of danger. It was good of him to take such precautions, but Varanus thought it unlikely that anyone would have the poor taste to disrupt a funeral with violence. More likely, the des Louveteaux would try to poison her in her sleep once they realized that she planned to reject their offer to buy her family's holdings.

Ekaterine was at her side, holding an umbrella above them both in case the sky saw fit to make its threats of rain materialize. It was comforting to have Ekaterine there, Varanus reflected. It reminded her that she was not alone.

She blinked away a tear as she watched Father's coffin being lowered into the earth beside his wife's gave. She felt Ekaterine place a hand on her arm.

"At least he is at peace now," Ekaterine said. "That is something."

"It is something," Varanus agreed without much enthusiasm. Father might be in Heaven, but until Heaven could be quantified, Varanus would not hold her breath waiting for it.

She looked across the small family cemetary and saw Alfonse watching her. He smiled at her. Varanus recognized that look: hungry and triumphant. She looked forward to disappointing him. Alfonse's high collar concealed his throat, but more than once he tugged at it, revealing the hint of a jagged scar. Varanus smiled. No matter what, Alfonse would bear that mark for the rest of his life.

The coffin finally reached the bottom of the grave, and Varanus approached slowly. She stood at the edge in silence for a short while. This was it. The end of her family. The end of her line. Grandfather was dead. Father was dead. Alistair was dead. She was the last Norman Varanus. Grandfather's line would end with her.

The family in England would fight for control of the holdings, just like Grandfather's neighbors in France. The English Varanuses had exiled Grandfather, but they still saw him as one of them—or more precisely, they saw his property as theirs. And she knew what they saw in her, what they all saw in her: a small, frightened woman, alone in the world, with a husband too busy fighting for the Tsar in Asia to attend her father's funeral.

She took a handful of dirt and threw it onto the coffin. Let them come. Let them try to take it from her. She would fight them all, and she would win.

Varanus looked away from the grave, toward the mausoleum where Grandfather had been interred. His will had been very specific about that. It seemed that in his old age, Grandfather had become obsessed with the idea of premature burial. Even the door to the mausoleum had been designed to allow opening from within as well as without. Such eccentricity seemed so unlike Grandfather, but Varanus acknowledged that people could change dramatically in fifteen years.

She saw a figure standing by the mausoleum, watching the proceedings. He was tall and handsome, beautiful even, with fiery red hair and the same vulpine features Korbinian had possessed. He wore a uniform that Varanus recognized immediately: the sharp black-on-red of a Fuchsburger hussar.

"Korbinian…?" Varanus whispered in disbelief.

Aside from the color of his hair, the man looked exactly like him.

"Yes, *liebchen?*" Korbinian asked, appearing at her side. He leaned over and kissed her on the cheek. "Be strong, my love. This will all be over soon."

Varanus looked at him, then back at the man by the mausoleum.

"If you are here, then who is that?" she asked softly.

Korbinian looked at the young man and stroked his chin as if deep in thought.

"He rather looks like me, doesn't he?" he asked. "Perhaps a few years older than I was, but near enough. But of course, how can I be in two places at once? And with red hair. That is simply ridiculous. My mother had red hair. You have red hair. But I took after my father in that regard."

"Stop speaking in riddles," Varanus said. "Who is he? That is *your* uniform."

"It is the uniform of Fuchsburg," Korbinian corrected. He placed his hands on her shoulders and kissed the top of her head. "You know exactly who he is, *liebchen*."

Alistair.

"It's not possible," Varanus whispered.

"Neither am I, *liebchen*," Korbinian said. "And yet, here I stand."

"Our son," Varanus said. "Alive."

"So it would seem," Korbinian said.

"Grandfather has much to answer for," Varanus said.

Korbinian kissed her on the cheek. "What a pity he is not here to answer."

"It is inconvenient," Varanus murmured.

"Death often is."

"What should we do?" Varanus asked.

"First," Korbinian replied, "we wait until the funeral is done. Then we speak to our son and find out where he has been all this time."

The strange man remained at the corner of the mausoleum throughout the rest of the funeral proceedings. Varanus waited until the dreadful ceremony was finished. A number of people came forward to offer their condolences with sincere, if uncertain, words. What could they say to relieve such loss?

The des Louveteaux were among the first to approach, led by old Louis with Alfonse following a step behind. Louis's beard was full and thick, gray in color just like Grandfather's had been. Even Alfonse had grown one in the years since Varanus last saw him. There was something altogether unwholesome about the cluster of ravenous-eyed, dark clothed men who approached her with expressions of the most insincere sympathy. Their eyes said everything. They thought that she was weak. They looked at her like mongrel dogs contemplating a meal.

“Lady Shashavani,” Louis said to her, biting the words. He was angry that she had been elevated above his station.

“Lord des Louveteaux,” Varanus replied. “Thank you for coming. I know that my father would have been touched to know that your family was in attendance.”

“But of course,” Louis said. “Your family has been a pillar of society since your grandfather arrived on our shores.”

A veiled insult that put her family’s respectability to a mere three generations.

“Very kind of you to say,” Varanus replied.

“Well, we must all support one another, mustn’t we?” Louis said.

“I recall that was Christ’s advice,” Varanus replied.

“When it comes time to manage the affairs of your family’s estate, I would be most pleased to offer my assistance,” Louis said. “I know the task of settling your inheritance must be daunting, especially at such a time.”

Varanus held back a laugh.

“It is very kind of you to offer, Lord des Louveteaux,” she said, “but I believe that my grandfather’s solicitors will explain it all to me.”

Not that it required much explaining. Varanus suspected that she understood it all better than the solicitors, but it would not do to make such a thing known. A woman of means who understood her own finances? God forbid.

“Of course,” Louis said. “But should you require anything in these trying times, my family will always be here for you.”

Korbinian peered at Louis from the side and shook his head.

“He really is a *schwein*, isn’t he?” he asked.

“You are too kind,” Varanus said to Louis, ignoring Korbinian. He was right, though. Louis was an absolute swine, all but leering in triumph.

“What a pity that your husband could not accompany you,” Louis said.

“Alas, he was in Khiva when word arrived,” Varanus said. “I was obliged to travel without him.”

“It must be very difficult for you to bear all this alone,” Alfonse said, interjecting. His voice sounded peculiar, higher than Varanus remembered it. Perhaps the throat injury from Sedan had affected him more severely than Varanus realized.

“One perseveres,” Varanus said.

“How very English of you.” Louis smiled and gave her a curt nod. “Well, our prayers are with you, Lady Shashavani. Good day.”

“Good day,” Varanus replied.

As the des Louveteaux withdrew, Ekaterine leaned in and murmured, "They are going to be trouble."

"I know," Varanus replied softly. "But once the estate is settled, there will be little they can do."

She glanced toward the mausoleum. The young man was gone, vanished into the crowd. Varanus searched for the scarlet among the black, but she could not see it. Had he even existed?

"Of course," Ekaterine said. "And fear not, Doctor. If they push too hard, Luka and I know what to do."

"And what is that?" Varanus asked absently, as the next group of mourners approached.

"We kill them," Ekaterine said.

CHAPTER TWENTY-SEVEN

Friedrich von Fuchsburg watched the des Louveteaux walk toward the graveyard gate. Such arrogant creatures! They were little more than murders and thieves, but they had the audacity to regard themselves as nobility. They strutted about like they already owned the place. And that fiend Alfonse... Had he looked like that the night he murdered Friedrich's father?

Friedrich slipped through the crowd, hunched slightly to keep himself hidden. He doubted that it had much effect—dressed as he was in bright red and standing six and a half feet tall—but he did not want to spook them until they were too close to escape.

He cast a look over his shoulder at the tiny woman standing by the grave. The men in town said that she was Babette Varanus, daughter of the late James Varanus. But that was impossible. Babette Varanus had died twenty-four years ago.

Hadn't she?

No matter. Friedrich had other things to attend to first.

He stepped out of the crowd a few paces from the des Louveteaux and rose to his full height. Walking in an arc, he flanked them so that he could come around from the front and intercept them at the gate.

He had dreamed about this moment for years, but how would it play out? How would his father's killer react?

To his great satisfaction, Alfonse des Louveteaux glanced toward him, at first dismissive, and suddenly stopped short. The old patriarch, Louis, the Count des Louveteaux, halted as well, and the rest of the family stopped behind him.

Alfonse stared at Friedrich, his eyes almost bulging. Friedrich smiled. He had always been told that he was the perfect image of his father. Apparently it was true. What must it be like for a murderer to be confronted by the very face of his victim?

"Who are you?" Louis demanded. "Get out of my way!"

Friedrich motioned for Louis to walk around him saying, "You may pass, old man. I have no quarrel with you."

"How dare—" Louis began, his face turning bright red with anger.

Friedrich turned to Alfonse and approached until he was only a half step away. Looking him in the eyes, Friedrich gave Alfonse a curt nod and said:

"Good day, Colonel des Louveteaux. My name is Friedrich Korbinian Leopold Freiherr von Fuchsburg. You murdered my father."

"What...?" Alfonse stammered.

He took a step back, but Friedrich advanced to match it.

"I demand satisfaction, Colonel," Friedrich said. "I demand a duel for the sake of my family's honor."

"Honor?" Alfonse asked. "Why...why, your father was killed trying to murder me!"

Alfonse backed away another step and again Friedrich advanced. Friedrich sensed the other des Louveteaux men circling around him. It was wise that he had confronted them in public. Without the crowd watching, they would likely have murdered him.

"Lies," Friedrich said. "And you know that they are lies. Now, if you are a gentleman, you will consent to fight me."

"A gentleman?" Alfonse looked astonished.

"Are you not familiar with the word?" Friedrich asked, taunting.

Alfonse bared his teeth and snarled, "I will not fight the likes of you, and certainly not for the honor of a disgraced murderer like your father!"

Friedrich paused. He had never really anticipated a refusal. He assumed that Alfonse's guilt, shame, and arrogance would be enough to goad him into a fight. Still, a von Fuchsburg was not a von Fuchsburg if he could not improvise.

"Very well," he said. "Then I shall give you provocation."

So saying, he spat in Alfonse's face. Alfonse let out a cry and clapped a hand over his eye.

"You damned German bastard!" Alfonse shouted.

"There," Friedrich said. "I spit upon you and upon your family. When you are prepared to defend your honor, you may send word of your challenge to me at the Hôtel Rollo in town. I will be staying there until you decide to become a man."

Alfonse lunged at him, snarling like an animal. Friedrich drew back a step and reached for his sword. If he could kill the fiend here and now, clearly in self-defense...

"Stop!" Louis snapped.

Alfonse froze and slowly looked toward his father, twitching with contained energy. Friedrich knew the expression on his face: it was the look of a man who, in that instant, knew nothing but violence.

"You will hear from us, Baron von Fuchsburg," Louis said. "You will soon have great cause to regret this insult."

"The Hôtel Rollo," Friedrich repeated.

He stepped around Alfonse and walked back toward the gravesite, leaving the des Louveteaux behind him. The first step to his revenge had been accomplished. Now all he had to do was kill Alfonse.

Alfonse watched Friedrich walk away. He was seething with rage, every instinct telling him to chase down the impudent boy and rend him to pieces. But his father's hand on his shoulder was all it took to keep him restrained.

"I will kill him," he growled.

"Perhaps," Louis said softly. "But if he truly is who he claims to be, I wonder if it would be best to deal with him in a more efficient manner."

"What do you mean, Father?" Alfonse asked.

"He may only be human, but we do not know what he is capable of," Louis said. "I would prefer not to take the chance of a duel, nor do I see any reason to pollute our family's dignity by pandering to his ego. And besides, if all of his family is as mad as he, we might have a legion of vengeful von Fuchsburgs crawling out of the woodwork after you kill him."

Alfonse bowed his head subserviently and gave a whine of consent.

"What would you prefer, Father?"

"Let us rouse Gérard," Louis said. "The Baron von Fuchsburg stikes me as the sort of man who rides wherever he goes. If he were to be set upon by a wild animal while on the road… Well, it would be unfortunate but of no great concern to anyone. And there would be no reason for a relative to come and seek revenge against us."

Alfonse smiled and took a deep breath.

"That sounds very wise, Father," he said. "I will make the arrangements."

Friedrich waited for the crowd to disperse before he approached Lady Shashavani. He spent the time pondering what he should say to her. Was she really the daughter of James Varanus? She had to be, of course. Why else was she there, the grieving sole survivor of the family? But how could she be Babette Varanus?

How could she be alive?

As the mourners drifted away, Friedrich approached and bowed. The Lady Shashavani turned to look at him, her face concealed behind a heavy veil. They stood there, watching each other in silence for a time.

The woman next to Lady Shashavani looked from one to the other but said nothing. She silently withdrew a step.

"Well," Varanus finally said.

"Well," Friedrich agreed. "Is it true? Are you truly Babette Varanus?"

"I have not been Babette Varanus for some time," Varanus said. "I am the Lady Shashavani now."

"Of course," Friedrich said. He hesitated. This confrontation was not one that he had expected. He did not know what to say. "Do you know who I am?"

He thought he heard Varanus catch her breath.

"Yes," she said softly. "Alistair."

Something about the name made Friedrich pause. No one had ever called him that before, he was certain; but for some reason it resonated with him. It was so familiar.

"No," he said. "No, I am Friedrich Korbinian Leopold von Fuchsburg."

"Alistair," Varanus insisted.

"Why do I know that name?" Friedrich asked.

"Because that is what I named you when you were born," Varanus replied. "Because you are my son."

Mother, Friedrich thought. It was she. He *knew* that it was she.

"I was told that you died," Friedrich said.

"Who said such a thing?" Varanus asked. There was a hint of anger in her voice.

"My aunt, Ilse," Friedrich said.

Why would Auntie have lied about such a thing? But then, she had always regarded him as her own. Perhaps Aunt Ilse's maternal care had been more calculating than charitable.

"It seems your aunt and my grandfather have much to answer for," Varanus said. "Alas, neither of them is here."

"Why did you never come to find me?" Friedrich asked.

"I was told *you* had died," Varanus replied. "I suspect that we were both deceived."

"So it would seem," Friedrich said.

"How have you come to be here?" Varanus asked. "How did you arrive in time for the funeral? And why did you not send word to the house?"

"When I left Fuchsburg, your father was still alive," Friedrich said. "Word arrived of my great-grandfather's death and of my grandfather's illness. I departed immediately, but I arrived the day after my grandfather's death." He cast a glance toward the grave. "Until the funeral, I had no reason to believe that you were alive. I assumed myself to be the only surviving member of our family."

"Why did you come?" Varanus asked. "Merely to pay your respects?"

"In part," Friedrich answered. "I assumed that I would be the sole inheritor of the estate. I thought it best to secure it before it fell into the hands of your English relatives. I am relieved to see that I need not concern myself with it."

"I saw you speaking to the des Louveteaux," Varanus said. "Are they a part of your business?"

She knew, no doubt. Friedrich's bloody revenge was written across his face. Well, no point in lying, least of all to his mother.

"I have come to kill Alfonse des Louveteaux," Friedrich said.

"You…what?" Varanus asked. She seemed surprised by the answer.

"I have come to kill Alfonse des Louveteaux," Friedrich repeated. "I have come to kill the man who murdered my father."

Varanus began to speak but stopped herself. After a short while, she said:

"I suppose I cannot dissuade you. You are like your father. You will do something whether it is wise or not."

"Now that I know you live," Friedrich said, "I would prefer to do it with your blessing."

"Where are you staying?" Varanus asked.

"The Hôtel Rollo," Friedrich answered. "I have rooms there. It is very…rustic."

Varanus laughed and said, "Yes, it is. No, this will not do. You will come and stay with me at the house. The company will be most welcome. And you and I must talk. We have much to discuss."

"We do," Friedrich said.

Varanus touched his arm gently.

"Walk back with me," she said. "I will send the coachman to retrieve your things."

Friedrich held up a hand.

"If you will allow me," he said, "I think I would like to walk for a little while, to clear my head. I will meet your man at the hotel and oversee the moving of my things."

"Very well," Varanus said, nodding slowly. "But do not dally. I have waited almost twenty-five years to find you, my son. I cannot bear to wait much longer."

* * * *

"My son lives," Varanus said softly, watching Friedrich walk away.

"So it seems," Ekaterine said. "You are certain of his identity?"

Varanus looked at Korbinian, who stood at her other side.

"Absolutely certain," she said. "He looks exactly like his father. And he has my hair."

"This is true," Ekaterine said.

"My son lives," Varanus repeated, "and now I watch him walk away from me." She looked at Ekaterine. "Is it wrong of me to worry so?"

Ekaterine placed a hand on her arm and said, "No, it is not, but what is it that you fear?"

"He's come here to kill Alfonse des Louveteaux," Varanus said. "And I saw him speaking to the fiend before he came to talk to me. I fear that on his 'walk' he will actually attack the des Louveteaux and try to murder Alfonse."

"You suspect?" Korbinian murmured. "It is what I would do, and he is my son as well."

"Do you fear that they will kill him?" Ekaterine asked.

"I do," Varanus said. Why else would she be concerned? Alfonse deserved to die.

Ekaterine nodded and said, "I will follow him and see to it that he is safe."

"No," Varanus said, catching her by the arm. "He is my son. I will follow him."

"Is that wise?" Ekaterine asked, glancing toward the sky.

"It is overcast and I am veiled, Ekaterine," Varanus replied. "I scarcely feel the sun. I will be perfectly safe."

"Doctor—" Ekaterine began.

"Do not try to dissuade me," Varanus said. "I am his mother. This is something I must do."

Ekaterine stopped herself from saying something and took a deep breath.

"As you wish," she said. "But I will accompany you."

"Ekaterine—"

"No," Ekaterine said. "I go with you, or you do not go at all. It is too dangerous for you to go alone."

Ekaterine paused, waiting for a response that did not come. Varanus was speechless. What could she say?

"Well?" Ekaterine asked. She motioned toward the receding Friedrich. "He is getting away."

* * * *

Friedrich walked out along the road to town, mulling things over in his head. What had just happened? When he had left Germany, things had been so clear. He would introduce himself to his grandfather James, find Alfonse des Louveteaux, kill him in a duel, and finally return home in triumph. Since arriving in France, he had lost his grandfather without ever meeting him, he had completely failed to guarantee his duel, and he had discovered that his mother still lived.

Madness!

He strolled through the village, ignoring the locals as they stared at him with curiosity.

Was she really his mother? But how could she be an imposter? She had taken the place of primacy at the funeral, and no one—not the priest, the servants, or the townsfolk—had doubted her identity. She had passed words with people who had known Babette Varanus from birth.

And she was very short, he reflected, as he wandered out along an empty country road beyond the bounds of the village. By all accounts, Babette Varanus was very short. Lady Shashavani was very short. Then again, he found everyone to be very short, but still…

Why had she allowed Aunt Ilse to take him away? Surely she had known. She had to have known! Lady Shashavani said that they had told her he died, but could he believe that? Then again, her voice had sounded so *familiar*. He had recognized it. How was that possible if they had never met?

And there was that name. Alistair. No one had ever called him that before, but he recognized it as if it were his own.

He walked with these thoughts for the better part of half an hour, meandering through the countryside. Then he turned from the road and cut out across an open field. The fresh air was good for clearing his head, though he would have preferred a forest to open ground. The forests back in Fuchsburg were rich and deep, and he felt a sudden longing for them.

Something in the air made him feel uneasy, as if he were being watched from afar. He paused in the middle of an open field and looked over his shoulder. He saw nothing but the line of the hedgerow. But something was amiss. He *was* being watched.

Friedrich placed his hand on his sword and looked in every direction. He knew the scent of danger. But where was it coming from?

He turned and looked toward the adjoining field, separated by a low stone wall. Eyes were on him. But where were they?

Suddenly Friedrich heard a roar from behind him, a twisted, guttural sound. He spun about, drawing his sword, and saw a hulking mass of dark fur charging in his direction.

Friedrich froze at the sight, not from fear but from utter confusion.

What is that? he thought. It took him a moment more for the realization to hit him: *I should move*.

But by then it was too late to run. The beast was approaching too quickly. Was it a bear? But why would a bear attack him? And in the middle of a field? Impossible—

Sword, he thought, catching himself. It would not do to be killed by this strange beast without some effort of self-defense. If he were to die, at least it would be fighting.

He raised his sword and held it out toward the beast, face set defiantly.

Come at me, then!

The beast leapt for him, jaws wide revealing rows and rows of teeth. This was surely the end. But what an end it would be!

"Get down you fool!" someone shouted.

Someone barreled into him and knocked him off his feet. Friedrich fell into the damp grass and struck his head on the ground. It did not hurt, not exactly, but his head swam from the impact.

He blinked a few times and saw the strange woman who had been with Lady Shashavani at the funeral now lying on top of him. He looked at her, she looked at him, and he saw the beast pass over them in its leap.

The beast landed a few feet away and turned. It glared at Friedrich with its pale blue eyes. It pawed the ground and tensed for another charge.

The small, black-shrouded figure of Lady Shashavani stepped in between them and faced the beast.

Good God, Friedrich thought. *I've just discovered that my mother is alive, and now we're both going to die*.

He looked back at the woman who lay on top of him.

"Hello," he said, smiling.

The woman looked at him in astonishment and blinked. She was rather pretty. A pity she was going to die as well.

Varanus stood at her full height and regarded the beast from behind her veil. It looked back at her, sniffing the air. It growled and tensed for another lunge.

Varanus felt her stomach clench. She recognized the beast. It was the same one that had attacked her and Korbinian in the forest two and a half decades ago. That was impossible, of course, but Varanus was sure of it. The particular shade and pattern of the gray fur, the look in the eyes, even the smell of the creature told her that she remembered it.

The beast leapt at her. Varanus took a breath and spun in place. She caught the beast on the side of the head with the back of her hand. The blow knocked it sideways, and it hit the ground in a heap. It rose quickly, snarling and snorting, but now the look in its eyes was one of confusion.

Varanus flexed her fingers and stepped around to keep herself between the beast and her son. She looked down at Ekaterine and asked, "How is he?"

Ekaterine looked at Friedrich and back at Varanus.

"Alive," she said.

"Keep him that way," Varanus told her.

Ekaterine climbed off Friedrich and knelt beside him. Friedrich tried to get up, sword in hand, but Ekaterine pushed him back down with the strength of a Shashavani.

"Stay there," she said.

Varanus watched the beast paw at the ground as it studied her. No, not "paw". It *scratched* with its claw-tipped fingers. Varanus looked again. Yes, they were fingers. Just like the creatures in Georgia. They had hands—

The beast lunged again, this time not past her but at her. Varanus ducked low and jumped to the side, tucking her arms before her face to keep her veil from flapping up. She hit the ground and rolled.

She was on her feet again in an instant. The beast took longer to recover, slipping on the grass before it righted itself. It seemed somewhat disoriented by the open ground and by the light of day. It kept sniffing the air, like a thing that could smell better than it could see. But the creatures in Georgia had shown very keen sight.

The beast advanced again, this time slowly and with measured steps. It snorted and grumbled, turning its nose from Friedrich to Varanus, unsure of whom to focus on.

I shall make that choice for you, Varanus thought.

She moved forward to meet it as rapidly as her skirts would allow. The beast opened its mouth and made to bite her arm. Varanus twisted sideways and brought first one fist and then the other into the beast's throat. It gagged loudly and whimpered, withdrawing again. Now Varanus had its full attention.

"Ekaterine!" Varanus shouted. "Get him away from here!"

Ekaterine pulled Friedrich to his feet and began dragging him away in the direction of the road. Friedrich struggled against her.

"No!" he shouted. "Unhand me! I must protect my mother! Where is my sword, God damn it?"

His sword!

Varanus struck the beast on both sides of the head with her hands in a tremendous clap that sent shudders through her. The beast let out a cry and scampered backward. It gnashed its teeth with rage and took a swipe at her. Varanus fell back, narrowly avoiding the blow. She would not be so fortunate next time. Though disoriented, the beast was fast and well coordinated.

Friedrich's sword lay on the ground. Varanus knelt and snatched it up. She held it out defensively as the beast advanced on her again. At least the sword gave her some range, though it was matched by the beast's long arms.

And so the dance began. The beast moved toward her, she withdrew. It circled to one flank as she circled to counter. All the while, Ekaterine managed to pull Friedrich further away, though he fought her at each step.

Varanus lunged with the sword and cut the beast beneath its chin. The tip of the sword drew blood, but the wound was shallow. The flesh of the beast was tough and unyielding. In reply, it lashed out at her, and she only just jumped backward in time. As it was, the beast's claws tore through her skirts.

But that was not to be the end of it. The beast pressed the attack further, bounding forward with its jaws wide and its claws slashing at the air. Varanus felt those claws tear into her arm and side, cutting cloth and flesh alike. The pain was tremendous, but worse, Varanus felt the creeping sting of sunlight growing from beneath the exposed skin.

Gripping Friedrich's sword in both hands, she brought it down on the beast's brow. She had expected, perhaps foolishly, to shatter the offending head from the force of the blow. Instead, the blade struck and slid away, leaving a shallow depression in the beast's skin that did not even draw blood.

No!

In reply, the beast swept her feet out from under her, shattering the bones in her left leg as it did so. Varanus hit the ground and struggled to maintain her senses.

"No!" she heard Friedrich shout.

Get him away! Get him away! she thought, though when she tried to speak, all she could manage was a low, guttural snarl.

The beast loomed over her, its mouth split open, its tongue hanging out like some overfed hunting dog. Varanus looked into its eyes. Like the beasts in Georgia, it thought it had won. Like the beasts in Georgia, it was mistaken.

As the beast bit at her, Varanus shoved the sword into its mouth, holding it lengthwise to restrain the creature in the manner of a horse's bit. The beast snorted and chuffed angrily, and it lashed out with one set of claws, striking the side of her head. Varanus gasped in pain. Her veil came away, and suddenly the burning sensation filled very last inch of her body.

But she was not finished. Shouting in anger, she smashed the side of her fist into the beast's nose. The beast howled in pain and ducked its head away, whimpering and growling in equal measure.

Varanus grabbed the beast by the snout with her free hand and drew back the sword. The air in her lungs escaped her in a single long scream of fury, pulling the beast's head down even as she thrust the sword into its throat.

The attack robbed Varanus of her last reserves of strength. Her head swam, confused by the impact it had suffered and by the endless shivers of pain that filled it. The sun, clouded though it was, burned Varanus's flesh and eyes until she could think of little else but agony. Blindly, she pulled the sword free and cast it aside. She was so very hungry, and she smelled the same rich blood that had nourished her on that moonlit night in Georgia....

Her lips found the flowing wound, and she drank deeply from it. The blood was so delicious she could not bring herself to stop, even as her body cried out from the harsh touch of the sun.

Suddenly, someone pulled her away. She heard Ekaterine speaking but could not make out the words. She felt a heavy cloak being wrapped about her head and body, shrouding her from the sunlight. Then someone lifted her into his arms.

"I have you, Mother," she heard Friedrich say.

"Alistair..." she murmured. One hand struggled to reach out and touch his face. "Alistair, is that you?"

"Do not worry *liebchen*," came Korbinian's voice. It was only a murmur, but it was as clear as if he were wrapped inside the cloak with her. "Our son has you. You are safe now. Rest. Rest and awaken."

CHAPTER TWENTY-EIGHT

By the time they reached the house, Varanus had regained her senses. At first she was confused—why was she being carried by Alistair? But no, his name was Friedrich, not Alistair—but she quickly remembered what had transpired. Friedrich set her down near the gate at the head of the drive so that she could walk the rest of the way on her own, still shielded from the sun by the heavy cloak she had been given. Varanus caught Friedrich staring at her, mesmerized by her miraculous recovery.

This was going to be difficult to explain.

"Come," she said, motioning for Friedrich and Ekaterine to follow her. "We will enter through a side door. I would prefer to avoid questions until after supper."

"Yes, my lady," Ekaterine said.

"I must change, of course," Varanus said. "Ekaterine, have Alis… Friedrich placed in one of the guest rooms and then come see me."

Ekaterine merely nodded.

While she changed into a new dress, Varanus mulled over what she was to say to her son. But what did one say under such circumstances? "Hello, Friedrich. May I call you Alistair?" or "I know you were told that I had died, but as you can see, I am both alive and immortal" or "Join me for dinner, if you please. I normally drink blood, but on this occasion we will be enjoying local fare."

She sighed aloud as Ekaterine helped her into a new corset. The old one was clearly beyond repair, both bloodstained and shredded along one side. It was a miracle it had stayed on her until the dress had come off.

"What am I to do, Ekaterine?" she asked.

"You should begin," Ekaterine said, "by telling him that you love him. I know it's not popular, but I have always been of the opinion that a mother's love ought to be known by her children."

Varanus laughed a little, which quickly turned into a gasp as Ekaterine pulled hard on the laces.

"Not so tightly!" she cried.

Ekaterine leaned around and fixed her with a stern look, saying, "It serves you right for wearing it. Such a beastly garment."

"It is the fashion," Varanus said.

"So you keep telling me," Ekaterine replied. "And yet, like your hats, it is nothing less than dreadful."

"Ekaterine, what am I to say to him?" Varanus asked.

"I do not know," Ekaterine said, "but I will tell you what you are not to say to him. You are not to explain what you are. He will ask, and you will want to tell him because he is your son."

"I know," Varanus said. "I will keep the secrets of our order. But what else am I to tell him?"

Ekaterine shrugged apologetically and said, "Explain to him that you thought he died. God willing, that will distract him from what he saw today."

"It won't work, will it?" Varanus asked.

"Well...." Ekaterine sighed. "Well, God is very busy these days." She smiled at Varanus and patted her arm. "Just tell him the truth...except when you must lie."

Varanus found Friedrich waiting in the upstairs library. The room was dark and the windows were shuttered, but Friedrich paced back and forth across the floor without once bumping into the furniture. He turned toward Varanus as she entered and looked at her expectantly.

"You could have turned up the lights," Varanus said, and did so.

"I was thinking," Friedrich replied.

Varanus turned toward him, and they regarded one another for a little while.

"You have questions," Varanus finally said. "I know that you have questions."

"I do," Friedrich said.

"Well...ask them," Varanus said.

Friedrich scowled for a moment, then smiled, then scowled again.

"I have so many, I don't know where to start," he said. "You are my mother. I know you are my mother."

"That is not a question," Varanus said.

"I was told that you died!" Friedrich cried. "Why was I told that you died? And how are you so young? You are my mother, yet you look to be my age! And the beast! What was that creature? And how did you kill it? And how did you not die? I saw it tear you to pieces, but here you are, alive and well! How?"

Varanus took a deep breath. She could hardly have expected anything else.

"Shall we sit?" she asked, motioning to a pair of chairs.

Friedrich nodded briskly and said, "Yes, yes, let us do so."

He sat quickly and folded his hands in his lap while Varanus sat opposite him.

"Now then," Varanus said, "I will do my best to answer your questions one at a time."

Friedrich nodded.

"Yes, that is good," he said. "And please understand, I do not wish to seem ungrateful—"

Varanus leaned forward and took Friedrich's hands. Friedrich started a little, surprised, but after a moment he smiled at her.

"Do not apologize," Varanus said. "Today has been a difficult one for me as well. I discovered that my son was alive. You see, several months after you were born, my grandfather, William, told me that you had died. And at the time, I was so distraught that I never thought to ask to see your body until after the funeral."

Best not to mention the attempted suicide. That was the sort of thing that would distress the poor boy.

"It never occurred to me that you had been taken away," Varanus continued. "I never thought that my grandfather would lie to me. Now it seems I was mistaken."

"We were both lied to," Friedrich said, frowning. "After I was born, my Aunt Ilse brought me back to Fuchsburg from Italy. And when I was old enough to understand, she explained to me that my father had been murdered by a Frenchman and my mother had died in childbirth. She said that your family did not want me, and I believed her. It was not until it seemed that the family was about to die off with your father that I even thought about coming here." He looked toward one of the gaslights. "I never believed that my aunt would lie to me either. I will have words with her when I return home."

Damn Ilse! Varanus thought, growing warm with anger. The blasted woman had conspired with Grandfather to steal her son! Grandfather was not alive to answer for the crime, but Ilse was!

"Perhaps we will have words with her together," she said aloud, keeping her tone level. It would not do to upset the boy.

"Tell me Mother," Friedrich said, "is it true that my father was murdered?"

"Yes," Varanus said. "I was there when that bastard Alfonse des Louveteaux struck him down, on Christmas morning no less!"

Friedrich nodded slowly and said, "That is what my aunt always said, but today I have been given cause to doubt her account of things." He paused. "How are you so young?"

"Young?" Varanus asked.

But of course, she hadn't aged in fifteen years. She had become so used to seeing those around her not change at all, she had almost forgotten that it was normal for people to grow old.

"You look my age," Friedrich said. "How is this possible?"

"A family trait," Varanus answered. "Your great-grandfather William scarcely showed his age."

Friedrich studied her for a little while before he slowly nodded. Varanus suspected that he did not believe her, but at least he was willing to set that point aside.

"And the beast?" he asked.

"The beast," Varanus said.

"What was it?"

Varanus sighed and replied, "I do not know."

"It was not a creature of Nature," Friedrich said. His tone was insistent and earnest.

"I know that," Varanus said. "I encountered such a creature before, many years ago. When your father was courting me, we were set upon by such a beast. We drove it off but did not kill it."

"You believe it is the same creature?" Friedrich asked.

Varanus considered this. It seemed impossible, and yet… No, it *was* the same creature. It…*smelled* the same, for lack of a better word.

"I do not know," she said. "But, I do know that it is well we killed it. The countryside is safer for that."

"*You* killed it," Friedrich said. "You beat it and stabbed it with my sword."

Varanus waited for him to mention the drinking of the beast's blood, but the question never came. She looked into Friedrich's eyes, but she could not see what he was thinking. Had he not seen? Or was he simply refusing to address it?

"How did you kill it?" Friedrich asked. "A creature of that size and you cast it aside like a bird buffeted by the wind."

Varanus shook her head and said, "No, you are mistaken. I evaded it, yes, and I did strike it many times, though I suspect it had little effect. It was your sword that killed it, Friedrich. I was merely lucky. The beast could have killed me."

Friedrich rose from his chair in a flash, arms upraised in agitation.

"It did kill you!" he shouted. "Or it ought to have done so! I thank Heaven that you are alive and well, but Mother, I saw it tear you apart! And yet here you are, whole and unharmed! How is this possible?"

"I was not badly injured," Varanus said. "You were some distance away. You must not have seen what you thought you saw."

"I know what I saw," Friedrich said firmly.

"I can give you no other explanation than the one I have given you."

"I cannot accept that!" Friedrich answered. "There is more going on here than what you are telling me, and I want to know what it is!"

He stopped, fist upraised, as the door opened and Ekaterine leaned into the room. She blinked a few times at the sight of Friedrich before exchanging looks with Varanus.

"My lady," she said, "dinner is served."

Varanus smiled pleasantly and rose from her chair.

"Thank you, Ekaterine," she said. "We shall be along presently."

"Very good, my lady," Ekaterine said.

Varanus turned to Friedrich, took his hand, and gently lowered it. "Come," she said, "we shall talk further after we eat."

It was dinnertime at the des Louveteaux house as well, and Alfonse sat carving apart his second beef steak of the evening. He would consume a third by the end of the meal, he knew that already. The rest of the family sat around the table, similarly devouring chunks of bloody meat with all the gentility of the French aristocracy. His father was the most voracious of them all, already calling for the servants to bring him a fourth piece of meat.

Such an appetite! It made Alfonse smile proudly. One day soon he would be just like his father, and his father would be...well, something even greater than a man.

"More wine!" he shouted, snapping his fingers.

One of the servants scurried forward to refill his glass. It was the home vintage: a hearty red mixed with blood, just the restorative he required.

At the far end of the table, his mother, Charlotte des Louveteaux, called out to his father:

"Louis, has the matter with those beastly Varanuses been settled yet?"

Louis wolfed down a mouthful of meat before replying, "Very nearly, my sweet. I give them a week's time before that bitch Babette succumbs."

"And how was the runt's funeral?" Charlotte asked.

She had not attended, of course. At her age, she had grown too fair and beautiful to be seen in public. Her teeth were sharp and long, and her side-whiskers had grown almost as thick as Louis's. By now, shaving was a wasted effort. It would not be long before the family would usher

her into the deep places of the earth. It made Alfonse so proud. And to think, one day his beloved Claire would look the same.

Claire. The very thought of her and her scent roused Alfonse, and he growled softly, tearing into his piece of beef to sate his hunger. Darling Claire had married that beastly banker, Bazaine, but her husband was not the master of his house. Nor was he the master of "his" children, for they all belonged to the des Louveteaux line.

"Alfonse, my child," Charlotte said, "I hear that a man came to the funeral claiming to be the son of Babette Varanus and that dreadful German."

"Yes, Mother," Alfonse said. "He called himself Friedrich von Fuchsburg."

"Is there any truth to his claim?" Charlotte asked.

"It seems so," Alfonse said. "He certainly looked like his father."

Louis laughed loudly, his mouth full of food, and said, "Yes, and it gave you quite the start, didn't it? Ha ha! You should have seen the boy, Charlotte. White as a sheet."

Alfonse felt the heat of his temper rising. He quickly changed the subject.

"The damn fool had the audacity to challenge me to a duel," he said. "'For his family's honor.' It was absurd."

"You do not mean to fight him?" Charlotte asked, frowning.

"By my order," Louis said. He washed his mouthful of food down with a swig of wine. "The German is not worth the effort, nor does he deserve the respect of being dueled. I have dispatched Gérard to deal with the problem." He glanced toward the clock over the fireplace. "I am surprised he has not returned."

As Louis spoke, the door opened, and the butler stepped in. He walked to Louis's side and whispered in his ear. Louis's face immediately fell into a scowl. Clearing his throat, he stood and snapped his fingers at Alfonse.

"Alfonse, come with me," he said. He smiled at the rest of the family. "Continue, please, until I return."

Alfonse stood and followed his father and the butler into the hall. He saw one of their groundsmen, Mercier, standing nearby, his back rigid like a soldier at attention. Mercier dared not look at them but stared straight ahead, waiting to be addressed.

"Well?" Louis asked. "What is it?"

"Master Gérard is dead," Mercier said.

"*What?*" Alfonse exclaimed. He looked toward the dining room and lowered his voice. "How?"

Mercier looked toward them and quickly looked away. He was afraid, which was good. His news was very bad, and that alone was reason enough for him to be killed and eaten.

"We are not certain, Messieurs," Mercier said. "We found the body in a field. He had been stabbed through the throat, probably with a sword. I believe he bled to death."

"The German?" Alfonse demanded.

"There was no sign of him," Mercier said, "so I believe he escaped alive after killing Gérard."

"Impossible!" Louis's expression was red with fury. "Von Fuchsburg is only a man! He could not have killed one of us! And he certainly could not have survived!"

"A sword should not have breached Gérard's flesh," Alfonse said to Mercier. "How could a man have possessed such strength?"

Mercier looked like a mouse surrounded by cats.

"I do not know," he insisted. "All I can think is that the German stabbed while Gérard pounced on him, and the force of Gérard's attack caused him to impale himself upon von Fuchsburg's sword."

"And von Fuchsburg was not there?" Louis asked.

"There was no body," Mercier said. "I called for him at his rooms in the village, but he was not there. They said his things had been collected by men from the Varanus house."

"Then he is there," Alfonse said. "His mother has taken him to her bosom, it seems."

Louis shook his head, almost salivating with anger.

"That boy must pay," he snarled. "Gérard may have been a bastard, but he was my grandfather's bastard. Von Fuchsburg will die for this offense!"

"I will kill him for you, Father," Alfonse said.

"No," Louis replied. "No, he deserves a more lingering death than that. Mercier, take your men and invade the Varanus house. Find von Fuchsburg and bring him back here alive. We will bring him before the assembly, execute him, and feast upon his flesh."

"Yes, my lord," Mercier said, bowing deeply. "But I must ask.... The house will be inhabited. What are we to do if we are seen?"

"Make it look like a robbery," Louis said. "If they resist, shoot them. I will attend to any trouble with the police."

Mercier bowed again and backed away, looking at the floor.

"As you wish," he said. "It will be done; it will be done."

Alfonse smiled at the sight. It was always refreshing to see humans who knew their place. And soon von Fuchsburg would know his place as well. And then he would die.

Alfonse hummed happily as he and Louis returned to the dining room. He could already taste the German's sweet blood on his tongue. It would be delicious.

Varanus poured a glass of brandy from a crystal decanter and handed it to Friedrich. Taking her own drink—a glass of sherry—she sat on the sofa beside him and gave him a warm smile. They were in the parlor, where they had retired after dinner. The meal had been a quiet affair and very awkward at first. Thankfully, by the time they had finished eating, she and her son had reached a sort of unspoken accord. By now, they seemed to have both agreed to set their uncertainties aside. Certain questions could not be answered, and they were not asked. But everything else was fair game.

"So you are a doctor?" Varanus asked.

"Yes," Friedrich said. "Science is my greatest love, you know, even more than war, which I understand is unusual for a man of my station."

"Most unusual," Varanus said. "But I approve nonetheless." She sipped her wine. It was an acceptable substitute for blood, which was in short supply in France. Without willing donors, it would have necessitated an unacceptable level of violence. "And you are the Baron von Fuchsburg?"

"That is correct," Friedrich said. He seemed surprised at the question. "Why do you ask?"

"Well..." Varanus began. "You were born out of wedlock."

Friedrich blinked and said, "I was?"

"You didn't know?" Varanus asked.

Friedrich shifted uncomfortably in his chair and took a sip of brandy. "No," he finally said.

"How could you not know?" Varanus asked. "Your father was murdered on the very night our engagement was announced." She gave Friedrich a quick smile and placed a hand on his shoulder. "We loved each other very much, and I know that he would have been very proud of you, had he lived. But he did die before you were born."

Friedrich was silent for a moment before he laughed loudly and said, "My aunt has a very different and—I see now—a very fabricated story."

"And what is that?"

"My aunt claims that there was a secret wedding," Friedrich said. "She even produced a priest and a number of witnesses."

"I'm certain she did," Varanus said. "And you had no knowledge of the truth?"

"None," Friedrich said. He did not seem particularly concerned. "Of course, I see why my aunt lied. My father was murdered. If I were illegitimate, who knows to whom the title would have passed. The lie allowed me to inherit. It was very good of her, all things considered." He drank some brandy. "But I wish she hadn't lied about you, Mother."

"We have both had a great deal of time stolen from us," Varanus said. Ilse would have to answer for that, she thought, but she said nothing on the matter.

There came a knock at the door.

"Enter!" Varanus called.

The door opened and Ekaterine looked in.

"Is everything well?" Varanus asked.

"Yes, Doctor," Ekaterine said. "I simply wanted to tell you that the household is retiring to bed, as am I."

"Yes, of course," Varanus said. "And Luka?"

"Luka is examining the grounds," Ekaterine said. "Evidently a man was spotted near the forest. Luka is taking one of the dogs to investigate. I suspect he will retire after that."

"Very good, Ekaterine," Varanus said, trying not to laugh. It was so peculiar speaking to her as if they were mistress and servant. "I will see you in the morning."

"Now then," Friedrich said, interrupting, "just a moment." He rose and extended his glass toward Ekaterine. "You could always join us for a drink."

Ekaterine smiled at him, then looked at Varanus.

"Good night," she said.

"Good night, Ekaterine," Varanus said. "Sit down, Alistair," she said to Friedrich. She waited for Ekaterine to leave before she added, "Alistair, I will thank you not to invite my maidservant to drink with you."

"My name is Friedrich, Mother," he replied, returning to his seat. "And she is no servant."

"Oh?" Varanus asked. "What is she, then?"

Friedrich took a drink of brandy and said, "I do not know, but I know servants, and she is not one. She carries herself like a woman of means, and whatever words you use with one another, you speak to each other in the manner of equals." He shrugged, smirking a little. "I am no fool."

Varanus hid a smile. Friedrich was proving to be an observant man. That was good. At least his mind had not been dulled by his long years away from her.

"You certainly are not," she said. "Still, I will thank you not to invite her to drink—"

She stopped mid-sentence, for at that moment she fancied that she heard the sound of glass breaking. The noise had been muffled, and it was very faint. Some distant part of the house perhaps? Or downstairs? Or was it just her mind playing tricks on her?

"Yes, yes, as you wish, mother," Friedrich said.

Varanus turned quickly to look at him.

"What?" she asked.

"I will refrain from asking Mademoiselle Ekaterine to drink with me," Friedrich said. He drained his glass and reached for the bottle. "Mind you, I am very good company after a few drinks."

"Yes, I'm sure," Varanus said. She stood quickly and walked to the door. "Will you excuse me for just a moment, Alistair? I must check on something."

Friedrich shrugged and poured himself a fresh glass.

"Yes, of course," he said. "I have brandy to keep me company." He raised the glass and looked at the richly colored liquid. "And what fine company it is."

Varanus smiled and slipped out into the hallway. As she shut the door behind her, she thought to herself:

Wonderful. I finally have my son returned to me, and he's a drunk. A charming drunk. A brilliant drunk. But a drunk all the same.

Ilse von Fuchsburg had much to answer for.

Varanus walked softly through the dark house, her ears alert for any sound. Alas, there were too many of them, and she turned this way and that at every creak, rustle, and murmur. She listened for voices, but she heard none. There was a curious scent that had entered the house, that much her nose told her. But it proved elusive.

As she entered the foyer, she heard the creak of a floorboard on the opposite side of the room. She quickly ducked into the shadows and waited, every muscle tense.

She saw three men cross into the dim light of the moon, which filtered in through the windows. The men were dressed in rough clothes, and a sniff of the air told Varanus that they were the source of the smell. One man carried a cudgel and a lantern while the other two had shotguns in their hands.

There *had* been an intrusion, and these men were behind it. But who were they, and what did they want?

Varanus slowed her breathing until it was almost silent. She waited in the darkness as the men approached, considering what to do. She could manage three men, even armed with guns, if she took them by surprise. The shotguns were a slight concern, but she was more worried about someone coming to her aid at the sound of gunfire and being shot by accident.

At that moment, there came a tremendous crash from the library followed by Friedrich's shouting:

"Swine! Who are you? Unhand me!"

The three men in the foyer looked at one another.

"They've found him!" the man with the lantern cried. "Quickly, help them!"

"No!" Varanus shouted.

She darted from the shadows and into the path of the men before they could make sense of her. The man with the cudgel reacted first. He drew back his arm and brought the weapon down at Varanus's head. She evaded easily and grabbed him by the wrist. She pulled with a single sharp jerk, feeling the shoulder dislocate. The man screamed in pain, and she punched him on the side of the head, knocking him to the ground in a senseless heap.

One of the remaining men turned his shotgun on her and fired. Varanus twisted away as quickly as she was able, but a cluster of buckshot still hit her in the side. She gasped for air and stumbled, but it was not enough to stop her. She grabbed the gun by the barrel and tore it from his hands. Stepping in close, she smashed him in the face with the butt of his own weapon.

Varanus was about to turn and attend to the third man when she heard his shotgun go off. She was hit dead center in the chest and knocked backward from the force of it. She fell against the wall and clutched her stomach. The shot had torn through clothing, corset, and body.

Good God, what bore were the men using?

The man adjusted his aim and fired his second barrel, hitting Varanus in the chest and throat. She was knocked into the wall a second time and struck her head. Her legs gave out, and she slid to the floor.

Varanus snarled and struggled to move, but the trauma made it difficult for her body to respond.

"By the Wolf, how are you still alive?" the man demanded. He broke open the shotgun breech and reloaded.

Varanus heard a door open and Friedrich shouting "Mother! Mother!"

She tried to respond, but blood welled up in her mouth, and she gagged on it. As if in a dream, she slowly looked down the hallway toward the library and saw Friedrich running in her direction. A gaggle of men with bruised faces and bleeding noses and mouths chased him.

Friedrich's eyes widened at the sight of her, and he began screaming obscenities in German.

"You swine!" he cried. "You whore-spawned pig-dog, how dare you hurt my mother! For this, I will cut out your bowels and force them down your—"

Friedrich rushed at the man with the shotgun, hands outstretched to murder him. The man drew back a step and struck Friedrich on the side of the head with his shotgun butt. Friedrich fell sideways and tumbled to the ground, senseless.

"No!" Varanus screamed, though it came out as a thick gurgle.

The man with the shotgun turned on her and fired both barrels. Varanus saw a flash and then everything was darkness.

CHAPTER TWENTY-NINE

"Doctor? Doctor, can you hear me?"

At the sound of Ekaterine's voice, Varanus awoke with a start. She tried to sit up, but Ekaterine quickly held her down and tried to sooth her.

"Calm, Doctor, calm," Ekaterine said. "You're safe."

Varanus tried to speak, but she found that a tube had been place in her mouth and partly down her throat. She choked and gagged and pulled the offending thing out. Fresh blood spilled all over her lips and face.

"What is going on?" she demanded, pushing Ekaterine away and sitting up.

She saw the body of one of the assailants on the ground next to her, a bloodletting pump attached to his arm. How like Ekaterine to think of feeding her at such a time.

Varanus felt her chest. The buckshot had torn numerous holes in her clothes, but her body had fully healed. Even the shot was now gone, pushed out by her closing wounds. The metal pellets now littered the floor.

"What happened?" she asked, pressing her hand against her forehead. She suddenly felt a tremendous headache.

Ekaterine knelt beside her and placed her hands on Varanus's shoulders.

"Doctor," she said, "I need you to promise that you will not panic."

Varanus frowned and repeated, "What happened?"

"Your son has been taken," Ekaterine said.

"*What?*" Varanus demanded.

"I came as soon as I heard the shooting," Ekaterine said, "but I was too late to stop them."

Varanus felt panic rising in her. Her son kidnapped? Who would have done such a thing? And in her home? In the dead of night? By force? Who could have possessed such audacity?

"Where have they taken him?" she asked.

"Luka followed them," Ekaterine said. "We will know when he returns." She picked up the feeding tube and held it out to Varanus. "Now please, Doctor, finish drinking. You will need your strength." She nodded to the corpse. "And he is hardly in a position to complain."

Varanus frowned, but she did as instructed. She could not deny that the taste of fresh blood was invigorating.

"What about the servants?" she asked, after her first swallow.

Ekaterine sighed and said, “They were rather disappointing, I am afraid. Most of them hid at the sound of gunfire, although that Vatel fellow came at once. He is a good man.”

“What must he think?” Varanus asked.

“Oh, fear not,” Ekaterine said. “I took care of all that. I covered your body so you didn’t appear to be shot, only unconscious. I told him that Luka killed the attackers, who were all anarchists seeking to outrage respectable people in the dead of night. It was quite readily believed.”

“I’m certain it was,” Varanus said. “Where is he now?”

“Looking after the servants,” Ekaterine said. “He promised to make certain that no one panicked.”

Varanus forced a smile and patted Ekaterine’s arm.

“What would I do without you?” she asked.

“You’d be lying half dead and starving on the ground,” Ekaterine replied. She looked up suddenly and stood. “Luka!” she cried.

Varanus turned and saw Luka walking toward them, a rifle in his hand. She quickly stood and hurried to meet him.

“What news, Luka?” she asked. “Where is my son?”

Luka’s expression clouded.

“I followed the men all the way to the des Louveteaux estate,” he said. “I saw them bring him into the house. I thought to intervene, but…”

“No, you did well returning to tell me, Luka,” Varanus said. “Saddle horses for Ekaterine and myself while we arm ourselves.”

“Very good, Doctor,” Luka said, bowing his head.

“Ekaterine,” Varanus said, turning to her, “I require trousers at once.”

Varanus could find no trousers in her size on such short notice—not that it came as any surprise—but she discovered a collection of her clothes in a chest in her room, including her old bloomer suit. It was more than a little absurd, but at least it was better than trying to fight in layers of skirts. And worse, Varanus reflected, she was rapidly running out of proper mourning wear. It would not do to rescue her son only to be left traipsing about the place in pastels. What would the neighbors think?

The ones who were still alive, that was.

She rejoined Ekaterine, who had stolen—“borrowed”—some clothes of Luka’s, which fit her well enough under the circumstances. Ekaterine also had a set of weapons and ammunition that Luka had brought with them. “For just such an occasion,” she said. Varanus was inclined to agree.

Luka had the horses ready when they joined him in the courtyard. He was armed as well, with a rifle, pistols, and a bandoleer of gunpowder charges wrapped in paper. He nodded at them wordlessly, and Varanus nodded back. There was nothing to be said, only things to be done.

They rode to the des Louveteaux house in a matter of minutes, hopefully, Varanus thought, compensating for the head start enjoyed by the kidnappers. There was no telling what the des Louveteaux would do to Friedrich. Varanus silently prayed that they planned to hold him for ransom, or that if they meant to kill him, they would first gloat over his captivity. She urged her horse on to greater speed, knowing that each moment brought her son closer to death.

At the edge of the des Louveteaux estate, she diverted from the road and led them cross-country. The front gate would be watched. Their best chance would be to enter the grounds from the side.

She stopped a short distance from the house and dismounted. Luka and Ekaterine halted behind her, tying their horses to the branch of a nearby tree.

"What are your instructions?" Luka asked.

"I am going to find my son," Varanus said. "The two of you remain here and protect the horses. We may require a fast escape."

"No," Ekaterine said.

"Ekaterine, it's too dangerous—" Varanus began.

"No," Ekaterine repeated. "I will not let you go in there alone. Neither of us will, will you Luka?"

"Neither of us," Luka agreed. He looked at his pocket watch impatiently and said, "And if I may, there is no time for argument. The young man has been in that house for nearly an hour. We are trying the Almighty's patience."

"You're right," Varanus said. "But be careful. Neither of you is as resilient as I am, and I won't have your deaths on my hands."

Luka looked at her sternly and said, "Doctor, if I can survive a century traveling the world with Lord Shashavani, I can survive a few Frenchmen." He handed his rifle to Ekaterine and drew a dagger from beneath his coat. With the dagger, he pointed in the direction of a darkened window along the side of the building. "Now," he said, "we enter through that window in two minutes. Bring the firearms and ammunition. I will clear a path."

"Two minutes," Varanus said, nodding.

It was two minutes longer than she wanted to wait.

* * * *

William waited in the shadows by the gate, watching the des Louveteaux's thugs patrol the grounds. He sniffed the air. They smelled of Louis's scent. Indeed, the whole house stank of des Louveteaux, even at that distance. Suddenly, he detected another smell approaching from his flank: horses carrying Babette and her two servants.

Most peculiar. Clearly Babette had come for her son. Good. The damned fool boy should never have tempted the des Louveteaux's anger. William had allowed the von Fuchsburg woman to take the boy away on the understanding that he would be kept safe from Louis and his family. And now, the damned fool had gone and gotten himself kidnapped by them! William's line was diminishing rapidly, and if something happened to his great-grandson…

Well, he was not about to see that happen.

William waited for Babette and her servants to act. It would not do to be seen by them. As far as Babette knew, he was dead and interred, and he saw no reason to dispel that illusion. He watched the manservant Luka cross the dark grounds and kill the three men on patrol without detection. A handy fellow, William decided, more a soldier than a servant. Where had Babette gotten him? William sniffed the air. Was he the same man who had accompanied Lord Shashavani in France fifteen years ago? He scarcely seemed to have aged.

Once Babette and her servants had infiltrated the house through a side window, William left his hiding place and ran across the lawn. It was so much easier moving on all fours at times, and much faster as well. Yes, he reflected, the change was quite advanced. He could not allow Babette to see him like this. She would not understand.

He circled the house and approached the kitchen door. A man was on guard there, standing with a lantern and a pistol. The man spun around to face William and raised his weapon.

"Who goes there?" he demanded.

William walked into the light and bared his teeth. At the sight of him, the guard relaxed.

"My lord," he said, "you are late."

Ah. The guard had confused him with one of the des Louveteaux. That was just as well—

The man paused and narrowed his eyes. "Wait a moment," he began. "What is your family?"

No matter, William thought. There was no point in bluffing when violence was just as effective.

He knocked the guard's pistol away with a flick of his hand. He grabbed the man by the throat and snapped his neck as easily as he had once broken a stick. How wonderful it was to be old.

William threw the body into the darkness by the side of the house and crept into the kitchen. Time to find the boy and then deal with the des Louveteaux once and for all.

Varanus found the des Louveteaux house dark and all but deserted. The lights were low and, aside from the odd armed man in the halls, the servants were nowhere to be seen. It was almost as though they had been locked away in their rooms. But that was an absurd idea, wasn't it?

She sniffed the air. The house was heavy with the scent of men and women and with a peculiar sort of musk that seemed familiar, yet she could not place it. Moving through the house with Luka and Ekaterine at her back, she finally came across Friedrich's scent. He had definitely been here. But where was he now?

The sound of chanting caught her attention. It was very faint, too faint for Luka or Ekaterine to notice, but she heard it creeping up from somewhere below them. Varanus knelt and pressed one ear to the floorboards. Yes, definitely below them. But not, she realized, from the basement.

"What is it, Doctor?" Ekaterine asked, kneeling beside her.

"Chanting," Varanus replied. "Chanting somewhere down there."

"So there are people here," Ekaterine said. "Good. I was beginning to feel unnerved."

Varanus rose and continued into the foyer. She spotted two armed men on guard there, watching the door. She indicated them and Luka nodded. He crept across the room, knife in hand, and struck one of the men on the back of the head, rendering him senseless. Then Luka turned in a flash and, covering the mouth of the second man, forced him to the floor.

"Keep going," he said quietly as he killed the man. "I will keep watch here. If you need me, shout."

"If we shout, we'll be discovered," Ekaterine said.

"If you have been discovered, shout," Luka said. "Then it will make not a bit of difference."

"Words of wisdom," Varanus said. She motioned to Ekaterine. "Come."

She led Ekaterine down the main hallway, the chanting growing louder with each step. Near the center of the house, she heard the voices drifting in from behind the wall paneling. She placed her ear to the wall and listened.

It must be hollow, she thought.

It took her only a few moments to find the seam where the wall met a hidden door and a few moments more to uncover the catch. A section of the wall swung inward, revealing a short passageway that ended in an ancient stone staircase, which spiraled down into the ground. Torches were bracketed to the walls, barely bright enough to light to steps.

Varanus sniffed the air. Amid the heavy layering of smells, she detected Friedrich's scent. He had been brought this way.

"I must go down there," she said to Ekaterine. "Stay here and watch the door."

"You can't mean to go there alone," Ekaterine said.

"I must," Varanus replied. "I have my rifle, and I am not without my own capabilities. And I cannot risk someone coming in behind us. Please, Ekaterine, do this for me."

Ekaterine frowned but nodded her assent. "Promise me that you will take every precaution."

"I promise," Varanus said. "And I promise that I will kill every last one of them if they have hurt my son."

"Go," Ekaterine said. "Go, and bring him back safely."

Varanus exchanged nods with her and made for the stairs.

Varanus followed the stairs down for what felt like ages. Though she could see well enough in the dim light, she hesitated to think what such a journey would be like for mortals. The musky stench grew stronger with each step, and it was worsened by the dankness of the deep earth.

At first she assumed the stairs would lead into the basement, but they descended past the lower levels of the house without opening or changing. It was simply an endless spiral that sank into the earth. Finally, as she traveled deeper than any possible part of the house, the confined pit opened up into a large stone chamber.

The room was as dark as the staircase, lit by torches and lanterns that could barely maintain a general glow. It was like perpetual twilight beneath the earth. The room was hewn from solid stone, carved in the manner of a great amphitheater. Varanus saw rows and rows of well-dressed men and women—the cream of Society, all from some of the finest families in Normandy. They stood in the shadows, eyes fixed on the broad pit at the center of the chamber.

Varanus concealed her rifle in the staircase and slowly advanced through the crowd. No one paid her much mind. She approached the edge of the pit and saw Louis and Alfonse des Louveteaux standing in the center, flanking a man sitting in a chair. Varanus caught her breath when she realized that the man in the chair was Friedrich and that he was tied in place by heavy ropes.

"Brothers and sisters!" Louis des Louveteaux cried. He turned toward a poorly lit shelf of rock overlooking the pit. "I bring this enemy before our exalted elders to beg their indulgence! This man, this mongrel human, has dared to murder one of the Blood! My own kinsman Gérard was struck down by this man, an offense that must be punished!"

Varanus heard a deep rumble from the darkness on the shelf. Startled, she looked again and saw several massive, hunched-over shapes lurking there. She could not see them clearly, even with her enhanced eyesight, but something about them was unwholesome and reminded her of the strange beasts from Georgia. She sniffed the air. Yes, definitely the stench of the beasts. The cavern was filled with it.

How could there be more of them? And at both ends of Europe?

"This offense must be answered," came a voice from the darkness. "You have right of retribution. Why do you bring the offender before us?"

Varanus was aghast. They could *speak?*

"Because, great ones," Louis said, "I wish to give the gift of this punishment to all those of our race. I invite my brethren to join me in this humble feast."

Friedrich cleared his throat loudly and said, "I do beg your pardon, but what in God's name is going on? Unless you've all lost your minds, you'd better damn well untie me!"

"Silence!" Alfonse growled, striking Friedrich from behind.

"Don't you dare touch me, you filthy, inbred coward!" Friedrich shouted back. "You haven't the courage to fight me properly, so you murder my mother and have me kidnapped?"

Alfonse fell silent and looked at his father. A collective gasp filtered through the crowd, and even the creatures in the darkness above the pit seemed startled.

"Silence!" Alfonse repeated, striking Friedrich again.

"Let the mortal speak," rasped the voice from the darkness. "What 'mother' does it speak of?"

"Babette Varanus," Friedrich said. "Who else would be my mother?"

"Impossible!" Louis cried. "Babette Varanus is childless!"

Friedrich looked at Louis and said, "Well, aren't you the perfect little idiot? Of course my mother had a child! *Me!*"

"If it is as it says," the voice rasped, "this one is of the Blood."

"He is not!" Louis replied. "He cannot be! And if it is true, then surely he is the child of a runt. A runt's runt!"

"It does not look like a runt," said the voice. There was a pause. "Are there any who can tell us the truth of this? Did the granddaugther of William Varanus bear a pup?"

A pup? Varanus wondered. *What sort of way is that to speak of a child?*

"It is true!" she shouted, moving into the light. "It is true!"

"What is this?" asked the voice.

The eyes in the darkness turned toward her, as did all of the assembled gentry, amid murmurs of shock and disbelief.

"I am Babette Varanus," Varanus said. "And I tell you truly, that man is my son!"

"Mother?" Friedrich shouted. He craned his neck in an effort to look up and see her. "You're *alive?*"

"It's all right, Alistair," Varanus called down to him. "I'm handling this."

"I—" Friedrich began. "My name is Friedrich!"

"Not in front of the neighbors, Alistair," Varanus said.

"Babette granddaughter of William," said the voice in the darkness, "you claim that this man is your son? That he is the great-grandson of William Varanus?"

"I do," Varanus said.

"Lies!" Louis shouted. "Where is the proof?"

"Hold your tongue, Louis son of Charles," the voice rumbled. "You know our laws. Of the Blood is of the Blood. The mother's testimony is sufficient to establish lineage. This man is of the Blood. He has the look and scent of a pup."

"I...I..." Louis sputtered. He looked from the dark figures to Friedrich and said, "Blood or no, he murdered one of our order! He must be punished for it!"

"Perhaps," the voice said. "But Alistair son of Babette—"

"*Friedrich!*" Friedrich shouted.

"—was brought here as a human," the voice finished, ignoring him, "to be killed and eaten, as must be the fate of all mankind. Now he sits before us, a child of the Wolf. Count yourself fortunate, Louis des Louveteaux, that he has not yet been consumed. The crime of cannibalism must not be tolerated. It is The Law."

"It is The Law," echoed the assembled gentlemen and ladies.

Louis turned red with anger and stammered. Clearly Varanus's arrival had interrupted his carefully laid plans. It made Varanus smile to herself.

"Even so," Louis said, "even if he is of the Blood, he murdered one of my house. He murdered a des Louveteaux! He, the child of a runt, the descendant of a dishonored house! I demand retribution!"

"You come before us to seek the death of another Scion?" the voice asked.

"I do," Louis said. He pointed at Friedrich. "I beg your permission to *kill him!*"

"*You* demand retribution?" Varanus shouted. "That beast tried to murder my son! That is why it was killed! It is I who should demand retribution upon you and your house!"

The figures on the ledge turned toward one another and conversed softly in what seemed to be a chorus of growls. Finally, the voice spoke again:

"Very well. As the truth of the matter cannot be known, it must be settled by The Law. There shall be a trial by combat. Let the young fight for their elders. Alfonse des Louveteaux shall fight Alistair Varanus."

"I am *Friedrich von Fuchsburg!*" Friedrich shouted. He paused. "But I accept the challenge."

Varanus felt sick. Combat? No, she could not allow her son to fight Alfonse. Alfonse had already murdered her beloved Korbinian; she would not allow him to murder her son!

"I do not allow this," she said.

"You do not allow it?" Louis asked. "How dare you, whelp? It has been decreed, and so it shall be."

"…and so it shall be," echoed the crowd.

"No," Varanus said. She jumped down into the pit and landed solidly on both feet. She crossed to the center and turned to the figures on the ledge. "I will fight in my son's place."

"What?" Friedrich demanded. "Mother, no—"

Varanus looked at him and pleaded with her eyes.

"Friedrich," she said, "let me do this."

Friedrich looked back at her and his face fell. He slowly shook his head, whispering, "No, no…."

"Let me do this," Varanus repeated.

"Alfonse son of Louis, is this agreeable to you?" the voice asked.

Alfonse smiled, showing his teeth, and replied, "Oh yes, most agreeable."

"Very well," the voice said. "Alfonse son of Louis shall fight Babette granddaughter of William until one or the other yields. Whosoever wins shall decide the fate of Alistair son of Babette. Begin."

"Wait a moment," Varanus said. "Are we not to decide terms? And weapons?"

"Weapons?" Alfonse laughed. "We use the weapons that Nature gave us and none other."

He snarled at her and approached, and for the first time, Varanus noticed his teeth. They had changed since she had last seen them closely fifteen years ago. They were sharper than was natural and more pronounced, halfway between those of a man and those of a wild animal.

What was this madness? Men and women obeying the orders of beasts? Men deformed and distorted, almost beasts themselves. And this talk of blood and scions? And the way they spoke of her and Grandfather and her son…

No matter, she thought. She would kill Alfonse, rescue her son, and only then would she allow herself to ponder the strange blasphemies that she had heard.

"Come Alfonse," she said. "Come to your death."

CHAPTER THIRTY

Alfonse laughed at her as he removed his coat and tie.

"Remember," he said, "when you yield, simply say so. You might survive."

"You forget, Alfonse," Varanus replied, "my better half is English. I would rather suffer in silence than admit defeat."

"We shall see," Alfonse said, removing his gloves. His hands were hairy, and his fingernails were long, sharp, and discolored, more like talons than nails. Alfonse smiled at her and flexed his fingers. "You can always yield."

Good God, what was he?

"Do not think of such things, *liebchen*," Korbinian whispered in her ear. "Think of our son. Think of me." He looked into her eyes and said, "Think of killing the man who murdered me!"

Varanus inhaled deeply and slowly exhaled. She planted her feet firmly and raised her fists as Luka had shown her.

"Come on, then," she said. "A gentleman does not keep a lady waiting."

Alfonse threw back his head and laughed.

"I will tear you to pieces, little runt," he said.

His laugh turned into a roar, and he charged at her. The speed of the attack took Varanus by surprise. Alfonse's maddened eyes and gaping jaws made her think of the terrible beasts in Georgia. There was something hideously similar between them, and it made Varanus think terrible thoughts about Alfonse's ancestry and the nature of the beasts.

A moment later Alfonse was upon her. Varanus shook herself to regain her senses and lashed out with her empty hand. Her block caught one of Alfonse's arms as it reached for her, stopping the attack in mid-swing. But Alfonse had seen fit to attack on both sides, and the claws of his other hand struck the side of Varanus's face, cutting almost to the bone.

Varanus cried out in pain and ducked away, clutching her face. Alfonse backhanded her, knocking her to the floor.

"No!" Friedrich screamed. Varanus heard him struggling against his bonds as he shouted curses and threats of violence in German.

Varanus looked up and saw Korbinian looming over her.

"Get up, *liebchen*," he said.

"I was planning to," Varanus said, taking his hand and rising.

"Well, well," Alfonse said, "the runt is more resilient than I thought. Or perhaps I am losing my touch. That ought to have killed you."

Varanus took her hand away from her face. The flesh had already begun to knit back together. She smiled, which was painful, but tolerably so.

"Nonsense," she said to Alfonse. "It was just a flesh wound."

Alfonse snarled at her, "Flesh wound? I will show you a flesh wound!"

He came at her again, tearing at her with his claws. Varanus threw up her arms to break through the initial attack. Alfonse's claws tore her forearms, but he could not displace her. Varanus dropped her guard and turned sideways, thrusting her shoulder into Alfonse's chest and blocking one of his arms.

Snorting in frustration, Alfonse brought his free arm in, grabbing for Varanus's throat. Varanus blocked the attack with her open hand, then struck Alfonse's upper arm with the back of her fist. Alfonse's arm was tough and heavily muscled, but he winced at the force of the blow. Varanus was not finished, however, and she struck Alfonse across the face with the heel of her palm.

Alfonse stumbled away, spitting blood. Varanus flexed her fingers and shook her hand. Alfonse had an incredibly strong jaw, and the blow had hurt; less than it hurt him, no doubt, but still…

Again Alfonse lunged at her and again Varanus evaded, blocked, and retaliated. Her fists pounded into Alfonse's chest to knock the wind out of him. Alfonse gasped for air and half doubled over. Varanus struck him beneath the chin.

Alfonse backhanded Varanus and retreated, hunched over and lashing out almost blindly in an effort to keep her at a distance.

"How is this possible?" he demanded.

"Surprised, Alfonse?" Varanus asked, advancing on him. "I am a Varanus. Never underestimate us."

Alfonse snarled loudly and roared, "Die!"

Eyes red with anger, he lunged at her and grabbed her by the throat. Varanus struggled to fend him off, but in his rage, Alfonse suddenly seemed incapable of sensing pain. Varanus struck him in the chest, feeling ribs break, but Alfonse did not relent.

Panic filled Varanus until she forced herself to remember that she did not have to breathe. Fighting her instinct to gag, she reached past Alfonse's arms and grabbed him by the throat, strangling him in turn. Alfonse's eyes bulged in amazement, and he began to gasp. Before long, his grip slackened and he dropped to his knees.

"I yield!" he said, barely able to manage a whisper. "I yield!"

Varanus smiled and said, "No."

She forced Alfonse onto his back and pressed him firmly against the stone floor. Alfonse struggled, ever more feebly with each passing moment. Varanus found it absurdly simple to hold him there as she choked the life from him. How incredible it was to hold his life in her hands.

Varanus stared into Alfonse's eyes, watching them fill with panic and then slowly dim. She leaned down and whispered in his ear:

"A touch."

Alfonse's eyes flashed with horrible realization. A moment later, they went dim and his body was still. Varanus looked at Alfonse's corpse, feeling a rush of warmth flow through her body. He was dead. The man who had insulted her, assaulted her, murdered her beloved, and presumed to regard her as his property was dead. And he had died by her hand. Varanus took a deep breath, feeling heady with elation and triumph.

"No!" cried Louis, falling to his knees. "No! It cannot be!"

"It is done," said the voice. "The granddaughter of William Varanus has proven the stronger. Her will shall be carried out. It is The Law."

"It is The Law," echoed the audience.

Varanus stood and said, "Give me back my son."

"I will destroy you, you bitch!" Louis screamed, his face bright red behind the thick gray beard.

"Alfonse des Louveteaux did not yield," the voice said.

They had not heard him, Varanus realized. Good.

"He fought unto the death," the voice continued, "as was his right. Blood has killed Blood according to The Law. The complaint has been answered."

"Give me back my son!" Varanus repeated, walking toward the figures in the darkness.

"Release the pup," the voice said.

A pair of men in frock coats rushed down into the pit as if they were servants rather than gentlemen. One of them produced a knife, and they quickly freed Friedrich from his bonds. As the last of the ropes fell to the ground, the men took Friedrich by the arms to help him stand, but Friedrich shoved them off and stood of his own accord.

"Get off of me, you swine," he said. He turned to Varanus and rushed toward her. "Mother, are you all right? I saw—"

Varanus embraced him tightly and whispered, "You saw nothing, Alistar." She released him and turned toward the figures. "My son and I are leaving now. Do not try to stop us."

One of the figures motioned with its hand. For a moment it passed from the shadows into the light, revealing a hideous, long-fingered mass of muscle, fur, and claws.

"Go," rasped the voice. "You are free to leave."
"Come," Varanus said to Friedrich.

She took him by the hand and led him up out of the pit. The crowd parted as they began to move through it, the well-born gentlemen and ladies bowing to her like she was a queen. Strangely, several even tilted their heads to show her their throats. Varanus looked at them in bewilderment and hurried toward the exit.

"My lords!" Louis cried. "I have a complaint! I demand retribution!"

"The complaint has been answered," the voice said. "You know The Law, Louis des Louveteaux. Your son was not heard to yield. He chose to die rather than submit. His death was noble. It brings honor to your line. But you cannot demand retribution for it."

Varanus quickened her pace even further, walking as fast as her short legs would allow. Louis would not let them leave if he could help it, and she had no intention of waiting around while he struggled to think of an excuse for their deaths.

"Mother, what is going on?" Friedrich asked softly.

Varanus clutched his hand tighter and said, "Hush. Just keep walking."

"Wait!" Louis shouted. "They cannot leave! They have not been initiated into our mysteries!"

There was a short pause, and then the voice asked, "What?"

"William never inducted her," Louis said, "and she cannot have inducted her son. Blood or not, they are *outsiders!* They cannot leave now; they will divulge our secrets!"

Damnit! Varanus thought. She slowly looked over her shoulder and saw the chorus of shining eyes turn toward her.

"Wait," the voice said, the command echoing throughout the chamber.

"Run," Varanus said to Friedrich.

She bolted for the stairs leading to the surface, dragging Friedrich behind her. A man loomed out of the crowd, grabbing at her, and she knocked him away with a slap of her hand. Another appeared directly in her path, and she simply put her shoulder into him and ran him down.

"Up the stairs!" she told Friedrich. "Ekaterine is waiting!"

She grabbed her rifle from inside the doorway and turned back toward the chamber. Now it was all in an uproar. The initial surprise of their attempted escape was gone, and the crowd of gentry rushed at her, arms outstretched. She could not tell if they meant to capture her or do her violence, but she was not in the mood to find out. Behind them, she heard a chorus of voices from the darkness shouting for Varanus to be subdued and brought before them.

Not bloody likely, she thought.

Varanus turned and rushed up the stairs. She saw Friedrich above her, hesitating lest he lose sight of her in the tight spiral.

"Run!" Varanus shouted. "Run!"

She felt someone grab her arm from behind. She looked back and saw a woman dressed in an exquisite Worth gown, whose face was covered by a thin stubble of gray beard. The woman snarled and snorted at Varanus, pulling on her arm to drag her back into the depths.

Varanus pulled her arm free and knocked the woman away with the butt of her rifle. The woman tumbled back into the crowd behind her.

At least that would offer some delay. Varanus continued up the stairs as fast as her legs would allow. She heard gunfire near the top and bounded up the remaining steps. She saw Ekaterine and Friedrich in the doorway, firing into the hallway.

"What is happening?" Varanus demanded.

"We have been discovered," Ekaterine said.

An explosion sounded from the direction of the foyer, followed by the screams of men. Luka appeared in the doorway and nodded at Varanus. He had a lit pipe clenched between his teeth.

"I have delayed the men from outside," he said, taking a powder charge from his bandoleer and lighting the fuse. He threw it underhanded in the direction of the foyer. "We should depart out the back."

Another explosion sounded.

"Good thinking, Luka," Varanus said. "Bring up the rear, will you?"

"Very good, Doctor," Luka said.

Varanus dashed into the hallway and ran for the back of the house. Ekaterine followed quickly, and Friedrich continued along behind her. Luka withdrew more slowly, throwing two more powder charges before switching to his firearm.

Near the dining room, another group of men confronted them, weapons at the ready. Varanus fired at them with her rifle while Ekaterine and Friedrich ran for the cover of the dining room. Varanus took two bullets in the chest and ignored them as she shot the gunmen down one by one.

How did the des Louveteaux have such an inexhaustible supply of men, she wondered. And where were they all coming from? Still, having seen that twilight pit and the teeming mass of unholy gentry…

Luka ran to her side and shot the last gunman, dispelling her thoughts.

"Hurry, Doctor," he said.

Varanus nodded and ducked into the dining room. She made for the doors at the far end and rushed out into another hall. They were near the back of the house now. It was only a matter of time before they found a window leading outside.

She ducked her head into an adjacent room, some sort of study. Good God, the house was like a labyrinth! But this room was on the outer wall, and it had a pair of tall windows looking out onto the grounds.

"This way!" Varanus cried.

She ran across the room and smashed one of the windows with her rifle. She helped Ekaterine through first, then Friedrich, and then Luka. She looked back and saw another of the des Louveteaux's men in the doorway. He stared at her for a moment and began firing with his pistol. Varanus dove through the window and out onto the lawn. There was shouting from the room as more men hurried in. They would start shooting from the windows in a moment. There was nowhere to run!

"Luka!" Varanus shouted, pointing toward the broken window.

Luka needed no further explanation. He lit two powder charges and threw them in quick succession. They tumbled through the open window and exploded in a great thunderous blast, shattering the remaining window and filling the air with glass and splinters of wood. Varanus threw herself onto Friedrich, knocking him to the ground and shielding him with her body.

She looked up again and pulled herself to her feet. She could see now that the house was on fire, both in the front and in the study where the latest explosion had gone off.

She helped Friedrich stand up and brushed him off.

"Yes, thank you, I am fine," Friedrich said, protesting as she fussed over him.

"Doctor, we must go," Ekaterine said.

"Yes," Varanus said. "To the horses."

As they ran for the edge of the grounds, Varanus looked back at the burning house. For a moment she fancied that she saw a figure standing in one of the windows looking at her. She narrowed her eyes for a moment, working to make out details at such a distance. The figure was tall and broad, dressed in—could it be?—one of Grandfather's expensive suits. The face was masked by shadow, but the profile was all too familiar.

"Grandfather?" she whispered, unable to believe her eyes.

The figure drew back into the darkness, leaving nothing but an empty window.

Varanus shook herself. Her mind was playing tricks on her. Grandfather was dead, and now was not the time to think about the dead. The living needed her.

She turned and followed the others in the direction of the horses as the House of des Louveteaux burned behind her.

* * * *

William turned away from the window. Babette and the boy had escaped. They would be safe. Now it was time to attend to Louis.

He walked into the hallway and made for the underground passage. The house was filling with smoke and heat. Servants and Scions alike rushed about the place, trying desperately to fight the growing fire. William ignored them, and they all scurried out of his way as he passed.

He entered the staircase and descended to the meeting chamber. A few gentlemen of the Scion order met him on the steps and tried to bar his passage, challenging him and demanding to know who he was. This was no surprise. None of the Scions had seen him since the change, and the smoke from the fire had overpowered his scent. He snarled and bared his teeth at them, and they quickly backed away, allowing him to pass.

In the cavern he found the great multitude cowering, terrified by the smell of fire that had somehow managed to infiltrate even that deep place. How amusing, to see some of the most exalted masters of Europe huddling together like frightened animals.

William ignored them and walked to the pit. He saw Louis at the bottom, kneeling on the ground and cradling his son in his lap. This intrigued William. Alfonse was dead? How could that have happened? Surely not by Babette's or the boy's hand. Neither of them could have possessed the strength to overpower him.

"Who comes before us?" demanded the chief among the elders from its position above the pit.

"I do," William said. He stepped into the light and stood his full height. "I am William Varanus, and I demand satisfaction."

Louis looked up from his son's corpse.

"William?" he demanded. Louis rose slowly, staring up at him. "Impossible!"

"Impossible?" William asked, laughing. "Do you think me incapable of feigning my own death without your assistance, Louis? I know that it is custom for our kind to assist one another in such intrigues, but that does not mean we cannot manage them ourselves."

"Why do you come before us, William?" asked the elder. "It has been some months since last we saw you, and now we see that you are soon to be one of us. We are intrigued."

"I have been detained by the circumstances of the change," William said. "It has been made all the more difficult by the antagonism of the des Louveteaux house, which," he added, "is the reason for my coming."

"Antagonism?" Louis cried. "Your great-grandson slew Gérard! And your granddaughter murdered my son!"

So it had been Babette. William smiled a little. Incredible. How had she managed it? Unlike Alfonse, she was no soldier, and Alfonse had been gifted by greater size, strength, and the improvements of age. Even if Babette had begun to manifest the change, Alfonse had several years on her.

What sorts of things has Babette been learning in Russia? William wondered.

"Babette killed Alfonse?" William asked the elders.

"She did," the chief of the elders replied. "They faced one another in combat for the life of her son, and she prevailed. Alfonse never yielded even as he died. Great honor was done to both houses."

"This is a remarkable turn of events," William said. He looked toward Louis. "It would seem Babette was not a runt after all."

Louis scowled back up at him.

"She is not," the elder said. "There can be no doubt that your granddaughter and her son are of the Blood."

"Blood or no Blood, they were not initiated," Louis said. He pointed at William. "*You* did not bring them into the fold, and because of it, they have left with knowledge of our secrets! They may be our undoing because of you!"

Impudent wretch!

William snarled at Louis and dropped down into the pit, landing on all fours. He stood and approached Louis.

"The affairs of my house are my affairs," he said. "I and I alone have managed them well despite the fact that my son made any induction impossible while he lived. I had planned to bring Babette and her child into the order, but *you* interrupted my preparations. *You*, Louis des Louveteaux, who have meddled in the affairs of my house for years! You invaded my territory and kidnapped my great-grandson, bringing him among us before it was time. You revealed our secrets to them without my consent. It is you who have put our order in danger."

"How dare you!" Louis snarled, frothing at the mouth in anger. He looked to the elders for confirmation, but he was met with silence. "My lords?" he asked.

William turned to the elders and said, "My lords, I must beg an indulgence."

"What would you ask of us, William Varanus?" asked the elder.

"Louis des Louveteaux has meddled in the affairs of my house for decades," William said. "He has offended my dignity, insulted my blood, and sought to murder my heirs. And all this I have borne in silence. But now, my lords, in his arrogance and disregard for my property, he has threatened to reveal our secrets to the uninitiated."

"Lies!" Louis shouted.

"My lords," William continued, "I ask for the life of Louis des Louveteaux as punishment for his crimes against my family, to be determined by a trial by combat, as is The Law."

"As is The Law," repeated the assembled Scions, as they crowded around the edge of the pit.

Louis looked at William, mouth agape in disbelief. He turned his eyes toward the elders as if expecting them to refuse the request.

William knew better. He began removing his coat and tie. It felt so much better to be free of the suit's confines. Soon he would no longer be able to wear his old clothes. It would be such a pity.

"This is acceptable," the elder said. "For too long there had been anger between your two houses. Let it be settled by combat to the death."

Louis stared at them in shock. Slowly he turned back to William and narrowed his eyes.

"Come then," he said, showing his teeth and removing his tie.

William calmly removed his vest and shirt, breathing deeply as he was freed from the confines of clothing almost too small to be worn. He would require new clothes if he were to dress as a man in future. Perhaps one of the cultists was also a tailor....

A matter for another day, he thought. *Vengeance first, fashion second.*

"I will not say that it has been a pleasure to know you, Louis," he said, dropping onto all fours. "I have always considered it bad form to lie to one's neighbors."

Louis roared in anger and rushed at him, clawed fingers outstretched.

William opened his jaws and lunged for Louis's throat.

A week later, Varanus stood with her son on the railway platform in Rouen, beside the evening train bound for Paris. Ekaterine was at her side, and Luka stood nearby, watching over Friedrich's luggage while simultaneously avoiding the familial conversation.

Varanus stood on tiptoes and did her best to reach Friedrich's collar so that she could adjust his tie. Friedrich made a face but did not stop her.

"Now then, Alistair," she said, "remember to get a good night's rest in Paris before you leave for Germany."

"My name is Friedrich, Mother," Friedrich reminded her, "and I promise to get plenty of sleep before my journey tomorrow."

Varanus wagged a finger at him and said, "Be certain not to spend all hours in some cabaret in Montmartre. Promise me."

"I promise," Friedrich said.

Varanus knew he was lying to her, but it made her feel better to hear him say it.

"Remind him to eat well," Ekaterine said playfully. "And not to speak to strange women."

"Do you mind?" Varanus asked her, sighing.

But Ekaterine was right: she was fussing. Varanus folded her hands in front of her and smiled at Friedrich.

"I am sorry Alistair—" she said.

"Friedrich," Friedrich said.

"Yes, Friedrich." Varanus shook her head. She would never become used to calling him by that name. "Have a good journey and don't forget to write."

"I'll make a point of it," Friedrich said.

"And remember," Varanus said, "send me a letter from Paris first thing—" She caught herself. "Nevermind. Just write to me when you arrive back in Germany."

Friedrich smiled and kissed her cheek.

"I promise, Mother," he said. "And you'll be fine here? You're certain you don't need me to stay?"

Oh, if only he could.… But no, the des Louveteaux were not to be trusted, even with Alfonse and Louis out of the way.

"I am quite certain," Varanus said. "And since the police have finished questioning us all about the break-in, there seems no reason to trouble you with a prolonged stay in France. We shall be dealing with nothing but paperwork until our departure."

"It will be very boring," Ekaterine added.

"Oh, I don't know," Friedrich said, smiling at her. "I'm certain I could think of something to liven things up for you."

Ekaterine exchanged a look with Varanus and said, "Thank you, no, Baron von Fuchsburg. I'm certain I don't know what you mean, and moreover, I have no need of it whatever it may be."

"Pity," Friedrich said. He picked up one of his bags and looked toward the train as it was being boarded. Looking back, he asked, "And the police truly believe the story about anarchists attacking us?"

"Apparently," Luka said, stepping aside so that the porters could carry Friedrich's trunk onto the train. "It seems the des Louveteaux confirmed our story." When the porters had gone, he added, "Why, I cannot imagine, but they did."

"Perhaps to conceal their own hand in things," Friedrich said. He looked at Varanus, and she knew what he was about to say. It would be one of five questions that he had asked repeatedly ever since that night. "Mother, what were those things?"

"As I have said, Friedrich, I do not know," she replied. "And, as I have said, I mean to find the answer." She patted his arm and smiled. "But not until you are safely away."

"But how did you…" Friedrich leaned in and lowered his voice. "How did you kill them? That man Alfonse and the beast?"

Varanus looked up at her son, wishing that she could tell him the truth. But she could not. For her own sake and especially for his, she could not reveal those secrets. Not now anyway. She would not think of bringing him with her to Georgia until he had given her some grandchildren. It was only sensible.

"As I have told you before, Alistair," she said, "I will explain when you are older."

Friedrich sighed and threw up his hands.

"Very well," he said, "I suppose I cannot force an answer." He embraced her tightly and kissed her cheek again. "But know this, Mother," he whispered in her ear, "this is not the end of things. I *will* discover what is going on, whether you wish to tell me or not."

Varanus kissed Friedrich back and patted his arm.

"Travel safely," she said.

Friedrich smiled and nodded. He climbed aboard the train and gave a parting wave before vanishing inside.

Varanus felt Korbinian wrap his arms around her from behind and rest his chin on her shoulder.

"There goes our son," he said. "Such a fine young man."

"He is," Varanus murmured.

"What was that, Doctor?" Ekaterine asked, glancing toward her.

"He is a fine young man," Varanus said.

"Indeed," Ekaterine said.

They watched as the train built up steam and slowly pulled out of the station. Varanus had the sense of someone watching her and looked down the platform. For a moment she fancied that she saw a tall, broad-shouldered gentleman watching her from the shadows. Varanus stared hard, trying to make out details, but all she could be certain of were a pair of pale blue eyes, gloved hands, and the expensive cut of the suit. The man's face was hidden in shadow.

"Is something wrong, Doctor?" Ekaterine asked.

Varanus looked at her, startled.

"Well, I…" she said.

Varanus looked back toward the shadows and saw nothing but the receding crowd.

"No," she said. "I was just thinking."

Luka cleared his throat and said, "Regardless of what you told the boy, I understand that the estate is very nearly settled."

"It is," Varanus said. "Grandfather was always very good with his paperwork."

"I take that to mean we shall be departing for home soon," Luka said.

Ekaterine looked at him, one eyebrow raised, and asked, "Are you in such a hurry to leave."

"This may shock you, cousin," Luka said, "but yes, I am. I long to return home to a land with good wine."

"Nonsense, Luka," Varanus said. "France is famous the world over for the quality of its wines."

But Luka was adamant, his face set firmly. Even his moustache seemed to quiver with determination.

"Forgive me, Doctor," he said, "but my forebears invented wine-making. The French vintners are charlatans."

"Oohhh," Ekaterine said, flashing Luka a smile. She put her hand on Varanus's shoulder. "Ignore him."

"Matters of wine aside, we shall be departing soon," Varanus said. "I must go to England to settle some matters of the estate. There is a whole branch of the family there that I must…speak to."

She would speak to them indeed, and not only about property. Perhaps the English Varanuses could help her unravel some of the mystery surrounding Grandfather, the des Louveteaux, and their relationship to the beasts.

"Come," she said. "Let us return to the house before it grows much later. I could do with some refreshments before attending to the last of the accounts."

"I quite agree," Ekaterine said, taking Varanus by the arm. "Perhaps we should open a bottle of your grandfather's best charlatan wine in celebration. Wouldn't you like that Luka?"

Luka's moustache twitched a little, but he did not respond. Instead, he said:

"I will go fetch the coach."

As he departed, Varanus and Ekaterine began walking more leisurely toward the street.

"I've never been to England, you know," Ekaterine said.

"Nor have I," Varanus admitted. "Most of my family lives there, yet I have never visited. Isn't that peculiar?"

"Most peculiar," Ekaterine replied. She sighed and said, "I wonder what it will be like."

"Oh, Ekaterine," Varanus answered with a laugh, "it's going to be an adventure!"

ABOUT THE AUTHOR

G. D. Falksen (author, blogger, man about town) enjoys the finer things in life, like tea, kittens, and swing jazz. A part-time traveling lecturer, he makes regular public appearances at events across the country, though he still finds time to moonlight as an MC up and down the East Coast. In his always dwindling free time, he has written a number of short stories, serials, and the novel *Blood In The Skies*. Having appeared in *The New York Times*, on MTV, and in numerous other media, he nevertheless endeavors to maintain himself as an international man of mystery who adores elephants. For those seeking more information on the peculiar eccentric, he can be easily located at his website: www.gdfalksen.com

Made in the USA
Middletown, DE
13 March 2015